PARIS HANGOVER

Kirsten Lobe

St. Martin's Griffin ❧ New York

www.stmartins.com

Library of Congress Cataloging-in-Publication Data

Lobe, Kirsten.
    Paris hangover / Kirsten Lobe.
      p. cm.
    ISBN 0-312-35568-8
    EAN 978-0-312-35568-5
    1. Americans—France—Fiction.   2. Dating (Social
customs)—Fiction.   3. Apartment houses—Fiction.
    4. Paris (France)—Fiction.   I. Title
PS3612.0235P37 2005
813'.6—dc22

                                     2005002211

First Edition: April 2006

10 9 8 7 6 5 4 3 2 1

For my mother, who taught me to believe in the words of Henry David Thoreau: "Go confidently in the direction of your dreams. Live the life you have imagined."

Contents

You're an expatriate. You've lost touch with the soil. You get precious. Fake European standards have ruined you. You drink yourself to death. You become obsessed by sex. You spend all your time talking, not working. You're an expatriate, see? You hang around cafés.

—ERNEST HEMINGWAY, The Sun Also Rises, 1926

Prologue: The Wake-up Call, Country Mouse—City Mouse, and Becoming Klein

Late March

Admit it. *Come on*. At some point in your life you came home from a long, crappy day and said, "Enough! I wish I could just pack up and leave this all behind! Everything! This job, this city, this *tired* relationship, this apartment, and just move somewhere. A-whole-nother country, another culture, a new group of friends, a new lover. Change my entire existence. Yeah, some place dreamy, beautiful, romantic, where life would feel like an endless vacation . . . Paris!"

God, wouldn't that be great? You'd startle the hell out of your friends and family with your courageousness and, most important, surprise yourself. This is my day to feel that gnawing desire, and you know what? *I am going for it*. It goes something like this. No, in fact, it goes *exactly* like this:

I'm home. Phew-ha!

Toss my purse on the Eileen Gray table by the door and quickly deactivate the alarm system. I code in C-R-A-B. Funny, I chose the code because I have a crab tattoo, but today, it better suits my mood.

Ooph! Long day . . . huge egos . . . boring to die. I kick off my Jimmy Choos, accidently sending one flying down the stairs to the first floor of my loft, and unknot my hair from its of-the-season low chignon. Pull off the Ted Muehling earrings and toss them in the marble dish on the glass table as my cat scurries up the stairs to do his usual routine of figure eights between my feet.

"Hey, Puccini, I missed you. Tell me, did you compose any operas today, kiddo? Or did you just lie in the sun? Would you believe I spent the better part of the day arguing with the design director over "the right" shoulder pads for the fall collection? . . . Intellectually stimulating? Oh, not so much, and don't even ask about the hemline controversy! Ooh-la-la." I bring my cappucino-colored hairball up to my shoulder. "Tell me, kitten, this isn't *all* there is to life, right? Oh, sure, put cat hair *all over* my new Hedi Slimane jacket . . . oh, who cares. Go ahead, knock yourself out.

"Come on, boy, dinnertime." We both hightail it down the two flights of stairs to the kitchen. I peel open a tin of tuna, "Sheba," scooping it into the sterling silver cat bowl engraved with his name. "Look at this piece of crap, Puccini. It's from Bergdorf's—a hundred and fifty dollars, for God's sakes, and it's tarnished in a week. Jesus, what am I doing even buying things like this?" I mutter.

Puccini's not listening, he's deliriously devouring smelly morsels of gelatinous tuna. "I think it's safe to say you wouldn't give a damn if I'd served it to you in a homeless man's *shoe*. Nope, tuna is tuna. Right. No more frivolous purchases. Total waste of money. Man, you're easy to please. I *used to be* . . . Hmm."

Passing through the living room as I head for my painting studio, I think to myself, *God, I never sit in here, never. Why do I live like this? As though it's a museum . . . as if the photographers from* Elle Décor *are gonna burst through my door at any minute* demanding *to publish photos of my apartment. It's nuts, all this stuff—Noguchi, Eames—no one ever sees it and I never use it. That's just "whackadoodle-do," as we used to say back in Wisconsin.*

Moving aside several paintings in various stages of completion, I finally make my way to the desk. Pressing the flashing new messages button on my answering machine, the android chick from God knows *what* planet announces in her usual unenthused all-business voice: "You have nine new messages."

What are the chances any of them are going to shake me out of this melancholic state? Oh, I'd say about zero. What *is* my problem lately? I just can't seem to get it up for this life of mine.

Be-e-ep!

"Hello, Klein, it's Liza (my fashion consulting headhunter). You've gotta go back to Oscar de la Renta tomorrow at 10:00 a.m. for a meeting with the head designer, and then Isaac Mizrahi wants you to scoot down to Soho at 2:00 for a chat about his new venture. Oh, and I'm sending out your paycheck from the trip to Hong Kong with Ungaro—it's a doozy. I recommend you think about incorporating. I know a great lawyer—Let me know. Take care, bye."

Be-e-ep!

"Dahrl-ing, it's me. (Thierry. My Big-Shot French Industrialist Boyfriend. THE Man of my dreams and yet after five years together, still refuses to have children. Utterly perfect in *every* way but that.) Did you get the note I left for you this morning? I didn't dare wake you, you were like a *croissant chaud* all curled up. I'm in London now and just finished my meeting with the English Heritage group. It went marh-vh-elously. We'll have something to celebrate when you arrive Friday. I've made reservations at Wilton's *pour déjeuner* Saturday, and then we're free to do whatever you wish until Monday. I'm voting for spending the entire weekend *in the room.* I got you something delicious at Agent Provocateur today, *mon ange.* You're going to lo-ove it. (No, *you* probably are. Let me guess . . . something obscenely sexy, ridiculously expensive *and* that will be beyond terrifying to put on.) *Comme d'habitude,* Anna will call with your itinerary. *Je t'aime, K. Je t'embrasse très fort et partout.*"

Be-e-ep!

"Lauren, it's your father. (He's so funny, like after thirty-four years I'd be thinking, *Who's that? . . . Familiar, but I can't quite place it.*) I am just calling to check in with you and make sure you arrived back in New York safely. We enjoyed your visit and thank you again for coming for my birthday. I love you. Remember, be careful. Goodbye, squirrel." (A childhood nickname. Something to do with me hoarding stuff, no doubt.)

Be-e-ep!

"Hey girl, it's Cameron. (Young, sexy art gallerist who's so damn hot, I'm just always one drink away from falling into his lap. Did I say lap? I meant arms. Oh all right, I meant lap.) Saw you in *W* magazine last week. Did you go platinum blonde? Mmm, I like. Just a quick call to confirm you're coming to the opening tonight. It'll be great, Patrick McMullan has sent word he'll pop by to take a few photos . . . Hey, wear that crazy Fendi ostrich feather coat, and if you could get your splashy, rich French boyfriend to buy something, I'd be eternally grateful. Kisses. Bye, babe."

Be-e-ep!

"Hi, Lauren . . . oh, sorry, Klein . . . right. I keep forgetting you go by *just* your last name these days. It's Julia. (A friend from high school, still living in our hometown in Wisconsin.) I heard you were in Madison. Marisa saw you on State Street with your dad. I really wish we could've seen each other. I hardly get to speak to you anymore. (True, but I send her postcards from *all* my trips. Guess that doesn't exactly qualify does it? "Guilt trip" noted and begrudgingly accepted.) Call me when you can. Miss you. Bye, sweetie."

Be-e-ep!

"Hello, Klein, it's Anna. I just want you to know you're booked on the Concorde to London Friday morning, and a car will pick you up at your house at eight-thirty to take you to the JFK. Thierry's at Claridges, of course, suite 710. This is all on the itinerary. I'm having it delivered to your house by Thierry's driver at seven tonight. Call me at home if there's any problem; you have the number. Have a good trip. (She says it deadpan; she so-o-o doesn't like me. I totally get it. If I were Anna, I would hate me, having to arrange this shit for my boss's fifteen-years-younger girlfriend too. Hey, none of this was my idea. I never had a Big-Shot Boyfriend before. This just all came with *him.* Responsibility, REFUSED!) Bye."

Be-e-ep!

"KLEIN! KLEIN, are you there? Pick up! It's me. (Yasmin, my bestest friend in New York City, a fabulous British girl I met working at Ungaro; the coolest, most entirely unfashionista earthy angel and the kindest soul who happens to look exactly like an exquisite wood fairy) Guess what? I'm pregnant!! It's so amazing, we're absolutely wild with excitement! I cannot believe it. I can't wait to speak to you! Call me! Bye."

Be-e-ep!

"Klein, it's Christopher calling. Saw you shopping at Takashimaya with your famous boyfriend last weekend. Didn't want to disturb you two lovebirds, you looked like you were having a ball buying up the place. Oh, and I love the hair . . . very glam. Question: I was wondering if you know anyone who has an apartment to rent for, say, six months? (Don't you just hate people who say "question" before they ask one? So pretentious. They tend to be the same people who say "knock wood" and tap their heads. *Unbearable.*) I need to move out while my townhouse is being redecorated. Of course they'd have to have a top-notch security system. You know I'd be a wreck if anyone snatched my Magritte or Bacon. I'm rather short on time, so please call if you can think of anyone. Perhaps I'll see you at Cameron's opening tonight. Bye."

Be-e-ep!

"Hello, Miss Klein, this is David over at Barneys. I just wanted to call and let you know your dress is ready. I think the tailor did an excellent job, and I am sure you will look fa-ab-u-lous in it at the Whitney benefit. Please don't hesitate to call me if you should require anything else. I am entirely at your service. Take care, Miss Klein. Goodbye."

THIS IS MY LIFE.

I should be happy. This is the life I wanted, the life I worked so damn hard to get. I ought to be *thrilled*. I know it. I'm so *not*. At the risk of sounding like a malcontent, I gotta say, this existence is *nowhere*. It all looks great from the outside; the inside is another life altogether.

I saw this coming from the moment I opened my eyes this morning. Awakened by the sound of a baby crying on the street below—or was that the sound of me crying?

It wasn't supposed to be like this. I was supposed to find the "right man" and he'd fall madly in love with me. We'd be sickeningly crazy about each other. Everyone would *want* to hate us but couldn't because we were still so goddamn grounded and "good." Yep, we'd laugh the eighteen hours a day we *weren't* shagging like minks. Then in a couple of years we'd have our first baby and grow *closer* and celebrate our third anniversary by splurging on a small country house in Brittany. Dammit! I have the "great man" part but not the "baby" part, and I *know* I have to lose the great man now if I ever want to get the baby. Because he's just never going to give in and years are flying by and I can't keep waking up every morning and thinking, *Now what?*

I swear I had a "life plan" once. But in all the excitement of what gown to wear to the next charity ball, and which bikinis to take to St. Barts, it seems, at some point, I must have misplaced that life plan in an absurdly overpriced must-have handbag.

The time had come for one of those not yet officially named, but soon to be overhyped social ills: The Midthirties Wake-Up Call of the Urban Female. I was quickly sliding from "optimistic, pretty-young-thing" to "jaded, haggard-lost-soul" (albeit with a fabulous wardrobe). None of the material trappings mattered anymore. I was thirty-four, essentially single, childless, *and* had inadvertently put my Paris dream in the mental file of "things I will eventually get around to"—somewhere behind learning to speak Japanese.

The two things I wanted *most* in life were to be a mother and to live in Paris. Somehow, I had let the years slip by, foolishly believing the future would figure itself out. I had forever convinced myself, *I'm just too busy, I've got that upcoming wedding in Venice and that project for Oscar de la Renta and then I'll sit down and make some sense of all this*. My stock of excuses had drained and now my life stared me in the face—and it wasn't pretty.

My yearning for motherhood had become so all consuming that each time I caught a glimpse of a child playing at the park or a baby cradled in its stroller, it took all the strength I had *not* to sweep that child into my arms. Pathetic. I was on the cusp of becoming that woman in the famous Roy Lichtenstein painting: "Oh no! I forgot to have a baby!"

I'd been to enough Costume Institute balls, benefits, gallery openings, and galas to last me a lifetime, and what did I have to show for it? (I mean other than the brilliant collection of killer Manolos?) Just about zip. I'd spent a dozen years in New York City, busting my ass to reach a certain level of income and acquire all those objects of desire society insists we must seek with a vengeance. You know, having the *perfect* outfit for every occasion (borrowed couture or prêt-à-porter as a backup) and of course the killer shoe-purse combo to match (generally, about the price of a compact car and disposable after one season). Fabulously luxurious sheets (Porthault, Pratesi), the coolest wineglasses (Baccarat, Murano), a few great pieces of art (Sam Taylor-Woods, Alex Katz), an obscene collection of accessories (from Fendi to Jade Jagger's collection for Asprey), groovy furniture (Christian Liaigre, Marc Newson), the "right" books (Phaidon, Taschen, Rizzoli).

With all that settled, the truth just reared up and took a seat (on a long-sought-after black Corbusier chaise, in my case) and said, *Okay, so now what? This isn't* all *there is in life. Didn't you have some* nonmaterialistic *dreams? I remember something about babies, a family, and moving to France. Does any of that a ring a bell?*

DING-DONG! Time to face the music. The Big-Shot Boyfriend in my life isn't coming around on the baby issue. We've argued it out for five damn years, and I've never managed to sway him. And the dream of living in France . . . gimme a minute, I'll find an excuse. Would you accept that I still haven't quite gotten around to taking those French classes at l'École Française? I have the brochure. I'm really close to making the call to enroll . . . really close. But now that I have *all* this furniture and stuff, it would be soo-oo expensive, and such a pain to move it all across the Atlantic. I mean that is *far*.

It occured to me that I had spent twelve years in New York City, proclaiming ad nauseum the trite "Carpe diem!" to rationalize my every spontaneous action, and I knew it was time to put up or shut up. It was time to leave the Big-Shot Boyfriend and go find a man who shared my desire to have a family. Definitely. And since I have a virtual obsession with dating *only* Frenchmen (I didn't mention that yet, did I?), maybe, just maybe, I could go to France and, as they say, "kill two birds with one stone."

Admittedly, the story that brought me to this crossroads reads like a cross between the children's book *City Mouse and Country Mouse* and a bad article in *Cosmo*. I'd grown up in Wisconsin, aka God's country (at least that's what they call it in umpteen beer commercials). The true religion in Wisconsin is the twice daily consumption of mass quantities of fast food and the ritualistic wearing of sweatshirts charmingly decorated with the state claim to fame— get this, *cows*. To be fair, it was a beautiful *Brady Bunch* kind of place to grow up, but as one gets older that "discerning eye" sharpens and some things just didn't jibe with my vision of the ideal life. Case in point: the culture revolves around state football games where fans don enormous yellow cheese-wedge hats of foam rubber and refer to themselves (proudly, I might add) as "cheeseheads." I don't think I'm going out on a limb here to say Wisconsin is definitely one of your less glamorous states, still a step up from, say, Alabama, but it's a tight race to be sure.

In college I did the English literature degree to have something to fall back on. (Fall back where? Into the unemployment line, most likely.) Then after a few years of realizing I was far more concerned with what to wear to class (is a cowboy hat, jodhpurs, and a full-length mink coat wrong for a lecture in geology?) than class itself, I took my corn-fed confidence and headed to New York City to study fashion design.

Phew! Finally I was at peace. No one in New York City sniggered at my big ambition of designing "couture." In Wisconsin, people thought couture was perhaps a new-fangled farm implement. In New York City everyone was like me: they had huge dreams, were escaping from somewhere, wore head-to-toe black, talked as fast as an auctioneer, and thought—as I did—that they'd make a million dollars by age twenty-five. I keep readjusting that, by the way. Now it's more like a million lire by age seventy-five. I think that's doable, possibly.

While in design school I shed my first name, Lauren, and opted for the modern Klein, my last name. Remember college? It's just a hotbed for bad ideas. (Many, upon reflection, evoke uncontrollable facial tics and cringes.) Frankly, "becoming Klein" is the *least* ridiculous thing I did in a long list of utterly senseless practices. The tattoo and getting black Italian hair extensions (keep in mind I'm blonde) were among other such clever and spontaneous acts born of a completely naive sense of self-certainty. Charming, endearing, and amusing—*when it's not you.*

Living in New York City during my twenties was exactly what I'd hoped it would be. With the exception of a few really bad do-it-yourself hair color jobs, including optic white roots with pee-yellow hair (yessiree, I said pee-yellow). Believe it or not I was shooting for a Sharon Stone look. Good God, I'm not even going to mention the year I gained twenty pounds and was mistaken for a man.

I lived in the West Village, on Carmine Street, with a gorgeous and witty writer. (A man, okay? The lesbian thing was just a week and I was much younger.) I'd met him in Wisconsin and imported him. Wisconsin does a few things great. Men, cheese, and mosquitoes, in that order.

After graduating from design school, I worked the required smattering of low-level designer jobs on Seventh Avenue. I think you'd have to agree that picking out zippers, buttons, and snaps officially qualifies as peon work. A thousand buttons and a few years later I finally got the high-profile bigwig gigs at Calvin Klein, Oscar de la Renta, etc. Prestigious, yes, but I often imagined that working on a prison chain gang on the interstate of North Carolina in the 105-degree heat might be more pleasant, actually. I got pretty sick of people who said things like, "Those shoes are *so* last week" and meant it.

By some inexplicable stroke of luck, I segued into just occasionally working on Seventh Avenue as a fashion consultant and managed to move up from the crap-hole apartment with mice above a bagel shop (which featured a built-in aromatherapy of cinnamon-raisin and pumpernickel-onion depending on the time of day).

After a few years and a few clever investments, I was able to move into a splashy Tribeca triplex. I had an ideal setup—great boyfriend, killer apartment, money—and like a character in a tacky Danielle Steele novel, I got greedy and took a wrong turn. Okay, a few.

I dumped my perfect boyfriend (he was perfect, no exaggeration) for a Big-Shot French Industrialist fifteen years my senior. As I possess nothing resembling patience, I suppose I got antsy for a more glamorous (read: expensive) luxury lifestyle. You know, the whole *Vogue* magazine–promoted package deal: flying the Concorde, vacations in Aspen and Mustique, a box at the opera, having a car and driver, blah, blah, money, overrated blah. By the way, I can blame fashion magazines, right?

Don't get me wrong, I did fall madly and completely in love with Monsieur Industrialist. Elegant, handsome, brilliant, witty—what's not to love? I'll readily admit he had told me from the start he didn't want children (and obviously I'm pretty much oh, aching to), yet I still went blazing into a five-year relationship knowing one day I would probably have to leave.

The epiphany made it all crystal clear. Here I was, thirty-four years old, with my years of fertility flicking the lights on and off yelling, "Last call," and it was time to pack up shop. I once again took my corn-fed (now caviar-satiated) confidence and decided to leave Thierry and this jet-set lifestyle, to move away to the other great love of my life: Paris. Time to get on with *my* life dream: kids, painting, a *younger* Frenchman, a smaller life.

So I gave it all up. (Don't be silly, I kept the jewelry.) I called my friend Christopher, who was in desperate need of an apartment for six months and said, "Take it, it's yours, I'm moving to Paris." Exchanged my keys for a lovely little subletting check and didn't look back. Now the 2,000-square-foot Tribeca triplex has been replaced by a 550-square-foot garret in Saint-Germain. What I used to spend on my dry cleaning is now my monthly budget. Two dozen evening gowns went off to be sold at a consignment shop and the Manolo Blahniks lie dormant under my bed, guarded by dust bunnies the size of sheep.

I made the decision to chase my dream and live a simpler life. Let's be honest, I do miss some things, like having a maid. There is no way to look at changing the cat's litter box as morally fulfilling or a character builder. *No way*.

The journal that follows is a monthly diary of my expat adventure of a lifetime. I have kept a journal since I was seven and while the entries from ages seven to twelve tend to recap episodes of *Happy Days* and my love for Andy Gibb a bit much, I'd like to think that occasionally I jot down some clever and/or juicy details now that I can stay out past nine o'clock.

In the words of Baudelaire (and, yes, this is a blatant attempt to appear literary, a counterbalance to the Andy Gibb reference), it's an "invitation to the voyage." An invitation to observe from a safe distance the painfully amusing missteps of my attempts at scaling the vast, unexpected cultural hurdles while I tried to create a new life in Paris that had some semblance of meaning and happiness, and hopefully find Monsieur Right. (Think of it as a double-blind experiment, a beat-the-clock game where I plowed through my savings at Mach 2 with my biological clock ringing in my ears.)

JFK—Paris with the Devil in Tow

Early April

I thought I pulled it off quite well, considering I gave myself only seven days from deciding to move to Paris to date of departure. I managed to sublet my Tribeca triplex, gracefully exit the three fashion consulting jobs, and pack ten pieces of luggage vital to my sanity—books, paints, clothes, favorite objects (which may or may not have included sex toys).

I knew that the one remaining detail was figuring out how to bring my semipsychotic cat, Puccini, with me on the plane. I was fully prepared. For once, I would follow the official rules and prepare all the necessary documents. I bought a cat airline ticket and splurged on the top-of-the-line "airline approved" cat transport carrier. I knew I'd have to knock him out (the cat, not the vet) for the flight, as even the two-block trip to the vet had made Puccini into a nervous wreck. The vet gave me cat tranquilizers, assuring me that "one pill an hour before you leave will have him sleeping soundly before you even get to the airport." Great. Done.

The day of departure arrived. Passport? Check! Obscene amount of luggage? Check! Okay, time to sedate Puccini; I thought the tough part was going to be getting that bloody pill down his tiny throat as he gagged and shrieked, surely one paw reaching for the phone to call the Cruelty to Animals hotline. After catching him pull the "fake swallow" followed by expelling the pill in a corner, I lassoed him and we had an out-and-out brawl. Twenty minutes, three Band-Aids, and one very pissed cat later, I had won "in a draw." I even succeeded in jamming him into the cat carrier bag as he performed a rather impressive violent moonwalk of resistance.

The minibus I'd hired to take me and all my stuff to JFK astonishingly arrived on time. Of course the driver was so thrilled to see so much luggage that he sat paralyzed in the driver's seat as I struggled to load everything inside. I was giddy to be on my way to a new life in Gay Paree. Then I noticed, the vet was slightly off in his estimate that Puccini would be . . . "sleeping soundly" was it? More like wild-eyed and meowing loudly in auto-repeat mode. *Très* annoying.

I arrived at JFK and dragged ten pieces of baggage relay-style to check-in, while Puccini provided a soundtrack of howling at thirty-five decibels to the delight of no one. With my new budget-minded economy ticket, I knew there was zero chance of trying to sneak eight *extra* pieces of luggage (Louis Vuitton, natch) onto the plane. Still, I approached the the female ticket agent with optimism.

"Hello, I'm on the flight for Paris. Would it be at all possible to get a bulkhead seat? I'm rather tall and I have my cat with me so I might need a little extra room," I asked above the incessant howling of Puccini.

"No, I'm sorry, bulkhead seats on international flights are reserved for mothers traveling with *enfants,*" she said with an entirely unnecessary scowl.

"He is kind of like a wailing child at the moment, wouldn't you agree?" I said, trying to amuse her into compliance. No dice. She wasn't the slightest bit charmed by me, Puccini's aria, or by my proud proclamation of "I'm moving to Paris."

"And is *all of that* your luggage? Do you mean to check it on this flight?" As though I were trying to sneak a pickup truck through as carry-on.

"Yes, I suppose I may be a bit over on the weight limit."

"Definitely," the crab apple in the Air France polyester uniform announced with annoyance, realizing she was now going to have to do some *actual work.* "Bring them all over here and put them on the scale."

I put the box-o-yelling cat on the ground and lugged all ten bags onto the scale piece by piece. She snorted and huffed at the weight and appearance of each one and stamped the statistics into the computer.

"Well, Miss Klein, looks like you owe another seven hundred forty-five dollars. Would you like to put that on a credit card?" She almost squealed with glee at my misfortune. I threw down my credit card as though paying another seven hundred forty-five dollars was the equivalent of a nickel to me. She handed over my ticket and credit card receipt with a brusque, "Gate 2a."

Not even so much as a "have a nice flight." Short on charm, that woman. Whatever, I was moving to PARIS! You couldn't rain on my parade, chick. Nothing could.

Unfortunately, Puccini had chosen the role Tasmanian Devil for his Air France debut. As I waited at the gate in economy class check-in, I clutched the cat carrier bag handles closed as he desperately tried to break the speed of sound doing frantic revolutions in a confined space.

Oh sure, people pointed and exchanged theories of whether I was carrying several rabid ferrets involved in a violent family dispute, or if it was in fact a Komodo dragon who'd ingested LSD. As we all filed into our economy seats, cattle-style, I was enduring, thinking only of afternoons spent drinking at cafés with beautiful Frenchmen. This was supposed to be the easy part: getting from Point A to Point B.

As they closed the doors to the plane, I noticed those little paws I could never bring myself to cruelly declaw were slicing and shredding the rip-stop window of the carrier. I tried desperately to hold it closed with my hand. I can't be certain, because my hand was below the seat, but I'm pretty sure a vicious hyena jumped in to assist Puccini by biting me with such force that blood began to pour from four very distinct puncture wounds. Fuckity fuck fuck! At this point, I would have gladly declawed and deteethed (unteethed, distoothed, what is the word?) Puccini with pleasure. Okay, fine, cat bastard. Go nuts. I desperately needed about a bazillion napkins for my gaping wounds. I pushed the stewardess button. She arrived a casual ten minutes later.

"Miss, is that *your* cat sitting on that gentleman's shoulder?" the second "Air France sweetheart" to cross my path asked me with cocked eyebrow.

Sure enough, Puccini had clawed a hole in the cat carrier and perched himself on the Indian man next to me. The notion of "denial of ownership" was momentarily considered but, damn it, I'd already been seen with the cat, so I was obliged to grab him and request the absurd (which, at the time seemed perfectly reasonable to me): "Might you have some container (even one of those goddamn beverage trolleys) I could put my cat in, because I see we're about to take off and he's already destroyed his *airline-approved* (that part I enunciate loudly, like it's her fault) carrier bag?"

She cheerfully replied, "Oh no, miss, I'm sure we have nothing like that. Good luck." Already on her way back to that riveting presentation of how to work a seat belt.

"Excuse me!! Miss!!? Could you possibly bring me several napkins? My hand's bleeding quite badly," I yell over the heads of all the seated passengers, who of course *all* turn around immediately to see what the hoo-ha is. Zip response until she returns ten long minutes later and without a word throws the napkins into my lap. Lovely. I considered explaining to her that her laissez-faire attitude toward having a savage cat loose in the cabin, might be a mistake. But I decided to take the high road.

After apologizing profusely to the Indian Gentleman, who I must say took the whole cat epaulet moment quite well, I realized my options were très limited. There was no escape and an eight-hour flight ahead. So for the safety of the other innocent passengers (selfless, yes?) I sacrificed myself to the cat gods. Off I headed to the toilet, my only feasible refuge: a contained space protecting others from feline fury. Being in a tiny, confined space with Puccini wasn't my favorite fantasy but I ruled out ensconcing myself in the cockpit— too many dials and activity.

I can *un*happily confirm that the powerful potpourri of urine disinfectant in an airplane toilet never does quite become tolerable. And while we all have been told it's illegal to be in a plane bathroom for takeoff, I discovered no one really cared. My fears of being jostled in heavy turbulence paled next to the reality that at some point I was going to have to actually leave the toilet with the cat.

We reached our cruising altitude (from what I could guess) and Puccini turned into a belligerent old drunk, staggering, hissing, and spitting. I tried to find a neutral corner as he began an eight-hour circuit-training routine of hostility blended with confusion.

As to be expected, fellow passengers began to knock on the toilet door, impatient to pee and curious as to whether someone had taken up residence in the bathroom. (Yes, thank you. Please have my mail forwarded to me here. Finally I feel at home somewhere.) As I squatted on the smelly floor, exhausted, blood oozing from my aching hand, the idea of letting in the guy pounding on the door seemed amusing: "Sure, buddy, I dare you to expose your most vulnerable body part to this drugged-out claw machine I like to call my traveling companion. Bring it on!"

The hours passed slowly (that's an understatement: I took to counting how many sheets comprised a roll of toilet paper). I imagined that *out there* movies were being shown, people were putting on their sleep masks, relaxing after a glass of red wine. The aroma of beef bourguignon seeped under the bathroom door, and I can tell you that, mixed with *l'odeur de la toilette,* it had absolutely no appeal, regardless of my hunger pangs.

God, I would've killed for just a tiny bag of peanuts, those ten delicious, precious nuts I'd taken for granted so often. At hour five, crazy thirst kicked in. You must remember all the times you've seen the sign in plane toilets stating NOT DRINKABLE WATER. You've laughed to yourself, *What fool would want to?* Suddenly I was that fool, parched, going bananas with dehydration. Water: yes, but access denied.

This was truly not the flight to Paris I'd envisioned. That was more along the lines of me toasting myself with Champagne, kicking back, eating *fromage* (yes, two points for you, that's right: cheese) and naming my future French-born children. *(Chloe: yes, that's a lovely name: No, wait, it's also a perfume . . . nice bottle, but smells like old ladies . . . okay then, Clotilde . . . perfect.)*

Hours passed like years as I nodded off for a second only to discover Puccini jumping from the sink onto my head. My black cashmere sweater was now several layers deep in beige cat hair, creating a 1970s angora look I'd normally be horrified to be seen in. My contact lenses had dried to corneal eye carapaces when finally I heard the landing gear descend. My thought of *Yipee . . . France!* quickly dissolved into, *Oh shit, customs.*

I stuck my head out of the toilet door and hailed a stewardess to beg to be moved to first class, cat in my arms, in order to get off this goddamn plane first. She told me it was possible. I thought, *There is a God—cruel with a twisted sense of humor but a god, nevertheless.* Any normal thrill of making a move of such comfort and magnitude from a toilet to first class was lost as I took my seat in 2B. I was on the receiving end of the terribly disapproving expressions of the elite first-class passengers (where, dammit, I normally would be with the Big-Shot Ex, for crying out loud). They were none too amused to have paid six thousand dollars for their seats only to be joined by the bedraggled bleeding girl in the tacky angora sweater, bleeding profusely, and her wild cat in tow.

So I wasn't a big hit in first class; I was okay with that as I had bigger issues ahead of me. After landing, the pilot waited ten minutes to tell us we'd have to stay out on the tarmac and be shuttled by bus to the terminal. Oh, genius.

As everyone filed into the shuttle bus I saw the Indian man I sat next to (briefly) and Puccini sat on (actually). I wondered if he'd eaten my dinner, gobbled down the peanuts designated for me. I was so starving by then, I would've eaten Puccini and used his claws for toothpicks.

At the customs booth, the inspector was unimpressed with the dishevelled girl and seething cat. After a visible mental debate on whether to give us a hard time, French laziness worked to my advantage as he decided it was way too much of an effort to interrogate me than, say, just grunting and stamping my passport.

Oh, the pleasure of hauling endless pieces of luggage, each the size of a Volkswagen, to two different *chariots*—that's French for "luggage cart." It's so chichi, don't you think? I believe I even asked Puccini if he concurred. *C'mon, I was delirious with thirst.*

Of course, as is always the case, one piece of luggage was being annoyingly elusive. Three quarters of my fellow passengers had already probably made it home by the time my last bag popped out. Finally, with all ten bags and one cat, I trudged to the counter where I was asked if I had anything to declare. "Oh yes, I *declare* I am fucking going to kill this cat, and the vet. One pill!? And the cat-carrier company is definitely getting a letter. They . . . I'm just getting started!" I was encouraged to, "Move along, mademoiselle."

It's a mean feat pushing two *chariots* of luggage and a cat through a re-volving door, to the . . . *Hey, wait a minute.* That long line of people couldn't all be waiting for taxis? God damn it, can I get a break?

I began negotiating my way into the umpteenth line in less than ten hours and was beginning to imagine this nightmare was almost over when a taxi fi-nally pulled up in front of me. The French taxi driver spotted the cat and an-nounced, "*Pas de chat!*" as he waived the businessman behind me ahead. As businessman and taxi drove off I felt a pitiful sense of loss. The next taxi dri-ver appeared, only to proclaim, "*Trop de baggages!*" (too much luggage) and tell me I would only be accepted by the *taxi minibus.*

As far as my eye could see (through the cat-hair veil) there were no such *taxi minibuses* in the airport. Approximately one hour and forty-three minutes after landing, the much coveted and rare *taxi minibus* made an appearance. The driver was a charming older man, quick to help me with the bags, and even friendly. Once we were under way, he ever so kindly informed me that, "Cats don't like to travel, mademoiselle." *Oh, really? What a helpful bit of information at this juncture, monsieur.*

I looked down at Puccini on my lap; he had quietly fallen asleep. Charming. Perfect. The vet was right on the money, those pills work like clockwork. I highly recommend them both. Oh, and the "airline approved" cat carrier, now there's a real piece of craftsmanship and durability. I want to officially thank you all for making it such a smooth, problem-free trip.

I knew right then and there we were not going to make another transatlantic trip together, Puccini and I. I was going to have to make this "Paris dream" work, because returning to New York City was clearly out of the question. Whoever coined the adage "Getting there is half the fun," I'm guessing, *never* went transatlantic with a drugged-out cat.

Pepe Le Pew, BYOA, and a Cuf of Copy

MONSIEUR RIGHT REPORT

I can't quite figure out why I've always been drawn to Frenchmen. Perhaps if I went into deep therapy or hypnosis I could find the origin of my obsession. I'd love to be able to say, "I saw an Yves Montand film when I was fifteen and that elegant, Gallic charm swept me off my feet." But in truth it's probably less 1950s black-and-white cinema than Pepe Le Pew.

Saturday mornings, plopped in front of the TV watching cartoons . . . that voice: "*Ooh-la-la, mon amour,* my lee-tel angel of luv." I definitely put that voice and the concept of being completely adored and sought after together. Even today, hearing the French accent twenty-four hours, seven days a week, I still can't get over its effect. I swear I climb the walls in rapturous desire just listening to the waiter read the specials of the day aloud. It can be a bit dangerous, as I often tune out to the content and end up melting into a blissful delirium until I realize, *Damn, he stopped talking. Did he ask a question? Is "huh?" going to suffice as a response while I come out of my auditory stupor?*

Living in New York City for so long, I'd run through the stock of imported Frenchmen. Word got out among my friends that I had a particular cultural inclination, and by age thirty-four I'd met every bloody Jacques, Pierre, or Philippe in town. I exhausted the supply while still maintaining my demand. (See, I DID listen in economics class and even extrapolated the useful supply vs. demand theory into my life—so that C in economics was completely unfair!) It was time to come to the source, the grand buffet of Frenchmen! I increased my odds by six million in one fell swoop.

Not being a spring chicken anymore, I'd had enough experience in relationships to have acquired a certain vague notion of the ideal man for me. Okay, let's be honest—it was actually a highly detailed, strenuously rigid mental wish list, pretty much specific down to chest hair quantity and arrangement. (I'm kidding . . . *sort of*). But I also knew I had to be a bit more flexible than I'd been in New York City. Dumping a perfectly charming man because he owned too-low-thread-count sheets does in retrospect seem a bit brutal (come on, though, it was like sleeping on burlap bags; okay, you're right, it was harsh of me).

The wish list is, in no particular order of priority, as follows:

THE NONNEGOTIABLES

1. Obviously, he must be French. I didn't come all this way to date a man from Kentucky.

2. He must have a very non-European appreciation for dental hygiene. I cannot tell you how many gorgeous creatures (already!) have been eliminated due to tobacco-encrusted, scary, brown teeth. (No teeth like Halloween pumpkins or the color of suede, in short.)

3. No reading material in his bathroom. Not even Balzac will be tolerated. Just do your business and get out; it's not a reading room for crying out loud. I once dated a man named Xavier who'd settle in to read every word in *Le Monde*. Before he got to the business section I was gone.

4. Absolutely no ownership of slip-on loaferlike, tassel-adorned comfort shoes. And I absolutely recoil in horror at the sight of those Birkenstock Jesus sandals, they're too Peppermint Patty crossed with Caveman for me. Any man caught wearing them is instantly unfuckable.

5. He has the much underrated skill of being able to tie cherry stems in a knot with his tongue. It speaks volumes of hidden talents and possibilities.

6. He should be funny. Not funny like Jackie Mason. Not slapstick funny. No "there's a coin behind your ear" routine. But Jerry Seinfeld/David Sedaris funny. Don't think I'm unaware this is a really tough request in the country that has embraced Jerry Lewis as the god of humor.

7. A strong nose. I have a thing for noses. Not any particular type per se, just unique. I guess you could say I'm a classicist: Gallic noses do it

for me, and large is good—within reason. Yup, I'm *that* bananas that I find Gerard Depardieu's nose sexy, actually *everything* about him is sexy. I know the "French thing" is an acquired taste; either you get it or you don't.

8. I will not partake in a relationship with any man who is a self-proclaimed sports fan. I can see, maybe, going to watch the French Open, a Polo match, or an occasional soccer match (only if David Beckham is playing shirtless), but following any other team sport is a deal breaker. If I wanted a sports buff I could've stayed in Wisconsin, thank you, and watched the Packers from a recliner with my beer-swilling pig of a husband.

9. He should be somewhat romantic. He doesn't necessarily need to recite the poetry of Pablo Neruda on a daily basis, but a few sweet notes, kisses on the neck . . . that's what I'm shooting for.

10. I'm rather firm on the issue of personality disorders. While men that are bipolar can be a blast when on the upside, generally the crash is not worth sticking around for. Multiple personalities as well are just too tricky and complicated. Schizophrenia is also a bit too tiring for me at my age—maybe if we'd met when I was an angry eighteen-year-old, but now I'll have to take a pass, thanks.

11. He doesn't have a job that involves wearing a name tag, crunching numbers, or working directly with a cash register.

12. (If applicable:) Embraces his receding hairline (no bathroom cabinet full of Rogaine, or brush-over maneuvers). Any resemblance to Tom Ford will be well received and highly rewarded, to be honest.

I'll admit, there's a lot more. *I know* I'm a smidge demanding. In truth, the older I get, the more I throw things *off* the list. It's getting to the point where it's pretty much any age of man will do (okay, between a pacemaker and ticket holder to a Britney Spears concert). And *any* level of intelligence above mono-syllabic. He must be *at least* as tall as he is wide. Honestly, when I arrived in Paris I thought, *Well, he must have a semi-decent car.* But I've quickly changed that to, *Well, he'd better have enough money for the métro, for two.* I've gotten the bends as I rapidly plummet down this hierarchy of hopes.

A FEW SLIGHTLY ANNOYING DETAILS I DIDN'T ANTICIPATE

Did I happen to mention that I arrived in Paris without the slightest lead on an apartment? After the flawless, carefree flight from New York City, I checked into a tiny three-star hotel on rue du Bac in the chic Saint-Germain. This was the part of Paris that I knew the best and liked the best, so I'd booked the cheapest room in the cheapest hotel I could find. I dumped my cat on the bed and dragged my ten pieces of luggage into this miniature version of a hotel room. With piles and pyramids of luggage taking up every square inch of floor space—not to mention blocking out the sun from the small window—I knew I'd have to spend all my waking hours trying to get out of this scenario and into my first apartment in Paris.

It should be noted that a three-star designation for hotels in France is completely not the same as three stars in the United States. Apparently the only requirements in France for this distinction are a bed, a door with a key, and a toilet—electricity is optional, curiously. I quickly learned how to bathe, wash my face, and brush my teeth in the dark since the bathroom light was a Studio 54 blinking strobe that, as a rule, trickled into a cinematic fade to black. Without fail, on my midnight trip to the bathroom I kicked the cat food bowls, Pelé style, all over the floor. *Amusant? Non.*

With my cat, Puccini, sniffing around in vain for a litter box, I was compelled to run out to the streets of Paris to begin the first of many scavenger hunts. There was no time to unearth my "bible" (the French-English dictionary), but I was confident that I'd surely come across cat litter at the local grocery store. When that didn't happen I had to resort to a popular method I've employed many times since: charades. I did my impression of a cat in a litter box while saying *"Pour merde de chat,"* over and over. And while my charade was ultimately successful, I was sad that this was my debut in Paris—I'd imagined something a little more chic, really. I set up Puccini in the broom closet that was our room, slapped a sign on the door with the warning DANGEROUS CAT INSIDE—DO NOT ENTER (again, portrayed in visuals alone) for the maid, and headed out to get a newspaper to begin my apartment search.

The little man who ran the front desk at the hotel, and who resembled Toulouse-Lautrec right down to the limp, suggested I buy *Le Figaro* to check out the apartment listings. After quickly flipping past the front page of the paper, where I could only understand the words *France, déteste,* and *Bush,* I found the unfurnished-apartment section. It was a mere two pages, for *all* of Paris. I was astounded. *The New York Times* always had innumerable options for habitation, and now I was faced with just three listings of apartments to rent in the entire 7th arrondissement. The other option was to consider apartments that were furnished, but it just creeps me out to imagine living with someone else's stuff, so I circled the first three ads. I thought I'd call, make a few appointments, and go to an open house or two. Instead I spent the better part of that day looking for a cellular phone. It was pretty obvious this whole process was going to be a hell of a lot more arduous than I expected.

The next day, phone in hand, I called to set up appointments. After each call, where I'd nervously try to speak in French (I think I may have said, "I'm looking for a cat with a view, but I have to tell you I have an apartment") and feebly try to interpret what they said back (usually I understood their first names, then nothing, and then maybe half of the address), I'd get off the phone, light about ten cigarettes and think, *Oh God, I hate this part.*

I finally got myself together and grabbed my checkbook and a file of bank statements and set off to an open house on rue de Lille. There was a crowd already waiting outside, made up of the same thirty people I'd see at every apartment viewing. The same desperate souls, all competing for the precious few apartments. I was given a form to fill out by the real estate agent and asked to wait my turn to enter. A "form" and "waiting," my two least favorite things. Hmmm. Let's see here . . .

Employer: I'd have to say, *"None."*
French Bank: Oops, is that important?
French Citizen: Nope!
Present Address: A cheap hotel, is that a problem?
References: Again, is that really necessary? Hmm, then I guess I'll have to go with "none" here.

Realizing I wasn't going to be able to talk my way into securing an apartment even if I could've spoken French, I crumpled up the form and took a tour of the apartment. It was absurdly tiny, quite dark, and had ceilings so low we were all cowering like Neanderthals, *and* there were absolutely no appliances. No refrigerator, no oven, no dishwasher—nothing. Just scraggly twisted wires coming out of all the walls. Wow, who knew that to rent an unfurnished apartment in France means BYOA (bring your own appliances)? *No way, that's crazy.* Who the hell moves through life with a stove in tow? And still the mass of apartment seekers were fiercely competing for this dark, depressing apartment that had a kitchen that resembled the inside of a radio. This apartment search process was really *merde de chat* all right.

Back in the hotel, sitting among the luggage with Puccini staring at me like, *Okay, what now, smarty-pants?* I took a few deep breaths and vowed to find us a place to live. Defeat was not possible. I spent the next week opening a French bank account and compiling a fairly convincing file that stated that while, yes, I was an unemployed, unbilingual expat with no stove, but with a cat, I was certainly financially capable of signing a lease.

I took old stock and mutual fund statements of accounts long since evaporated, whited out the dates, and made a dossier claiming I had loads of money, if not a visa. I seriously contemplated putting in the file absolutely anything that might possibly sway them: nude photos, money, my "best dressed" award from high school. While being a tall blonde American girl may be a success at cafés, I accepted it was working in absolute opposition to my getting an apartment. I was losing out on apartments left and right. My wish list of what I wanted in an apartment was quickly narrowed down to any apartment with electricity and a door (and I wasn't that firm on electricity.)

I spent two weeks seeing that same crowd of apartment seekers at every appointment. I guess they weren't having any more luck than I was. Then one Wednesday morning we all found ourselves at an apartment on rue de Verneuil. It was a gorgeous seventeenth-century building that had been under renovation for the past two years. Apparently it was one of the oldest buildings in Paris and had spent the last few hundred centuries leaning progressively into the street, until one day it took a death plunge and collapsed completely, blocking the rue de Verneuil for ages. But now all five floors were freshly restored and sold, and this little prize on the third floor was to rent. I knew it was going to be a great apartment because you could sense the tension in the crowd outside. Listen, at this point I *knew* these people. When I got in the door, I said to myself—for the first time in this whole exhausting search—*This is it!*

It was love at first sight. Everything was perfect: terracotta tiles on the floors, classically French wood beams on the high ceilings, brand new everything, and beautiful big windows with antique closures. And what was that behind the kitchen door? Could it be? *A new fridge. A new stove.*

The place was only 550 square feet, but every inch was truly charming. With the masses distracted filling out the *de rigueur* forms, I put my new strategy to work and strode directly up to the man who clearly owned the apartment. Summoning my full repetoire of French skills as I nervously stood before this short balding man clad in a cheap brown suit, I tried to express the following: I have a lot of money (lie!); I live in New York City and want this apartment just for a pied-à-terre (lie *numéro deux*). What do I have to do to get this apartment? But this is how the *real* conversation went:

"*Bonjour, monsieur. Excusez-moi, avez-vous un moment s'il vous plaît?* (No real errors yet.)

"*Évidemment, je suis occupé, mademoiselle.*" (I'm busy, lady, what do you want? By the way, lousy accent.)

"*Est-ce que c'est possible de parler intime?*" (Giddyup, here we go. I botched the formal use of *parler* (speak) and instead of asking to speak privately, asked if I could speak to him *intimately.* You may be thinking he would've interpreted that as possibly a sexual offer, but I'd already come to understand Frenchmen prefer their sexual liaisons infinitely more *indiscreet,* so it didn't even occur to him to consider it might be sexual. I assume that out of sheer curiosity he broke from the pack of wannabe renters, turned to me and gave me a minute of his precious time. Of course, I stole the moment to further embarrass myself.

"*J'habite à New York. Je seulement cherche un espace pour un peu de temps. J'ai trop de* money. *Qu'est-ce que je besoin de faire pour toi? Je suis* desperate." And I handed him my dossier. (As it poured out of my mouth, I cringed at the battering I was giving myself and the language. I'd butchered the formal address and launched into a babble: "I live in New York City, I'm merely looking for a *space* for a little *time* I have *too much* money. What do I need to do for you? (again informal, without respect) I'm desperate." Oh yeah, that's all *highly* intelligent. You'd never guess I went to college. Have two degrees, in fact. Wasted money.

As I watched the mob "ooh" and "ah" over the apartment, I felt myself becoming more and more fiercely determined to outsmart this group of strangers in my dream apartment. Then the potbellied proprietor with the bad comb-over said, with an amused smile, "*Donnez-moi un an de loyer plus un dépôt de garantie aujourd'hui, et c'est à vous.*" HUH? I wasn't so good at translating responses yet. WHAT? WHO? Is that sexual? Is that a reasonable suggestion? Staring at Monsieur le Propriétaire with a blank expression, I realized the entire negotiating process would go a whole lot smoother if I knew what he was saying. No chance we could mime this out is there, mister? By the grace of God, a young woman standing behind him jumped in with (in flawless English, thank the Lord above), "He's requesting you give him a check for a year's rent and the security deposit—*today.*"

I had a shot! I chose to completely ignore the fact that I didn't have the money and began to pull out my checkbook (look, everyone, I have a French checkbook!). Seeing this gesture he wagged his fat finger furiously and added (I translate), "*Non, mademoiselle.* A cashier's check, depositable today." Today? Ouch.

That verged on the impossible, but I think a few neural transmitters found each other and I immediately replied, "*Ça va.*" (Wishing I had a clue how to say the proper coherent response in French: "Fine, I'm going to my bank on the Champs Elysées and I'll bring back that cashier's check. This apartment is mine, get it?")

The young woman, who'd only seconds ago been my translating savior, threw a dramatic twist into the already challenging process. Leaning close to Monsieur le Propriétaire, she asked, "*Si je vous apporte un chèque d'abord, est-ce que je peux l'avoir?* (If she were to bring a check to him *first,* would he give it to her.) *Bitch.*

Clearly starting to enjoy the bidding war and ensuing chase, the proprietor announced to all, "*La première personne avec le chèque!*" Like I didn't already have enough pressure, now for all I knew Mademoiselle Troublemaker's bank was across the street, and she might even have the money. I *so* didn't. I had about seven thousand dollars and needed another ten thousand.

"*Charmante,*" I muttered in her direction. Nice one, girl, thanks a lot.

I literally ran, heart racing, out into the street to begin the first stage of the Race for Habitation competition. I was losing time and dashed from street corner to street corner in a hectic search for a taxi. Eventually I got one of the handful of taxis in Paris, jumped in and practically yelled, "Barclays, Champs Elysées!" I was ready to jump over the seat and slam his foot against the accelerator. "Faster, faster!" I couldn't keep myself from saying. If I interpreted his expression correctly, he would've preferred I say it during sex with him, rather than screaming in his ear from the backseat.

Finally, on the Champs Elysées, I sprang from the taxi in a wild sprint to Barclay's. *Shit, I left my new cell phone in the backseat. Oh, whatever, the apartment is so much more important, I'll get another one.* I flew into the bank, pulled out my stack of credit cards and asked for credit card advances on three of them to cleverly, instantaneously acquire the necessary funds. I was so convinced this was the sure-fire, can't miss, genius idea of my life that I was already beginning to decorate the apartment in my mind, when the bank clerk said, "I'm sorry, mademoiselle, but that kind of transaction would have to be approved by the bank manager and he is away at lunch."

No! No one else can sign off on this? No, this is France, Klein: Business comes to a standstill during the lunch hour as every bloody soul in town goes to load up on *steak frites* and *crème brûlée.* I hate to admit I pulled out the "crying card," but I was sincerely desperate and the idea that some guy was leisurely drinking his Bordeaux while I lost the apartment of my dreams just made me hysterical.

She correctly deduced that my sobbing in the lobby wasn't going to be good for business. She called the manager on his cell phone and got clearance. She called my credit cards and tapped them out (so much for paying the hotel bill!). Mission accomplished. Gigantic cashier's check in hand, I raced into traffic, ready to throw myself in front of a car and steal it if I had to. Unbelievably, I found a taxi and allowed myself to catch my breath, so hitting lunch-hour traffic at the Place de la Concorde just seemed a cruel twist of fate. I was writhing in impatient agony in the backseat as I saw visions of that damn French girl arriving just seconds before me, handing over her check. *Oh Christ, if I have to witness it firsthand—her excitement, her gloating perfect Parisienne smile—I will die.*

Minutes before I was about to have a stress-induced, brain aneurysm we pulled up in front of the building. I threw a wad of euros at the driver and pounced from the cab into the building. I ignored the mob of people jostling in the apartment, *still* filling out forms, and trying to get the owner's attention. My rival was nowhere in sight—fabulous. I thrust my check through the assembled crowd and announce, "*Voilà!*" The owner nods approvingly and I restrain my victory dance until later (it went on for hours back at the hotel; the cat thought I'd lost it) and then he says, "Well done, I'll expect you to do the same thing next year." I'm thinking, *Yeah, sure, whatever. You get my first-born child, I don't care. I have the apartment! Tra-la-la!*

I was given the keys, and signed some stack of documents—frankly, I could've been voluntarily declaring myself clinically insane (fine, I'm an insane girl WITH an apartment)—and we shook hands. I smiled at the apartment hunters, thirty I would never have to see again. The "American girl" had finally persevered!

I skipped onto the street just as my female competitor got out of a taxi and looked right up into my triumphant face. She glowered. I smiled—with that *Don't fuck with me, I'm a New Yorker* expression I'd earned in the Big Apple—and ruthlessly offered, "*Bonne chance la prochaine fois.*" (Good luck next time. I know, I *am* such a bitch.)

I stood a moment and looked up at *my* new building, in the heart of Saint-Germain, and felt complete and total joy. Being a New Yorker I also hoped like hell the owner wasn't going to disappear with all my money, and I'd arrive the next day to see the key wouldn't even fit in the door.

The following day I ripped the Do Not Enter sign off my hotel room door, put my hotel bill on yet another credit card (I had thirty whole days to figure out that financial debacle, no problem), and made the grand exit from my three-star, disco-bathroomed, Toulouse Lautrec–run hotel.

Hauled luggage and cat up the rickety staircase (hmmm, didn't notice that yesterday) and I was in. Another victory dance (can you blame me?), but no one to call to celebrate with, no friends or even a phone, for God's sake. So I gallivanted around all 550 square feet of my very own apartment until sunset. It started to get cold; apparently the heat wasn't turned on yet. Hell, I didn't care, I was just thrilled to have actual light in the bathroom again. I stood at my window looking into the dark blue sky over the Louvre and said to myself, *I did it!*

I climbed onto my makeshift bed of a garment bag jammed with winter

coats, pulled out the fur-trimmed Prada for a blanket and drifted off happily
into sleep. At 5:00 a.m., I was rudely awakened by what literally sounded like
the Louvre being torn down under my window. No, just the daily truck deliv-
eries to the Proxi grocery store across the street. Saturday night in Times
Square is quieter than this extravaganza. But you know what? By the end of
the first week I kind of grew to like it. That, my friends, is the magical power
of Paris.

SUBLIME PLEASURE DU JOUR

Living in Paris is an experience like no other. It's like being on a ride at an
amusement park: wildly exciting, a bit scary, a little overpriced. Sometimes
you're so thrilled you could wet your pants and sometimes you're left feeling a
bit nauseous. With that same shaky trust in the people who have set up the establishment, I might add.

But this adventure is so chock-full of stimuli that I have to carry around a
journal to jot down every gorgeous moment as it comes. Just quick, random
notes of any bloody thing that makes my day unique, complete, fabulous,
memorable, etc. You get the gist.

I only write in "Sublime Pleasures" when I'm truly compelled. Whether it
be drunk as a skunk, half falling off a bar stool at La Palette (okay, I *did* fall,
but then I had the good sense to order a "cuf of copy" to sober up a smidge).
Or I add to it while taking an afternoon tea at a deserted Café de Flore. Here's
the first entry:

*This dream has the perfect soundtrack. To awaken each morning to the
sound of doves cooing and church bells ringing. C'mon, it doesn't get any
more beautiful than that. The sirens and car alarms of New York City are a
distant memory.*

*The first sounds I hear as I come into consciousness are usually the ten-
der voices of mothers and their children, up early and out on their morning
outing to the* boulangerie *down the street to buy brioche and croissants. The
gentle,* "Maman . . ." *followed by,* "Comment, ma chérie?" *is like music.
I've woken up to find myself living in the children's book* Madeline. *All the
struggles with Puccini on the flight, all the exhausting days of traipsing*

around looking for an apartment, all the moments I wanted to burst into
tears of frustration . . . So entirely, deliciously worth it.

FRIEND COUNT

Okay, here's a question: If your cat's bipolar, can you count that as two
friends? No? All right then. Zero, for God's sakes. Do you think I have time
to drum up a friend right now? I'm hip deep in luggage, cat depression, and
the struggle for existence. I'm lucky if I can get out the door without tucking
the back of my skirt into my pantyhose. So, as far as friends, I'm still trying to
get Puccini to talk to me. He's bitching that the language is too hard to learn
at his advanced age, the cat food in France is subpar, the cat litter is too rough,
etc.—the usual expat cat complaints no doubt.

Viagra in the Air,
a Dwarf in a Top Hat,
and Baby Dior

Late April

MONSIEUR RIGHT REPORT

What's with this city? I swear it's making me into a sexual predator. It's *not* my fault. If you've ever been to Paris you *so* know what I'm talking about. The second you get off the plane, you just get swept into this maelstrom of mad, wanton desire: for croissants, for shoes, for men. For the love of God, I've got horns so big, I could fall over. Dear me. It's something in the air. Maybe they're pumping Viagra into the atmosphere. Beats me. Whatever it is, it instantly envelops you and catapults you into becoming a ravenous lioness in heat. I've learned you can't fight it; just be *damn* careful who you saddle up next to.

That said, time to dress to the hilt and blaze into the Parisian dating world. Friday night, Paris, seven o'clock: "Let the games begin!" I actually said out loud as I searched my closet for one of those "I feel good in this" outfits. I opted for the "never let me down before" chocolate brown leather pants, a tobacco silk bias-cut camisole with a cappucino three-quarter-length lamb-suede jacket tossed over it. (Guess it's kinda obvious I used to work in fashion, huh? Unfortunately my color references are forever altered. Which can become absurd when you find yourself telling the veterinarian, "Yes, it seems Puccini is throwing up a mélange of terracotta vomit with hues of vermilion and cinnabar.")

At twilight I set out for Le Fumoir, a chic bar-restaurant just behind the Louvre. I'd been turned on to this joint by an article in French *Elle* two months ago, and had made a big mental note in the file of "places to go if I ever move my ass to Paris." And now I was escorting my ass over there.

Passing over the footbridge Pont des Arts, I am struck by the incredible sky, all vibrant purples and vivid fuschia as the sun is just beginning to dip below the horizon. I feel at once entirely anonymous, entranced by the beauty and yet a little anxious. The awareness that I don't know a living soul in Paris is a constant source of anxiety. Sometimes it's a delicious sense of rebirth: getting the chance to discover your true self, listening to your innermost thoughts, and other times . . . *it just bites.* But I tell myself, *I went to all the trouble of moving here, so I'd better keep a stiff upper lip and persevere, and frankly, I have no other option.*

All right, maybe the silk camisole was a bit optimistic, brrrr! It's a tad cold so I wrap my Fortuny scarf around my neck another time. I stroll past the groups of young Beaux-Arts students who I've come to notice constantly hang out in small clusters all over the bridge. They sit sharing a bottle of wine, a joint, laughing uproariously as nearby a few straggling tourists try to eek out the last photos of the day. I smile, thinking, *God, I love Paris, it's breathtaking, all the . . . What the . . . ? Dammit!*

My boot heel anchored itself between the bridge's wooden planks and I'm violently yanked backwards midstride as my other foot shoots forward from the momentum. I fall forward onto my hands and knees with nothing resembling grace, and unconsciously yell out loud, "FUCK ME!" as I try feverishly to extricate my heel from its trap. The stoned students fall on their backs, pointing and laughing. Great. Yeah, this is a confidence builder . . . killer start to the night. Could I be more embarrassed?

Up again, having left the black plastic heel plate as a souvenir for the ravenous shoe-eating bridge and as a tangible reference for the high-as-kites students to illicit yet more waves of laughter. Okay. Great mood: Slightly diminished to be sure. Optimism: Shaken. Cue: Bright red face. Perfect. I pick up the pace as though, "Sure, that's fine I'm just in *such* a hurry!"

Turning now onto the quai du Louvre, I hear click, SCREECH!, click, SCREECH!! *Jesus, is that noise me?* I lift up my right foot to see the metal-exposed heel is now grinding into the concrete with a sound akin to a finger cymbal attached to my shoe. *Oh, genius, this is just chic to die. Whatever.* I click-screech over to Le Fumoir, enter the double doors, and saddle up to the large central wood bar. I plop my purse down on the shiny bar and skooch up on a leather barstool. Pp-ff-ftt! Charming, my leather pants sliding across the leather stool have, in one entrance-killing moment, managed to sound like I've expelled a gigantic fart as my mating call! *For the love of God, can I get a break over here?*

"*Bonsoir, qu'est-ce que vous desirez?*" the waiter shouts from four feet away, clearly trying to avoid the imagined (I swear!) pungent personal space of the American Fart-Machine Girl.

"*Un verre de vin blanc, s'il vous plaît. Et avez-vous des allumettes?*" (I ask for a pack of matches everywhere I go. I always take them home, throw them in a drawer and then on slow nights, I can look at the heap of matchbooks and say to myself, *Hey, I have been a social girl. I'm allowed an off night.* It's clearly a pathetic game of self-delusion but occasionally surprisingly effective.)

I sit for about half an hour, noticing that once again, I'm the only person alone among packs of couples and groups all happily engaged in animated conversations. This is HARD. I'm simultaneously proud of myself and dying to get the hell outta there. Drink number two, cigarette number four. *Wait a minute, do I look like a prostitute? No, maybe I just look like I'm waiting for someone. I am waiting for someone, I just don't know who the HELL it is yet.* I'm quickly depleting the "I'm fine here by myself don't feel stupid at all" facade when I notice the arrival of three rather interesting-looking men. All of them smiling and confident, well dressed and mid to late thirties. Bingo! Hmmm. I like the tall one. Dark shiny hair the color of espresso and blessed with impossibly blue eyes. He seems quietly elegant and inexplicably intelligent looking. Always a charming combination. Standing at the bar about six feet away, they order a round of mojitos, apparently the speciality of the house. In no time the tall one notices I'm half—all right, entirely—staring at him. He turns and says something to his friends (which of course I'd give my right arm to have heard), and they all come over to my side of the bar.

"*Bonsoir,* are you waiting for someone?" the short one asks. Is there a right answer? If I say yes they'll move away, but if I say no I'm revealed as a single girl out on the prowl. Bloody hell.

"I was, but she just called my cell phone and said she can't make it." (Quick thinking. Well done, Klein.)

"Well then, can we join you?" he responds, not missing a beat. I gesture the equivalent of "please do" and in the blink of an eye I am in one of my favorite places in the world, surrounded by Frenchmen. Cool. A round of introductions, *et voilà*—Philippe (the shorty), Frederich (the least attractive), and Gilles (the tall, shy target). Gilles, eh? Not a great name but it'll do. Philippe quickly becomes the interpreter as Gilles speaks not a word of English (predictably, as is my luck). We go through the famously traditional spiel of "What do you do? Are you visiting? Oh, from New York? How great!" About thirty minutes into this, I realize I'd better make it blatantly obvious I've set my sights on Gilles, or this is all gonna get really fishy. Cutting back on the flirtation-for-all, I brazenly reach over and push a stray hair off Gilles's forehead and smile with a look that says, "So? Are you with me?" . . . And I wait.

Like clockwork, two beats later Gilles takes my scarf and in some feeble gesture to connect, drapes it twice around *his* neck. Apparently this move has released a waft of my perfume into the air, and he swoons in mock ecstasy. I'm charmed. Don't know why I find this so endearing but it works. Case closed.

"*Dites-moi, êtes-vous célibataire?*" he asks me with imploring eyes.

Am I *celibate?* I'm thinking that's a *très* personal question. Man, are they direct here! My stunned expression is immediately read by Philippe who offers "No, Klein, *célibataire* means 'single' in French."

"Oh God, then, yes, *je suis célibataire*," I say, gagging on the phrase. They all look at one another and obviously this is the correct response, as they raise their glasses and toast, "Chin-chin!" in unison. (A bit cheesy, boys, but whatever, maybe that expression is not as queer *in France*.)

"Your glass is empty, Klein, would you like to try a mojito? We're getting another round," Philippe offers as he raises his hand overhead to summon the waiter.

"Actually, I've never tried one." (I say, thinking, *Mixing alcoholic beverages never bodes well for me. Once, at Pravda, in New York City, I drank three Cosmopolitans, a glass of red and a glass of white wine, and ended up borrowing—okay, stealing—someone's limo and breaking two ribs by night's end. No good can come of this.* And yet, as is often the case, I completely ignore my better judgment and proceed into hedonism.)

"All right, but just one." Four mojitos arrive and are raised with ceremony in my direction, toasting my virgin taste-testing of this drink famously chock-full of ice and enormous green mint leaves. Like a nervous cocky girl, I take way too big of a gulp and as the cool, refreshing alcohol glides down my throat, a handful of thick leaves lodges itself securely in my windpipe.

With Gilles, Philippe, and Frederich awaiting my review, I'm attempting to utter, "It's fabulous," but I'm suddenly aware that *neither* speaking nor breathing are in my repertoire. I try desperately to swallow, once, twice. No luck, all systems are at a standstill. Plan B: choke them back up. Ahhh, shit. "Ka! Ka! Haack!" I can't. The godamn leaves have jammed in some sort of flora dam, and it's quickly becoming obvious I'm turning into a prime candidate for the *très* unsexy Heimlich maneuver.

Gilles suddenly grasps the extreme urgency of the situation, and in one fell swoop is behind me and swatting my back with hearty blows. I feel at once the immediate attention of all eyes in the room and the surreal reality . . . I AM CHOKING! Things are starting to go out of focus. I literally *can't breath*. The manager rushes over to see if he can help; people stand up from their tables to gauge if they can assist in any way. Total pandemonium.

Philippe, Frederich, and Gilles are all pummeling me in succession, yelling repetitively, "Ça va?" and then ridiculously, Frederich is unconsciously offering me a sip of mojito. I may be losing all oxygen to my brain right now, but you win the stupidity prize, boy. About eight good hard blows later, I'm sputtering a voiceless version of "I'm okay," quite unconvincingly, as I spew bits of leaf to the four corners of the bar and all over the floor. Phew! The worst is over: my eyes are teary, I'm drooling spittle, I've surely got mint in my teeth, and I'm feebily trying to reclaim a sense of cool by shakily lighting up a cigarette. Pathetic *and* scary. Two things I try to avoid in life.

Philippe hands me a tall glass of much-needed water. Frederich elegantly lights my cigarette as Gilles discreetly reaches over and gently puts his hand on my shoulder. "Klein, wow, that was rough. Are you okay? You gave us a bit of a scare. Dramatic? Yes, you're an interesting girl for sure," says Philippe as he kindly plucks mint from my hair.

"Perhaps mojitos aren't your drink," jokes Frederich.

"Right, I'll stick with white wine," I choke out, and we fall slowly and gratefully back into our lighthearted chatter. An hour goes by, I scooch off to the bathroom for a quick pee and to do one of my thrice-nightly traditional makeup checks (to just confirm that the concealer has indeed evaporated, revealing the red spot on my chin and that, yes, I have mascara pooling under my eyes). Looking in the mirror in the dimly lit bathroom, squeezing between two young girls clad in skirts so short that they could be mistaken for belts, I survey the damage. I'm a wreck as expected. Well, that's reassuring. Dabbing another layer of Shiseido concealer on the hopelessly obvious blemish, I steal a moment to assess the night in progress. *Damn near died but other than that, not a bad night. I'm loving this Gilles. He's terribly polite and shy. Never had me a shy one. He's being terribly subtle, hardly even flirting with me . . . that's new. Gotta say it's making me a little crazy. Oh, I so do love a challenge. If he fell at my feet I'd have been* très *disappointed. Maybe he doesn't even like me. No, he digs me . . . right? Oh God, who knows. Why is my skin so bad? Wish I spoke French better. Gotta say the mint leaves were like a natural mouthwash. I'll probably have fresh breath for a month. Well, better go back to my boys.*

Sauntering through the restaurant with all the confidence of a girl who has both tripped and choked in front of a great many people and still managed to survive, I realize despite myself that I am having a ball with the Three Musketeers. The long dining room is hazy with the gray smoke of a thousand exhaled cigarettes and the music by Air bellowing over the din of animated dinner conversation. This is all *new.* How cool. I love "new."

Back at the bar with my three French boys graciously welcoming me back, I slide back onto the bar stool ever so carefully (having learned my lesson with the leather pants one humiliating time too many, and knowing there's only so many embarrassing moments a girl should have in a single evening). Philippe pipes up with, "If you're not busy, we're going to meet a few friends for dinner at Chez Omar in the Marais. Want to come?"

"Pourquoi pas!" I answer, realizing this has replaced my previous often repeated motto of "Carpe diem." Thank God, because that was *so* tired.

Gilles offers to take me in his car, which turns out to be an elegant black Jaguar. Still feeling the aftershocks of my New York City lifestyle, I dig the car. I get in and look at the Gilles's beaming smile and think, *Sexy man, sexy car, I'm in Paris. Now we're talking.* I return his smile, and he takes my hand and gallantly kisses it while uttering something in French. Which I'm hoping was something like, "You are very beautiful, what a pleasure it is to meet you," but just as easily could've been, "For God's sakes girl, don't fucking scratch the floor mat with your tacky metal heel."

We zipped off into the cool night air, Philippe and Frederich following behind in their black Audi, arriving at the restaurant in a big production as we hook up with six of their friends. Dinner was great fun as Gilles made shadow puppets in the candlelight to clue me into the menu. The rabbit, cow, duck, and lobster were a cinch, while the rendition of mussels and sea skate definitely fell flat. But we got along marvelously and I loved being so graciously welcomed into this circle of witty, exuberant friends, not to mention that I was beginning to think Gilles was "the cat's pajamas" (as we say in Wisconsin).

Joining the Three Musketeers, we became a Gang of Four and went out almost every evening for two weeks. It was like the accelerated crash course of Parisian nightlife: aperitifs at Mathis Bar, dinners at Pershing Hall, Thiou, and Hôtel Costes followed by dancing hard at Baron and Castel. Nonstop decadent fun, endless laughing, crazy kissing, and one very memorable night of spontaneous passion, pressed up against the cold stone of the Louvre as gendarmes hovered close by.

With each moment we spent together, I was falling more and more for Gilles as he just continued to charm and impress me at every turn. Which is amazing because he, honestly, had a rather everyman face. Not an exceptional feature save his intensely blue ("Tiffany" robin's egg blue, as we'd refer to them in New York City) eyes. And although he enjoyed posing as though he had the body of an Adonis (God, I'm a good sport for not bursting into tears of laughter), he had serious love handles. But what he lacked physically he made up for in other, more important (read: less superficial ways). He owned a beautiful gallery of fifteenth–seventeenth century tapestries (try finding that in New York City—fat chance), had exquisite taste in clothes, music, art, and furniture—*all my major criteria.* So even though I had the French comprehension of a doorstop and he had the verbal English skills of a mute, we were beginning to embark on quite a love affair. I loved his lively spirit, that he busted his ass working (*so-oo-o* un-French), and while not being exactly handsome, he was classically French looking. He had something really sexy going on (other than the Jag, okay?) some *je ne sais quoi.* Ha! I finally found the perfect opportunity to use that phrase . . . cool.

A FEW SLIGHTLY ANNOYING DETAILS I DIDN'T ANTICIPATE

After the thrill of finding an apartment abated, it was screamingly obvious I was going to have to get some serious furniture. As I had arrived in Paris with nothing more than a flight-induced freaked-out feline and ten pieces of luggage, I had to quickly and cheaply furnish my apartment.

The budget-born theme of Modern Nomad interior, utilizing various pieces of luggage as furniture (valise = table, soft duffle bag = chair, train case = side table) was better in romantic theory than in execution. Not to mention that sleeping on a garment bag jammed full of winter coats fell short of any semblance of comfort. Clearly I needed to choose some kind of interior theme, as it is quite possibly illegal in France not to do every damn thing in one's life without a commitment to style. This decision was the easy part.

My five-year boyfriend (it was a five-year relationship; he wasn't five years old, in case that's what you were thinking) from New York City had a pied-à-terre in Saint-Germain. We'd stay there each time we came to Paris. His pied-à-terre was in a beautiful seventeenth-century *hôtel particulier* on rue de Grenelle, with lavish gardens and an interior dictated by its architecture, in the style of Louis XVI. (Cool detail: it had once been the home of the milliner to Louis XVI. That *kills* me.) The apartment was charming as hell and I guess I'd always dreamt of having an apartment of my own in Paris in the same style: totally French, very feminine, and with an opulent canopied bed. It was completely *not* my personal style, but somehow my little French dream got all convoluted with this image I'd had all the years I lived in New York. All during my twenties I'd been accumulating files of magazine clippings of what I envisioned my Paris apartment would look like one day. Among them was "the bed." I'd torn it out of the visual bible of French style, *Côte Sud* magazine. It was a reproduction of the wrought-iron canopied bed of the writer Colette. You don't get more French than that.

Now, finally in Paris, I unearthed the photo and tracked down the little boutique that created them on rue d'Assas. I'll never forget how bizarre it was upon entering the shop to see that, strangely enough, the older woman who owned the shop was a dead ringer for Colette. Talk about getting carried away with a theme. But the bed was magnificent, piled with boudoir pillows and antique linens of cream and ivory.

It was the only bed in the store, and it was *tiny,* a "single." Impossibly small for what I was sure were going to be innumerable nights of sexual gymnastics with Monsieur Right, or even Monsieur Right Now.

Inquiring when I could have the same bed, but in a queen size, delivered,

I encountered one of my first wake-up calls to the reality versus the dream. The faux-Colette boutique owner said it would take *three months* for a queen-size bed to be made *sur commande* (to order). Damn it! Another glitch.

Seeing as I'd been sleeping like a contortionist on the garment bag, waking up achy and crabby as all hell, and this was *the* bed, I put the cash down and had it delivered that evening. In the tiny shop it looked terribly quaint, but in truth it's a miniature version of a real bed. While it does make a charming daybed to recline on while reading or day dreaming, it *so* wasn't made for two. (Except maybe two midgets and I'm not going to invite two midgets to sleep over *and* give them my bed. This much I know in life.) So, on the occasion I had Gilles stay over, it would have to become an altogether different gymnastic routine than I'd imagined. The process was as follows:

1. Interrupting passionate kissing to flip on the lights and begin the creation of a bed big enough for two. Which involved . . .
2. Moving furniture out of the way to accommodate incoming mattresses. A complex redecoration of apartment, really.
3. Ripping off the bed linens to expose two futon mattresses and dragging one futon onto the floor.
4. Pulling out the second futon mattress and aligning it in center of apartment floor next to the first futon.
5. After having redressed linens on top of two side-by-side mattresses, both members of couple exhausted and dripping with sweat from expending last morsel of energy, collapse on bed, *too tired* to have sex. *Voilà!*

After acquiring the so-called dream bed, I still had a zillion other things to buy for my apartment. In keeping with the interior theme of romantic Louis XVI, I had fixated (another fixation? *mais oui!*) on finding a proper French boudoir table. It all went back to my fantasy of applying that last dab of lipstick as my lady-in-waiting secured my diamond choker while I made the court attendants at Versailles await my arrival. (So I have an active imagination. Sue me.)

I had read in my plethora of guidebooks that a whole smattering of antiques could be had cheaply at the flea markets on the outskirts of Paris. The cheapest being the Puces des Vanves on the southern edge of Paris, where you could apparently haggle your voice hoarse and get some great deals.

The first Saturday of living in my new apartment, I set the alarm for 6:00 a.m., to arrive early to the flea market and get the really good stuff before the rest of Paris even woke up.

I stuffed my pockets full of euros and went out to find a taxi. On a cold Saturday morning in Paris there isn't a soul on the street, so I got first dibs on the dozing drivers waiting at the taxi stand on rue du Bac.

The driver was in a vile mood. I didn't know what destination would've pleased him, but the flea market certainly wasn't on the top of his list. We drove through neighborhoods I'd never known existed, deserted and eerily desolate. It felt a little like we were suddenly in war-ravaged Baghdad. It can be terribly disconcerting to be in a car with an angry driver, not having a clue where you are. I remember feeling quite sure this was like the beginning of a bad movie where the foreigner ends up chopped up into little pieces or sold into white slavery. I could already see my father pleading with congressmen for assistance to get my body parts shipped back to the States.

Then abruptly he stopped the taxi, pointed to the left, saying, "C'est les Puces des Vanves," and demanded about ten euros. The flea market wasn't exactly bustling with activity. In fact, it didn't so much resemble a flea market as much as a street strewn with crap. The streets were full of Beverly Hillbilly–esque trucks piled high with a sorry collection of secondhand furniture. The bleary-eyed vendors were a sad lot, resembling a casting call for a Fellini movie. A one-time torch singer perhaps, now with a cigarette in one hand and a Pastis gripped in the other, with the fingernails of a hyena. A dwarf in a top hat arranging his display of old corkscrews and chipped tea sets. I had wanted cheap, and clearly this was one small step above garbage; I settled in to peruse the goods. I was seeking a mirror, two armchairs, and my coveted dressing table.

Eventually, behind half of a rusty gate, I spotted my pièce de résistance: the makeup table. It couldn't have been more perfect. Dove gray with a round mirror encompassed by wood scrollwork, with four pretty little drawers for storing tiaras and the like. A bit weathered and a few chips, but I decided I'd explain that happened during the French Revolution, thus adding to its charm. The man with croissant on his whiskers and red-wine breath was asking for 400 euros, a bit too steep for me. So I pulled out all the stops. Reverting to "poor (literally in this case, with my new budget in place) little American girl trying to make a go of it in your beautiful country" (I'm pushing it there). The whole big smile, batting eyelashes, charm at full throttle gig. Ha! I hornswoggled it down to 250 euros.

Ecstatic and self-congratulatory at my effective bargaining skills, I eagerly began bidding on damn near everything. Luckily, common sense kicked in at some point, or I'd now be the proud owner of a circa-1900 gynecological chair, which I'm sure would be a bit shocking for guests at family dinners. But clearly it has its uses.

A bit later, after accidentally reaching into a bin of old scraggly wigs (are those big sellers—could you even give them away?), I came across two little Louis XVI chairs. All spindly, delicate, and reupholstered in a fabulous gray toile de Jouy. So what if one of the legs was broken and the other ill-balanced. It's not like I was going to have André the Giant over for tea. And so for the thousandth time in my life, I bought chairs that were (as friends and family remind me constantly) attractive but utterly uncomfortable. Fine, at least I'm consistent.

In my frenzy of furniture acquisition, I had not really plotted out the system of getting this stuff back to my apartment. No huge surprise that the vagabond junk dealers don't offer delivery and my inquiries were met with dismissive laughter. But being Independent I Can't Be Stopped Girl, I began a long, laborious shuffle of furniture from the market to the corner of the street where the taxi had left me three hours ago.

Obviously items left unattended in this godforsaken part of town have about the same chances of surviving as David Duke at a rap concert. So I was dashing back and forth proclaiming to all in the vicinity, "This is mine, I'm coming back for it in one minute." (I've had chicer moments in life to be sure.) Still, someone managed to swipe my new walnut-framed mirror, and I couldn't even get a soul to acknowledge it ever existed. Or that *I* even existed for that matter. My self-congratulatory mood disappeared with the mirror.

Fine, you French furniture felons, I'm outta here. I need a taxi immediately to escape this whole situation. I waited ten minutes, twenty minutes, not a cab in sight. I guess it makes sense that taxi drivers don't exactly line up at 10:00

a.m. in front of crap furniture markets in bad neighborhoods, giddily awaiting someone throwing old junk in their cab. Without a clue, I continued my furniture drag-a-thon about a hundred feet up the street to a busier intersection, hoping this locale would improve my chances.

As I spotted a taxi, I did the progressively humiliating performance of whistle-yell "Taxi!," frantically wave arms around, chase taxi down with the grand finale of the taxi driver looking right at me, then at heap-o-furniture, and hitting the gas. Charming, really. Does life get any more fun than that? My Paris dream was taking a beating.

Finally a good old soul stopped his taxi and even helped me to heave the furniture into the trunk and backseat. Faith in humanity redeemed! I gave him my address, rue de Verneuil (you guess how that *neuil* bit should be pronounced; I gave it my best French accent), and off we went. If I'd thought we were going to Baghdad on the way to the flea market, now we were going back by way of Kabul. And damn, it was taking a long time. And nothing was even looking remotely familiar. Hey, wait a minute, I've got a rather efficient internal compass, and I was completely sure he was lost—or *I* was. Then again he was Parisian so it had to be me.

I asked the driver again, *"Je voudrais rue de Verneuil, monsieur?"* He thought I'd said rue Verdun, an entirely different part of Paris. Fabulous accent of mine. Entirely my fault as I can't even pronounce the street I live on! I deserved to pay the extra eight euros as a pronunciation penalty. We traversed Paris in a grand tour, trying to get back to civilization. I was flushed beet red, feeling suddenly quite ill-prepared for this life I'd thrown myself into. Why the hell was I at thirty-four years old still doing all this crap alone? It'd be funny as hell if someone was with me, but alone, it just felt pitiful. *Merde!* (At least I could swear in French).

I paid the driver literally the last centime I had. The money I'd put in my back pocket to save for food for the weekend. I dragged the furniture up the three flights of tiny stairs, piece by excruciating piece. I was spent. Literally, physically, and emotionally. I just left the furniture in the entrance and crawled back into bed hoping I'd wake up later and discover it had all been a bad dream.

SUBLIME PLEASURE DU JOUR

My neighborhood—the "7th"—is just storybook charming. The gorgeous architecture, the beautiful little shops, it's all *parfait*. I can hardly believe I'm within three blocks of the Louvre, Musée d'Orsay, and my adored Café de Flore, where Sartre, Hemingway, and Simone de Beauvoir used to write, hold court, and get hideously drunk. And now I can too, anytime I want. (Get drunk there, that is; the "hold court" part? Not so much yet.)

Every little shop in my *quartier* (district) is so precise, defined. The greatest cheese shop in France, a quaint little establishment named Barthélemy, is just a few blocks over on rue de Grenelle. I've come to believe cheese is like adult candy. At a certain age you stop craving Mars bars and find yourself salivating over a divine *Gouda*. This kicks in sometime around age twenty-five, at the same time you discover the appeal of a fine red wine, older men, classical music, and a good night's sleep.

At Barthélemy you're almost knocked off your feet by the deliciously fragrant aromas of hundreds of fresh cheeses. Enormous rounds of *Comté* as big as tires, tiny hearts of *chèvre* sprinkled with peppercorns, oozing *Camemberts* in twenty varieties. Strange blocks of crumbly, mold-covered *gloriette,* and blue slabs of *fleur du maquis*. Heaven.

The yellow flat sheets of "American cheese" individually wrapped in plastic are quite frankly criminal once you discover what cheese, *real* cheese, can be. The unique difference to French cheese is that because it isn't regulated by stiff pasteurization laws, it develops flavors that are literally *illegal* in the United States. I recently read a marvelous quote by the famous restaurant reviewer Patricia Wells. She said that the three most important components of French cuisine—bread, wine, and cheese—are all a result of the same magical process: fermentation. Let's hear it for letting things go to rot! I'll drink to that!

FRIEND COUNT

The Three Musketeers: Gilles, Philippe, and Frederich. I'm pretty damn pleased to have met these generous souls, because it's wildly difficult to make friends at this age, in a foreign country, with zero contacts and minimal language skills. It got to the point, I kind of considered just walking up to people who looked interesting and handing them a typed copy of my "friend résumé," "See, if you'll look at the list there, you'll notice I have many fine attributes: I'm punctual, a good listener, and rather well read. At the bottom are the names of people who can confirm this. Feel free to give me a call, I'm available CONSTANTLY!"

The Three Musketeers,
Asshole Decoder Ring,
and Petit Bateau

May

MONSIEUR RIGHT REPORT

After two glorious weeks of being joined at the hip (*literally* . . . I won't even go into the "spontaneous sex in the parking garage" story; thanks to the video security cams, I'm sure by now it's available on the Internet anyway) Gilles invited me to join him on a tapestry buying trip in Brussels and the quaint village of Bruges. I bravely accepted. Hell, I had no friends to talk me out of it and I *did* come to live an adventure, didn't I? Kicking back in the Jaguar, it was beautiful to see the French countryside whiz by and be dashing off to discover a new place. But it would've been just a tad nicer if we could've, say, HAD A CONVERSATION. (Mental note: *Try to find boyfriends with whom you can speak a common language other then sex.*)

At one point I thought Gilles was trying to tell me about a dream he'd had, only to discover he had been explaining a song on the radio. *Hell-o!* After that we just played music and abandoned verbal communication.

I flipped for Bruges. A fabulous suite in the elegant Hôtel de Tuilerien overlooking the canal, long walks around the beautiful village at dusk, gorging on mussels served in big black pots with huge platters of crispy *frites,* visiting twelfth-century churches, and such great sex I glowed in the dark. Shellfish, apses, and screaming orgasms—what more could I ask for? (Okay, a flow of coherent communication would have been nice.) A gorgeous setting can really enhance or, dare I say, even create a sense of romance, and, by God, you know it's pretty damn hard to fight with someone when communication is limited to words of one syllable.

A week later Gilles's birthday arrived. He'd been so generous with me, so

I planned to flourish gifts on him and cook a whole romantic meal for two. He'd told me he had no plans to see anyone but me on his birthday, so I was shocked when suddenly around eight o'clock throngs of his friends began to arrive, just as I was setting the Champagne on ice. Within an hour, forty people were stuffed into his apartment, all carrying gifts, dressed for a party, and it quickly became obvious he'd *prearranged* a party for himself and not told me. Okay. That's a bit wackadoodle. Not exactly sure why he didn't tell me. Who knows, maybe he did and I just didn't grasp it in French. Beats me. The other two Musketeers, Philippe and Frederich, arrived, and confirmed that Gilles had in fact, asked everyone to come and that apparently we were all to go to dinner at the hipster restaurant Pershing Hall. Hmm. All right, Gilles, you are officially bizarro, verging on rude, to let me slave all day cooking knowing a dinner tête-à-tête wasn't in the cards. Then again, perhaps Gilles had correctly anticipated that the *lotte avec crème beurre* was, at best, going to taste like an old shoe. Fair enough. I switched gears to superhostess since I was "the girlfriend," and it was actually quite fun, since everyone was very warm and claimed that Gilles had told them all about me and that he was madly in love. I laughed it off, not even sure if I was really that crazy about him or if I was just in love with having a group of friends and a social life. Champagne corks popped left and right, a Franz Ferdinand CD was turned up, and people were starting to dance. I headed off to the bathroom to fix my makeup and steal a moment of privacy.

Touching up my MAC spice lip liner, I tried to tell myself maybe this was all for the better. Maybe it would be more fun than the private romantic night I'd planned. Clearly it took the pressure off *me*. It's not my country, go with the flow. Back in the *salon* (living room) I see Frederich has jumped up on the *guéridon* (table) and is leading the assembled crowd in a painfully French version of "Happy Birthday." "*Hoppy Burrthday tu ewe . . .*" Amusing. Gilles is just thrilled to be the center of attention, master of the house, and I'm happy for him. Hey, who's that chick by his side with the huge birthday present? I didn't meet her and she is just a *little* too pretty to be glued to my boyfriend.

"Hey, Frederich. Hi, kiddo, great party, *non*? Do you have enough Champagne? Tell me, who is the girl next to Gilles in the black dress?" I try to say casually as I watch her stroke Gilles's lapel.

"Oh, she's his ex, Sandrine."

"Really?" I respond. Then, through clenched teeth: "How long were they together?"

"I think three, maybe four years, but don't worry, he dumped her when he met you. And I don't even think he invited her tonight," Frederich says, trying to be reassuring as I glimpse *my boyfriend* and *his ex* whispering to each other. Sandrine takes the enormous gift she's been holding and hands it to Gilles as the assembled group stops as if on cue to watch the unveiling. Well, this certainly sucks. No one was here to see all the fabulous things I gave him earlier (like the crocodile wallet I *so* shouldn't have splurged on, as now I'm halfway through next month's budget).

I stand in the doorway, half listening to Frederich try to convince me I've got nothing to worry about as I try not to go ape-shit watching this reunion. Obviously I would be cool with this if, say, Sandrine were a bearded old cow. But she's sickeningly cute, one of those gift-to-men babes with long blonde cascading hair (thicker and shinier than mine, the wretch), huge dark eyes, a perfect bee-stung mouth, and a devastating body perched on a pair of heels I would kill for. *Grrr-rr.*

Most of the crowd has stopped dancing to watch as Sandrine and Gilles rip off the wrapping paper together (nauseating) and he tenderly places the gold bow atop her head as she beams to the guests. (Anyone have a dagger?) The empty box falls to the floor as Gilles lifts out a gorgeous full-length Christian Dior camel-hair coat with an enormous collar and deep pockets. It's wicked chic. Everyone "oohs" and "ahs." Someone takes photos as he poses, and Sandrine rises up on her princess heels to give him a kiss—on the mouth. I AM SO HATING THIS! IS THIS SHIT ACCEPTABLE IN FRANCE?! Be cool, Klein. People are starting to look at you to see how you'll react. More Champagne for me, oh yes indeedy. I go to the buffet and Gilles's sister scooches over to pour me Champagne and scrutinize my face for any signs of jealousy. I refuse to fall.

"So, I guess we're all headed to Pershing Hall for dinner. Have you been there before?" I ask, not caring at all what her response is.

"*Oui, seulement une fois.*" Whatever, SISTER, I've got to get back in eyeshot of Gilles and Sandrine. I guide her back into the salon and hunt for my kill.

"And you, Klein, where do you live?" she asks.

"Ah, in the 7th by Musée d'Orsay, kinda." (Listen, chicka, I'm about to blow over here. You'd better stand clear because I've got my boyfriend and his ex in my sights and this ain't gonna be pretty.) Sandrine has proceeded on her mission of Operation Boyfriend Return, pushing her perfect body up against Gilles and gently caressing his much-delighted cheek. *Okay*. Time's up! I've had enough! I home in like a heat-seeking missile. Target: One or both of them, depending on how much the alcohol is going to fuel my fury. Just as I set my jet propulsion into high gear and start my descent, Gilles (living in some parellel universe where apparently neither I nor the party exist) leans in and kisses the beckoning mouth of Sandrine as he slides his arm around her tiny waist.

I barge in between them like a referee at a boxing match. Move it, princess, before I take my big American ass and sit on you, crushing all your delicate bones. I face a stunned Gilles with venom in my eyes.

"*Excusez-moi, Gilles, qu'est-ce que tu fais?*" (What are you doing?)

He smiles sheepishly—and then smugly, once he notices his friends are all watching. *Oh, you think this is funny do you? Two women fighting over you?* I'm thinking. I try to be cool, say nothing, just mimic his move of laying a kiss on her and the slithery way he moved his hand around her waist.

"So?" I demand as I look at him sternly. "*Ce n'est pas gentil!*" (This isn't kind.) I wish like hell I knew how to say *motherfucker* in French.

SM-AA-C-K!! Out of nowhere Gilles just smacks me across the face with an open palm. My brain flashes into white lightning and I slap him back hard. Without a word I turn on my heel and haul ass to the bedroom to get my purse and coat. A stampede of people—Frederich, Pierre, Gilles's sister, faceless others—fly after me in turn asking, "Are you all right?" "Oh my God, I don't believe he did that to you!" "Don't leave, Klein!" I make a dramatic exit as I sweep on my huge coat, throw my hair over the collar, and stride out the door, rushing down the six flights of stairs. Like *hell* I'm waiting for the elevator.

He just SLAPPED me!? That's INSANE. What the hell did *I* do? Total asshole. Complete and total asshole. I *so* didn't see that coming. God, no one has so much as ever pushed me before. Jesus. I can't believe I've been slapped by my first French boyfriend. I burst into tears and begin the long three-mile walk home, trashing my Fendi heels as I stagger through the streets of Paris. I pass the foreign embassies on rue du Faubourg Saint-Honoré, and the guards don't even so much as blink an eye as I walk by howling in despair. Thoughtful bunch. This is *too* hard. I want to go home, back to New York. *Now!* Where did I lose my asshole decoder ring? I gave up my jet-set life and divine French Industrialist for this? I must have lost my marbles along with my ring.

I go to bed that night with blistered, throbbing feet from the long walk home, eyes so puffy I almost have to lance them to see, and thinking, for the first time, *Paris . . . dumb idea.*

A FEW SLIGHTLY ANNOYING DETAILS I DIDN'T ANTICIPATE

It turns out there is an unfortunate issue of different electrical voltages in Europe. I can attest to this after sitting down to dry my hair one lovely morning and discovering my blow dryer had been transformed into a handheld booster rocket shooting red-hot flames at my cranium. Had my hair not been wet, I'm sure I would now be living in Madagascar, hiding from my own reflection in tide pools.

Maybe it's not so surprising that in my all of two-minute final decision to move to Paris, the technical details of voltages bypassed neural storage. It was with not so much as a blip of forethought that I'd brought my Bang & Olufsen stereo and three lamps and two phones. I assure you that no matter how hard one hammers a two-prong electrical plug into a three-hole outlet, it never quite creates a flow of electricity. Although once in the dark I did accidentally touch my keys to the same outlet and damn near spontaneously burst into flames.

I set off to BHV department store on one of my increasingly frequent Euro-obstacle problem-solving missions. This famous department store is as well stocked as it is overwhelming. Classically French in that there is absolutely zero sense of logic to its internal layout: suits sold next to confiture, towels jumbled near handbags. I immediately started talking to myself (in English, of course; don't be stupid, in French I'd have had an aneurysm), trying to calm down and shop.

After an hour of wandering through six floors in hopes of stumbling across the hardware section, passing through the Create Your Own Toilet and quite possibly the Make Your Own Tombstone sections, I finally discovered—*ta-da*—the AC-adaptor display. Cleverly located, as all French people must know, behind the pet department by the drapery rods. Since absolutely nothing looked familiar—or cheap for that matter—I finally accepted that I would have to break down and ask for help. Impressions of miming electricity are much harder than you'd think. (Although I am sure Marcel Marceau could've pulled it off.)

Eventually I hailed down one of those elusive salesclerks who, I might add, wear the same snazzy hardware aprons as they do back at Home Depot. With my vast knowledge of hardware and appliances, I tried to explain that the problem was a difference in what I thought was "Hergenvolz Zoltage." Which yes, come to think of it, does sound like the name of a German engineer in the 1940s. Hmm. As it turns out it's a 220-volt, 50-hertz system deal. Hey, give me an A for being relatively close.

After a lot of repeating "volt" and "hertz" back and forth in various accents, it was established that because a strong voltage is necessary to power a stereo, I needed to purchase an adaptor roughly the size of a small microwave oven. This black box of dense electronics weighed, oh, just slightly less than I did and cost forty euros. It seemed wrong. Aren't there little pieces of beige plastic with three prongs costing, say, a buck? I argued my case for a smaller, cheaper option to no avail, powerless as usual in the face of an insistent salesclerk.

In retrospect, my La Samaritaine experience may have been one of those all too common instances of what is known as "Ameriscrew." This is when a French citizen takes pleasure in persuading a naive American into an unnecessary expensive purchase. Being a trusting soul, and knowing there was no way I was going to play out this adaptor scavenger hunt again in another store, I purchased the two-ton adaptor brick-o-fun and began one of my famous long journeys through Paris with a large, cumbersome object in tow.

Not having a car (because the last time I drove was seventeen years ago, so it would be the equivalent of a suicide attempt) and being careful with my money (okay, cheap), I rarely spring for a taxi. So each large-size purchase makes the scenic, maddening excursion home with me on foot. Each time, without fail, I'm foolishly optimistic, thinking it'll be a cinch. Then after the first block, the easel, clothing rack, ironing board, or chair becomes such a goddamn obstacle to battle through the throngs of tourists that I'm tempted to chuck it over the closest bridge into the Seine. But this time, I endured in the desperate hope of once again getting to hear actual music.

No more listening to the sound of my own heartbeat or the racket of the neighbors fighting, which just doesn't have a beat you can dance to. Car alarms? Sure, they call for a semi–New Age interpretive dance, but random shouting—not so much.

Once I connected something close to one hundred cords, the adaptor was a roaring success even though the sleek, streamlined aesthetics of the Bang & Olufsen stereo were murdered by what resembled an old car battery parked next to it. I convinced myself it was a small price to pay for moving to paradise and giving it my own soundtrack.

Unsure if I'm going to spend the rest of my life *en France,* I'm a bit hesitant to splurge on a vast array of French appliances. So for the time being, I am using a lint brush in lieu of a vacuum and, let me tell you, keeping the floors clean can take the better part of a weekend on all fours (and I think we both agree there are more fun ways to spend a weekend on all fours). No problem can't be solved when you're desperate, cheap, and creative. This phrase has managed to become a daily mantra.

SUBLIME PLEASURE DU JOUR

I'm in love. Nope, it's not likely I'll end up married but it is serious. I'm in love with Monoprix. This chain of stores is literally a daily habit that I look forward to with something bordering on delight. They are inexpensive and pretty groovy, considering they stock everything from Dom Perignon to Brillo pads. And everyone shops there: supermodels, famous actors, well-known artists, the odd bourgeois aristocrat. (Who I like to refer to as "aristorats" because they always have attitude beyond words. So what, your ancestors brought down the Bastille? Right, okay, that is pretty fab.)

Monoprix even has clothes. Maybe the styles are slightly less sexy than John Galliano but, hey, at twenty euros for a cashmere scarf, who's crabbing? I bought my first and only Wonderbra there. (Could someone tell me why as I get older my boobs are getting smaller? That doesn't make sense *at all.*)

With its juice bar, restaurant, bakery, great produce, fresh flowers, cheap socks, it's no surprise Monoprix is addicting. At Monoprix I can buy prepackaged sushi *and* Windex *and* a great bottle of wine *and* printer cartridges all in one shot. I perpetually replenish my stock of Petit Bateau tiny white T-shirts that have the cute rib trim. I mean please, at seven euros each, I feel positively decadent buying three at a time. Hey, it's the last thing I can fit into in the kids section (yes, I'm cramming into the 12x like a goon) and there's something fun about that. Not to mention I'm going through batteries by the dozen (which may or *may not* be for my vibrator; I'm not saying).

FRIEND COUNT

For a few weeks there I had a healthy handful of buddies. The Three Musketeers gave me a rare oppurtunity to actually answer my cell phone rather then just use it as a clock. Alas, after the left hook from "Didier," I had to give all of the Three Musketeers the heave-ho. I'm sad to report that despite my best intentions I'm back down to just one feline friend. Printing up that "friend résumé" is starting to get some serious consideration. Or maybe I could make up a sandwich board that I could wear and hand out flyers. *Mon Dieu,* who knew it would be so hard to find friends!

Nicolas,
a Gazebo of Bed Linens,
and Poison Pastries

March

MONSIEUR RIGHT REPORT

I'm definitely over that toad Gilles. *Completely*. Not sure slapping him back was the greatest exit. In retrospect sleeping with his best friend might have had a sharper sting, but not even I am that evil (not to mention that his best friend isn't hot enough or I probably could've been swayed). Whatever. I feel a bit beaten (literally for God's sake) so I'm not doing the *de rigueur* "pull out all the stops, dress to kill" gig that's expected on Saturdays in Paris. I'm just throwing on a pair of old Levi's, and a white T-shirt and heading out with wet hair in a messy chignon. Where? Beats me, I just need air and the immediate distraction of the streets of Paris. It's like a drug, really. The world simply feels safe and beautiful once you're walking down boulevard Saint-Germain. I love this city. And what a perfect sunny day. Only noon and already I've witnessed so many beauitful images. Running through the Tuileries gardens, seeing all the flowers in full bloom, the beautiful children pushing their little sailboats in the fountains as the ducks flitter about in the sun. A gorgeous to-die way to start the day.

I walk by Café de Flore and Deux Magots and see all the Parisians are elated to resume their spots at favorite café terraces after a long winter inside. It makes me think, *Never before have I lived in a city where the entire population just seems, well . . . happy, relaxed, content.* New York (for all I love about it) is one giant panic rush, an endless weight of pressure: "Go-work-harder-make-more-money-keep-moving-up-nothing's-ever-enough!" Here, most people are simply fine with their lives the way they are: a little work, a small apartment, a normal car, a few intimate friends.

A feeling of calm permeates my skin, and I'm instantly feeling optimistic again. My days begin with a delicious menu of possibilities. Museums? Shopping? Book stores? Art galleries? Well, it usually depends on how much money I have in my jeans pocket.

Ah, *merde,* in my haste to hit the streets I brought only five euros, so good mood or not, it's gonna be a cheap-girl day of nonacquisitional pleasure. Window shopping on rue du Four will have to wait. It's one o'clock and that means time to head over to my latest creature-of-habit lunch ritual, the nameless cheapo Chinese resto on rue de Buci. Rats, that means I have to walk past the packed terrace of the Bar du Marché, and that always makes me feel so strangely self-conscious. What's with that place? It's always throngs of artsy hipsters spilling out all over the terrace and the kind of place I'd love to go but would be the only person *alone* among all the groovy Parisians. *One day I'll penetrate that little world,* I think, *just not today.* That will take a tad more confidence than I've got *aujourd'hui.*

I duck into the Chinese place next door to order my traditional lunch of six pieces of sushi, two steamed veggie dumplings, and a Coca Light. The young Chinese guy behind the counter knows me on sight and says, "*Comme d'habitude?*" (The usual?)

"*Oui, pour sur place.*" (To stay.) I still don't have any friends, but this guy just might notice if I dropped off the planet.

"*Quatre euros dix, madame.*" Great, that leaves me ninety centimes for the day. Can't even get a pack of gum with that. And I'm not a madame, I'm a mademoiselle! Everyone assumes at this age I *must* be married. Grrr.

I turn around to try to find some not so terribly painful place to sit alone and . . . oh . . . my . . . god. *That* man is perfection. Sitting alone in the corner is the single most beautiful man I have ever laid eyes on. Holy Shit. *Wow.* He looks up at me and smiles with the most beautiful brown, sexy, sparkly eyes I've every seen. *Klein, don't drop the tray, do remember to breathe . . . hello! Don't just stand there idiot-girl, sit down somewhere, you're starting to look stupid. Really stupid. And shutting your gaping mouth would create a slightly more appealing look.* Right. Right. Right. Sitting. Sitting would be good, as my knees are starting to buckle. I sit parallel to Mr. Perfection at the only available table and can hardly concentrate. *Okay, you're here to eat. Try to remember how that works.* I am struggling to remember what a fork is used for when

I glance at him again and he . . . *Jesus* . . . is still staring at me. This isn't possible. I look a total wreck, as though I've been sleeping in a cave and have zero—no, negative zero—idea how to dress.

He is so completely gorgeous, like a conglomeration of all the most beautiful men I've ever known put together. Dark brown hair and light mocha skin, perfect thick horizontal eyebrows over the biggest eyes, the sweetest, happiest eyes imaginable. He must be over six feet, with delicious full lips the color of a plum over perfect white teeth. And oh, I'm fairly sure a body like Michelangelo's *David* hides beneath that . . . Polarfleece? *Yow*. How is it possible I'm attracted to a man wearing *Polarfleece*? Oh, I so don't care he's sporting a Polarfleece pullover, the jeans are *so* working. Actually, everything about him is completely working.

Okeydokey, gotta give eating a go here. All right, it's just ridiculous, I'm so self-aware and flushed red I can hardly swallow. It's just some textured object. Seriously, sushi has never been so unappreciated or cumbersome. Amazingly, I find I am capable of semi-ingesting food, but when it is finished what is there left to do? I can only sip my can of Coke for, oh, another five minutes if I have to. I take slow micro-sips and try to send Mr. Delicious Eyes mental messages to suggest approaching me would be *really* appreciated. Message received! The jeans are suddenly in motion and—oh yeah, baby—comin' this way. Bring it on!

I slowly raise my head, extricating the straw from its flight path up my nose, to see him standing right in front of me, casually, hands in pockets. Smiling. *Perfect.*

"*Bonjour,* you are American, *non*?" I nod. (Hate that, when it's a dead giveaway, like I've got U.S. GRADE A stamped on my flanks.) "Would you like to go somewhere for a coffee?" the voice attached to the jeans says.

A dumbstruck mute, I point to my now empty Coca Light can and blurt, "I have a drink already." (What the hell am I saying? WHY AM I SUCH AN IDIOT?!) I look down and look up again, dying of retarded embarrassment. A second later, we both laugh out loud at what a clever, clever girl I am. I stand up, and some smattering of intelligence seeps back as we leave the restaurant together. The young Chinese guy behind the counter apparently has seen this all unfold and yells out, "*Bonne journée, madame!*" Funny.

We pause just outside on bustling rue de Buci and Mr. Perfect says to me,

"I'm sorry to interrupt your lunch, I just was compelled to speak to you. My name is Nicolas, but everyone calls me Nico." (*Whatever the hell your name is I can hardly bear that your deep, smooth voice with the slightest French accent is simply as delicious as you are.*)

"I'm Lauren, but my friends call me Klein." (*You can call me anything,* I'm thinking, *just CALL ME!*) I'm blushing. Stop that. That is not a pretty color. I go crimson-purple as a rule.

"Shall we?" Nico says, gesturing to the left.

"Absolutely," I say, breathlessly. The sun dances on the flowers at the corner shop, over the oysters, crab legs, and lobsters on ice at the fish market across the street. The little cafés and *boulangeries* are doing brisk business as a newspaper hawker yells, "*Le Figaro! Le Monde!*" in a husky voice.

Nico and I stroll down toward the Seine. Turns out he's thirty-four years old (excellent), really fucking funny (imperative and *très*-rare!), and has a really interesting job (vital and fabulous!). He explains to me that he invests French money in developing schools and businesses in third-world countries (definitely admirable), nonprofit (definitely low paying—oh, who cares, look at this man's lips, hips; God, does he have a single flaw?).

He begins to tell me how he's not actually Parisian; he was raised in the Basque region of France. As he starts speaking about the countryside that is so dear to him, I'm watching his mouth and thinking, *I could seriously base an entire religion on those lips, monsieur,* he looks at me for a second and apparently repeats, "So, Klein, where should we walk?" and then I snap back into reality.

"Would you like to go to the flower market with me?" I ask. "I have actually never been, and it's just behind Pont-Neuf, isn't it?"

"*Bonne idée, avec plaisir,*" he says, smiling. Perfect. We cross over Pont-Napoléon to the flower district tucked away near Notre Dame. The smell of succulent flowers blossoming and budding in the sun greets us a block away. We smile at each other and I offer, "Lavender?"

"*Oui, lavandre, très bien,*" he responds, tapping me on my nose. We immerse ourselves in the flower stalls, one after another overflowing with possibilities. Just as we admire the pots of dahlias, garden roses, and boxes of daffodils, I begin to worry that maybe this market is just too girly-girl for my tremendously masculine companion. He suddenly says, "Do you know these

flowers? They are the herbs of tampa, or these *genets*? They're from my countryside. I have a large garden there." A perfect ass *and* a perfect green thumb.
I'm entirely smitten with this boy.

Nicolas wanders away for a few minutes as I sift through a basket, feigning
an understanding of what makes a decent narcissus bulb, when suddenly he
returns with a huge bouquet of rubrium lilies wrapped in yellow tissue for me.
Me! They are my favorite. He is IN. *So* IN. You could have hit me over the
head with a two-by-four and I wouldn't have felt it. I give him a kiss on the
cheek, and with his sparkly eyes shining in the sun, standing in his nubby Polarfleece, I can imagine him as a five-year-old boy. Darling. It is all so sickeningly cute, I feel like we are starring in some cheesy deodorant commercial.
That's Paris for you. Moving here is the smartest decision I've ever made (better even than buying Microsoft stock before it split 3 to 1, which was the previous titleholder).

The afternoon is flying by and a cool breeze is starting to slip off the Seine.
"Let's go to Le Comptoir for something warm to drink," Nico suggests. I'm
thinking, *I'd go damn near anywhere with you right now. You could suggest
walking to your bloody Basque region, and I'd happily skip off into the sunset
with you.* He offers me his Polarfleece as it's getting nippy (yes, pun intended).
If you'd told me this morning that under any circumstances I'd be thrilled to
put on a pilled, stained Polarfleece pullover I'd have fallen down laughing. I
don't even know where Le Comptoir is, but I am a slave to this day. I have
beautiful flowers in one hand and—check this out—the beautiful hand of
Nico in the other. Conversation flows easily and there is a warmth and famil-
iarity in his face that is comforting. Then I suddenly remember, *I look like
shit. I should address this, really.* I mumble, "I'm sorry, I really look scruffy today, no makeup and terrible outfit and everything . . ."

"No," he said, "You look like a ballerina who's just changed out of her
tutu, and you should never wear makeup, it would mask your beauty." Oh
come on, that was precisely, completely, music to my ears. (Dude, if you can
stomach me like this, it all goes up from here.)

Turns out Le Comptoir is kind of a hike to the Carrefour de l'Odéon in
the 6th, but so worth the walk. It's a classic French café—all antique mirrors,
cozy and romantic with small marble tables and a zinc bar. We take a seat inside overlooking the small square and sit the lilies on a chair next to us. We or-

der espressos and settle in to some light chatter and serious swooning. When I tell Nico I am a painter he, like everyone, asks in what medium do I work, what style. I give my traditional answer: "Oil, somewhat abstract expressionist. I'm influenced by de Stael, Twombly, Kline, Motherwell—"

Nico jumps in, "Do you know the work of Clifford Still?" I could slide out of my chair. *No one* I meet knows Clifford Still. He is my hero, my icon. It is all I can do to not throw myself into Nico's arms and bathe him in kisses. Who created this man? He is fucking astonishing.

It is almost seven o'clock. Passing from afternoon to evening, the sun is gone and darkness begins to fall like a dark veil. Nico slowly and casually gets up and comes over to plant a long, warm kiss on my lips. Pouf. I'm gone. Lost. Who am I? Where am I? And where DID you get that mouth, monsieur?

"Sorry, Klein, I've been wanting to do that all day." My lips are pulsing with joy; never have they ever felt so alive. Speaking in *any* language becomes tricky. Luckily he jumps in with, "I have an idea. Why don't we split for an hour and I'll come over to your house at eight o'clock, and we will properly celebrate your arrival in Paris." All right, admittedly I did fudge earlier when I said I just arrived in Paris. I milk that idea a bit longer than is legal, but take note, girls, giving a man something to celebrate is really effective and generally results in a festive Champagne-enhanced dreamlike state.

I give him my address and don't for a second feel it is a dangerous or too-fast move. I am old enough to know when something is right and this *is* so right. I run home with the energy of ten horses and delirious with excitement. Generally, I don't have anyone over until I've spent a good two hours making everything, spice cabinet included, absolutely perfect, but what the fuck? Carpe diem! Scratch that. *Pourquoi pas!*

I prep Puccini: "Be nice, no hissing or biting, this one's a keeper okay?" As usual, Puccini feigns not to understand English and continues to clean his whiskers. "Oh, and if you could, Puccini, try not to make any of those stinky chocolate kisses in the litterbox while he's here. Are we cool?" Zero response.

Nico arrives promptly at eight o'clock (unheard of in France). I buzz him in and try to keep it together as he climbs up the three flights to my door. *Klein, you look good. Suede shirt and 501s, hair down and just a smidge of eye makeup. A hint of color from the afternoon sun. Decidedly casual. He digs that (I think). Calm down, girl.* I open the door to see . . . Damn it, if possible, he's even more gorgeous than I remember. God damn, boy. You are hot. Way, way, crazy hot. He's changed into a French blue shirt open at the neck, revealing just the perfect, slightest hint of chest hair against that mocha skin. I somehow refrain from ripping it to shreds and taking him in the entrance. Miraculous, really.

"*Bonsoir,* Klein!" Oh, yes, *and* you're French. Oh man, this is so great. "This is for you," he says and hands me a bottle of chilled Veuve Clicquot. Genius, we drink the same Champagne; it's not cheap either. Well done, monsieur. Before I even finish saying "Come in" he is on his knees making friends with Puccini. To my utter shock, Puccini climbs up into his arms and gives him a "whisker kiss." Okay, who's exchanged my psycho-nasty cat for this love machine?

"Great apartment, Klein, love the layout." And he proceeds to . . . What the hell *is* he doing? . . . A cartwheel. Not the greatest in form or execution, but impressive all the same. Not generally on first dates but . . . "I know I will embarrass myself at some point tonight," he says, "so I thought I'd get it out of the way." I'm charmed. We pop open the Champagne and thank God I bought Champagne flutes two days before, because otherwise we'd have to share the bottle like a couple of old winos. We sit on the floor because there really is nowhere else to sit (mental note: *Get sexy, comfortable furniture one day in your life*). We toast, and sitting Indian style across from each other, begin talking animatedly. I'm loving him. One moment he's explaining the evening sky from the top of Machu Picchu, the next jumping up on my kitchen counter.

"Have you seen the view from up here since you moved in?" he bellows from the ceiling.

"Well, no, to be sure, I haven't." I leap up next to him as Puccini rolls his eyes—"Human courtship, so absurd"—and you know what? It is a damn fine view. Kind of a bird's-eye, God-like point of view on my expat Parisian dream apartment. I look over at Nico, all endearingly childlike and entirely masculine at the same time and think, *I bet you will show me a lot of interesting points of view in this new life of mine.* If you can fall in love in a single evening, we manage it.

He tells me stories of swimming in the Amazon and sleeping in trees in the rain forest. I tell him stories of how I got suspended from the cheerleading squad for beating up another cheerleader, and even about my terrible shoplifting habit when I was twelve years old. We take photos, holding the camera at arm's length to document forever what definitely feels like a magical evening.

Around three in the morning we are all talked out, when Nico says, "I don't really want to leave, this is such an amazing night. Can I stay with you? I promise to be good."

"Stay," I find myself saying, ignoring my hard and fast rule of "No sleepovers, no sex, not *ever* on a first date." All those rules go flying out the window after he starts kissing me. Those fleshy lips! Soft, warm pillows of scrumptious pleasure. With his hard body pressing against mine and grinding our hips in insane, taunting rhythm, he isn't going anywhere. I pull him onto my tiny bed and slowly take off all his clothes. He bursts into a big smile as I get to his white boxers. *Mmm.* I slide them off with my foot as I bite his lower lip. *Whoa . . .* Man, I would be smiling too if I were a man with *that* between my legs. I beg you to form a picture in your mind of the most perfect, gorgeous male sex you can fathom. Nico's is *that* image, in the flesh. In the hard flesh. He is looking at me so intensely, I want to dart my eyes away, but his look is so adoring, so caressing I find that for one of the few times in my life I hold his gaze and keep my eyes open. With one hand tucked into the small of my back and the other guiding my hips, he slowly lowers me onto him and deliciously enters me. I feel myself slipping into a trance . . .

The next morning, after a sleepless night (did I mention he's hung like a horse?—no, a really big horse, possibly a Clydesdale), he leaps up to announce, "Where's the closest *boulangerie*? I want to make you breakfast in bed."

"It's around the corner on rue du Bac, but the owner's nasty and always charges me double so be careful," I warn him. The second he leaves, I jump out of bed and race to the bathroom to do the whole teeth-brushing-spritz-of-perfume-jump-back-into-bed routine—faux wake-up pefection. When Nico comes back, he makes me a breakfast fit for the queen of France: fresh strawberries in crème fraîche, warm croissants and two kinds of confitures, peaches in creamy yogurt sprinkled with *muesli* and tea with lemon and a dollop of *miel*. Bliss. Fuck me and feed me—not a bad start to a day, frankly.

Monsieur Right? . . . *Peut-être.*

A FEW SLIGHTLY ANNOYING DETAILS I DIDN'T ANTICIPATE

Of course I knew there would be a few cultural hurdles to stumble over when I moved to Paris. I just didn't expect them to be so goddamn high and lined up like an army of dominos. While most cultural differences are harmlessly amusing, others are downright nonsensical. One of the most interesting is what the French consider to be "absolute necessities" versus what are construed as "luxuries." For example, it absolutely blows my mind that I have never once met a Parisian who owns a clothes dryer. (Nico doesn't have one and he doesn't even know anyone who does, either!)

True, the French all own the classic washing machine, but it's a distant cousin of the gigantic American Sears Kenmore models I grew up with. Here in France, washing machines are always ridiculously tiny; they resemble the Fisher-Price washer I had when I was six years old. To the French it is apparently inconceivable to understand the necessity of its twin: the dryer. Call me a spoiled American (you wouldn't be the first), but I don't believe these two machines should be uncoupled. They need each other and I need them to be side by side and preferably larger than a box of cereal.

As I did the first wash load at my new apartment, a tricky choice had to be made. Due to washer size limitations, will one sheet or ten pairs of socks be the lucky first load? After the ninety-minute cycle where the washer shook so violently, I thought, *Okay, it's either possessed or I've accidentally trapped a Tasmanian devil in with my socks. Voilà,* yet another Euro-dilemma presented itself.

I found myself at a loss as to how to dry everything without turning my apartment into a wet-panty museum. Does everyone in France dry their sheets in tent-forms, suspended between the shower rod and the bathroom door? Are twenty pairs of socks drying in the oven and a pair of underwear on every doorknob the traditional system of drying? Does Hubert de Givenchy do this? Because I am frankly tiring of the gazebo of bed linens at my hacienda.

I finally decided to ask Nico. He graciously informed me that everyone uses drying racks (are you thinking *How primitive*? I did too), which are available at all of the monstrously large department stores.

So once again I set out for BHV to acquire my first, *très*-Euro, environmentally friendly drying rack. I bought the biggest one I could find, a waist-high white metal number. A mere twenty euros. Two points for the anti-dryer brigade in cost savings versus the price of an appliance. It took me roughly fifteen minutes to untangle and set up this rickety, ill-balanced armature, and it immediately collapsed under the weight of one pair of wet jeans and a sock. (Negative two points.)

As with everything in France, I was sure there were some important details I wasn't being told that would make everything work seamlessly. Apparently not so (again); as I understand it, the French don't mind that when your clothing is finally dry after three days of coexisting in your living space as a pseudo-art installation, you are left with a crisp sculpture of what was once a plush, supple towel. They readily accept that putting on air-dried jeans feels like you're pulling on plaster leg casts, and once-cozy sweatpants are now fleece slabs of steel with embossed imprints of rack marks. Not to mention the sensation (now I'm on a roll) that slipping on rack-dried socks is exactly like putting your foot into sandpaper-lined envelopes. C'mon, there's something I'm not getting. Bath towels shouldn't crunch when you fold them. Sometimes, to be honest, I miss a dryer more than some family members.

SUBLIME PLEASURE DU JOUR

As I sit here having a cup of tea, on the corner of my street stands a seventyish old man who has established a little outdoor florist business. Claude is a cheery and chatty Parisian who pulls up his broken shopping cart and sells day-old flowers to everyone in the neighborhood. He wears the same thing every day, an old cotton fisherman's shirt and matching pants, in what was once probably marine blue. With his scruffy gray moustache and loud gravelly voice (more like gravel rubbed on sandpaper, actually), he begins each day at seven and leaves at sunset.

Everyone knows Claude, God knows how long he has been an institution in the neighborhood. From tiny children to elegant older women, everyone stops and shares a few words with Claude. He always has just a few bouquets to sell, usually tired roses or wilting daffodils, and he does brisk business despite his ridiculous prices. I decided to buy a few white tulips from him and wasn't prepared for the whole charming experience.

A whole formal introduction process was followed by the flowers-for-euros exchange, and then, with his weathered dirty hands, Claude reached into a small, beaten-up plastic bag. Claude handed me two tiny pastries, like nothing I'd seen before or since, and told me in earnest seriousness, "You eat this pastry at two o'clock today, and the other at six." The ex–New Yorker in me thought, *Yikes! Could be poison?!* but I realized, no, it's just all a part of this little microcosm of Parisian charm. The tulips died the next day, but I lived. And now Claude and I are old chums. This is the stuff that makes Paris a dream come true. I still couldn't tell you what's in those little pastries he makes.

FRIEND COUNT

You can of course add my new and impossibly beautiful boyfriend, Nicolas. And perhaps the old man Claude who sells me day-old flowers. Can I throw in the guy who asked directions to Musée d'Orsay? No? Fine, it's a count of two then. Unless you'll let me add the writer Charles Baudelaire. I'm spending every night with him *in my bed*. So what if he's been dead about 140 years. Still I'm falling in love with him. Here's why:

PARISIAN DREAM

That marvelous landscape of my dream—
Which no eye knows, nor ever will—
At moments, wide awake, I seem
To grasp, and it excites me still.

Sleep, how miraculous you are—
A strange caprice had urged my hand
To banish, as irregular,
All vegetation from that land;

And, proud of what my art had done,
I viewed my painting, knew the great
Intoxicating monotone
Of marble, water, steel and slate.

Staircases and arcades there were
In a long labyrinth, which led
To a vast palace; fountains there
Were gushing gold, and gushing lead.

Tall nymphs with Titan breasts and knees
Gazed at their images unblurred,
Where groves of colonnades, not trees,
Fringed a deep pool where nothing stirred.

Blue sheets of water, left and right,
Spread between the quays of rose and green,
To the world's end and out of sight,
And still expanded, though unseen.

Sex at the Opera, the Gyp, and Monsieur Despont

June

MONSIEUR RIGHT REPORT

There is nothing better than this. Okay, to be honest, I have been thinner and have had more money in the bank, but in the love department, this is right up there. Tops. Recovering from a whirlwind love-fest weekend with Nico, my whole body ached from (1) two solid days and nights of a non-stop swinging-from-the-rafters sex-a-thon and (2) absolutely gorging on Nico's divine cooking. You'd think all the aerobic activity would've kicked my metabolism into high gear, but apparently not so much, as my tummy closely resembles the bunny hill at the ski resort back in Wisconsin. Frankly, I don't care, I'm in love. Officially. Where do I sign?

Nico called last Friday afternoon and said, "I'm sick of restaurants. Come over at eight o'clock and I'll cook for you, my Kiki." How cute could he get? Kiki as in "Kiki of Montparnasse" from the twenties, the bonne vivante diva who inspired Man Ray and Picasso. Nico dubbed me "Kiki of Saint-Germain." Call me queer, I think it's some sweet instant passport to pretend I'm oh-so-French now (hey, I'll take it where I can get it; feeling a part of this culture ain't so easy, cowboy, when I see not one familiar face all day and the phone never rings). So, at seven o'clock I stood before my closet, Puccini curled on the bed ready to offer opinions on outfit combinations. "So what's it going to be, Puccini, casual-sexy or dressy-slutty?" Puccini replied with his standard flick of the right paw. "Ah, yes, I'm in full accordance, the casual-sexy gig. You are so right, Nico's complete and total ignorance of fashion warrants I shelve the Alberta Ferretti strapless suede dress with eyelit hem for the more understated white Helmut Lang jeans and simple Ungaro halter."

You've got to love a man who tells you, "You don't have to be all glamourous for me. I love the way you look in any old pair of jeans." That left me twenty minutes for hair and makeup and my traditional boudoir drink. Boudoir drink, you ask? Oh sure, let me explain. One day, don't ask me when, I read that Cary Grant always had a single glass of Champagne while dressing for an evening out. It may make me a little on the butch side, but Cary Grant is my god not to mention it adds a certain sexy element to an otherwise routine experience. (And admittedly I tend to get nervous for any event, even the arrival of the FedEx man, so a little nip simmers me down.)

I threw on silver hoops, a dash of mascara and with a kiss to Puccini's whiskers I was out the door by 7:40. My dear Nico lived just eight blocks away. While in LA that's definitely a car ride, in Paris it's a quick, pleasant walk.

Walking down rue du Bac, the pale sun was beginning to set, and the whole sky looked like a beautiful Maxfield Parrish painting, indigo blue with white cottony clouds sprinkled with gold and pale pink rays. Exquisite. A gentle warm wind blew softly through my hair. *Mmm.* Paris in early summer, walking to my drop-dead sexy boyfriend's apartment, passing all the lovely little shopkeepers closing up for the evening . . . divine. Exactly what I was hoping for when I dreamt of Paris.

I popped in to the little florist by the *poissonnerie* (fish market) and picked out a small bouquet of orchids. The young proprietor is a short, rather homely soul, and I was charmed to see him try to flirt with me and ask my name. Frenchmen, God love them, never see any barrier—height, age, marital status, tourist or resident, rich or poor, they pursue with abandon. He offered me a single yellow rose as he wrapped the orchids for Nico. When I asked why I deserved this generosity, he responded simply, *"Parce que j'adore les blondes, c'est ça."* (Because I love blondes, it's like that). Hilarious.

Am I the only woman in the world who feels a certain ridiculous pleasure carrying a bouquet down the street? Men and women passing smiled at me. I think it's always lovely to see people walking with beautiful flowers—you know they're off to a marvellous evening.

At exactly 8:00 p.m. I arrived at Nico's building, a gorgeous stone maison with an enormous iron gate. Secret smile, that I already know the door code by memory: 7292. The door clicked and I pushed open the heavy gate and entered the stone-paved courtyard. It was a charming and pretty little courtyard with potted geraniums scattered about and one large oak tree in the center where a little bird chirped a fevered welcome. I passed through an ancient wood door that creaked on its hinges, and climbed up the five flights of tiny stairs. Was I breathless with anticipation, winded from the hike, or did I just smoke too much last night? Probably all three. Nico, being a rather cheap boy (should I be saying "frugal" to be nice?), lived on the top floor—two tiny inexpensive *chambres de bonnes* (maid's rooms) combined. So what if he doesn't have much money? He does have killer thighs to show for this low-rent, five-floor walk-up deal. He hears my heels pound the wooden stairs and has whipped open the door before I'm even at the landing

"*Bonsoir, mon amour,*" Nico says as he sweeps me into his arms, and showers my lips with kisses. *Mmm.* He always smells like . . . a dream, *exactly* how you hope a man will smell. Clean, warm, masculine. With his sparkly eyes, all chocolate brown and sensual, I'm once again overwhelmed and stunned that this gorgeous devil has chosen me. He's already got dinner under way in the tiny closet of a kitchen and says to me, "Choose a wine and help yourself, I'm going to change out of my suit," and he trots off to his bedroom. I examine the kitchen; a kitchen can speak volumes about a man. Despite being almost small enough to be referred to as a diorama, it's perfect. Nico moved in six months ago, and immediately ripped out the dated, dilapidated stove and counters and redid the whole kitchen in glistening chrome and polished steel. An old butcher block shipped up from his Basque countryside with three tiers of fresh vegetables hanging in copper baskets. I kneel down to peruse the wine rack. A few bottles of Champagne, some Bordeaux blancs, and dozens of great Spanish wines he buys by the crate just over the border in San Sebastián, Spain. I choose a Rioja I remember as full-bodied and smooth . . . just like Nico's body, come to think of it. I uncork it with an old basic metal waiter's corkscrew, a *de rigueur* object in every household. I've learned no true Frenchman would ever dream of having one of those tricked-out, high-tech, corkscrews, my Big-Shot Ex used to swear by. To a true Frenchman, using one would be as repulsive as, say, drinking from plastic cups or eating cold Brie.

Nico returns. How did jeans and an old white surfing T-shirt ever get so sexy? He puts on a Cesaria Evora CD and heads back to the kitchen after giving me a sweet pat on my ass. I get two wine stems from his vast collection in the kitchen cabinet and pour us each a glass. He takes his, sips, and goes back to the stove.

"Feel free to light some candles," Nico says over his shoulder. I bring all the candles I can find and arrange them as though I'm illuminating a medieval castle in the center of the table. It's surprisingly pretty. Not bad, Klein. If I do say so myself. A tantalizing smell of simmering vegetables is wafting through the air as I go back, wineglass in hand, to watch Nico cook. Men love being watched in the kitchen—the whole ritual of chopping the tomatoes in perfect proportion, the flipping of the sautéed onions as they drizzle olive oil into a simmering pan. It's a performance and they are the artists. I'm a particularly appreciative audience, not having any real culinary skills. (You can't really count giving blow jobs in the kitchen, can you? Nah, I didn't think so.)

I set the small oak table (that was Nico's grandmother's) with the gorgeous blue and violet pottery he bought in Argentina. Everything in Nico's apartment was brought back from some adventure in an exotic locale. A blue feather headdress from Guatemala hangs by the door, an old opium pipe from Vietnam sits on the mantel, and he's hung elaborate Indian embroideries above the huge bed he bought in Bali. I lo-o-ove this about him. Give me a man with little money and a curiosity about other cultures over a rich man who hires some joker to decorate his flat *any day*.

Just as I'm eyeing his zipper, wondering if I can't make some contribution to the kitchen activity, Nico smiles at me and says, "Kiki, hold that thought; stir the sauce until I tell you to stop." A man so involved in cooking a gastronomic dinner for me he refuses an oral opportunity . . . hmm. Very impressive. To leave me with my mouth simultaneously watering *and* starved. Clever boy.

Nico and I sit down to a beautiful dinner of coquilles St. Jacques in a *ciboulette* (chives) and cream sauce with a fantastic warm vegetable tart and a simple bowl of fat strawberries sprinkled with brown sugar for dessert. The conversation goes from his insistence that I start a new movement in art (yeah, sure, that's a cinch) to an invitation to take me to the opera this week. This, my friends, is the clincher. I love opera (hence, obviously, Puccini), and if I can find a lovely man who's actually as passionate about it as I am to go with me . . . oh my, *seriously* potential husband material. We talk about opera a while, agreeing that neither of us can endure the Wagner *Ring* series, and that

Tosca is simply the most beautiful opera ever. If he had said Strauss's *Elektra* I might have had to get up and go home.

After we've eaten every last crumb, dishes are ignored on the table, the CD left on auto return, and candles left to burn to their wicks. Nico tells me, "Do you know what I did this afternoon?" as he pushes me up against the door to his bedroom with his hips. A thousand things rush through my mind. *What? Did you close some big business deal, steal off to sleep with someone else, buy me new shoes, fall asleep at your desk . . . ?*

"Tell me," I say, hoping for the shoes.

"I was so crazy with desire for you I went to the men's room and came, thinking about you," he says. Hmm. Is that sexy? On some level I'm sure it must be, but the immediate mental image of him in some UV-lit generic men's room isn't the hottest scenario I can think of. Even so, it certainly implies his longing for me, so I smile (giving up the hope of new shoes) and delve into his chest hair, pulling his shirt over his head. Nico's whole body is just excruciating bliss to me. I'm delirious at just the sight of his forearm, so to see him now sprawled out on his bed, buck naked . . . *Ooh-la-la.* I'm taking thousands of mental photos for the day when I'm eighty years old and a dried up, wrinkled old bag; I can stare out the window from my rocking chair and think of these moments, this man.

We make love for hours. Touching his skin is like swimming in velvet and he kisses me with just the most exquisite tenderness, the most beautiful expression in his eyes. Mmm. Nico's gaze makes me feel so utterly adored. As though I'm the most desired, beautiful woman alive. He's a magnificent lover; his ability to tantalize areas of my body I didn't even know were sensual is a dream. When he gently kisses the inside of my arm or behind my knee I melt in rapture. He "listens" to my body and loves to bring me to the brink and slowly pull back and build my desire up again from there.

"I love you, madly and completely," I tell him when we finally finish, unable to stop myself. I'm a bad girl. I'm not holding anything back, not protecting my heart at all. I'm going full-on one hundred percent into this relationship and it's (deliciously) scary. Screw it, I'm too old to play games, be coy, act cavalier. I'm in love and living every moment fully, passionately.

"*Je t'aime, je t'aime, mon amour,*" Nico whispers again and again as I fall asleep in his strong arms.

The morning comes slowly and quietly (Nico too actually, hee-hee). One advantage of fifth-floor apartments—total silence. As always, he awakens me with sweet kisses on my eyelids and scoots off to the kitchen to make yet another sumptuous, enormous breakfast.

We pass the weekend crazily in love. When we're not in bed, we go out to a marvellous exhibit of Oscar Niemeyer at the Jeu de Paume museum in the Tuileries. I love this modernist architect; his work is so sexy it's like architecture porn. We both love the show and as we walk through it, Nico stays close and steals kisses all afternoon. Nico has begun to amaze me with his life, his stories. That he has actually been in Neimeyer's masterpiece building, Copan, in São Paulo, Brazil, I'm both jealous and impressed (rare). After the exhibit, we go for tea at a tiny café in the 2nd arrondissement. One of those backstreet old-timers' joints, with primitive coffeemakers and cigarette butts all over the black-and-white tile floor. Nico loves taking me to little-known places, always off the beaten path. He took me salsa dancing (*so* against my will) in one of the scariest parts of town, but he was right, it was completely great. We were the only non-Latinos, and as we danced in what seemed to be somebody's basement, I felt as though we could've been in a tiny village in Brazil.

He also took me to a crazy regga (not reggae—who knew there was a difference?) concert in the 10th. These are outings I would *never* have dreamt of, and honestly cringed at the notion of. But Nico has opened up my world and introduced me to so much I never knew existed in Paris. Or in myself, really.

Which brings me to this evening. We have tickets to the opera. Truthfully, Nico kind of killed the charm of this invite when he called Monday to ask me to put it on my credit card: "It's time you took me out for a change, Kiki." Not exactly elegant, but I tried to be a sport with my penniless suitor. Yes, my days of flying first class and running away on spontaneous trips to Mustique are definitely a distant memory.

I tell myself it's all fine because I still get to go to the opera and with a gorgeous Frenchman I'm crazy about. *So there, Klein, don't be a poop.* I haven't been to the opera in Paris yet (horrifyingly true; don't tell a soul!), so I'm not exactly sure just how fabulous to dress. I opt for "wildly overdressed" rather than underdressed, as is my habit. Puccini and I agree on the Carolina Herrera black one-shoulder sheath and my beloved black-velvet Blahnik mules. I put on some Marin Marais music composed for Louis XIV and sit down at my dressing table. *Love this shit*. This is exactly what I used to dream of when I'd play dress-up in my mother's closet. To live in Paris, sitting ever so carefully, mining my jewelry box for just the perfect pair of chandelier earrings as I await my prince to pick me up for the opera. So what if I looked like Mrs. Doubtfire all day, wearing my beat-up corduroys and some old knit sweater and glasses as I changed the litter box and scrubbed the bathtub? This, no one knows, and will hopefully never fathom as I emerge at the opera *ce soir*. A final spritz of perfume—collarbones, wrists, and, yes, behind the knees. *C'est fini*.

With my traditional boudoir drink in hand and a fluttering tummy of butterflies, I check my watch. Nico had said, "Pick you up at seven-thirty in my car. Prepare yourself, it's a piece of crap." I'm fine with the idea of some clunker of a car, but oh, not so fine with the fact it's seven-fifty. No. No. No. Late is unacceptable. *I hate* late. Everyone in France is late. Pacing, smoking like crazy, and trying to not flip into an evil mood, I snatch up the phone when Nico finally calls.

"I'm downstairs, come down." Finally, rude boy. No apology (never from Nico). I grab my purse and dash down to the street to find Nico standing next to the shittiest car in the world. With his big smile and dumb off-the-rack suit, he's still just breathtaking. You know you're in love when you happily plop your thousand-dollar dress down onto the rusty springs of your boyfriend's ancient Deux Chevaux. *That's* when I knew.

Nico's lateness issue isn't explained or discussed; we are just happy to be together, beside ourselves excited. When Nico looks over at me and says, "My Kiki, you are the most beautiful girl I have known," (biblical sense I'm guessing) I am so happy we could've just changed course for a drive-thru McDonald's for all I care.

We zip through traffic as though we have a death wish and still arrive unfashionably late, after the curtain has been raised. Our seats are in the nosebleed section just under the roof. I couldn't care less. I am delighted to see I've let go of the New York City snob-demanding bitch I used to be when I'd throw a hissy fit if my seats weren't in the first row (CENTER!) of the orchestra. We climb staircase after staircase looking for the "poor-folk mezzanine" and try to not giggle as we race like lost children around the elegant interior.

We finally find the proper floor, proper door, and push the velvet curtain back to begin the seat hunt. It's so damn dark, I can't see anything, and the upper-upper-tier must not have ushers: maybe the air is too thin for them to work safely. I can hardly see Nico or the seats . . . when . . . *what's that*? Nico whispers in my ear, "Just stay where you are," and his hands begin to glide up from my ankles to my waist, quietly lifting my dress up along the way. *Oh dear God, he's not serious.*

"Nico, no!" I say, and he replies with lust-induced assurance, "Shush, it's dark. No one will see."

I try to balance on teetering heels as he bends me over the balcony balustrade. I can't believe this. Are we mad? Only *this man* would get me to consider this. Christ, he's like a male lion. Authoritative animal passion that reduces me to a passive, accommodating creature without reason.

I can feel him unzipping his pants and taking his sex in his hand behind me. A drug—I feel the first wave of inebriating delerium when he pushes my black silk thong to the side, and Nico's hot hard flesh meets mine . . . my eyes close in total bliss as he enters me as the aria crescendos . . . (Or is that me screaming? Nope, it's a beautiful voice, can't be me.) Nico's strong warm hands on my hips, he tips me forward, gliding into me, then thrusting deeper and deeper. The sound of the music disappears as I am pulled into his hypnotic rhythmn. I grasp the rail frantically, trying to support myself against the force that's about to push me over the balcony. As my legs begin to tremble and my arms start losing their hold, I reach back with blind mad desire, grabbing him to pull him deeper inside me. I feel his wet mouth on my bare shoulder, then teeth biting at my neck. My head falls forward, weak from passion. Cymbals crash and Nico shudders in ecstasy; I semi-collapse on the railing, drunk with pleasure. The blood has all rushed to my head, and I slowly open my eyes allowing conciousness to gently seep back in. I see Nico's smile sparkling in the darkness beside me. Mmmm. I muster the strength to pull my dress back down over my hips. Nico tries to help, but neither of us has quite acquired hand-eye coordination again and it's all feeble fumbling. We catch each other's eye and I realize I'm laughing. God, I love the opera. Shit, it's not as dark as I thought it was. I look out at the orchestra below and then back over my shoulder at Nico in a semi-panic. He understands immediately.

"Kiki, it seemed darker when we arrived, didn't it?"

"Yes, baby, I think we've just given the audience a live performance they weren't expecting. Oh, my God!" We realize literally all eyes are on us, some bemused, some not.

"Fuck, we've got to get out of here," Nico says, laughing. We race out into the hall and collapse in giggles.

"I thought it was darker, didn't you!" we say at the same time. We decide there is no way to go back in and resume our seats, and what? Are we going to have to confront these people at intermission? So we do what any other two normal people in love would do. Hand in hand, we rush toward the nearest alcove to kiss. An usher walks past and we all smile at each other. I love France. Passion is expected in Paris. Encouraged, celebrated, and permissible everywhere. Nico asks, "What do you want to do, Kiki?" I take his face in my hands and say, "Follow me." A quick visual check of the closest men's room reveals all stalls empty, no video cameras or bathroom attendants. Play through! Nico makes quick work of the stall lock and lifts me up against the closed door. He's slamming me so hard against the metal door I'm convinced I'm going to be black and blue for a month, but I don't care. I don't care about anything, just him, this moment, the expression in his eyes. This is a great fucking night at the opera, *literally*.

A FEW SLIGHTLY ANNOYING DETAILS I DIDN'T ANTICIPATE

Every goddamn time I go to buy a newspaper or a magazine at one of the street newsstands I'm gypped (yes, I still use this fourth-grader word when applicable). The Sunday *Times* of London is clearly labelled four euros and I'm given back six euros out of a twenty-euro bill. I get intentionally ripped-off—all the time. Yes, I'm blonde, American, and bad at math, but c'mon, I'm not an idiot (nor am I a real blonde, come to think of it). But whether it's the newsstand by Café de Flore or the one on boulevard Raspail, once they see the English newspaper or catch wind of my American accent, I'm given back some ridiculously reduced change. Then begins yet another performance of the skit of me pointing out this grievous crime and the vendor doing a lousy line-reading of "*Ooh-la-la, mon erreur, pardon!*" Yeah, sure, I believed that the first *five times*. Now I just hand over a prepared handful of exact change and scoot off. Life's tricky enough already without that unnecessary routine, for crying out loud. *Grrr*.

SUBLIME PLEASURE DU JOUR

You can really only spend a few months settling in to your new apartment in a foreign country, and then you have to curb those long meandering strolls and lazy afternoons reading in the sun and get back to work. That's generally easier when you have some established job or profession. But I was just an ex–fashion designer and wannabe painter so it wasn't easy.

After years of working on Seventh Avenue in the fashion industry, I had really exhausted my passion for fashion design. It wasn't so much that I actually lost interest in creating the clothes, I just tired of the shenanigans that go with it. (Inflated egos, massive superficiality, brutal backstabbing, and screaming arguments over a quarter-inch difference in a hemline—and that's all *before* lunch.)

In my loft in Tribeca I had designated one huge room solely for painting. For two years while I worked consulting, I had made a series of paintings and found it to be a perfect balance of *maintaining* an income and *maintaining* self-respect. In New York City that's not always easy.

The first series of paintings was called Confessional Letters, and was admittedly somewhat inspired by the strong success of British confessional female artists like Tracey Emin. Each five-by-seven-foot canvas was an enormous graffitied "letter" to an ex or current lover. The colors, whether violent blood red or soft gentle grays, made clear the tone of each letter. The typeface varied in size and scale and was mixed in with splashes and drippings of color pigments and various oils. I photographed each letter before I'd start painting again, obscuring the legibility and resulting in an abstract smattering of letters and type. I would send the photo to the man the letter was written to, so only he and I would know what it had at one time expressed. I loved that the series combined my three favorite things: men, painting, and writing. Cool.

Now I wanted to figure out the whole Paris art scene. I can't tell you how many Parisian power dealers and French gallerists looked at me with one eyebrow raised, as if to say, *You moved to Paris to* paint?! Not exactly, but yes, I wanted to paint and show my work here, which I guess seemed like going back to a game of touch football after playing in the Superbowl. Whatever, it's not about fame or money for me, it's about creating and living a balanced lifestyle. (Balanced? Yes, there is a balance in my life: ten cigarettes for every bottle of wine and one new boyfriend every two weeks. *Voilà!*) Anyway, I got the idea. Paris wasn't the big leagues. Noted. With the exception of a few fabulous galleries like Karsten Greve and Xippas, it was a quieter, less cutting-edge art world than New York.

I began to spend each afternoon going to all the galleries I could find. The more modern contemporary galleries in the 13th arrondissement, around rue Louise Weiss, and the galleries in the Marais, which were fabulous and the most like the ones I knew in New York City. I inspected them all and took notes. But I discovered the smaller galleries on rue de Seine and the rue des Beaux-Arts really charmed me. Not only were they were smaller, more intimate, and specific, but the people were friendlier and more relaxed. So I got to work and puttered around with some ideas on paper, hashing out a new concept. Because my apartment was now so terribly small (Puccini is still bitching about being unable to go from zero to forty miles an hour in a high-speed run), I needed to reduce the size of the canvasses and the scale of the idea. I walked the two short blocks to the famous Sennelier art supply store on quai Voltaire and filled baskets with impasto pastes, pigments, and smaller canvasses (*toiles*). When I carried them back home, the wind off the Seine whipped up and made me into a human kite for a few steps. Once it even slammed me in the face, resulting in a bloody nose that splotched on the canvas in a surprisingly beautiful *tache*.

I think I was inspired by my long visits to the Egyptian and Asian sections of the Louvre, because the new series evolved into a somewhat primitive version of the *écriture* (gestural writing) of these two cultures. Vague symbols of a forgotten language, in short. Or as I would've said in New York City "a non-codified language that the individual can interpret freely based on one's understanding of artistic and historical ancient cultures." Blah, blah, add a few more zeros to the price, blah.

I experimented, ground pigments, carved into wet impasto with Chinese wood tools, and sanded away at layers of encrusted paint. There were as many failures as successes, but it felt great to struggle and occasionally hit on something I liked. Finally I had three that I thought weren't bad. I scraped up some confidence and a handful of photographs of the new paintings and headed over to the Galerie Despont on the rue des Beaux-Arts, an absolutely tiny gallery whose work I'd drooled over and walked around in circles for months. *I think Patrick Despont will get my work,* I told myself. Despont wasn't even there, when I finally screwed up the courage to go in, which was good and bad. Good, in that I could just leave my little envelope and possibly avoid the horror of watching him burst out laughing at the absurd notion he'd show work as "young" as mine, and bad, because now I had to leave a note—in French.

The next day I tried not to think about the art I'd left "out there" and went on with my usual routine. After my morning run, I wrote in my journal of what gloriously embarrassing thing I'd done the day before and then went for a walk down rue du Bac to La Grande Épicerie at Bon Marché. Allotting myself only four euros for lunch, I picked out a small container of *céleri remoulade,* a *petite déjeunette* (small baguette), and a Coca Light and walked over to the little park just in front of the department store Bon Marché, chosing a bench in the sun to eat my lunch and watch the children play on the jungle gyms.

I was just settling in for some heart-wrenching pining for motherhood when I got a call on my cell phone (this was a *rare* event—oddly enough, when you have no one to give your phone number to, no one calls). Against all odds, it was Patrick Despont, the owner of the gallery, who I deciphered was asking me to bring my paintings over to his gallery *maintenant,* NOW. I literally ran down rue du Bac, knocking over old ladies, to get home. I grabbed the three paintings and, like a desperate art student, paraded them unwrapped through the streets over to his gallery. (What? No one's stopping me to inquire about the fine artwork I'm carrying? Fuck. Maybe they're crap.)

Monsieur Despont turned out to be a warm and elegant man in his fifties, who immediately got down to business. He knelt in front of my paintings, took his glasses out of his pocket and put them on to inspect my work. Luckily my lack of French kept me from making the nervous, nonsensical chatter I would normally use to the fill the silence. After about ten minutes of pouring over every square inch of each canvas, he announced, *"Pas mal,"* (not bad) and suggested we go to lunch around the corner to talk about the details. I quickly agreed to go eat another lunch. (So what! I'll be a *fat, successful* artist. It will be my own personal ironic twist on the poor, starving artist image.)

Patrick Despont and I walked around the corner to rue Mazarin, to Casa Corso where he was greeted like royalty. As we waited for our table to be set up, he saw several of his fellow gallerists from the area and introduced me to each of them as—did I catch that right?—"a talented young artist." How cool. (And it sounds even better in French.) We sat for two hours over sole grille and entrecot, talking about his background and mine. I was blown away—he used to be close friends with my personal god, Francis Bacon. We ate and talked until I was going to burst right out of my jeans, but I was just loving this; he had marvelous theories on art, and fantastic stories of the Paris art world and its inner workings. God, what a kick to hear firsthand of how Francis Bacon would keep all his money in empty paint cans and how much he would struggle with each painting. Heaven.

I showed Monsier Despont my portfolio of work from New York City; he hated it all. Somehow I was glad. The new paintings were entirely different and less flashy, and it spoke of where I wanted to go with my work. He asked me to leave the three paintings, to exhibit immediately and suggested I try to do the same *écriture* idea in bronze. Yes, this is exactly what I wanted, someone passionate about art who would support and nurture my growth. I was so excited when I left Monsieur Despont that I even called my parents backs in Wisconsin on my cell phone (which I think costs about forty-four dollars a minute).

Within a week's time Monsieur Despont had put the all-white painting I'd done in his window. The gallery to the left had a *Picasso* in the window. I think I might have walked down that street a good hundred, hundred fifty times a day just saying to myself, *That's a Picasso and . . . then that's* my *painting*." For some reason this was all much more exciting than it would have been in New York. But then again, *everything* is more exciting in Paris.

FRIEND COUNT

I tried like hell this month to add another name to my friend list. Really. The most promising opportunity came during an afternoon with Nicolas, his best friend, Stephan, Stephan's wife, Anaïs, and their son, Étienne. I tried a thousand different ways to connect with Anaïs and she just wasn't having it. Oh no. She was a mistress of the cold shoulder and the queen of condescending glances. *So* not fair or deserved. I even took great photographs of their beautiful two-year-old Étienne, and sent them to her with a note inviting her for tea sometime. Not even a thank-you note. Rude. I'll keep trying. There have *got* to be some open-minded, kind Frenchwomen out there. Haven't there?

Pamela Anderson, Suppositories, and Anteater Whiskers

July

MONSIEUR RIGHT REPORT

I'm head-over-heels about Nico, and heels-over-head too—at least that's how I found myself with my Prada slingbacks parked up against his bedroom wall as he rode me into the ground last night. Gravity means nothing to this man. Forget running, just trying to keep this boy satisfied is a triathlon unto itself. Get it? "Let's *try* it this way. Why don't we *try* it from this angle?" I get flashbacks to fourth grade gym class doing the crab walk and the wheelbarrow maneuver, with all the stunts I'm performing. But that doesn't mean it's been all insane blind love (although that bit on Tuesday night with blindfold certainly qualifies). Truthfully, Nico and I have had a few snafus and blowups. And for all this being *madly* in love, sometimes I end up just being mad. I'm trying not to be such a demanding, intolerant girl, because oddly enough men just don't seem to love that in a woman. Go figure.

And as my father's always telling me, "You can't expect someone to be perfect unless you are perfect." (Hey, wait a minute, I thought dads were supposed to think their daughters *were* perfect). I mean, Nico is pu-ur-fect in the sexual department, like last Saturday night when in a passion-induced frenzy we managed to dismantle my canopy bed into a pile of rubble. But for all his apparent tribal knowledge about previously unknown erogenous zones, he really pissed me off tonight.

He came to get me in the Kiki-mobile. Yes, the ancient Deux Chevaux has been named after me. Cute, but I'd be a smidge more flattered if my name graced a two-hundred-foot racing sloop from the 1940s, decked out in teakwood and complete with three masts. But what can you do? Nico is a non-profit beautiful sex machine with no money. (I guess though, I am profiting, come to think of it.) He said he'd come get me at 7:00 p.m. so like the impatient girl that I am I went to stand on the corner in front of my building to wait for him. The streets in my neighborhood are tiny and quaint, but tough for someone to pull over and wait for me to scamper down unless they want to cause a minor traffic pile-up. So here I am waiting for Nico. *Well, maybe I'll have a cigarette.* I know Nico thinks it's terribly déclassé to smoke on the streets (and he's a smoker!) but my life is my own. A bit of nervous humming, a little pirouette on the curb, a glance at the antique shop windows, and that makes it 7:20. Great. Tra-la-la. A call to my cat three flights up: "Puccini!." Good boy, he knows my voice and has taken up a rather elegant pose at my apartment window. "Hi, my love!" "Meow!" I so don't care if everyone in the area looks at me like I'm bananas, that's my cat up there. He's the greatest. Puccini looks at me like, *What the hell are you doing down there? Come home this instant.* Sorry, kitten, I got a date with a love panther. A bit more humming. More lip gloss. And it's now 7:35. No call. This is *so* Nico. First date: on time and never again. Maybe I'm overreacting. In France, *c'est normal.* I should chill . . . but . . . I can't. Hating this. With a capital *H.*

At 7:45 I call him. "Nico, where ARE you?"

"I'm still at work, Kiki." (Notice, no "Sorry, my love.") "I'm leaving now." I don't even answer, I just push OFF on my phone. Fuckity fuck fuck. How rude is he? No, really? I march back up to the apartment. Puccini is thrilled his "meow" has apparently summoned me. Not exactly sweet cat, I'm going to pace and snort and storm around a while. I look in the mirror and say to myself, *You are insanely impatient, he's working. Not drinking with his buddies, or seeing someone else, or—heaven forbid—standing you up. Relax!*

I vow to be cool. Nobody likes a nag and I know I have the singular skill of fucking up perfectly good evenings by switching into insta-crab. Ten minutes later Nico calls my cell phone. "I'm downstairs, baby!" Fine. I'll be cordial, civil, whatever, but he'll owe me one. I climb in next to him and get one of those warm tender kisses I so love, and somehow manage to forget just how great they are until I'm getting another one. "You look pretty," he says. Yes, the acid in my blood does tend to turn my eyes a rather becoming green I've noticed (really, no joke). "And where, my little gourmand, would you like to go tonight?"

"I'm thinking Chinese tonight. Are you up for it?" I ask.

"Great, I know just the place, it's a hole-in-the-wall but the food is really fantastic," Nico replies. Hmm. If it's a hole-in-the-wall to Nico it must *really* be a dive. This boy has taken me to a plethora of seedy but oh-so-authentic joints, and frankly I'm tired of low-end fare every night. (Warning: SNOB ALERT!)

Nico drives like a bat out of hell and the seat belts must've disappeared around the time of the Roosevelt administration so I'm holding on to the door for dear life as we go up rue Monsieur-le-Prince the wrong way. "Nico, *watch out!*"

"It's okay, *ma chérie,*" he tells me as he zips half onto the sidewalk, plowing by an old couple to avoid an oncoming motorcycle. Well, I'll give it to Nico, life is never dull with him. *Never.* Moments later we arrive at—you guessed it—some Chinese dump by Jardins du Luxembourg. Tacky neon red Chinese characters à la Vegas by way of Peking and all the charm of a subway station. Terrific. Luckily, watching Nico cross the street in front of me, all sexy in his suit, revives my mood. Hungry? Oh, yes! Food? Not so much, suddenly.

Nico greets the surprisingly stunning Chinese girl who acts as host with a kiss on both cheeks and asks if they have a table for two. Well, seeing as not another soul is dining at this fine—what was it again, "fantastic"?—dining establishment, yes, I'd say we have our pick of the Naugahyde seats. Dinner's all right. Not great. And I'm pretty forgiving when it comes to food. I'll eat anything that doesn't enjoy sex more than I do (for example, fish, snails, potatoes, yes. Horses, bulls, rabbits, *non*).

Over unrecognizable dim sum mystery balls, Nico tells me that his best friend, Stephan, is splitting from his wife of ten years. Honestly, I saw this coming because recently they had a dinner party and for all their beautiful furniture and enormous house in Saint-Cloud, the relationship was clearly dead. How am I so perceptive, you ask? Because Stephan's wife spent the better part of the evening glaring at her husband, making sex-eyes at Nico, and proceeding to grind her tiny hips into *my boyfriend* while they danced together as a finale. I went blind with rage when I saw that. Oh yes, blind! Until

Stephan grabbed me and did some ridiculous French version of *Dirty Dancing* against my disinterested thigh. A really dumb evening. Yep, that marriage has lost its lustre. It's sad. The divorce rate of couples in Paris must be 80 percent and if you consider one or both members being attractive . . . oh god. Then it's doomed from the day they say "I do." Paris is just *seething* with seduction and scandal. It's a curse to live in such a beautiful place among such beautiful people because the sexual tension is so thick you could cut it with a knife. Listen, I've already lived here long enough to understand the underlying essence of Parisian men. They all (okay, *almost* all) have this large appreciation for other beautiful women. So it's completely common to be sitting at an outdoor restaurant, madly in love, and watch your boyfriend check out every beautiful girl that is in the four-block radius (which in Paris adds up to quite a few!). They'll tune out of the conversation briefly and you'll see a haze pass over their faces (much like women's faces glaze over in desirous craving when we see ice cream cones). It is, in a word, *hell.*

Nico and I have finally departed the deserted dim sum world and are out on the street. It's quite nice out, the buildings have held the warmth of the day's raging sun and the air is still. Nico takes my hand and says, "Let's go for a walk. Just over in the 5th is a great little café where we could get dessert." All right, Mr. Tour Guide, lead the way. We hold hands and turn the corner. The gorgeously lit Pantheon towers over us.

"Have you been inside the Pantheon yet, Kiki?" I abhor having to answer no, hate appearing as anything other then the most cultural, literal, über-informed girl that I want to be. In truth I'd attempted to go to the Pantheon a month ago but was thirty centimes short of the five-euro entrance fee so had to mope home disappointed in self, bank account, etc. I pull a "Nico" as I call it now—a silent response, vague, noncommittal.

"Voltaire is buried there," he says. (Ha! I *did* know that.)

"Yes, and Rousseau too," I say as my eye spots a poster for some cheesy men's magazine on a kiosk. Once again, Pamela Anderson's breasts fill the entire cover. Detest that woman. Not because she possesses a killer body, but because she perpetuates women as purely objects, brainless, silly Barbies (where is my pulpit; don't get me started, because once I get going on this subject I'm like a blonde version of Al Sharpton, all a gesturin' and spittle-flying as I rant and rave). But I'm thinking Nico is an intelligent man of the world, who'd sooner scavenge with aborigines than glance at an artificial woman like that, so I foolishly say, "Do you know this woman? Is she also famous in France?" while pointing to one of her nipples (c'mon, they're hard to miss). He doesn't miss a beat and blurts, "God, what I'd give for one night with her!" Please scoop me off the pavement. I'm floored. Stunned.

"Jesus Christ, Nico, what are you—twelve?! She's plastic from head to toe, and wears so much makeup you'd slide right off her." He's ignoring me, staring at the poster, fantasizing about fucking her. All right, everyone stand back, I'm going to unleash hell. Novices beware, I'm a professional in this arena.

"Jesus, Nico. Well, if that's the kind of woman you want, you are *so* with the wrong girl. I can't believe you. Why are you with me, telling me not to wear makeup or dress too sexy when that's what you're pining for? Fuck you. Go find a silicone bimbo. Fuck this!" Nico snaps out of his dreams and says, rolling his eyes, "Come on, every man would say what I've said. You're totally overreacting, Klein."

"Yeah, well, maybe I am, but if you think that makes me feel like going home and taking off my clothes, knowing you want *that* . . . Never. Go to hell." I storm away, not even a hundred percent sure how to get home. I walk about twenty paces, fuming. *Pfff . . . Fool . . .* And after another twenty paces, *Where is he? This is where he runs up, apologizes, drowns me in kisses and I half forgive him.* I look over my shoulder and he's gone. *Gone?* No. No. No. Can't be? Yes, gone. Doesn't he know anything? *I'm* the one with a temper. He's supposed to chase after me the *second* I'm the slightest bit displeased. This little temper tantrum bit of mine doesn't seem to translate into French. What a fucker. I'm never calling him. *Never.*

I walk down rue de Tournon and thank, fucking God I know where I am again. Terrific, I have another ten blocks and I'm pissed, and my feet are killing me and my gorgeous boyfriend just abandoned me by the Pantheon. *Hate* the Pantheon. As I walk home alone, past a million lovebirds hand in hand (what's with this city, do they put *Ecstasy* in the water?). I begin to unravel the whole cultural snag this evening. I'm willing to wager that in Nico's eyes I'm just flipping out but here's the kicker: in my culture, the great country of the home of the free, we lie and we like it. We say things like, "Sure, we smoked pot, but we didn't inhale." We offer, "I did not have sex with that woman," when we're skirting the fact oral sex is indeed sex. In France the policy is brutal honesty. ALWAYS. The men have no qualms about saying, "You look like you've gained a few kilos" or "You really don't look good in that," etc. In the States, men may think these things but they lie and say, "You're perfect, I could never look at another woman," and we smart but sometimes insecure women accept this courtesy as our due. Paris, nope. The truth pours out of every orifice. No matter how brutal.

Of course Nico would be attracted to Pamela Anderson. Hell, I am even. And I all but impaled him on the fence. Oh dear, what's going on? Where did that "I'm right. I'm always right!" philosophy of mine go? Could this be maturity sneaking up on me? What next? Sensible shoes? God, don't let me start buying sensible shoes! Then again, I'd kill for sensible shoes right now. Oh no! It's starting . . . yikes! What's next? Gigantic cotton underwear? Flossing after every meal? This can't be happening. I'm even considering calling Nico to apologize for exploding. Somebody stop me.

A FEW SLIGHTLY ANNOYING DETAILS I DIDN'T ANTICIPATE

My first experience with a French pharmacy was memorable. Not memorable-pleasant like remembering your first sip of Champagne. More memorable-horrible like your first killer hangover, falling into the mental file of "things to avoid if at all possible."

The "massive cultural misunderstanding" with Nico resulted in (1) an ongoing mental debate if I should call and apologize and (2) a dramatic plummet in my immune system resulting in one of those "I think I may well be coughing up a lung" colds. You know, the kind when you're so achy-sick even blinking is painful. You're lying in your sweat-soaked bed in the official Olympic One-Man Luge position. It was then that I realized, living alone with not a soul aware of my declining health. (If Nico really loved me he'd sense I was ill and rush to my bedside, *non*? *Merde*-head.) If I didn't get medicine soon, I'd expire.

It occurred to me, well, yes, maybe it is glamorous to die in Paris. This wasn't to be as triumphant as Oscar Wilde's departure, clearly, but certainly a step up from Voltaire's, to be sure. Who, if I'm not mistaken died insane, ranting and raving having eaten his own feces. Now each time I pass the distinguished sculpture of him on rue de Seine, I think, *Dear God, my man, couldn't you have come up with something a bit more refined? Yikes.*

So I summoned all my meager strength to drag my pre-carcass to the pharmacy for medicine. Seeing a doctor was out of the question. I'd sooner die than have to negotiate the verbal labyrinth of my medical history and symptoms in my preschool French. I was fairly sure I could survive an enter pharmacy, grab product, pay outing. I knew the ultimate cure-all; I have an almost religious trust in TheraFlu. This is based on a lot of trial and error, having suffered, to be exact, a gazillion colds in my life.

Having grown up in Wisconsin, I was climatically trained to endure the long, brutal winters of flu season. I would go so far as to say I am a connoisseur of cold medicine. Some people are wine experts or cigar afficionados, but this "cold thing" is my bag.

The pharmacy was across the street from my sickbed-cum-apartment. While I haven't done any formal studies, I think it safe to say there are pharmacies on every damn block in Paris. It's staggering, you can't swing a cat without hitting one. (Not that I've tried; it's really just a theory for the moment.)

Fair warning: upon entering, you will (as I soon discovered) be absolutely immediately (the word *nanosecond* is accurate) descended upon by a pharmacist who will implore you to divulge your health problems. I guess, as an American this intensely personal demand seems is a bit confrontational and embarrassing. I prefer the American method of being ignored, and being allowed to peruse the aisles of antidotes and antifungals privately. Free to discreetly hide the box of Gas-X under the body lotion in my shopping basket until check-out, where I send mental messages to the salesclerk defying him to make *any* comment that puts flatulence and me in the same sentence.

This anonymity isn't remotely possible in France. The only things that are put in the public shopping domain are makeup, combs, and five-euro bars of soap. For any medicinal need you have to chitchat, at length *and* descriptively, with Monsieur le Pharmacien. The French are amazingly unselfconscious and will proudly and loudly announce all their bodily dysfunctions. It might even be a nationalistic source of pride to proclaim the finer details of your bowel movements to everyone within earshot. (Are there really "finer" details in this regard? If so, I don't want to know the *less*-than-finer details.)

This is one thing I will never be able to partake in. I will do the required dressing to the nines to just go mail a letter. And even the occasional squatting over the old-fashioned hole-in-the-floor toilet. But describing a yeast infection to a total stranger (you, of course, realize that's hypothetical, right?), oh, I think not, *mon ami.*

I was capable of expressing that I had a simple, albeit debilitating, cold with the usual innocent symptoms. The pharmacist stood in a silent and dramatic posture for several minutes, contemplating my diagnosis. I realized he had assumed—like a lot of the French really—an exaggerated sense of authoritative self-importance. As though he was, in fact, the leading scientist in the medical field. Then he took my arm in his, leading me to the counter to offer his expertise orator style. (Unlike an actual physician, pharmacists tend to offer very vague, noncommittal diagnoses. I call this a *pharmagnosis.*) I was told, "Well, it sounds like it could very well be influenza but it could also be bronchitis, and we shouldn't rule out the possibility of tuberculosis." That wasn't entirely helpful or well received, I might add.

He disappeared to the back room for several minutes, returning with a wicker basket chock-full of fun and expensive products. This is my favorite part: the ludicrously vast array of medical concoctions I was encouraged (strongly isn't *strong* enough a word) to purchase. It included an ointment, a box of pills, a box of effervescent discs (okay, I like bubbles as much as the next girl, but preferably in Champagne, not in foul-smelling stink capsules), an inhaler, and *(mon Dieu!)* a gigantic box of suppositories.

From experience, I can bloody well guarantee you that whatever your illness in France, you will be presented with a "Jumbo Pak" of suppositories. I swear you could go into a pharmacy with a bloody nose and they'd slide a box of dinner-candle-sized suppositories your way with the advice, "Jam one in your nose and one in each ear and the rest up your ass, three times a day." Needless to say, the box of suppositories was taken directly from the pharmacy to my trash can. (Discreetly wrapped in a newspaper for disguised disposal, of course.)

I'm here to confirm that the French are indeed the unchallenged world champions of hypochondria. At the sight of a hangnail, they will indulge, ingest, and imbibe an all-u-can-swallow buffet of homeopathic medicine. The quantity of herbal remedies that are available and that are sold virtually everywhere is astonishing. I just discovered a homeo-pill display at an underground gas station. I think you'll agree the phrase "fill me up with unleaded and throw in a treatment for herpes" isn't going to be heard (*ever*) in the United States.

I, for one, am not tempted by the racks of, what is it? Bark of fig tree. And is that really anteater whisker capsules? As well as being crazy-expensive, it's all so damn specific; who can keep track of these witch's brews of herbs? Do berries of dogwood cure bad breath *or* reduce gastric juice? I swear to God I saw a big poster advertising drops of "saliva of the Gila monster lizard" to aid in memory loss. For the love of God, when I get sick just give me some straightforward penicillin and let's call it a day.

I *will* admit to trying one homeopathic aid: the L-72 liquid drops. Many of my French friends (all two of them) were wildly convinced that these herbal drops were like "Nature's Prozac." As an expat's life in Paris isn't, shall we say, always the nonstop festival of fun I'd imagined, I was more than a little willing to give them a go. L-72 purchased and in hand, I began reading the instructions. *What the . . . ?*

"Take 32 drops in a glass of water, 3x a day." Go ahead and call me an impatient American, but who the hell has time to sit and count out . . . what is that? . . . Bear with me, I'm lousy at math; I used to literally sob in math class as a child . . . 96 drops?! Hey, HomeoMed Company, why don't you make the eye-dropper opening bigger than an atom and save me the thirty minutes a day counting each slow drop. The word efficiency doesn't exist in the French language. Oh, all right, it does, but nobody has an example of it. (C'mon, if you've ever been to France, you know, truer words have *never* been spoken.)

Two weeks into the L-72 regime I chucked the idea; it was neither working nor amusing to drip-count your way through the day. Not to mention that it resulted in breath that could strip paint. But back to that flu from hell: after dropping the equivalent of forty-five dollars on the bountiful cornucopia of topical, oral, and anal medicine, I tried to go the "French way." (We can apply the "When in Rome . . ." cliché, right? It's still a European city.) Well, save for the butt-plugs and you know what, I got increasingly *worse*. So much for pharmagnosis. And as for those suppositories, oh, I think you know where you can shove them.

SUBLIME PLEASURES DU JOUR—DEUX

• That living in a tiny apartment in Paris is considered—by all levels of society—both charming and normal. Whereas in New York, anyone at my age without a doorman or a terrace is considered a poverty-stricken social outcast.

• The sound of small children coming home from their preschool down the street. This ritual at 3:30 p.m. of jubilant little voices yelling *"Maman!"* and excitedly relaying the details of their day, charms me to no end. By the way, four-year-old French is the maximum level of comprehension I have, so at least once a day I can semi-understand what's being said. I mean *really.* Sometimes I'll hear someone talking to their dog in French, and I'm standing there thinking, *Wow, you're one helluva a smart dog. I have no idea what that lady just said to you.* These are scary moments.

FRIEND COUNT

Yeah, I thought this category would be filling up by now too. Amazingly, Nico came crawling back—okay, not crawling . . . Oh, all right, I called him—and we fell back into step together (read: shagging-a-plenty). He took me with him to a couple of small dinners with his friends. And while all Nico's male friends are engagingly warm and charming, their wives and girlfriends are *equal* in their dislike of me.

The women are mostly a demure lot, passively accommodating and doting to their mates. Things I've *never* been accused of, frankly. So I'm always the loud American girl hanging out with the men as the women either tidy up or form some impenetrable circle that I can't for the life of me find an entrée into.

The one comment I did recieve from a Frenchwoman at dinner only added to my fears that American women and Frenchwomen are different species altogether. At one point I casually mentioned to Nico that he might want to wait for everyone to be served *before* he started eating, and the French wife next to me said in a whisper, "Never criticize a Frenchman until you have a ring on your finger." *Jesus.*

Stupid Show Pony,
Solo Sundays,
and *le Rémouleur*

August

MONSIEUR RIGHT REPORT

You be the judge. Check this out. After spending one of the most exciting days of my life, I called Nico to share my over-the-top excitement. It's three o'clock and I know he's at his office but he always takes my call when he sees it's me on his caller ID. As the "girl who fucks him," I have clearance.

"Nico, it's me. Guess what. You're never going to believe this. I'm so-o-o thrilled!"

"What? What's up, *ma chérie*?"

"I've had the greatest day! You know that gallery I told you about that I was hoping to show my paintings in?"

"The one on the rue des Beaux-Arts?"

"Yeah. The guy called me today, asked me to bring a few paintings over, took me to lunch, and is going to put ALL three up in his gallery. Isn't that cool? We have to celebrate tonight!"

"Kiki, I don't know why you're so excited. Honestly, you have nothing to celebrate until you *sell* them." Pause. Mental computation of surreal response.

"What? Are you serious? My paintings are in a *great Parisian gallery*!"

"That's hardly an accomplishment. Have you seen some of the crap in these art galleries? Look, I'm busy. I'll call you later." Click. Is he a huge party pooper raining on my parade or what? So maybe I don't have a painting at the Louvre, or the cover of *Artpress*, but this is something. *Grrr*. I'm starting to hate this boy.

When he's good, he's very very good, but when he's bad, he's AWFUL.

Like last weekend when I went to meet him at a café in the Tuileries gardens. It was perfect out, warm and blue skies, and I couldn't help myself. I completely overdressed for our lunchtime rendezvous. But I'd wanted to make an impact on arrival, a kind of knock-your-socks-off moment because I'd spent too many dates with Nico in casual non-hot babe looks. So I poured myself into the pale blue Fendi strapless dress with matching mules and treasured aquamarine earrings my mother had bought me. I looked good. *Damn* good, *merci beaucoup.* (I say this only because it's too damn rare lately.)

I pranced off to go show my gorgeous boyfriend, who looks good in anything (the best in *nothing,* frankly), that I clean up rather well. Sauntering over the Pont-Royal, I do my traditional "stop and turn slowly 360 degrees," looking east to the Pont-Neuf . . . what a view! The bold silhouette of Notre Dame, the turret of the Conciergerie, the elegant spire of Sainte-Chapelle— astonishing. And then back to the west, the sparkling Seine reflecting the image of the Musée d'Orsay and the Tour Eiffel peeking around the corner. It's always magnificent, day or night, raining or sunny. I adore this view. But my boy awaits, gotta get going.

Perfect, a green walk light. I don't even have to break stride as I cross the quai and enter the Tuileries. Oh hell, I forgot, it's dusty gravel. Fabulous. I'm going to arrive looking like my shoes have been dusted for fingerprints. (Mental note: *Avoid wearing mules in Tuileries ever again.*) I walk past the beautiful spouting fountain where little children are playing with their little wood sailboats. How gorgeous is that? I can't wait to have children to share that with. Nico would make beautiful babies. Love that boy. A glance at the opulent gardens of flowers blossoming in the sun—irises, gladiolas, black-eyed Susans, tulips. How magnificent is this? What a dream. Oh look, that little flower is exactly the color of my dress. It's perfect. A little violet-blue. They won't miss one little flower. Pluck! I tuck it behind my ear, gravity takes hold and it falls to the ground. Fine, you're going into my chignon, mister. I secure its stem into my elastic hair band and convince myself I'm the image of serene femininity. Ah . . . there's my boy, stride like a runway model. Work it, girl. I bend over at the waist, to flash a spilling-over décolleté and give Nico a big, long kiss.

"Hi, my love," I say in my infrequently used and, I'd like to think, seductive voice.

"Kiki, you look like a stupid show pony with that flower in your hair. Take it out!" My expression wilts instantly. So *not* the desired or expected welcome. I leave the flower in, because I like it and that's enough. Man. What a disappointment. Nico, you suck in the charm department. Apparently that Gallic charm exists only in movies.

We went on to spend a terrible day of him fuming that I "defied" his wishes. Yeah, well, I wish you were *rich* and that's not happening, so lay off. *Grrr.* We're supposed to go away this weekend to his famous Basque countryside, but I'm feeling a little sore throat coming on (really, not just an escape plan) so I'll catch up with you later.

The following Monday, après le weekend

That was . . . hmmm . . . a *memorable* weekend. It all started on Friday morning when Nico called.

"Kiki, are you packed yet?"

"No, I'm not feeling so well, not sure it's a good idea . . ."

"No, you're coming. The fresh air will be good for your throat and my aunts and mother are expecting *us*."

"Okay, I'll try, but I may be quiet as a church mouse."

"Kiki, do me a favor. Don't bring your pretentious Vuitton luggage, diamonds, or designer clothes, okay? My family are simple people and it would be rude."

"Fine, Nico. Whatever. I'll see you at Gare Montparnasse at five o'clock, right?" (Insert hacking cough here.)

"*D'accord, ma chérie.*"

Oh great. I feel fluish, I have to pack my (crappy) luggage and drag it to a taxi stand *and* get to the train station; and what's this stupid shit about "pretentious"? I guess that would in fact apply to my current state of "God, I miss having a driver." Fine. I've got to shed that diva mentality, it's so not an option anymore.

We meet on the platform at five and it's hard to miss him as he's changed into a bright red Lacoste shirt. This guy has no sense of fashion, it's ridiculous. Ridiculously sexy . . . look at that bulge in his jeans. Dear me, that's all mine. Mmm. We buy two train tickets, second class of course (back with the cattle in hell class) for Agen, where his mother will come pick us up. Nico's mother and two aunts live in a tiny village in southwestern France—as we'd say in the States, in Bo-Fuck Nowhere.

It's a five-hour train ride. The first two hours we're all giddy to be going on an adventure together. Taking photos of ourselves like crazy, much to the dismay of the other second-class (I mentioned that before, right?) passengers. Hour three is passed drinking little bottles of Bordeaux in the snack bar and illegally smoking cigarettes in the vestibule. It's like a gas chamber in French trains; everyone smokes with abandon and I'm almost sure we'll all arrive at our destination in a body pileup, dead from massive carbon dioxide poisoning. Drinking and smoking, France's two favorite pastimes. And the third . . . yep. That was hour four to four and a half. Sex in the tiny train toilet. What is with us and sex in toilets? They're not even sexy environments, more like bacterial stink dens but still there I am, jeans around my ankles, my butt on the cold metal sink, Nico in that absurd red polo, pounding me in triple beat to the train's speed. That's three hundred kilometers per hour, for your information. Strangely enough, it's a personal best on the pleasure meter. To be crass—no, very crass—Nico is a fuck machine. Sorry, but when it comes to sex, eloquence is lost in favor of pure raw commentary.

Finally we disengage and pull ourselves together, laughing the whole time at our insane lust, and the train pulls up in Agen. I try to fix my lipstick and make myself presentable when Nico says, "I have to tell you my mom hates Americans, so prepare yourself." My post-orgasmic glow fades fast as I see his *maman* drive up in her old Peugeot. Great. Bring on the hate, here we go!

Actually, his mom was very friendly, but it was quickly obvious this was going to be a loo-ong weekend as my request to stop at a *pharmacie* for more cough medicine was received with, "Oh no, we'll just dig up some hawthorn root and make you some strong tea." (All in French, of course; she spoke not a *word* of English, tragically.) After a thirty-minute drive we arrived at a small ramshackle wood house with knickknacks all over the yard. Wacky verging on cool. The aunts had the table set and we were told to sit and eat immediately. Dinner was piles of some local neighbor's homemade *saucisson*; luckily it was charred black so I didn't have to glimpse the scary contents which surely included an odd ear, a piece of pig tail, the usual. I cut it up and moved it around the plate just enough to not be revealed as the vegetarian that I am. Conversation was in rapid Basque so my silence was forgiven or possibly unnoticed. Full of meat and local wine, everyone got tired quickly. Then Nico took my bag and said, "I'll show you the upstairs loft, that's where we'll all sleep."

"Umm . . . sorry . . . we *all*?" I spluttered between coughs. Oh yes, apparently this whole Basque countryside experience was going to be topped off with a communal group-sleeping arrangement. Yes, we all five sleep in the same room. What is this, 1854? So much for privacy. A round of *"Bonne nuit"* to *maman* and the two kind but *très* butch aunts (who between them had maybe ten teeth), and I climb into a tiny twin bed next to Nico's, which I'm sure is chiming with Basque centipedes and countryside daddy longlegs. I so wanted to yell "Good night, John-Boy!" but knew that joke would've died a horrible death. Whatever, it amused me for two minutes, until a hideous wave of cough attacks swept over me. Do you say you're sorry after coughing? I am guessing, yes.

"Pardonnez-moi," I hack. Oh Jesus, my throat feels like I'm swallowing shards of glass. This is killing me. I hack and cough into the circa-1940s horse blanket I've been issued and still it won't stop.

"Kiki, shush!"

"Sorry, Nico, I can't help it, I swear," I whisper. Another choke-fest and Nico flips into a psychotic rage.

"Kiki, you're keeping everyone up, stop it!"

"I can't, I'm sorry." So despite it being pitch-fucking-countryside-black in the family sleep vault I get up and try to make my way downstairs to cough in privacy. Fuck, it's so dark, I'm sure to smack my head on one of those pine beams and, damn it, is this that old chest or am I stepping on one of his aunts? All right, who moved the stairs?

Then Nico yells at the top of his lungs, "Where the hell are you going?" Oh, like that's *not* going to wake the two toothless aunts. Christ.

"I'm going to sleep on the couch downstairs rather than cough all night up here." Naked Nico (hello, what are you doing naked?) storms over, turns on the light and marches me downstairs (thanks, I have a dad already). He yells at me that I'm trying to be a martyr and that if I wanted to, I *could* stop coughing. I can hardly respond as I'm coughing up my trachea, so he turns and storms back upstairs, turns off the light and gets back into bed. Charming man. Really.

I curl up on the couch, which is really more of a loveseat and covered with pieces of leaves and wood chips, and try to abort the next cough. No dice. Nico yells, from upstairs, "Kiki, goddammit, *stop* coughing! If you're going to continue this performance go sleep in the car!"

I'm so hating him. Man if I *could* drive a car, I'd grab those keys and high-tail it out of here. I'd drive straight to the Hôtel du Cap and never look back, but that's a non-option, so it looks like Plan C. This isn't pretty. The only way to smother the sound is to shut myself up in the bathroom. Come on, how could I have possibly reasoned with Nico, he was just being a complete freak. So I take a few scruffy towels to make a pillow and reluctantly lie down on the bathroom floor mat that is more old-lady pubic hair than terrycloth at that point. Disgusting, but at least now I can cough in peace. Man, this is light-years away from my nights in the Buckingham Suite at Claridges in London with the Big-Shot Ex, for God's sake. In the morning, get this, everyone acted as if nothing had happened. Phenomenal tunnel vision, gang. If someone should stumble across my esophagus, please let me know.

The weekend had its painful silences (often broken by my coughing) and its highlights—sex in a field of wheat underneath an old fig tree. Despite being thoroughly disenchanted with Nico's lack of nursemaid skills, I was compelled not to let that opportunity go by. It was just too beautiful.

After a long lunch on the sunny terrace *avec la famille,* I'd drunk enough local red wine to stop caring that the family wasn't sold on me as suitable-girlfriend-material for their precious Nico. What? Communicating in French is required? Isn't it enough that I did all the dishes and shucked the corn until my hands bled? Oh, you guys are awfully judgmental, considering you still all sleep in the same room. With raisinesque dishpan hands and a belly full of countryside cuisine, I saddled up next to Nico standing in the garden.

"Let's go for a walk, wanna?" I say raising an eyebrow. He gets *it.*

"Sure, let me just get a blanket and another bottle of wine." He says, smiling mischieviously in full agreement.

"*Allez,* baby!" I yell after him and proceed to walk down the gravel drive to the main dirt road. It's absolutely idyllic weather. A warm gentle breeze. The only sounds are of little birds flitting through the trees and bees buzzing in the flowers. Sunlight beats down on the treetops and dapples the lower tiers in a golden light as the fifteenth-century church bell on the hill strikes three. An extraordinarily lovely place to find oneself drunkenly in love, or just drunkenly in lust. (So even if I was packing up my heart and seriously considering this the *last* weekend with Nico, I—romantic that I am—wanted to end on a high note, *as in hitting a high C in a screaming orgasm.* God only knows when I'd ever or if I'd ever find a man that talented again. My old rallying cry of "Carpe diem!" rang in my ears.)

Seconds later Nico races up behind me in a full run and grabs me quickly around the waist—"C'mon, Klein, get movin'!"—as he dashs on ahead and into a field below. Love this man but is he or is he not always commanding me? I follow speedily behind in a sort of stagger-jog, realizing, *People who are drunk shouldn't really race; inertia can certainly wreak havoc in moments like this.*

Coming upon the deserted dirt road I see Nico has catapulted on and headed down the gently sloping hill directly below. He's already holed up under a marvelously regal fig tree whose branches span at least twenty feet. With great care, Nico's spreading the blanket just partly in the cool shade of the dipping braches and half in the shimmering sunlight. I barrel through the thorny brambles that scratch at my bare legs and saunter up to him just as he's uncorking the wine.

"You enough of a country girl to drink directly from the bottle?" he asks with a sweet smirk.

"*Bien sûr.* I'll have you know I grew up in Wisconsin surrounded by cows and farms, monsieur." I grab the bottle and take a gusty swig that in my full eloquence manages to pour out of both sides of my mouth and trickle down my neck, all over my white camisole dress.

"Smooth," he says, taking the bottle from me and placing it between the tree's gnarled roots. "Well, this will have to come off, it's a mess now." And he grabs the hem of my dress and pulls it over my head before I can argue (not that I was *going* to, of course).

"You've managed to drench yourself, dear girl." And with his strong arms craddling me in their clutches, begins to lick the wet wine from my warm shoulders.

"Mmm . . . not a bad vintage . . . a '68, *non*?" he jokes as his lips begin to trail down my collarbone and land on my bare breast. Using the thumb of one hand and his mouth on the other, tracing my nipples with his soft, warm tongue and sending shock waves down my spine. Damn, he's good. My head rolls back with the ache of desire, and I see only the billowy clouds rushing by as he falls to his knees and pulls me down to him.

"A bit more wine, maybe?" he asks, getting up to retrieve the bottle.

"No thanks, I'm . . . oh . . . Ah-h-h!" I should've seen that coming. In one gesture, he's thrown me on my back on the blanket and begun pouring cool wine all over my body. "Nico, you're insane, *completely* mad," I murmur, wallowing in complete bliss.

Sexy as all hell, he says nothing, just climbs on top of me, ravenously lapping at the wine pooled in my belly button and licking furiously under my arms, the nape of my neck, my toes. With my eyes closed, I feel him sit up. He gently spreads my legs and pours wine between my legs. I quiver in delight as he bathes me in kisses . . . As he senses I'm on the edge of exploding he sits up, slides his sticky hand under me and slowly slides inside me, his face wet with wine as he tenderly bites at the underside of my chin . . . We come together in a crashing wave of delirium . . . With my head tilted back in ecstasy, I gently open my eyes to relish the extreme beauty of the moment and I see . . . Nico's mother.

Tell me I'm mistaken. I'm *drunk,* that's all! Looking *upside down!* Nico's mother is watching us?!! I'm just hallucinating with desire, right?! I blink and the image unfortunately reappears, only *closer.* Impossible . . . Bloody hell! Sitting up in a panic and pushing Nico as far off as I can, I shriek, "Nico!! Is that your mother behind me?!!"

"Merde! Pas vrai!" He blurts out, just catching the image of her turning and walking back up to the road.

"Jesus, she was there for like, a really long time. Oh God! No! What a nightmare. What the hell . . ." I say, starting to burst into nervous laughter, collapsing back onto the blanket writhing in hysterical agony. "Oh God, she's gonna hate me now. *For sure.*"

He says, beginning to laugh, "And she's gonna kill us for all these wine stains on her blanket!" In each others' arms we giggle like naughty children and soon fall fast asleep in the afternoon sun.

That afternoon, under the fig tree in the Basque countryside . . . Incredible. Such a beautiful memory. But the moment I hear the word *Basque,* that revolting bath mat immediately pops up in my mind. Don't think I'll be partaking of that region for a while. As for Nico? For as much as we always loved having sex in bathrooms, I think our love has just gone down the toilet.

A FEW SLIGHTLY ANNOYING DETAILS I DIDN'T ANTICIPATE

It's really getting annoying that everything is closed on Sundays. As though it's a government-enforced day to stay home and marinate in the juice of reality that (in my case) you still don't have a family to spend the day with. You get to spend some serious quality time deciphering just exactly when you took the wrong turn on the path of life that brought you to *not* having a husband to share breakfast in bed with, or kids to take to the Jardins du Luxembourg. It's a crap deal to have one whole day each week to suffer, trying to tell yourself, *Yes, but I get to do whatever I want, all the time.* Which is absolutely no consolation when your biological clock is ringing in your ears like a high-pitched dog whistle.

You can't even escape for "retail therapy." Come on, open a boutique so I can acquire yet another pair of exquisite shoes I have absolutely no occasion to wear and no way to pay for. Even grocery stores are closed on Sundays. This would *so* not go over in the United States (as inevitably some overweight teenager in Mississippi would shatter a Piggly Wiggly storefront in a frantic feeding frenzy to maintain his daily quota of Hostess cupcakes).

Occasionally I will drag myself to the one place that is open: church. I pop in to Saint-Sulpice or Saint-Clotilde to piously pray that one day I may wake up on a Sunday and have a family that runs me ragged all day to the point where I wistfully yearn for the days of being single. Until then, I continue to endure with ridiculous blind hope and optimism. (*So* American, I know.)

SUBLIME PLEASURE DU JOUR

Man, this is one of my favorites and if you have a clue what a *rémouleur* is, go to the front of the class. One day I was awakened in my bed by the sound of a cart and a clanging bell. I quickly ruled out my first thought—*ice cream truck*—but as the clanging got closer and more annoying I got up and went to my window. To my total joy, it was a tiny old man, with what looked like a seventeenth-century wood cart, in which a wheel of slate sat in the center. He was a "knife sharpener," a throwback to some lost century where . . . what? We'd all rush out with an assortment of dull cutlery at the sound of the bell??

My God, what a quaint and dying profession; not something I had ever considered as a career choice but what bliss to discover it exists. Whenever I hear the *rémouleur*'s bell in the early morning I am so damn happy to live here.

FRIEND COUNT

Definitely NOT on this list is Nico's mom, who has had the unfortunate luck of discovering her son fucking (like a wild lion) the visiting American girlfriend. Returning to the house with straw in my hair and the wine-stained blanket, I was on the receiving end of the single MOST disapproving look I've ever seen. Yipes, dinner that night on the patio was strained, to say the least.

My God, it just occurred to me that I need to find a boyfriend AND a girlfriend! What are the odds? Something along the lines of being-struck-by-lightning moments *after* winning the Lotto . . .

The Almost-Countess,
Money Out the Window,
and a Diet Coke and a Blow Job

September

MONSIEUR RIGHT REPORT

Because trying to find a female French friend is as hard as trying to find a French cheese that doesn't smell like a litter box, I was amazed when a real *Parisienne* gave me her phone number. I had met her at a cocktail party when I was with my then-boyfriend, Nicolas. Could it be I had actually been accepted by a Parisian girl?!

Alex was a few years younger (everyone in my life here is, strangely enough) and seemed nice and intelligent. After seven months in France and a million attempts to have a Parisian girl pal I wasn't exactly discriminating. Her love life had just taken a dive, as had mine, so we commiserated over this single thread that connected us. She casually offered up an invitation that on my end seemed like a complete gift. She invited me to a large dinner her father was throwing at his château in Versailles, for all his banker associates. This kind of evening was probably very common for Alex, and I assumed (correctly) I was just invited to balance out the male-to-female ratio. But I still couldn't help being thrilled. I hadn't had a single opportunity to get dressed up in months, and to meet new people on top of it . . . God, what a coup.

As the summer sun was waning I strolled out onto rue du Bac to pick up a small bouquet for Alex before I set about the hellish task of trying to drum up a taxi. I popped into the the florist shop, Au Nom de la Rose, and chose a small bouquet of pale pink garden roses ignoring the condescending expression of the older woman who wrapped them up for me. What? You've never seen a girl wildly overdressed at seven in the evening? Give me a break. So I'm wearing a dress so tight you can see the blood coarsing through my veins.

Have you never been single? This isn't *my* choice. It's expected, okay? It's your dumb country, your dumb men who demand this "sprayed-on" attire. I'd definitely prefer Levi's, okay?

"*Merci beaucoup,*" I say, as I turn with silent conviction and trot off to the taxi stand to begin my traditional half-hour to four-day wait. Taxi stands bite. There's nothing to do but stand around like a dope. Generally I spend the entire time trying to will the five people in front of me to become instant friends and decide on all sharing one cab as they dash off to dinner together. (This has yet to prove effective but that doesn't keep me from trying.) Ten buses go by, pausing just long enough to expel dark, noxious clouds of exhaust into my face. Generally I prefer a spritz of Evian to set my makeup, thanks. Finally, with eight minutes to spare, I'm at the front of the line and a little old man taxi driver welcomes me into his cab. Dude, can you even see above the dashboard?

"*Bonsoir, monsieur, rue de New York, s'il vous plaît,*" I say as I buckle up and put the roses in the seat next to me. We speed off into traffic and, as always, I feel an enormous thrill as we zip through Paris at night, over the extraordinary Pont-Alexandre III, past the sparkling Grand Palais and beautiful place de la Concorde.

I arrived exactly on time at Alex's apartment in the chichi 16th, took the elevator up to her flat, and realized I was swept up in excitement. I knocked on her door and damn if she didn't take a leisurely long time to come to the door. And then greeted me with a dull, "Oh, hello."

Alex wasn't at all as friendly as I had remembered. She looked me up and down and without a word of thanks threw the flowers in the kitchen sink. Hmm. I was neither late nor early, what did I do to deserve this cool reception? Alex grumbled that I looked nice with a strange emphasis on the word *nice* and then announced she was going to change her outfit. Then it hit me: I looked *too* nice. When I'd met her I was about five pounds heavier and dressed rather casually. Now I was possibly upstaging her and she wasn't pleased at all. So despite the fact she'd already been in a great dress, she had now barricaded herself in her enormous closet, obviously in search of something equally as tight and revealing as the dress I'd chosen.

"You have such a gorgeous view, Alex!" I yelled toward the closet as I gazed over the Seine and to the Eiffel Tower smack-dab in front of her terrace balcony.

"Yeah," the bored-to-die voice replies from behind the closed door. She was a charmer. All the personality of a toaster. I glanced around the apartment and realized that for all her money, she had shit taste in furniture. Jesus, it looked like the cheesy Maurice Villency furniture store in New York City. Get some style, girl, for heaven's sakes. *Buy* some if you have to. I mean, who the hell puts a big-screen TV above a marble fireplace? Whatever, she was the only French girl who's ever been the slightest bit nice to me, so I vowed to be about a hundred times nicer to her then I would be to a French *guy*.

I couldn't believe it when she emerged from her closet. She was wearing virtually the exact dress that I was. What? Do you have a couturier hiding in there? That's a cool trick. Actually her dress was by Azzedine Alaia, and mine by the cheapest of shops, Zara, so she evened the playing field and visibly perked up. *Fine,* I thought as I put the flowers in a vase, *I should've known it wasn't going to be "easy" with a French girl.*

As we climbed into her Maserati (a gift from *papa;* wow, must be nice, I get CDs) and sped off toward Versailles, she turned the music up insanely loud and said nothing to me except, "You'll have to find a ride back to Paris tonight with someone else." Just lovely. She knew I wasn't going to know anyone there except her, and at this stage I wasn't laying odds she was even going to speak to me again. Twenty minutes later we pulled up to her father's terribly bourgeois château. Magnificent exterior, Palladian style with carved topiary trees and a guesthouse with a pool. The phrase "Dorothy, you're not in Kansas anymore" occurred to me as a servant met us at the door.

Alex blew past me and up to her bedroom, yelling over her shoulder, "Give yourself a tour." Gracious is not a word I'd use to describe her. Alex's father was apparently some heinously wealthy businessman who owned his own bank. As I peeked around in the library and salon I was disappointed to realize this house was proof that "those with the most money often do not have the taste level to enjoy it" was oh, so true. *And clearly hereditary*. The interior and all the furniture were hideously "Vegas, baby." Big white leather sofas and glass with chrome coffee tables in the shapes of flowers. Dear God, it's almost painful and possibly criminal to see so much money go to waste. I was just trying to stomach the billboard-sized TV with a recliner in front of it when Alex's father came into the room. He was about sixty years old and re-sembled a shorter version of the singer Charles Aznavour . . . and Charles Az-navour is already very short. He was polite (apparently Alex didn't inherit *that* gene) and took me out to the terrace to introduce me to the other guests.

Wow. This is marvelous. Christ, is that a clay tennis court behind the gazebo? And this, *this* is a terrace. Sixty feet long and about fifteen feet deep, all paved with enormous flagstones of slate and extending the full length of the house as it cascades into a classic French garden of manicured hedges and flowers. The terrace, with its pergola of ivy and blossoming vines formed a ro-mantic canopy overhead, and held a long teak dinner table set for about twenty people. Alex's father took me in hand and made introductions to the dozen guests already assembled.

I met a vast array of men in suits with smug expressions of self-satisfied wealth. I also met Alex's father's stunning girlfriend, who was definitely a model, and definitely forty years younger. She was twice his height, black, with the legs of a gazelle. One could safely wager she enjoyed his fat check-book more than his Brezhnevian eyebrows. This type of couple is so common, it just gets funny.

When the waiter (FINALLY!) arrived with a tray of Champagne flutes, I may have run to embrace him or possibly knocked him down. I was in des-perate need of someone to talk to; all the men were standing in a huddle, com-paring notes about money, *and* in French. That was not a conversation I could've just jumped into. The black model was glaring at me and *that* wasn't looking too inviting so, of course, I began drinking Champagne like water and tried my best to appear relaxed. Then the doorbell rang and from about twenty meters away . . . I saw the silhouette of a truly gorgeous man.

Holy smokes! Suddenly this party was getting interesting. Who the hell was he? Even if he's another waiter, arriving late to serve hors d'oeurves, I'm so loving him. Grab your apron and silver tray, baby, and hightail it over here *tout de suite*. At that distance it was entirely possible that my eyes were de-cieving me. But as he grew closer and closer, things just got better and better. He was very tall and slim with dark straight hair and bone structure that could cut glass. He stood at the entrance to the terrace and said hello to Alex's fa-ther. *Mmmm.* He was a young one for sure, thirtyish, I was guessing, wearing a crisp blue suit over a pink checked shirt with French cuffs. Generally I abhor pink, yellow, or any other pastels on men, but this was working, and he was so chic and handsome he frankly could've pulled off a pink jumpsuit. He was *divine*. He walked over, smiled broadly, and introduced himself, "I'm Jean François de Vallois." *And so you are. Well, whatever your name is, you're exquisite . . .* as I searched my brain for my own name.

When I'm nervous, I tend to hit the nervous-chatter switch and off I went into a sea of fragmented, ridiculous ramblings. Amazingly, François turned out to be just as skittery-chatty. Take two people with that gabbing-nonsense ability, add Champagne and you've got yourself a festival of fun banter. Alex finally surfaced and came over to join us, steely expression intact. François greeted her and then went to say hello to the pack of banker antisocialists. After reading my face (subtlety is not my strong suit I guess), Alex said to me, "Don't even think about it, Klein." With that she made a beeline to the black model and once again I was left alone. The Champagne had worked its magic, so I felt fine just observing the crowd, and then François came back and resumed his place at my side. We turned our backs on the group and leaned on the terrace wall to create a more intimate party within the party.

"So . . . Klein, is it?" he asks as he sips ever so sexily from his crystal Champagne flute. I quietly nod, trying to be demure for all of a millisecond as I've heard this works with Frenchmen. "I like it, it suits you quite well. Well, *Klein,* how is it that you are here at this party this evening?" he inquires as I notice his lips, wet with Champagne, are glistening in the violet light of the setting sun.

"I'm friends of . . . well . . . Alex invited me."

"Really? She doesn't seem so friendly to you. But then again, I can imagine why," he says, looking at me with a gentle smile.

"I don't get it. Frenchwomen hate me. I try and try and they simply refuse to be friends."

"Oh, don't worry about it, they can hardly stand each other," he says, touching my arm ever so slightly as we both laugh.

"François, how is it your English is so amazingly flawless and without the slightest accent?"

"Thank you. I studied at Harvard Business School, actually, and English is imperative for my job." He paused, looking out over the garden which was now bathed in a fading golden light. "I'm a banker, I guess that's obvious. But you, Klein, what *are* you doing in Paris?" (Would answering, *Waiting to meet a man like you. Even a man half as sexy, a quarter as charming,* be too honest?)

"I'm an artist, actually. I'm currently showing my work in a gallery on the rue des Beaux-Arts." Ha! Love that line. My new favorite phrase. In one fell swoop I am legitimized. *I think.*

"An artist?! Marvelous! I always wanted to be an artist, but my parents insisted I go to business school. Do you get to spend your days painting? What an idea! Whenever I'm in some boring meeting or lunch I often fantasize about being in front of a canvas, painting with ferocious intensity. Ah, it must be heavenly."

"It's pretty great but, honestly, it can get a bit lonely, and obviously not having an office to go to and mixing with people has really slowed down my learning French. Do you paint at all now?" I ask, stifling an involuntary coo of pleasure at how beautifully this is all going.

"Not often enough, mostly when I'm at my family country house in Uzès in the south of France. The light is just breathtaking; I set up an easel in the vineyard and paint *en plein air* as they say. Would you consider showing me your work some time? I'd be honored to glimpse the private world of someone living *my* dream." (Okay, you just cannot be this perfect, this sweet, this exceptional! I've got it! You're gay. That must be it, because straight guys are *never* this good. I gotta listen closely for him to let it slip that he and his "partner" are going to the Greek Isles.)

We talk on and on, drink a few more glasses of Champagne and I finally throw the gay theory out the window after I catch him staring a little too long at my décolleté. Suddenly the conversation becomes not as important as the subtext and the message we are telling each other with our eyes.

"Did you move to Paris by yourself?" (do you have a bunch of kids?) he asks.

"No, I came with someone—my cat, Puccini." (I'm free as a jay bird.)

"So, François, you're a vice president at a bank in Geneva?" (You do of course realize that I'm single and that you're unbelievably handsome and fascinating. If you continue to look at me this way, *I am* going to melt into my shoes.)

"Yes, but I try to come back to Paris every weekend." (I am available on weekends.) "All my family and friends are here and, of course, I'm hired out to parties to entertain American girls who can't speak French," he jokes as he taps his flute against mine. Cute joke, boy, and I coyly look down to glimpse . . . No *way*. Is that a wedding ring? Shit, he's taken-taken, not just straight, not just a girlfriend but a *wife*. Some woman is married to my dream man. How cruel is the world? I raise my eyebrow and compliment his wedding band. He looks at me, drops his eyes and says, "Yes, I am, but we are separated," with a look that speaks of true unhappiness. Unhappiness at being separated? Or that I'd seen the ring? Oh fuck. What a tragedy. I have a moral code tattooed on my conscience: NO MARRIED MEN.

Like every modern single woman, over time and with an array of painful experiences under your belt, you acquire a mental list of Nonnegotiable Dating Rules. My list is as follows, and not in any order of importance, because who can really prioritize stuff like this? A deal breaker is a deal breaker.

- NO MARRIED MEN, regardless of sexy eyes, perfect ass, wealth, sense of humor, or bulge in pants.
- No men who still live with their mother. Sure, she's a great cook and tidies up after you but, hey, time to get a life and/or a therapist.
- No playboys. No gold chains, white suits with red shirts, invitations involving wording like "Join me and *the six other girls* I've invited on my boat in Saint-Tropez."
- No sex on the first date EVER. Okay, right. I did with sleep with Nico *immédiatement*. Hmm. Technically, it was our second date after having spent "the day" as our first date. (You're not buying it? Fine then, please apply the tired but applicable cliché—rules are made to be broken.)
- No men who have dabbled, "experimented," or been actively homosexual. Hey, I lo-o-ve gay men, I just don't want to have to compete with every woman *and* man on the planet for my boyfriend's attention. That's just *way* too exhausting, because no matter how thin or pretty I may be, I'm just not physically equipped to help you out.
- No men who are physically obsessed with their bodies. You gotta admit men on diets, men who go to tan spas, and men who have liposuction or plastic sugery are not sexy. I will not put up with a man who

spends more money than I do on beauty products. Or gym buffs. I cannot bear hearing, "I'm gonna be late for our date because I have to put in a couple hours at the gym." Please. Listen, kiddo, just take those love handles and get your ass over here and fuck me.

But back to the predicament at hand. I came to a screeching halt and took an assessment of the situation: 100% sexy, smart, boy + 100% clever, witty, chic—MARRIED! = Operation Seduction aborted.

Just then Alex swept in and with not even a glance to me, grabbed François's arm and placed him next to her at the dinner table as far from me as possible. I was in no man's land, stuck between two men who clearly wanted to sit together merging and acquiring. Dinner was served immediately and the meal was, if I'm not mistaken, a carcass of some fine cow. Still fighting diligently to maintain my vegetarian status, I was left with just bread and olives. Throughout dinner François kept looking at me and I couldn't resist watching his every move until Alex's father got up and went to check on the dessert. I took this as an opportunity to make a mad dash to the loo. I popped my head into the enormous kitchen to ask Alex's dad where I might find a bathroom.

"Pardonnez-moi, monsieur, où sont les toilettes?"

The mini Charles Aznavour took my hand in his, I assumed to lead me through the house to one of the twenty-two horribly decorated facilities—but no, this is France. Frenchmen do not miss an opportunity to flirt with abandon. I think it might be a genetic disorder. Alex's dad kissed my hand ravenously, blathering on that I was so beautiful, adoring my shoes (yeah, they are good, aren't they?), my nose, my hair—in fact everything but my nose hair, come to think of it. Then suddenly in a wild flurry of little hands he managed somehow to push me up against the refrigerator. Whoa, shorty, back it up! I am *so* not interested. Just as I extricated myself from his incoming kiss (headed, given his height, right at my ribcage) his statuesque girlfriend appeared and witnessed this ridiculous scene. I think I'm saved. *Phew!*

But no. She unleashed a tirade, *en français,* whipped around and stormed back to the terrace. He said he didn't care, made lip contact with my belt, and searched for a piece of paper to write down his phone number. Jesus, half-pint, let me go. I've got to pee like a racehorse. He wrote it down on a hundred-euro bill from his wallet and jammed it in my purse (how terribly gauche). I laughed, thinking that if Alex didn't hate me already she'd *definitely* hate me if I started dating her father. That might be funny revenge, but he was such a cad; it wouldn't be worth the torture. After my trip to the bathroom (solo), where I took stock of this strange evening and tried to stop laughing, I resumed my seat at the table, trying to ignore that *I* was the reason there was loud arguing at the other end between the lecherous dad and his very pissed girlfriend.

I looked over at François, all smiley, and he mouthed. "Are you okay?" I responded with a face that suggested I could be happier and François, twin of decadence that he was, uncorked another bottle of Champagne. I caught the flying cork. Like idiots with crushes we began tossing it back and forth over the heads of the painfully serious, clearly unamused fellow diners. Tipsy and silly, we couldn't stop this cork-tossing affair. In short order we were both standing up, retreating to opposite corners of the terrace, whipping that cork with such force you would've thought our lives depended on it. Laughing and giggling like a badly behaved kid, I threw it into the garden below. Without missing a beat, François scaled the stone balustrade and leapt into the grass.

"I got it!" he yelled as he looked up from the now dark lawn. With the broad, gold moon shimmering above, both of us exhausted and intoxicated with desire, we just blissfully smiled at each other for a full minute, not saying a word. Delicious.

By now the party was wrapping up and I realized my sweet new Parisian friend, Alex, was giving me a faux-polite wave goodbye. All right, between her and the model girlfriend I didn't exactly have the makings of a fan club, but I didn't care. French girls are no fun. *French boys, on the other hand . . .* François realized I had no way back to Paris (and absolutely nobody who gave a damn), so he offered to give me a ride home. Yep, that's pretty much what I was hoping for. That or just "taking me" right there on the dinner table. We bid our adieus quickly and went out to the pebble driveway in a state of silent happiness.

We were alone and it felt exciting and at the same time strangely familiar. I was pleased to see François didn't have some vulgar rich playboy car, just an extremely elegant BMW. Like a charming prince, he opened the door for me, pausing for a moment to say, "I had no idea that this evening was going to be so splendid. You are an absolute joy. Really, you made this night quite magical for me, Klein."

I was drunk with, yes, Champagne, but also the knowledge I wasn't alone in believing there was some extraordinary accordance between us. We climbed in the car and headed back toward Paris, listening to Stabat Mater and stealing glances at one another. François took my hand, tenderly kissed it and told me he felt compelled to explain the situation with his wife. He said they had married too early, had already been together seven years (scratch, scratch) and were growing apart. The traditional story, I suppose. I just sat quietly listening, thinking, *Just how separated are you, mister? Separated like, it's over or separated like, she's just out of town?*

He claimed his wife was superficial and materialistic, too busy shopping and partying all the time. She was spending the entire summer in Ibiza with friends. (Aha! The "separated, out-of-town" idea. *Hmm*. Not so over-over, apparently. *Rats*.) The biggest problem, he said, was that she was uninterested in starting the family François so desperately wanted. Then he stopped his car right in the middle of the highway (you can do that?), looked at me and said, "I haven't felt this way in a long, long time. I am overtaken by the way I feel. I want to know everything about you. Give me one month, no sex, just talking, and if we fall in love, I will divorce her immediately."

Wow. Then I could have . . . YOU. That would be a dream come true. I pulled a "Nico" (the noncommittal answer of simply sitting and smiling). I had to change the subject. I wasn't exactly prepared for this confession and definitely needed to consider it all in a less intoxicated state. As we continued on through the dark, deserted streets, I tried to lighten the conversation. I described the ridiculous scene of Alex's dad's sneak attack, showing him the hundred-euro bill with his phone number scrawled on it. François laughed. "You know he's a billionaire? There aren't many in France, little lady!"

"Well, he should take his billions and buy better furniture." I laughed as I threw the bill out the window. I figured this dramatic gesture was worth losing the windfall of a hundred euros. (Remember, I was drunk.) François laughed and sneaked a kiss at the next stop light. A kiss that was very worth a hundred euros, I might add.

Total reason went flying out the window right along with that phone number. A month together (hell, a life together) sounded like fun; not a hundred percent safe, but how could I NOT give it a try? I hadn't met anyone like François since I came to France and—with the exception of that goddamn wedding ring—he filled every criteria I had, and *then* some.

As we passed by Les Invalides the idea of getting dropped at home didn't look so tempting so I said, "Do you want to go to Hôtel Costes?" I believe he replied, "Brilliant idea." I meant for a drink in the bar, but somehow we opted for a suite. Unwise spontaneity is my specialty. My love for staying in hotels is only nominally surpassed by my love of Champagne. The two *together*? Now we're talking! Checking in to a hotel after midnight, in heels, a tight dress, and no luggage is always funny. It's so completely blatant: *We're just here for a spontaneous night of unbridled passion.*

Sometimes I like to throw gas on the fire and ask if they could send up a bottle of Champagne, a box of condoms, and two toothbrushes. It simply screams, "We just met and we're gonna fuck like dogs!" But this time I said nothing. I let François take care of it all as I stood behind him like a good discreet girl (rare).

He gave his name and slid the credit card to the man at the reception desk who suddenly had some name recognition epiphany and all but kissed François's shoes. So I asked François, "What was *that* about?" His reply was straightforward, neither pretentious nor modest: "Well, you see, I am a count from one of the oldest four families in the history of France. I'm the seventy-fifth Count de Vallois." Sure, and I'm the Marquise of Wisconsin. But I knew he was serious and at that moment began the absurd mind game of, *He's a count; if we married, I'd be . . . a countess.* I beg you to find a woman who didn't dream, as a little girl, of one day growing up to be a princess, a countess, an anything with a title. I apparently still lived in a world of endless dreams and fantasies; I immediately imagined going back to my high school reunion, to all the girls who were so dismissive and cruel (Maria Mahaney, that's you) and announcing I was the Countess de Vallois. It was a sweet revenge I could almost taste. I'll admit it's terribly shallow and immature—call it what you want—but I was already quite fond of François and this little detail was definitely *la cerise sur le gâteau* (the cherry on the cake, *merci beaucoup*).

We went up to our suite and fell into each other's arms, kissing like maniacs. The open bottle of Champagne remained untouched as we smooched until we couldn't see straight. I swear to God we fell asleep fully clothed and just happy to be together. (All right, not *exactly* fully clothed, but we definitely slept . . . a little.)

The morning sun arrived in a few short hours and I realized François was getting up to wash his face. Struggling into consciousness, I glanced around the hotel room . . . God, what a headache. Who has been jumping up and down on my head? . . . And I guess those would be my stockings hanging from the light fixture? . . . Least they'd better be. Let's see here . . . Slept in makeup? Check! Slept in contact lenses? Yessiree! Ouch! They feel like crunchy eye shields. Never again will I do that. Who's taking a shower? Dream Man. Make that Separated Dream Man? Option no. 1: get up and speak to him, ignoring how shitty I look. Option no. 2: lie back in bed, hide under hair, pretend to be asleep. Oh, for his sake, I'm opting for no. 2, no question. Surely I have scary flammable morning breath and puffy eyes.

François returns and is already clad in his suit and that surprisingly sexy pink checked shirt. He kneels down by the bedside and gives me a gentle kiss on the forehead. Oh Christ, this is where he makes his escape, the French version of the getaway; a kiss and *poof*! Back to his wife, leaving me to kick myself and compare all the men I meet in the next six months to him. Yuck. What am I doing here? Then he whispered, "I have to go to a meeting, here is my cell phone number. Can we meet for lunch later at the Ritz? Say yes, Klein. I adore you." And he gave me another kiss as he tenderly ran his hand across my cheek. Aaaahhhhh. There IS a god. Sobreity hasn't diminished his ardour (that's always my personal test of sincerity of *my* interest). I suddenly want to be alone, so I can try to figure this all out.

"Maybe," I mumble, feigning semiconsciousness.

"Bye, my love," he says as he closes the hotel room door behind him. Oooph. This is all crazy and GREAT, but God, does it have "bad idea" written all over it. Remember, Klein, you have rules. Right, by this age there's no time to lose, can't risk it. Count or not. Perfect man or not, he's married. And—horror of horrors—I have to leave this hotel in broad daylight in the most blatantly obvious eveningwear and three-inch heels.

I have nothing to work with here. It's either the white hotel robe or the dress. Can't go barefoot, too bohemian. Shit, this dress just screams, "I've been a slutty girl, obviously put this on a good eighteen hours ago." My attempt to look like a smart businesswoman by securing my hair in a chignon with a pencil was perhaps just a wee bit offset by the black feather purse and plunging neckline. I wrapped the ostrich plume purse in a *Wall Street Journal* and tried to put on an air of businesslike seriousness. Futile. They've seen it *all* at this hotel, and no one was fooled as I teetered on my heels out the front entrance. I began the dreaded "walk of shame" home, past the throngs of khaki-clad tourists. "Look, Mom, there's a French prostitute!" "No, Jimmy, she's definitely too haggard, she must be the madame of a brothel; should we get a photo?"

Once home, I began agonizing in earnest. "Well, he really was great. Can't I see him just one more time?" This was *not* one of those moments you can call home for advice. Nope. Married. That didn't leave much of a gray area. I called François and told him I really (really, *really*) adored him but that I couldn't do it. He begged me to reconsider. I refused. That clever boy did some serious research, because he read my phone number on his cell phone and somehow tracked down my address. This is virtually impossible to do (trust me, I've tried many times since). He sent over a bouquet of red roses that was obscene—six dozen, it wouldn't even fit in the elevator—with a single word on the card: *Love*. He called for days professing love and adoration, offering exotic trips and shopping sprees. I held firm (MIRACULOUS). I've never heard a story of a cheating married man changing his ways, nor have I ever craved having the title la Comtesse de Marriage Wrecker. I told him if he really was so unhappy in his marriage, he should divorce and start anew. And that if he did, I would be there. Hmm. I wasn't holding my breath on that hope though; something tells me men always stay in the marriage, if you want them out of it. Pity. HUGE PITY VERGING ON TRAGIC, ACTUALLY! Dammit, if only he hadn't been married. It would've been a beautiful story, so romantic, *so* what I've been looking for. Life can be unfair. And as for that high school reunion, I guess I will have to come up with something else, although you have to say a "French countess" would have been really, really cool.

A FEW SLIGHTLY ANNOYING DETAILS I DIDN'T ANTICIPATE

I'm so fucking embarrassed. For more than six months I've been marching around Paris humiliating myself at least once a day with the same faux pas. I'd confidently march up to a snack bar vendor and ask, *"S'il vous plaît, un Coca Light avec une pipe."* This was always met with puzzled, semidisenchanted expressions. I took this to mean that, oh God, like napkins, straws are virtually hoarded, and somehow it upsets French businesses to relinquish them. (Really, if you ask for two napkins they glower at you, snort and moan like you've asked them for a sperm specimen or something.)

So when the vendor would shoot me this questioning look, I'd follow up my request with, *"Oui, une pipe, monsieur,"* while gesturing in a stroking gesture as though I had an invisible straw in my mouth. I'd get the Diet Coke and straw and pay and move on, thinking, *Oh, those crazy French people.*

I did this yesterday in front of a bilingual man who overhead me, gasped, then laughed and pulled me aside to share a precious bit of wisdom. I had been asking each day, all over this fine cultured city, for a Diet Coke and a blow job. Great. That's just great. (It turns out a straw is a *paille* in French, not a *pipe,* just so you know). Humiliating is an understatement. And it just keeps coming, wave after wave. *Quel nightmare!*

SUBLIME PLEASURE DU JOUR

Painting. I worked like a dog on my new Écriture series and loved every minute of it. Each morning, with a cup of tea in hand, I plodded over to the easel and looked at the previous day's work with a fresh eye. Some "thing," *some* area or line always jumps out at me: develop that; ooph, that was a bad idea, or, maybe this looks like it needs more depth. I used to think it would be nice to have another person's opinion to steer me when I feel I'm at a standstill but with time I've come to realize it's *my* idea I'm trying to express. No one can know where it has to go *but* me. Even if it sometimes goes awry and I end up killing it, it was my idea. (There is no greater frustration then having something you really like, that's going in a good direction, and then you push a little too far and it's irreparable. This is generally followed by a scream.)

Today the tea gets set aside unfinished as I pull the easel to the sunlight streaming in through the double windows and stand a while in deep thought. I always have an extreme reaction, never, *Oh, it's fine.* I'm always surprised it looks far better then I'd thought—or far worse. This new big one, sixty-by-sixty centimeters, is getting away from me. Getting too dark. I started it three weeks ago, by priming (laying gesso) on the prestretched raw canvas. I used to make my own supports and stretch the canvas *myself,* thinking you're not a real artist if you buy them ready to go, but damn, they were all wonky-torked and unusable. (I'd be swearing, sweating with frustration and my hand would swell from the pressure of simultaneously trying to pull the linen tight and shoot industrial staples in before it gave. That's a crappy, stressful way to start, so now I'm a big believer in prestretched, even if it costs a zillion times more.)

A day after the gesso dried on this one, with a palette knife I rapidly slathered on a thick layer of polymer medium mixed with an impasto paste. It was almost like a plaster and I needed to carve in the images I wanted in relief within an hour's time or it would get too dry to work with. If the phone rings or Puccini gets underfoot, *You're all on your own.* I'm ruthless about ignoring any distraction when I'm working.

Next comes the fun part, really, creating random images that I've fixed in my mind as some unknown language, symbols of meaning, and always laid down with lightning speed. Carving away at the impasto with a reed or bamboo pen, I end up leaving the images semi-lost in the depth. Some are *chinois* in feeling, some like Mesopotamian scrollwork, others hash marks and obscured primitive alphabets. While it dries, I take a break to smoke a cigarette or have a quick *thon baguette* (tuna sandwich, *en français*).

Then back to work again mixing the pigments that will fill in the deep hollows I've created. I know I'm supposed to wear gloves when I'm mixing the powdery toxic pigments, but it's like sex with a condom; yes, we all agree it's smart and safe, but it definitely diminishes the fun. (Which is in NO way a promotion of unsafe sex, simply a metaphor that's totally *inappropriate* yet effective in expressing an idea, *ça va?* At least I'm not suggesting smoking a cigarette while mixing pigment—that *would* be bonkers.) I've already applied layers of the dreadfully too somber *brun de Madère,* and tried to reduce the strength by diluting it on the canvas with white spirit but that didn't really work so I'm mixing an *ocre-jaune* color to lay on top, trying to lift the tone.

Next is "mulling," the part where I feel like a wild eighteenth-century alchemist, taking a handful of dry pigment and mixing it with cold-pressed linseed oil on a glass slab. I use a mortar to grind the particles in to the binder oil. This color-saturated oil gets brushed into the crevasses with a horsehair brush and when half dry, I run a pass over the whole painting with a frenzied haphazard swipe of a rag. The idea is that this results in the effect of an ancient tabula or artifact of a lost culture. I've done about six in different colors, styles, and sizes that worked and about twelve that died a horrible death, resembling dinosaur vomit captured for all time. Would you believe these twelve were *so* damn bad, I wouldn't even put them in the Dumpster of my building, afraid someone would see them and realize *I'm* the painter on the third floor, and know this shit was *my* doing. Or worse still, they'd sit there free for any passerby to take, and no one would. Oh, that would just *kill* me.

Today the *ocre-jaune* saves me, yet I still have to tone down the yellow so I take an *indien rouge* and an *ocre de ru* and rub them into areas that need to be pared down. I heap coffee grinds and tobacco into various areas to give it more texture. I'm grabbing any old thing these days to throw on the canvas, just to see the results. I've discovered spraying Windex makes the oil coagulate in cool Klimt-like discs. I also gave salt and cold tea a go on watercolor paper recently and that makes a magical fairy-tale mist effect. Not my cup of tea (oh, I guess it was, actually), but a cool discovery. A huge miss was an experiment using sand. Anselm Kiefer does it. It *seemed* a sure-fire idea, but it looked like something that should hang in a Holiday Inn hotel room in Florida for, God's sakes.

A few hours later, as Puccini moves his nap spot yet again to follow the sun's warm rays, I think I have finally achieved the colors I was aiming for. I'll have to let the painting dry for a few weeks until I'll go at it with a fine-grade sandpaper to further age—or *fuck it up,* as I say to myself. But for the moment it's gettin' there and like my little Paris dream, that's all I can hope for from a day's work.

FRIEND COUNT

I'm still counting Claude the florist and continuing work on the old bitch who owns the *boulangerie*. And of course there's my faithful Puccini. Alex, who I'd met through Nicolas, came and went in the blink of an eye so she didn't even have time to fill a friend slot on my chart, unfortunately. I'm starting to think that with Frenchwomen the best you can hope for is friendly condescension. And at this point I know not to even shoot that high.

Mr. Perfect,
Lime Tree Topiaries,
and the Delightful Floris

October

After the fleeting dream of becoming a countess went poof, somehow I still kept my faith in Frenchmen. Just when I was wondering if my ongoing unshakable optimism in the face of stark reality was the eighth wonder of the world, I might have met my ideal man. As luck would have it I found him one block away, just when I looked my absolute worst, back from my morning run through the Tuileries.

Red-faced, dripping with sweat, on my final ten meters and I locked eyes with the sexiest man I've *ever* seen. No shit, he makes Johnny Depp look like a Pekinese. I know occasionally I'll reference some actor or celebrity as an example of how someone looks, but in this case, it was a dead-on, *precisely* perfect example. This man was the French version of fashion designer Tom Ford. Completely. From the closely shorn gray-flecked hair to the crisp shirt with a tantalizing glimpse of chest hair to the beautiful jacket and the sexy stubble on a staggeringly gorgeous face. *Mmmm.*

In a terribly elegant gray suit, he strode into an antique shop with a cigarette in one hand and a glass of wine in the other. It's eleven o'clock, so even in France the wine is a bit on the *trop tôt* (too early) side. He lifts the glass up to jokingly toast me, and we both burst into gigantic smiles. You know how sometimes when you see a handsome man you sort of go weak in the knees or feel your heart race? This was "that"—times ten thousand. I swear to God, I felt every synapse in my brain explode, every cell of my heart accelerate, felt like my feet weren't making contact with the ground, and as though the sky opened up and a golden light fell down on just the two of us. It was one of those moments when not a word's been spoken but you *know* this person will play a big role in your life. He knew it as well.

His name was Alexandre. (pronounced Alex-ahnd-drhh). Perfect Alexandre. He was everything my mind conjured up when someone said "imagine your dream man." Thirty-one years old, six foot two, and with a divine body he earned kick boxing twice a week. It was his antique shop that he was going into and it was just twenty paces away from my apartment.

As fate would have it, the next evening I was walking by on my way to an art opening in the Louvre as Alexandre was climbing onto his motorcycle. Seizing the moment, ignoring my short tight skirt, I (who do I think I am?) pranced up and pretended to climb on the back of it without saying a word (a semi-queer move, but it was "beyond my control" as John Malkovich endlessly claims in the film *Dangerous Liaisons)—and it worked*. I introduced myself and asked a Frenchman for the thousandth time, "*Parlez-vous anglais?*" Well, *of course* he spoke English; he was perfect. He said he was going home to the 17th arrondissement but muttered, "Maybe some other time." I, brave but blithering, replied, "Whatever." The seed was planted and, amazingly, after not having *ever* seen each other once in the previous eight months, we ran into each other again the next Monday.

It was twelve-thirty in the afternoon and we both were buying cigarettes (the fifth food group in France) at the *tabac* on rue du Bac. Taking a break from painting, I was wearing some sorry ensemble of baggy jeans and a T-shirt, my glasses, and—horror of horrors—penny loafers. What the hell? I wear them like house slippers and thought, *Oh fuck it, I'm just going one block,* and there I am in *penny loafers,* the least sexy shoes known to man (no, actually, that's Birkenstocks, but penny loafers are a very close second) standing next to the sexiest man, I *most* want to know.

I'm standing behind him, unbeknownst to him, debating if it really would be *totally* inappropriate if I planted my lips on the sexy back of his neck where his hair makes a little swirl, when he feels my eyes on him and turns around.

"Hi, it's you . . . Klein, right?" he says with a flash of megawatt smile that liquidates me into a pool of self-conscious awe. Am I Klein? Huh? What are you saying? I'm entirely too focused on your face to comprehend anything but the movement of your lips. I'm sure I would feel pure and utter joy if you would just so much as touch my sleeve . . . or let me smell your neck. I know I could die a happy woman, if you'd just allow me that.

"*Oui, je suis Klein.*" (Dear God, I sound like a retarded parrot trying to speak French—and he's speaking in English, you dork.)

"Hey, are you busy right now? Wanna get a coffee?" he asks with this heavy French accent that inflames my underwear.

"No—yes," I stutter. (Really knocking him dead with intelligence.)

We sit down on the terrace of le Bar Bac Café and I try to imagine if I can find some way to ditch these fucking loafers into the street without being too obvious. He's dressed impeccably in a ruthlessly sexy white shirt open at the neck and a beige cashmere jacket over jeans. We order two espressos and light cigarettes instantly.

"Sorry I didn't offer you a ride wherever you were going the other night. You just completely surprised me and I wasn't thinking straight," he offers through a haze of exhaled smoke. "You live in the neighborhood I imagine?"

"Yes, just a block away, on rue de Verneuil. Is the antique gallery yours?"

"Yes, I have a partner but we don't get along anymore. I'm thinking of selling my share. It's a long story . . . So, why are you in Paris anyway?"

(Oh, this is always tricky. *To meet the father of my future children* doesn't exactly fly in conversation.) "To paint. I lived in New York twelve years and I have always wanted to live here, so one day I just decided, 'Today's the day.'"

"That's brave. Did you come with someone?" Alexandre asks, looking at me intensely. I just want to lean over and kiss his fleshy lips. He has, hand's down, the mouth of *all* mouths. The most sensual full lips over the whitest perfect teeth France has ever produced.

"Ah, yes, I brought my cat, Puccini. He's finally over the culture shock and really starting to dig the whole expat-cat lifestyle."

Alexandre laughs and the tiny lines by his eyes crinkle into little exclamation points. Drop-dead gorgeous. We chat away, unearthing details about each other, coyly flirting, and time flies by. My shyness has evaporated after three cups of espresso and I catapult into caffeine hyperspeed chat mode, trying to say every clever and interesting thing I can come up with. He's just being relaxed, cool, with his legs crossed languidly with an air of extreme elegance.

"It's almost two o'clock. Want to join me for lunch? Do you ever go to Le Rouge Vif down the street?" he asks, standing up.

"No, but I'd love to. Let me just run home for a second and I'll meet you there in five minutes, okay?" I say, thinking, *God, I am dying to pee and lose these fucking loafers.*

I almost sprint up the stairs to my apartment, and despite running four miles a day I'm completely out of breath. Yee-ha! I love this guy. This is amazing. Yikes, I have five minutes to change and slap on some powder, perfume, and lipstick. I swap the T-shirt for a tight black cardigan and toss the loafers in the trash to never ever endure that embarrassing "look" again. Hmm. Black boots with the tiny heel? Sexy but not slutty. Perfect. I cram some money in my pocket, take a slurp of mouthwash to kill the scary cig-coffee breath, then leap down the stairs to go meet the sexiest man on the planet, who, thank you very much, is WAITING for me!

I arrive at the table barely able to contain my enthusiasm. "I'm back. Were you sure I'd return?" I say, trying to act all sassy. He stands as I come to the table, kisses me on both cheeks, and luckily there's a chair for me to fall into when I brush my cheek past his warm face.

"Terribly sure," he replies cockily.

Like a smart boy with a taste for decadence he has chosen a table discreetly in the back of the quickly emptying brasserie. *And* already ordered an entire bottle of red wine. "Hey, you changed. I like those boots, they're very feminine. But don't they pinch your . . . finger-foot?" he asks, not sure if he's found the right word in English.

"Finger-foot? What?" I say, laughing.

"You know, the fingers of your feet? What's the word for that again?"

"Toes? You mean toes? I say, taking a sip of wine, charmed right down to my finger-foot.

"Yeah, sorry. In French they're called the *les doigts du pied*, 'fingers of your foot.' Sometimes my English isn't *so* perfect."

Yeah, well, everything else is. Phew-ha, boy, you are killin' me. And thank God drinking an entire bottle of wine at lunch is normal in France, because I couldn't have survived without it.

I discover Alexandre is charmingly devoid of pretence, funny as shit, and obviously successful at a young age. Bring me a straight, sexy man interested in fashion and interiors and I'll graciously fall at his feet. And I did. As the waiter took our plates away and replaced the ashtray, Alexandre said, "I have to say it's strange timing to meet you. I just asked my girlfriend to move in with me." (Ah, yeah, slightly inconvenient and devastating. I smiled, trying not to collapse from disappointment.) "Does that make you unhappy, Klein?" he adds.

"Do you *want* it to, Alexandre?"

We just smiled at each other like naughty little kids. A distinct acknowledgment that we were embarking on something big here and this was going to get *really* complicated . . . and *really* dangerous . . . and *really* fun.

Lunch went on for three hours. We were the last people in the brasserie, telling each other stories, trying to make each other die laughing, and totally oblivious to the rest of the world. Finally they kicked us out and Alexandre invited me over to his antique gallery to continue our flirt-a-thon. Man, oh, man, you couldn't have pried me away from him for anything. The whole time I was just thinking, *There is nowhere else in the world I'd rather be.*

Each time a client would enter the gallery, I'd say, "Maybe I should go?" And, God love him, every time he'd say, "You're not going *anywhere*." I generally despise that authoritative command stuff, but here I just rolled over. Talk about whipped, I was poster-girl. At around seven o'clock. I thought, *I better leave before I bore him or his girlfriend comes or anything happens to alter the total magic of this day*. I gave him a quick kiss goodbye and walked back to my apartment. (Hey, cool short walk, one minute). Once home I said hi to Puccini and just sat down on one of my pretty impractical chairs staring into space, thinking, *Ooph! What a genius day. What an amazing man. We have a serious contender here.*

I played it cool in the sense that I vowed to not pursue *him*; he had a girlfriend. A model. *Christ.* Over the next ten days Alexandre would call to say hi, to laugh and play that coy verbal banter that catapults you into obsessive adoration. We met for a coffee, for another lunch, an after-work glass of Champagne. He told me he knew his girlfriend was "physically perfect" (I believe I've heard that phrase about a hundred times too many, thanks) *but* she was boring and he was thinking of leaving her. I backed away, gave him no pressure, and crossed my fingers. But I wanted this man like no other.

Alexandre was just cool, inherently cool, with great taste in everything. He had style coming out of his ears; every piece of furniture, every piece of clothing, painting, or CD he chose was great, unique. It was ridiculous to try and compare other, normal men with this icon. Everybody got the short end of the stick against him. I was sure he was "the One"; there was no question about it. Girlfriend or not. Case closed.

One night after about two weeks Alexandre called me. "Can you come over to the gallery? We could go to Le Grand Colbert for a drink. I've got something to tell you." Ah, that would be a "yes."

Sitting in the pretty Belle Époque restaurant in the Passage Vivienne, a chilled bottle of Champagne on ice, me on pins and needles. *Christ, if he tells me he can't see me anymore, I'll die, just fall down dead . . . Anyone know the number for an ambulance? It might be wise to call ahead . . .*

"Klein, I did it. I left her, I told her I met someone and the whole moving in thing, everything . . . it's over."

I thought, *Ha! No way, I've won.* Generally, I'm all for solidarity among women, but the vicious love monster inside me wasn't exactly sympathetic to the plight of his girlfriend's (perfect-boobs-model) fate. Seriously, in her eyes, her boyfriend asks her to move in, she's half moved in, and then he tells her it's over. I was sure she'd be fine, being perfect and all. As for me, I'd met Mr. Right. I couldn't imagine any other man could ever be so unbelievably sexy, smart, or funny.

Alexandre was exactly what I'd dreamt of. He loved kids, and had left his girlfriend to be with *me*. Martha Stewart, you can take your no-bake cookies and ten ways to carve a pumpkin because, honey, this is *a good thing*.

A FEW SLIGHTLY ANNOYING DETAILS I DIDN'T ANTICIPATE

Ah, at *this* point, in this *mental state*, I can't find a single complaint. NOPE. Because I'm out of my head "in love." In fact, so much so, I think we can take the quotes out. I'm in love.

SUBLIME PLEASURE DU JOUR

I went out early for a walk through the Jardins du Luxembourg one morning. The park had just opened its gates and was virtually deserted save the odd jogger and a few gardeners setting to work. Two workmen had climbed an enormous old wooden ladder they'd placed next to the boxed lime trees.

They were busy trimming and clipping the twelve-foot-high trees into perfect spheres and piles of leaves and limes were strewn all over the gravel. It was beautiful unto itself and made more so by the powerful scent of fresh lime. The wind carried the fresh crisp scent to me, well before I came upon them. It was so beautiful in every way. With a big smile on my face I looked up at the workmen. They smiled and tossed me a ripe, green lime that I took home. It filled my apartment with the sweetest perfume for a month.

FRIEND COUNT

Against all odds, I'm proud to report I have another friend. That's two in the tally box now, thank you. (I'm counting Alexandre as well of course.) A few weeks ago I was sitting with Alexandre in his gallery having an after-lunch cigarette together when the most energetic and wonderful man came whirling through the door. His name was Floris, an *antiquaire* friend of Alexandre's, and he just swept in with all his exuberant energy and filled the room with his grand presence.

Alexandre says, gesturing in my direction, "*Floris, je te présente Klein, une amie américaine.*" (By the way, that's *a* friend not *my girlfriend. Grrr.*)

Floris bends at the waist deeply, in an over-the-top bow. "*Bonjour, mademoiselle. Vous êtes un rêve pour mes yeux.*" He kisses my hand or rather, the air above my hand. "*Alexandre, quelle femme. Elle est magnifique.*" (A general smattering of very generous but unwarranted compliments.)

"*Enchanté,*" I reply, entirely charmed and intrigued in equal measure. As he and Alexandre discuss various antiques I lean back in the leather armchair to drink in this larger-than-life man.

Floris was strangely intimidating yet playful and warm. He was extravagantly dressed in a beige poplin hand-tailored suit with a brightly colored striped silk handkerchief in the breast pocket and a crisp aquamarine dress shirt complete with French cuffs and garnet cufflinks. And the hair. No one wears their hair the way he did. His wheat-blonde hair fell to his shoulders in a surprisingly haughty fashion accompanied by, equally uncommon, thick and curiously long sideburns (*très* nineteenth century). He had a boyishly charming face punctuated by a devilishly sexy beauty mark just above his lip. He emphasized points in conversation with gestures not unlike a ringleader at a circus. In a theatrical turn, he faced me with a challenging piercing stare.

"Klein. What an absolutely modern name. Wherever did you acquire it?" Floris asks with an affected tilt of the head.

"I chose it myself, in fact. And thank you," I reply, somehow feeling as though we have all become quite proper characters in a turn-of-the-century play. "And, Floris, yours is an extremely elegant name, I must say. How ever did *you* acquire it?"

"It is an old family name I am Dutch aristocracy, as a matter of fact. Don't think too much of it. *Our* châteaux have long since fallen into ruin," he claims as he tosses his hair back with a blatant wave of his gold-signet-ringed hand. Hilarious. I adore people who create themselves extravagant personalities rich with eccentricities and unique style.

Floris continues, "You are American? I should say you don't look very American. I mean that as the highest compliment, of course." He puts a fore-finger to his lips and raised an eyebrow.

"American. Yes. But I live just over on rue de Verneuil, actually."

"Charming address. You know that the renowned furniture designer Jean Michel Frank lived at number 11? So, you're here living a *new* life? How di-vine. That reminds me of one of my favorite quotes by Oscar Wilde (I should've seen this coming, right?). Floris pulls himself up to his full height and bursts forth with, "I myself would sacrifice everything for a new experi-ence and know that there is no such thing as a new experience at all. I would go to the stake for a new sensation and be sceptic to the last. There is an un-known land full of strange flowers and subtle perfumes, a land of which it is a joy of all joys to dream, a land where all things are perfect and poisonous." He finishes with a triumphant nod of his head and a click of his heels.

"Marvelous, absolutely marvelous," I say, stunned, smiling and exchanging a glance with Alexandre who's equally amused by this spontaneous performance.

"I must dash. It's been a distinct pleasure making your acquaintance, my dear Klein. I shall look forward to our next meeting with impatience. *Adieu,* Alexandre." Floris twirls around and sashays out the door, leaving us both speechless.

A week later, as fate would have it, Floris and I ran into each other again at the charming little park next to L'église de St. Germain. Both of us had bought baguettes for lunch and found seats under the flowering magnolias. We struck up a lively conversation and exchanged phone numbers, vowing to become fast friends. Floris was one of the most marvelously amusing men I'd ever met. He would rattle off witty repartee like a stripper disrobing, and though one might have thought him to be over the top, in fact he was entirely down to earth. I decided the pretentious act was simply employed to keep people at bay and occasionally used to entertain wealthy clients. Fine by me, as I just instantly adored him.

Every girl needs at least one gay man in her life, for a million reasons, one of which is they will always tell you the truth and another, that when straight men reveal their terribly disappointing sides you can always find gay men that are perfect in ways straight men are not. It renews your faith in "men," so you don't just swear off the whole sex *entirely*.

The Alexandre Experience, Making a Bronze, and Stella to the Rescue

November

MONSIEUR RIGHT REPORT

The Alexandre experience is a delicious yet complicated thing to describe. I know this is going out on a limb here, but work with me. I started to think that Alexandre was not unlike the 'push-me pull-you' from *Dr. Doolittle*. On one hand, he was utter perfection, fabulous, as amazing a man as I could ever have hoped for, and on the other, a nightmare, apathetic, dismissive, a *total* creep. And thus I lived with a tag-team duo of Le Bon Alexandre and Le Creep Alexandre.

I offer you an example of Le Bon Alexandre and a romantic evening dining at the exquisite jewel box of a restaurant, Laperouse. (I must explain, this is one of the oldest restaurants in all of Paris, splendidly romantic, where you can reserve private dining rooms that look out over the Pont-Neuf. In fact, in the 1700s men of smart society used to secretly take their mistresses and courtesans there, and the mirrors on the walls are quite famous for the "scratchings." The scratch marks were made by women who received diamonds at dinner and would run them over the glass to confirm they were real. Only in France, right?)

Alexandre came over at seven o'clock after closing his gallery. We polished off two bottles of Ruinart Champagne, laughed until we cried, and jumped on his scooter. He wrapped my arms around him. We shot over to Laperouse on the Seine. Arriving hand in hand, we climbed the velvet stairs, ensconced ourselves in the charming *deuxième salon* private dining room (gilded in gold leaf, floor to ceiling); sat in the lap of luxury on red velvet Louis XV chairs, and scratched our initials into the antique mirror with the diamond ring from my Big-Shot Ex. We sipped Dom Perignon Champagne, ordered and devoured lobster bisque, salmon in a delicate *fenouil* cream sauce accompanied by a fine 1986 Château la Tour. Alexandre closed the door to our private room, beginning a session of mad kissing, Gucci heels against door, partial disrobing, my head somehow in *fenouil* sauce, the waiter's gentle knock on the door to bring chocolate torte, partial redressing. Waiter disappears, leaving gâteau drizzled with warm chocolate sauce. Dessert eaten off Alexandre's tummy doubling as plate. All physical desires satiated, we reopened door, I reapplied lipstick, paid the check, rushed back to his apartment, fucked like demons. Yeah, I'd say that works.

By the way, Alexandre is, wow, how shall I put this? Like having sex with the Concorde. There's this terribly unforgettable, supersonic element to his lovemaking. Titanium hard, elegantly designed, and those hips, dear me, moved with lightning speed and expert precision. Ooh-la-la, indeed. That night, I believe I had to be scraped off the ceiling. Twice. You know the level at which you *peak* in volume when you're screaming in the throes of ecstasy? I *started* there. Need I say more?

In the morning, after sleeping "in spoons" (you get it—nesting in proximity, not literally with cutlery), then (this where the Le Creep Alexandre part starts) he became all distant and treated me like I was a "buddy" or, worse, someone who might have sneaked into the apartment in the middle of the night uninvited. He would hardly even speak to me. Creep. *Beyond* creep.

Here's the deal. I admit, I had fallen hard. Harder than I ever had before. Sometimes I tried to say it was because of my age, that I was so ready for what was next, and that I was so alone in Paris. So I devoted all my energy to being the girlfriend of Alexandre, who would actually say to me after a long night of wild lovemaking, "I love being with you, but I'm not sure we should be a couple." *What?!* That was new for me. I'd kind of developed a notion that went something like this: *Listen, if I choose you, you fall madly in love with me. See? That's how it works.* Not with this boy. All the confidence and faith I had in my ability to attract men was dissipating as I saw him fighting against the idea of being with me. It was an exhausting game where I'd almost have him in my lasso and then he'd fling it off and gallop away. None of my old tricks or methods were working. I was turning myself inside out trying to figure out why he held back.

To be honest (maybe too much so), Alexandre was really unstable and readily admitted he didn't know who he was, or what he wanted. That red flag flew up early and yet I think I must have taken it and made it into a scarf or something, because I was in love, and determined. He said he'd never loved *any* woman before, which—as every woman knows—is a challenge set before you like a crusade.

I became his lover, and his best friend, and fell deeply into the role of being his counselor, advisor, and cheerleader. I wasn't about to give up and begin the search again for someone who'd just roll over and worship me. I had decided on HIM, chosen our fate of being together forever, and now I just had to convince him it would all be perfect. I'd never had a commitment-phobe boyfriend, and I was sure this would all just take a lot of love and a little patience (and about a thousand blow jobs).

A FEW SLIGHTLY ANNOYING DETAILS I DIDN'T ANTICIPATE

It sucks to have a gorgeous, divine boyfriend you're crazy about but who waffles back and forth on you. Annoying? Yes. Anticipated? Nope. *Et voilà.*

SUBLIME PLEASURE DU JOUR

For once I took someone's advice, and by Jove ("by Jove"? who am I, Alec Guinness?) it was bloody good advice (again with "bloody;" I'm reading too many British newspapers). The gallerist Monsieur Despont, who exhibited my *Écriture* paintings, suggested I try to create the same exact concept in bronze. I don't know what you think, but to me bronze is terribly sexy. Some people love diamonds or fast cars. For me, it's bronze, baby. All the way. This was going to take some doing, though, since I had never made even a paperweight in bronze. I had cast a few rings in silver but (1) that was in New York City, in English! and (2) they were about one-millionth the size of what I wanted to do now.

Despont suggested I go to the famous foundry at Saint-Denis where a lot of French artists produce their sculptures. Despite being totally intimidated, I found the phone number and called. The owner of the foundry was abrupt and brusque until I said I was working with the Galerie Despont. Then he became instantly friendly. (Fabulous! My first connection in the French art world!)

Fabrice, the proprietor, not so much suggested as *demanded* I come the next morning at eight o'clock. "Okay, great. Bye." *Damn,* what a dope. I didn't even get the address. Called back a minute later, like a disorganized flake. "Ah, yes, where are you located, monsieur?" All right, I couldn't make out any of the directions or street names as he gave me the address in rapid-fire French. "*Très bien, monsieur. À demain. Au revoir.*" Still, no idea what in the hell he had said. My "boyfriend" (as I liked to refer to him) Alexandre said, "Well, it won't be hard, I'm sure it's the only foundry in Saint-Denis and the taxi driver will just find it for you. Don't worry." Trying to assume the French system of relaxed, nonorganized planning (talk about an oxymoron?) I opted for believing him.

I knew Saint-Denis was just outside of the Paris city limits so I figured, *Oh, about thirty minutes in the taxi, that should do it.* The next morning it was raining, thus reducing the available taxis from the usual quantity of ten to maybe two. It took me forty minutes to just get one and the woman taxi driver (no, seriously, possibly the only female taxi driver in France) said, "Relax, we'll find the foundry." She made about ten phone calls on her mobile phone, consulted other drivers, took two laps around Montmartre, and rotated her map a few times until almost an hour later we pulled up at a huge gated building in God knows where.

The owner, Fabrice, buzzed me in and, suddenly I stood in a dream, in front of a fantastic nineteenth-century foundry in France. Pretty cool. The heat from the ovens was like a dry sauna, which with all the chemicals and toxic vapors that *completely* cannot be good for you. Still, I inhaled deeply; the room smelled like bronze. Delicious. Fabrice spoke *zero* English; in fact, no one there did, so we began a gestural performance of what I wanted to do and how it could be done. I wanted to make large two-by-three-foot sheets (or *plaques,* in French) of thick bronze. I wanted to make, essentially, flat bronze paintings. "Not a problem," he said. Looking up at the fifteen-foot equestrian sculpture cooling on a pedestal, yes, I guessed that a flat slab of bronze was going to be a cinch for them. But not for me, no sir. I was just totally lost.

Fabrice led me into the molding room, a two-story-high room where four workmen polished and buffed bronze sculptures in various stages of completion. The walls were lined with shelves holding hundreds of bronze sculptures, busts of Louis XIV, small horses, a man's hand, birds, lions' heads, and modern abstract forms. It was like a movie set, right down to the workers covered in plaster dust. Fabrice was extraordinarily helpful. He introduced me to all the assistants, who looked at me like, *A tall blonde American girl; sure, sure, you're an artist,* smirk, smirk; and he cleared a worktable where I could set myself up. I smiled at the workers, tried to be both nondisruptive but curious about what they were working on, and tried to blend in. (Fat chance in my three-hundred-dollar Donna Karan boots.)

Fabrice brought down a large sheet of wax about the size I'd hoped and laid it in front of me on the table. Great, thanks. Then he left and went to his office. Uh, anyone have a clue how I'm supposed to make this piece of wax into a gorgeously fabulous work of art? Someone? *Anyone?*

One of the assistants, who seemed to be the master of the group, looked over at me and sensed my complete bewilderment. He introduced himself as Franck and asked me where I was from. "New York?!" He bellowed it to all the others, who all repeated, "New York!" enthusiastically, as though I'd said Saturn. Somehow that was either impressive, amazing, or entertaining enough to make us all suddenly become friends. Who knew? Usually people instantly formed some other kind of judgments, not entirely always flattering. Franck saw I had not brought my own tools (should I have? I still can't imagine if that was expected or required) so he put together a collection of various metal utensils which resembled the tools on a dental hygienist's tray for a turn-of-the-century cavity extraction. Huge scrapers, knives of every size, large wood handles with blackened silver points, and a couple of sheets of thin metal screen were suddenly at my disposal.

He showed me, by way of example: you take the small sheets of screen, dip them in alcohol, shake the excess fluid, warm it over an open flame, and rub it on the wax to soften it, to make it malleable. And then I could proceed to use the utensils to engrave my desired motifs as I wished. Okay. I got it: screen, alcohol, hold over open flame—start gigantic fire! No, no, that wasn't right, I realized, as the entire room rushed over to douse out the two-foot flames. I apologized profusely: *"Oh, God, sorry. I forgot to shake the excess alcohol I guess, really sorry. Really."* I'm red-faced with total embarrassment and, yes, a bit from the red-hot fire I've started as well. I vow to "shake alcohol off," and that's about all I can think of as I try again. And then I get the hang of it, and the wax is starting to become pliable and I use every damn utensil within reach to carve and shape the images I want. Hours go by. It's great. I am a hundred percent into this, cookin' right along.

Then Franck nudges me and points to the clock on the wall. It's one o'clock, time for lunch. Right. It's not like I can say I packed a lunch or even have a clue where to get "food units," and goddamn it, after that long taxi ride, I don't even have enough money for a croissant.

Franck waves me to follow him and the other workers to the lunchroom upstairs. (I don't suppose you have a cafeteria here, where I could set up a credit account? No, I guess not.) We march up the stairs, which are dusty with plaster, to a windowless room with the stench of sweat and cigarettes. Appetizing? Not so much. About a dozen workmen arrive from the other stations in the foundry—the patina room, the plaster room, the casting room. What a bunch of friendly characters. Everyone's filthy; hey, I notice, so am I. My hands are sticky and covered in black wax and I realize I'm the only woman in this whole group of men with hands like old tires and the worst dental work I've ever seen. But it is amazing, as they all set me up with a little of their own lunches: a chunk of hard cheese, a ripped half of a baguette, a slice of ham handed over to me by the dirtiest fingers I've ever seen. I eat it every morsel gratefully. *Screw the vegetarianism, I'm bonding over here!*

A labelless bottle of silty red wine is passed around to fill chalky, calcium-crusted glasses, and this great group of dirty, sweaty workmen, toast me— "New York!"—*clink, clink*. Down goes the red wine. This is fantastic. For all the big deal chichi meals I used to eat in sha-sha locales, this is a totally unique, marvelously pleasing moment. I'm eating God-knows-what, with *seriously* French workmen, in God-knows-where, France, drinking who-knows-what wine. Bliss.

"To St. Denis!" I shout, toasting the group of workmen, and they fall into gales of laughter. That was the best lunch I ever had in France. Every time I look at the bronze I made that day I remember it all, and think I could never, ever part with it. The memories it gives me are priceless.

FRIEND COUNT

No way. You're just not going to believe this. I. Yes, this friendless female of almost nine months, has made friends with another girl! No, be serious, she's not French, that's ridiculously unattainable, but even better. She's *American*.

One Friday night Alexandre and I were out at the club Castel, dancing hard and drinking hard (and I generally spend the better part of the evening doing a global positioning on all the gorgeous models, hoping like hell he doesn't see them), when I heard a pretty blonde girl next to me saying in English, to her tall, dark, and handsome companion next to me, "The music is terrible tonight, why do they play this? It's *totally* undanceable."

Adhering to the steadfast rule of alcohol making you braver, chattier, I offer, "No kidding, what's with the back-to-back Michael Jackson medley? I swear, if he puts on "Ebony and Ivory," I say we storm the DJ booth."

The girl giggles delicately into her graceful hand, the picture of the girl *I'd* always thought *I'd* grow up to be—feminine, demure, gentle, and sweet. (Yet, somehow I turned into an aggressive, overreactive bruiser with a laugh that shatters bulletproof glass.)

"Ah, a fellow American. Hello. Are you visiting or do you live here?" she asks above "Thr-i-ll-er! . . . Thr-ill-er . . . !" bellowing from the huge speakers.

"I live here, in fact. I'm Klein, and this is . . . Alexandre," I say tugging at my date's arm to try and shake his attention from the nipples of the waitress handing him a vodka tonic.

"*Bonsoir.*" Alexandre says without sincerity or interest. Nonplussed, she returns, "I'm Stella. I'm studying at the Sorbonne and this is Antoine, my boyfriend."

Antoine gives a flip to the cascade of his overgelled hair that intentionally falls over one eye and semi-scowls. "*Salut.*" Stella and I look at each other and smile in complete empathy and understanding. Well, we've established we have two very attractive, tall, rude French boyfriends who could care less about our monumental meeting and we're two blonde American girls loving and trying to endure *them*. We step toward each other to talk without yelling.

"He's cute, your boyfriend. How long have you been together?" Stella asks.

"A few months, but don't ask *him,* he'll probably say we're just friends. It's complicated. He doesn't know if he wants to be my official boyfriend. Flattering it is not."

We both look over at Alexandre, oblivious and perfect in his Gucci white shirt and jeans, emitting sexuality right down to his fingertips.

"Yes, I think I get it. I *promise* you I understand what you're going through." She gestures her eyes over to Antoine, who's scanning the room with a studied air of apathy.

"Antoine is great, but Frenchmen are a different breed of animal, entirely frustrating beautiful creatures," Stella adds.

"Truer words have never been spoken, Stella."

"We *have* to get each other's numbers, we have so-o-oo much to talk about," she suggests. We both pull out our cell phones from our purses, each of us noting I have a better purse (tiny Dior saddlebag, from my long-gone rich boyfriend) and she has a better cell phone (Nokia flip-top with color display).

"I love your name, Klein. It's so unusual," says Stella.

"Thanks, I covet your phone, mine is like the first cell phone ever made. Look at this thing, it's hu-u-uge, like carrying around a brick in my purse." With numbers entered into phones, purses handed to tall, dopey boyfriends who stand like mute mannequins, Stella and I hit the dance floor for Grace Jones's rendition of "La Vie en Rose."

We skank about, fake-flirting with each other, and we dance until we're dripping with sweat. At least I'm sweating; she's "glowing and glistening." Each of us periodically glances back at our boyfriends, who are both caught up in the gazelle stride of some beautiful teenage model with breast implants like grapefruits. Stella and I look at each other, roll our eyes in sage recognition, break from dancing and take each other's hands. "We SO have to talk!" we both say at the same time and burst out laughing.

"No fucking kidding. You *must* call me!" I say shaking my head. Slowly we make our way back to our giant boyfriends with roving eyes and resume our positions as female bodyguards to our masculine companions. Soon after, I grab Alexandre to take him home and pour him into bed. What's the point of having such a sexy boyfriend if he gets so drunk he can't perform?

Stella and I meet for lunch a day later at the charming outdoor café Seraphim by Saint-Sulpice and immediately fall into hours of girl-talk and gossip. I've got *months* of stories to unload—all the trials and tribulations of Parisian men and Stella's with me at every turn.

"I don't even remember American men anymore, since I've been living here six years, but I think they choose women for their intelligence, not solely on their appearance, right?" she asks earnestly.

"Frankly, I have always been obsessed with Frenchmen, but occasionally I think I've been too romantic. A lot of them seem to have weird fantasies of what women should be, how they should act, and how they should look. It's staggering, really. And for all that they criticize Americans, I have to say, the 'gung-ho, go after what you want' attitude is really preferable to all these Frenchmen who rattle on like, 'I don't know who I am, what I want.' Ooh-la-la, I've had it with some of those lost boys."

"Precisely! They take ages to make the smallest decisions and they really don't push themselves like American men. Not to mention, they're terrified of marrying their mothers but want women to cook, clean up after them, and still look like models."

"And fuck like a porn star!" I add with a flourish of vulgarity. Stella laughs so hard she almost wets her pants, and I lean back against my chair thinking, *God, I missed this. This is divine.*

Stella was just twenty-nine years old and initially came to France as an au pair. She fell in love and stayed. We connected instantly in our American-girls-trying-to-endure-Frenchmen existences. What a total relief to see that she too, even with her six years of living here, has a hard time trusting these Gallic charmers. I left our lunch absolutely jubilant. I have a female friend! Someone to hang out with, go shopping with, go to lunch with, confide in—*a girlfriend!* I marched back home literally whistling with joy. I haven't been this happy to make a friend since third grade, when Lynn Fitschen invited me to come over and trade Barbie clothes. Amazingly, the main topic of conversation is still *boys*—liking them, not understanding them, and hoping one day we'll find Mr. Right.

Monsieur Smarty-Pants from Turin, Public Pee Pods, and *Hôtels Particuliers*

December

MONSIEUR RIGHT REPORT

Alexandre calls at seven-thirty. "Did you get my *texto*? Are you almost ready?" "What? Ready for what? My cell phone battery died. Why didn't you just call me on my land line?" I say, confused.

"I was too busy today to call you, Klein. We have to go to a birthday dinner for Sebastian. Can you be ready in a half hour because it's at La Grande Cascade in the Bois de Boulogne at eight-thirty. I can come get you and we'll be meeting everyone there."

"Alexandre, I'm in the middle of painting. I'm absolutely *covered* in oil. There's no way! Just when did you *know* about this dinner? I could've used a bit of warning." (Alexandre was the king of last-minute *command*-evenings. It made me crazy. But maybe he did it because he knew otherwise I'd come up with an excuse to *not* go. Some nights, trying to keep up with rapid dinner converstion *en français* was too much work. Perhaps he was more clever than I thought.)

"Klein, he's one of my best friends, we've *got* to go. I know you can pull it together. Please. It's dressy." (Note use of the ubiquitous French skill of never directly answering questions one doesn't want to.)

"Oy. All right, fine. You're wearing a suit, right?" I say, annoyed, looking down at my ink-black fingernails like that of a car mechanic. "I should wear a dress then, *n'est-ce pas?*"

"Yeah, whatever. Pick you up in thirty, *d'accord?*"

"*Oui, mon ange.* You're gonna owe me," I add, thinking, *And payback better be sexual.* I race to the kitchen to scrub my hands to the raw with turpentine. Oh, and that's a sexy smell. Terrific. Grab my black Oscar de la Renta dress with the deep back and the silver Dior necklace with the dangling *D* in diamonds. Toss lipstick, cash, cell phone, and cigarettes in my faithful black-fur Fendi purse as my cat jumps up on the bathroom counter to watch. "You know what, Puccini? I *can* get ready for a chic dinner in thirty minutes. How cool is that?" He looks at me like, *I don't know why you ever even leave the house; we have everything we could ever want right here.*

"Not *everything,* stinker. Sometimes I think you don't even comprehend where we live now. This is *Paris.* It's so beautiful, sometimes it's just painful to be indoors. Wait a minute, you're a cat. Why am I having this chat with you?"

I spring back into reality, and into my closet. With my newly acquired knowledge of motorcycle temperature versus real temperature I know I'm going to freeze my petunia if I don't bring a three-quarter-length jacket. Hmmm. Michelin-starred restaurant? That would be a "no" to the Cavalli and a "yes" to the black wool crepe Chanel with the signature camellia on the lapel. Done.

BZZZZ.

"*J'arrive, bébé,*" I yell into the intercom. I don't know if *everyone* feels this way, but whenever I speak French I feel like I'm playing a character in a play. I hear my voice and think, *Who* is *that?*

I love this moment: coming out to see Alexandre already back, straddling his motorcycle, helmet on, those muscular thighs pressed against the metal, smiling as he holds out my helmet. Drop-*dead* sexy. It's a great start to any night. I always let him adjust it on my head and do up the buckle under my chin. (Because I never like to ask for help, or for someone to take care of me, *this simple act* is the perfect exchange of my relinquishing my steel will *and* someone looking after me.)

"Nice jacket. Is it new?" he asks as we speed off.

"No, a million years old," I say over his shoulder, thinking, *Will I ever have money to buy nice clothes again? It seems terribly unlikely. Whatever. I do have this delicious man.*

We zip through traffic, catch a glimpse of the Tour Eiffel, all sparkling like Champagne bubbles, by the streams of shimmering lights on the Champs Élysées, through the dizzying maelstrom of the Arc de Triomphe, whipping in between cars all the while. We head toward the Bois de Boulogne and its dark, beautiful forests just on the edge of Paris.

The ride is a visual feast. It's like flipping through a stack of Paris-by-night postcards. I'm deliriously happy, even if I do smell like turpentine. I wrap my arms tightly around Alexandre's waist and lean into all the turns just the way he taught me to. This rocks, traveling by car in Paris is nowhere near the same experience. The dizzying fragrance of his warm skin feels my lungs like a drug and I bask in the pure beauty of this, the simplest of experiences—going to dinner. I've come to believe the greatest pleasures in Paris are *always free*. What an incredibly refreshing discovery.

La Grande Cascade is set deep within a wooded park in the Bois de Boulogne, sitting at the foot of a waterfall, like a glowing glass cube nestled in the darkness. The surrounding forest exhales its cold clean air as the trees sparkle with hundreds of glittering little lights. A regal glass awning spans the entrance and turn-of-the-century golden lamps softly illuminate the path. A peek behind to the glass-roofed terrace reveals starry skies above. I am enchanted!

Once a grand hunting pavilion for Napolean III, La Grande Cascade retains the historical elegance of the opulent Second Empire: the facade's large rectangular windows appear like gilded frames offering a theatrical view of a lavish and animated performance. Sommeliers assume studied poses as they ceremoniously decant the finest of wines with aplomb. Dozens of formally attired waiters bustle about, pushing glass-domed trolleys laden with cheeses of every region and multi-tiered dessert carts overflowing with glistening fresh fruit tarts, exquisite pastries, and decadent cakes. I feel I've stepped back in time. Instead of hopping off a motorcycle, I feel like I'm alighting from my carriage to dine with the court at Marly.

"Alexandre, this is am-*az*-ing. How incredibly exciting. Can we come here for *my* birthday too?" I ask, all giddy.

"Perhaps, if you're good," he says with a coy grin, gesturing for me to enter the restaurant first.

"That is such a 'you' answer," I say. I'm smiling, but I'm also seriously tiring of this Mr. Never-Commit-No-Promises man bit. Slightly embarassed to be carrying our nicked-up helmets, we leave them at the coat check in the *entresol* and walk toward the dining room.

"*Bonsoir, monsieur, bonsoir, madame. Bienvenus,*" the maître d'hôtel says cordially, followed by a subtle nod of the head.

"*Bonsoir, monsieur. Merci. Nous avons une reservation pour huit heures trente, sous le nom de Sebastian Gayral,*" Alexandre replies. God, I *adore* his voice.

We are escorted to the *salon privé* reserved for the *petite fête*. What a magnificent room! Gilded floor to three-meter ceiling, a romantic Boucher-inspired fresco adorns the ceiling while rich red drapes fall in pools of velvet. Ten gilded chairs surround a long Empire-style table bathed in white damask. Faint music, by Lully, dances in through the open door and resonates off the walls of carved *boiserie*. All of my senses are at once stimulated and tantalized. I love this shit—*crazy* for it. Okay, maybe not *all* the pleasures of Paris are free.

Everyone but Sebastian and his girlfriend, Emmanuelle, have taken seats and are already sipping Champagne. There are a few familiar faces among the gathered guests: Emmanuelle's brother and his girlfriend (they've never said two words to me, other than *bonsoir* at the beginning and end of the night, so I'm not expecting much) and Cédric and Amélie, a young and handsome couple who recently got married and are smart and lovely people (God, let me sit next to her), and two other couples I don't know.

The attractive woman with long chestnut hair has already followed her hideously unattractive husband's eye to me and she shoots a scornful look *tout de suite*. There's also a very handsome dark-haired man engaged in a serious discussion with a woman who's a dead ringer for Lilith Crane from the TV show *Frasier*.

Hmmm. Sitting next to Amélie isn't going to happen; she's already ensconced between Cédric and Lilith. A round of "*bonsoir*" and "*enchanté*" and "*tout va bien*" and Alexandre says to me, "Klein, why don't you sit there and I'll sit across from you?" "*Ça va,*" I reply curtly, realizing that once again he's chosen to sit *exactly* where I least want him to: out of hand-holding-safety in couple-proximity and, of course next to the one woman in the room pretty enough to be a rival, Madame Chestnut Hair Rude Glare.

I take my *designated* seat next to the handsome man with very short dark hair, taking off my coat and draping it around my shoulders. This little move has just become second nature to me; I think I must've seen it done by Grace Kelly in some movie as a kid and have always believed it looks rather chic. *Could be all wrong on that, though.*

Alexandre and I smile at each other, as if to say, *Well, here goes,* and we each strike up conversation with our dinner partners. Turning to the man on my left, stunned to see how beautiful he is on closer inspection: "*Je suis désolée, votre nom est Fabrice?*" (I kinda didn't know if I'd caught his name in the lightning-quick introduction round)

"*Non, en fait, c'est Fabrizio. Vous êtes americaine, non?*" he says looking at me like it's a dare.

"*Oui,* and you, you're French?" I reply, thinking, *I'm such a chicken, always switching to English as soon as I can. And damn, boy, you look a lot like a younger version of Alexandre. That's weird.*

"No. *Italian.* Fa-*bri*-zio." he says slowly as if he thinks I'm retarded.

"Ah, sorry. The *origin* of your name got somewhat lost in the idea that we're *in France* and you're *speaking French.* Vraiment désolée."

"It seems Americans always insist on speaking English, *whatever* country they are in. Can we speak in French or do you know perhaps, Italian? You *do* speak other languages, yes?" he asks, pouring me a glass of Champagne. (Hmm. Seventh-grade pig latin comes to mind as an amusing if ridiculous answer. No, that's out. This guy's painfully uptight. Lie? Yes, when in doubt, lie.)

"Frankly, my French isn't quite up to par yet and no Italian except *piccolo bacio* (little kiss). Sorry." (What the hell? I told the *truth* . . . where did that come from?) "I don't suppose you speak pig latin? I'm fluent, I can assure you." (God, I *did* make the pig latin joke. What kind of idiot am I?)

"Well, I speak six languages *including* Latin. But pig latin? No, I can't say that I do," he says, slightly amused, as he turns back to his date.

Terrific, really impressed him there, Klein. Whatever, Mr. Smug-Pants. Still, I am such a nervous nelly, gotta *not* let all that silly shit fly out of my mouth. It annihilates me. Hmmm. Maybe a cigarette will help me relax.

Fabrizio swivels back to me. "You really shouldn't smoke, Klein. It doesn't suit you and it's frightfully unhealthy." What is he, the surgeon general?

"What a revelation. I had no idea it was bad for you. Are you going to ask us *all* to stop?" I say, gesturing at the other guests, practically everyone of whom is exhaling a gray cloud. "But if it *really* annoys you, I can put it out." (Why in God's name am I catering to his wishes? *Connard!*)

"We all make our own choices in life, Klein," he replies, looking me straight in the eyes, as if transmitting a secret message.

"Yes, we do, *dear* Fabrizio," I counter, not getting his precise message but implying that his choice of an uptight girlfriend *seems as appealing as lung cancer.*

Sebastian and Emanuelle make a lively entrance. They are an absolute joy, full of life and generous spirit. As gorgeous physically as they are inside, they always radiate life and make every evening they're a part of fantastically fun. We all stand to greet them, bid a wealth of *bon anniversaire*s to Seb, and run the air-kiss gauntlet.

Two bottles of Perrier-Jouet Champagne are brought in and placed in silver ice-filled buckets at each end of the table. The young waiter in a black jacket with a long white crisp apron wrapped at his waist begins to announce the chef's *spéciaux du jour: "escargots à la Beaunoise, oeufs pochés en meurette, estouffade de cèpes confits, civet de langouste à la Catalane, et enfin langues de mouton aux navets"* (What? Generally Restaurant French I can speak, but this is haute-couture Restaurant French. Yikes, help!)

I feel Alexandre's gaze on me and hear him whisper, "I miss you, you're too far away," ending with pulling a sad-clown face. Nice timing and very sweet. I'm touched. I slip off my heel and slide my bare foot discreetly between his legs, watching his expression as he starts to blush and tries to play cool. Maybe sitting across from him isn't *all* bad. At the same moment, Madame Rude Glare on his right (with lips like Angelina Jolie) looks at me, leans over and says something close in Alexandre's ear. He bursts into a laugh. *Hate her.* Fine. I'll chat up handsome Mr. Smug-Pants next to me in that case.

"So, Fabrizio. What are you doing in Paris?"

"Such an American question. Are you going to ask me how much I make next?" he asks, chuckling as he unfolds my napkin and places it in my lap. Hey, stranger, that's *my* lap. Get your hands—*beautiful hands at that,* I must say—away from my privates.

"Ahh, that's very nice of you, but I think I can manage *my own napkin.* And if you have something against Americans, we can just abandon the idea of polite conversation. I was just trying to be—"

"Polite conversation?" he says, interrupting me. "That phrase is amusing. No, I do not have anything against Americans per se. It would be absurd to make a sweeping generalization and dislike an entire culture. I just have had an unpleasant *experience,* shall we say, with American women, so perhaps that's why I'm wary of them. You aren't from New York *as well,* are you?" he inquires with an expression akin to asking if I'm a convicted felon.

"Mmm, not directly. I did study fashion and design at Parsons in New York City. But I also studied for a year in Firenze. That was fantastic, an amazing experience, reading in the Boboli Gardens every Sunday, walks in Fiesole at night. Where did you go to school?" I add, thinking he's got to be *slightly* impressed I lived in his mother country and that I said "Firenze" instead of the usual American "Florence." Damn, this guy is hard to crack. But why am I tring so hard?

"I studied at Oxford and Haute École de Commerce—but *fashion* school? That explains it," he says after giving his order to the waiter.

"Explains what?"

"It explains why you dress like you just stepped off the catwalk. Designer labels head to toe. I personally wouldn't dream of *paying* to promote some designer or company."

"Well, I'm sorry if a woman taking the time (a brief five minutes *ce soir,* by the way) to carefully choose a becoming ensemble to express herself, her personal style and to give an evening a certain sense of festive celebration. If this is somehow lost on you, that *is* a pity." I turn away from him and smile at the waiter, ordering *"les oeufs et le poisson"* (the eggs and the fish) because these are the only words I've deciphered and unless they're served on a bed of cow brains (not impossible), I should be safe.

"It's just it all makes you *appear* to be a . . . high-maintenance girl. Am I so off the mark?"

"Pfff. You have *no* idea what you are talking about. You're a highly judgmental man. I wonder what occured in your life to make you distrust American women so much."

Monsieur Smug-Pant's expression pales. Apparently he's run out of clever insults and turns back to Lilith on his left.

Whatever. The two of you are probably having a chat about *chemical* compounds. *Enjoy!!* Listen, okay, you're smart to die, buddy, I *got it.* You don't have to look down your nose at me . . . hey, that *is* a great nose by the way, asshole. I sip Champagne and look across at Alexandre, who mouths, *I kiss you,* and blows me a smooch. Now *there.* Alexandre may read Harry Potter but he's lovely and fucks like a wild man, something I'm sure smarty-pants over here is terrible at *and* probably considers a waste of time. Why get all sweaty and untidy when he could be reading Dostoyevsky aloud to Lilith over there, in the original Russian!

I check him out, notice his hideous slip-on loafers and cheap tie. I get it. He doesn't know *how* to dress, so he puts it down. What a classic response. It seems *whatever* it is people are insecure about, they often condemn it with over-the-top intensity. And that would be you and fashion, rude boy. As I'm eyeing his shoes, he notices and turns to me. "Yes?"

"Well, your shoes . . . frankly they are a bit on the pragmatic side. Let's just say, had I seen your shoes *earlier* I would've known to expect your attack on *my* fashion sensibilty. I know you'll adamantly disagree but some people think that not only is fashion a mirror to history and society, but that the way one dresses is also an extension of one's personality. And *especially* a shoe. A shoe speaks volumes about a person." I exhale with feigned authority but real indignation.

I realize my speech sounded painfully like I was quoting body copy in a fashion magazine, but I attempt to cast off self-criticism with a deep sip of the Chassagne-Montrachet that's just been served.

"You hate my shoes?" he lobs back. "Really? They are completely comfortable, which is the *sole,* sorry about the pun (we both laugh, faintly) requirement for me. My girlfriend Céline picked them out," he says gesturing to Lilith. "We're also celebrating tonight. She was just made the head of derivatives at Société Générale," he says all proud, looking over at his schoolmarm of a mate who has all the sex appeal of a calculator.

"How very American of you to speak of job titles. Next you'll be telling me how much she makes." (15-Love, in my favor.)

"*Touché!* You win," he says with a churlish smile that makes the tiny lines by his eyes wrinkle charmingly.

"I *always* win," I reply, attempting to be confident.

"Yes, winning is an obsession for Americans, isn't it? Do they teach you how to be ruthlessly competitive in school?" (15-All)

"I thought *you said* stereotypes were absurd and ridiculous. But I'm gracious enough to let it go (obviously not). So, Fabrizio, let's talk about you. Maybe you'll be generous enough to tell me what *you* do." (30-15)

"You first." (Lob!)

"I'm an artist, a painter. And I sculpt in bronze. *J'expose mes tableaux à la Galerie Despont maintenant. Et toi?*" (Ace!)

"An artist? I'm surprised. You don't look like an artist." (30-All)

"You weren't kidding when you said you didn't care for polite conversation but you do seem to be the master of *impolite* conversation. Or are you evading my question intentionally?" (40-30)

"Me? I spend my days writing, actually. My latest book is about to be published." (Deuce)

"Really? Let me guess . . . a scathing exposé of the evil consumerism of superpower countries focusing on America's obsession with objects of status, and that this acquistion of material goods falsely signifies success and fullfillment at the cost of destruction of the family unit and morality." (Advantage, me.)

(Laughing) "An excellent idea for a book, Klein, but you'd have to agree that particular social criticism has been written numerous times before. Several not bad, such as David Brook's *On Paradise Drive* and Malcom Gladwell's *The Tipping Point,* he says. "But, no, actually, I've written a small book about . . ." (unconsciously I'm nervously rearranging my silverware when he reaches over and puts his fingers gently on my harried hands, continuing ". . . Mozart's years as a child, living in Turin. But I can't imagine that would be something you're interested in."

Embarrassed about being caught fidgeting, I say defensively, "It's just the fork was in the wrong place." (Game to the Italian player. But I've got a wicked serve in store.) "Mozart? Something I wouldn't be interested in, eh? I'll have you know, I went to Vienna last year solely to see a rare performance of his *Adoramus Te* at the Konzerthaus." (15-Love)

"That's a charming story, but Quirino Gasparini actually composed that mottetto, not Mozart." (15-All)

"As I understand it, Fabrizio, Mozart's lost original draft was the inspiration for Gasparini who, yes, is attributed as the composer, but that is very much a controversial argument." (30-15) Slave to fashion or not, I *so* got you there, kiddo.

"Well, you surprise me. Nevertheless it's a debate we won't solve tonight. Musicologists still are disputing the theory and will continue for years to come. Tell me, Klein, your boyfriend there (gesturing to Alexandre, and clearly doubtful), is he *also* an opera lover?" (30-All)

"Um, no, he's not. I went to Vienna before I met him. I went with my father." (So what if Alexandre knows nothing about opera; he's got G-spots as a hobby, *ça va?!*)

Luckily dinner is served and I can seek distraction in haute cuisine. I take small bites of the fragrant *poisson* still sizzling in its oval porcelain platter. Mmm. It's fantastic, with perfectly grilled skin, warm and delicately flaky meat with the slightest hint of tarragon, surrounded by tender *petits pois* in saffron *beurre*. French food is so sensual, your tongue just aches for the next sensation. Yeowts. Careful, girl, you're getting all hot and bothered. Right. Serious conversation. Back to that.

"The focus of your book is *just* the years Mozart spent in Turin? Why have you chosen that period?"

"Because I am from Turin. And like all Italians, I suppose, I'm passionate about my city."

"Yes, Turin sounds enchanting. Do you know *Nietzsche in Turin* by Lesley Chamberlain?" (15-Love)

"*Bien sûr.*" (15-All)

"Well, I have to say, I read it last year and fell wildly in love with the city *simply* from her descriptions: the cathedral, the small markets, the snow-capped Alps as a backdrop to the beautiful architecture," I expound, having clearly veered from clever to drunkenly pretentious. (Foot fault)

"Yes, it is quite a great city. In fact, Céline and I just returned from a week there. She's a brilliant woman. You should try to speak with her this evening." (15-30)

"Oh, yes, I *must* try to find a chance to talk to Céline." (Sure, I'll catch up with her later, like when her face thaws.)

I take a break from the tennis match to nibble at my fish, running chunks of bread through the creamy sauce and bringing it up to my mouth, when I feel a hand on my brow. Still with bread to mouth, I turn to see Fabrizio has brushed something off my face and is smiling. I swallow and demand, "What *are* you doing?"

"You had an alfalfa sprout on your eyebrow. I didn't think it suited your carefully chosen oufit," he says with a small laugh, holding a huge sprout aloft between thumb and forefinger. (Ace! 15-40)

Eeeh. I'm *totally* embarrassed. I've been sitting here with an alfalfa sprout on my head?! That was part of the *oeufs* plate twenty minutes ago! He let me chatter away with this squiggly vegetable adhered to my forehead?! Oh dear God. Interesting man, but he is killing me in every way!

"Thanks," I reply limply.

"Don't mention it." He returns slicing into his côtes de boeuf. (Second game to the gentleman from Turin.)

Such a pity Fabrizio is so arrogant and clearly *relishes* making me uncomfortable. He's an intelligent man I could really like but, NO way, too rude and too Italian. And those shoes! I thought all Italians were supposed to dress well. What is this guy's story? He's terribly handsome, actually, and it's entirely wasted on him and his unfuckably bad taste in clothes. Yes, well, *my* Alexandre is perfect, funny, vibrant, dresses to kill, and smart in *his* way. *Brilliant* in many ways, "in bed" being in the top three; the other two I can't think of right now. So, there!

"Fabrizio, when does your book come out in the United States? I'm sure it'd be an interesting read some night." Attempting to belittle him now, as though his subject matter is so slight it's the equivalent of "Puss' n Boots." (15-Love)

"At the same time as in France, in two months. Then I go on a book tour for a while and a well-needed holiday to Madagascar." (15-All)

"Wow, Madagascar. I'm sure you'll love it." (Madagascar? Number one on my list of places to go . . . And you're taking that hyperserious sourpuss mathematician next to you? I bet she's just *buckets* of fun. Look at her, she's drinking Evian, for God's sakes. I bet she looks like an asparagus in a bikini. Grrr. Fine! Go off with your brilliant stick figure; you have terrible taste in women *and* clothes.)

"Oh, so you've been there, Klein?" he says, rather excited, which for him is expressed by a raising one eyebrow and putting down his fork. Oh, what a wild man. "Tell me your impressions." (Lob)

"No, I haven't been, not yet, but I am sure it will be absolutely incredible. I'm waiting to share that experience with someone . . . someone really precious who will appreciate it as much as I know I will." (I'm drunk now, speaking *way* too freely, but trying to imply Lilith over there, will probably be spending her time in Madagascar creating charts of the barometric pressure at various sea levels.)

"And you think that *precious* person is *not* your current boyfriend?" he says just before Alexandre bellows, "*Ah, oui! Kylie Minogue est magnifique! Ooh-la-la!*" to Sebastian across the entire table. (15-30 Nice timing, Alexandre. Could you be *more* ridiculous?)

"I never said *that*. No, I'm sure *we will* go together. I'd love to go there for my honeymoon." (Ball out!) Just where am I going with this? What is my point? This guy's got me saying every last thing I shouldn't be saying, dammit.

A tremendously large cake on a silver tray is brought to the table and placed in front of Sebastian, as we all clap in a distinctly *proper* display of festivity. The dark chocolate cake is an amusingly precise replica of a nineteenth-century chaise lounge, an homage to Sebastian's profession as an *antiquaire*. A few standing Champagne toasts are made (*très* chic) and we all resume our seats to feast on cake and tiny rich cups of espresso. After polishing off a second helping, I reach to light up my much-savoured after-dinner cigarette.

"I'm making a choice here, Fabrizio, *to smoke*. Unless you object strongly," I say in hopes of warding off criticism. (30-All)

"You do as you please. Clearly I'd lose that battle." And he turns back to Céline, who's obviously fuming that her boyfriend talked so long to another woman. Oops! Looks like we won't be getting around to that chat, huh, Céline? *Quel dommage*. I'm *sure* we had *so* much in common. Nice briefcase. I've never even *owned* a briefcase.

It's late and I'm feeling weary, having partaken in enough richly divine food and wine to last me a while, at least until morning. I miss being beside Alexandre and Monsieur Smarty-Pants has thrown me into a mental tizzy—so judgmental, so handsome, so challenging. My God, and that bit when he put his hand on mine, essentially telling me to calm down?! The *nerve!*

Alexandre and I catch each other's eyes and make it known we are ready to begin the long, drawn-out departure part of the dinner program. The *bonsoirs* echo off the walls as cheek kisses fall sloppily on earrings and noses. Promises to see one another again soon are made as everyone leaves large piles of euros for their share.

I reach behind me to drop my jacket a few inches, enabling me to slide my arms in the sleeves, and briefly expose the small tattoo of a crab on my shoulder. Fabrizio has, once again, traversed all paths of personal space and with his hand on my bare shoulder, blurts, "A tattoo? Is it permanent?" Probably aghast. (Backhand point)

"Well, it's not a decal from a box of Cracker Jacks," I reply sarcastically, thinking, *Here goes. This is where he rips me to shreds as the finale.*

"You are an insolent woman—I like it," he says as he helps slide my jacket on, smoothing it over my shoulders. (30-40)

"Oh? So *now* you *like* me? I hardly believe you, after all the—"

"No, I meant I like your *tattoo,*" he says, smiling coyly. (Advantage)

"Really? Fabrizio, do you ever just speak in a relaxed, unchallenging way?" (Deuce)

"As I told you, I think polite conversation is vastly overrated . . . *and* nearly impossible with a woman like you." He winks and immediately turns away to help Céline on with her coat. (Game, set, and match to the man in the bad shoes.) *Hrmph!!*

Alexandre whisks over and lays a bunch of kisses on my neck. "Baby, I missed you, and . . . Ooph, I ate too much. I'm a *hip-po-pa-tome,*" he says, patting his tummy. "Let's go home." He gives my butt a gentle swat. Love that. I wave a final goodbye to Sebastian and Emmanuelle as we head toward the door; out of the corner of my eye I see Fabrizio. Céline is by his side, talking away to him and he's just standing there, smiling, staring . . . at me.

A worthy opponent, yes . . . but exhausting as hell.

A FEW SLIGHTLY ANNOYING DETAILS I DIDN'T ANTICIPATE

Believe it or not, there *is* a downside to the charming idea of going for a pot of warm Earl Grey tea at the famous Café de Flore and then setting off for an afternoon of shopping in Saint-Germain. Once you've taken in all the people-watching you can stand, and paid the ten euros for the small pot of tea (oh sure, that's a fair price; after all, you did heat the water . . . *please*), you'll merrily stroll out, perhaps with the intention of doing some serious damage at Louis Vuitton, and you'll inevitably find yourself in the all-too-familiar position of . . . dying for a bathroom. Suddenly, drinking that entire pot of delicious Mariage Frères tea doesn't seem to have been such a good idea. One lovely autumn afternoon I found myself in just this scenario.

I hastily weighed the options: *I can't make the mad dash back to my apartment before my bladder will burst, so that's out. I can go into another café and use their facilities but then I'd have to order something. Something cheap, like a Perrier. But then if I take in more fluids I'll start the whole damn process all over again*. Out of options, I accepted my fate of having to—dear God, no—find one of those freestanding public-access toilets.

Perhaps you've seen the modern "pee pods" that dot Parisian streets. Without fail, they are always located at major thoroughfares and make no effort to be discreet. I should explain: I'm one of those people who try to go through life without anyone ever considering that I actually have any need for toilets. (Someday I will grow up; I've recently become "okay" with buying tampons.)

So then, yes, standing in front of the Maison de Pee, scrambling for exact change, and trying to decipher the instructions before I pee into my boots is my personal idea of hell. Luckily, I had the required fifty centimes, dropped it in the slot and the door glided open. Hmmm, the maison is surprisingly spacious and groovy. Kind of a cross between an airline toilet and a NASA space capsule. I enter and the door automatically closes behind me, *et voilà!* It's like I'm in my own private little apartment in the heart of Saint-Germain. Imagine, just for fifty centimes! No time to peruse the interior aesthetics. I virtually rip the buckle clean off my belt in my haste to relieve my bladder, which I'm sure must be the size of a hummingbird's to have put me in this predicament. With my pants around my ankles, I'm doing the don't-let-any-skin-or-personal-clothing-touch-the-toilet-seat hovering maneuver, when, for the love of Pete, the automatic door slides back open and I'm literally exposing my bare ass to the throngs of chic Parisians passing by. Dear God, what a horror (for all of us).

Perhaps if this worst-case scenario were happening anywhere else in the world (for instance, Montana) I so wouldn't care. But *Paris!* Argh! My audience was composed of refined people to whom anything less than a *100 percent* cashmere scarf is appalling.

In an absolute panic I'm fumbling to pull up my pants with one hand, and with the other simultaneously hitting random buttons in an entirely feeble attempt to close the goddamn door. I must have inadvertently hit the game-over button because suddenly I am inundated with a mist of deodorizer spritzing from above, as well as the crashing roar of the toilet continuously flushing. But *of course* the door is still open to the masses of curious onlookers. (*Bonjour! Ça va?*) In full-blown panic, I desperately wish there were a "hyperspace" button to push, or at least a trapdoor, or even that I could will myself to spontaneously burst into flame—anything to escape my starring role in this spectacle.

Finally clothed, I'm all too aware "exiting" is my only means of departure. Sadly, it's not even possible to nervously laugh this off with a friend who, come to think of it, also could have acted as a great door block. Nope, just me leaving the "pod," having definitely lost my dignity somewhere inside, forcing myself to assume an expression of fake calm, as if, *Oh sure, that went flawlessly; so the door opened, so what? I needed some fresh air and daylight anyway.*

But, as is my luck—would you believe—I never even *got to* pee.

SUBLIME PLEASURES DU JOUR—TROIS!

• That you can order a white wine at a café at ten o'clock in the morning and no one blinks an eye. Not that I do, but it's a nice option. (I wait the *long* three hours until lunch, thank you.)

• The famous Berthillon glace sold at its original shop on Île Saint-Louis. The flavors are exotic—cantaloupe, cinnamon, mango, baked Alaska. It is so unbelievably, deliciously decadent and makes Häagen-Dazs taste like frozen spit in comparison. But don't head over to Berthillon for a cone in August, as it will be *fermez* like every *vrai Français* establishment.

• Walking past the old *hôtels particuliers* on rue Bellechasse and passing under an arched vine-covered entrance that leads into a private courtyard. It's entirely transporting, the cold of the old flagstones underfoot, all moss covered and worn with age. Standing under a canopy of trees, the air is chilly and blows softly into the street carrying with it the delicate smell of very old timber. A small fountain of a young boy in cream Carrara marble flows and gurgles as it has for hundreds of years. To the right a large copper trough, deeply patinaed, stands as it has since horses used to gather to feed in the evenings . . . You can almost hear the liveried carriage turn into the courtyard.

FRIEND COUNT

Alexandre, Floris, Stella, Sebastian, Emmanuelle, Amélie, Cédric—seven! Yipee! I'm guessing here, but I imagine Fabrizio's girlfriend, Céline (Mademoiselle de Rivatives), wouldn't be interested in applying for a position number eight *avec moi.* Nope. Fine.

Dinner with the Parents with No English Subtitles, la Poste, and Outdoor Terraces

January

MONSIEUR RIGHT REPORT

I knew it would happen one day; I just thought I'd be a lot more prepared when it did. One afternoon Alexandre said, "Oh, by the way, we're invited to my parents' for dinner on Sunday." Oh dear God. While normally this kind of thing would be "nerve-racking level-5," in France, with my hyper-underdeveloped French language skills it was an off-the-charts event on the stress-o-meter. What were the chances that they'd be content with my reciting the days of the week and introducing myself over and over? Slim to none, I was sure, and I became a basket case of nerves just thinking about it.

To be honest, before I moved to Paris I had envisioned that by merely co-existing with French citizens I would, through osmosis, become marvelously fluent in the language. That completely *didn't* happen and while I had been brave enough to move to France, the idea of taking French classes strangely scared me, and so I kept putting it off and making sure all my French friends spoke English.

As Sunday loomed, I sat down with my tome of French grammar, Barrons, and *French the Easy Way* for a mini–crash course. Curiously enough, wearing the beret, the Picasso striped shirt and smoking a pack of Gauloise cigarettes just did not increase my comprehension. I was getting progressively more tense as I tried memorizing the French words for *monkey, table,* and *horse* and thinking it was going to be very unlikely that I'd have the occasion to use them. "Well now, you parents of my lover man, that table is larger than a monkey and the color of a horse, *non*?" Uughh!

Sunday arrived all too soon and "tense" evolved into "full-blown panic."

An hour before our expected arrival *chez les parents,* Alexandre and I were still hanging out at my apartment after having spent the day, as the French would say, as *flâneurs* (wandering aimlessly around Saint-Germain, looking at buildings, store windows, stopping for coffee, the usual Sunday routine).

"Alexandre, this dinner with your parents tonight, what do you say we just tell them we split up, I'm history, gone, moved back to the United States?"

"Oh come on, relax, it will be fine. They'll love you, don't worry," he said adding, "But perhaps I should tell you they don't speak a word of English, so if there's a problem, I'll translate, okay?"

"Zero English?!! *Merde.* Alexandre, somehow I don't think a bewildered mute is your parents' first choice for their son. For God's sake, my French is so bad, last week when I was shopping for new vacuum bags I translated it into *poubelle sacs* (garbage purses). I'm going to make a total ass out of myself, I'm just warning you."

"I thought you generally made an ass out of yourself *every night* anyway," Alexandre said, laughing as he began tickling my waist.

"Stop it. I'm serious. I've seriously only recently mastered idiot phrases like "where is the book?" and "the vase is on the table." If you really cared about me you'd let me stay home and eat cookies."

"No, it's because I really *adore* you that I want you to meet them," he said. I melted a little.

"Oh, sure play the old Gallic-charm card, but remember you'll have to jump in with verbs because I only got through the nouns chapter," I said under my breath as I huffed off to my bedroom. He wasn't going to let me slip out of the dreaded shindig. All right then, it's inescapable, I have to go. No opportunity to feign laryngitis I suppose. No, Alexandre would kill me. So what does one wear to meet French parents? Something French, I'm guessing. Nope, this is definitely not the evening to drag out the Ralph Lauren American flag sweater. French, huh? Prada? No, that's Italian. Gucci? No, of course not, too sexy, plus Italian. God, I don't believe this but for the first time in my life I'm going to ask for help choosing an outfit.

"Alexandre!" He comes into the room with a cup of tea and sits on my bed next to a dozing Puccini who can't be bothered with either of us as he's in deep REM cycle, whiskers twitching and probably dreaming of killing and/or fucking the female cat across the street.

"What the hell am I going to wear? I should be kind of demure for your mom, right? But still not house-mouse matronly, so your father thinks I'm pretty enough, yes?"

"Easy, Klein, you're thinking too much. Well, let's see here. You have a million clothes," he says, getting up to rifle through the racks. "Why not this blouse . . . and this skirt?" he offers, handing me a black crepe shirt and a simple black skirt with a small pleated hem, both Agnès B (French).

"Well done, boy. Let's hear it for an innate sense of French style. And I'll wear the necklace you gave me with the little gray pearls and . . . these shoes!" I say holding up a pair of ink black Marc Jacobs mules with a modest two-inch heel.

"Perfect. See, Klein, everything's going to be fine."

"Since when did *you* become the optimist of this couple?" I say, half joking, pushing him back on the bed. "Now, hit the road, cowboy, I gotta get changed. Here's an idea. Why don't you pour me a glass of wine. Hey, we should probably bring something tonight, right? Flowers? Chocolates? Wine?"

Alexandre returns with a cold glass of white wine for me and says, "Not chocolates. My mother's allergic; she'd collapse in a coma and then, yes, I'd say my family would indeed hate you. Flowers, though, that's a good idea."

I dress quickly, down the wine, do a bit of light makeup and easy with the perfume when Alexandre appears in the doorway. "You look fine. Let's go," he says with one hand on the front door and a cigarette in the other.

"Fine." I look "fine"? God, could he ever give a compliment? That would be a big, fat no. We climb in his car and make a mad dash around Paris looking for a florist, any florist open on a Sunday at seven-thirty at night. Betting odds: easily 20 to 1.

"Dammit, they're all closed. We'll have to give up this search or we'll be late, Klein."

"Ah, no. One, I'm not arriving empty-handed and two, since when is it important to be exactly on time in France anyway? Strike that. Of course we'd better not be late for your parents. Hey, what about the florist by the Madeleine? I think I've seen them open on Sundays. Turn right! Here!"

Alexandre hightails it to place Madeleine like a demon with a death wish. Sure enough, the florist is open, albeit with a sorry collection of garishly dyed daisies and ludicriously expensive orchids. We drop forty euros on four pitiful tired orchids surrounded by some cheesy sparkly silver branches and race back to the car.

"We've got ten minutes to get to Neuilly. Can we do it, Speed Commander?"

"Never doubt a Frenchman in traffic, Private Klein," Alexandre says with joking authority. (More frightening words I have not heard.) Pulling up at his parents' apartment building in this smart suburb north of Paris, with two whole minutes to spare, I realize I've never been to this part of town before. It's beautiful. There are enormous gardens on every block and gracious lawns between charming nineteenth-century buildings. The whole neighborhood has a friendly, welcoming air. *Tra-la!*

In the elevator going up to their apartment, I'm nervous and tell myself *not* to go blank as is my usual move when faced with French conversation under pressure.

"You're holding the flowers. Let me, okay? It'll seem like they're from me if I hold them. It's better that way, right? I think it is," I plead.

"Careful, Klein. You're doing that blithering, rambling stuff."

"Thanks for the ego boost. Why do I feel like Dead Man Walking over here? What a pity my final meal was a tuna baguette. Would it really be so rude to leave the flowers at the door and run?" This is all a foolish endeavor. I definitely should've postponed until I could string three words together in French. Wonder what the French translation of "rain check" is?

Alexandre knocks at the door and from the other side of the door we hear, "*Alexandre? C'est toi?*" (*Oui, avec my American simpleton girlfriend*). Alexandre's mother, Michèle, opens the door and welcomes us inside with a big smile. She's lovely, petite, in her midfifties, with dark short hair and well dressed in a pretty blue pantsuit. I hand over the orchids in a semi-bribe gesture and hope they will serve as a source of brief, simple converstion.

"*Bonsoir, Klein. C'est un grand plaisir de vous rencontrer enfin.*" His mother gives me a kiss on both cheeks and takes my hand in hers. (So far, so good. *Phew!*)

Interestingly, their apartment's a dead ringer of the split-level abode of Bob Newhart in his 1970s sitcom. Modern furniture, a few cool paintings, a little terrace, and invitingly smells of divine cooking. (Nice contrast to the smell of my apartment: cat, cigarettes, cat food.) Alexandre's father gets up off the couch and comes over. "*Bonsoir, Klein. Bienvenu.*"

"*Merci,*" I say, wishing I had thought of some object or gift to offer *him* as a semi-bribe gesture. Something like cash, for example. Everybody's smiling *way* too much, yet I feel myself calming down, as they're making every effort to make me feel welcome. We all sit down on the couches and aperitifs of Champagne are quickly brought to the coffee table by Alexandre's mother. (Second phew!—available alcohol.)

"*Donc, Klein, où habitez-vous?*" asks Claude.

(I can pull this off.) "*Je habite dans le septième, rue de Verneuil.*" (Why am I so proud to just be able to say what street I live on? How ridiculous. Any three-year-old can do that. *And* with a better accent. But I feel like I'm on a roll, so here goes. "*J'aime beaucoup ton appartement.*"

FUCK! I did it again! I have the singular talent for instantaneously choosing the informal *tu* with people I should be *vous*-ing. Well done, Klein. That lack of respect is really going to win them over. God. Two minutes into the evening and I'm addressing his parents as though we're old buddies that used to hang around getting stoned together.

Nevertheless, Claude plays along and doesn't call me on it. Luckily, he starts talking with Alexandre, leaving me time to breathe, blush with embarrassment, and sip my Champagne. Man, I could *so* slam this glass *and* the three others on the table right now.

Michèle set about arranging the orchids in a tall vase, placed it on the dinner table and thanked me again. The chitchat about the flowers ran far too short though, leaving the floor open for all kinds of tricky subjects. And dammit, there was neither a monkey nor a horse in the room to comment on. Claude and Michèle made more simple converstion directed at me and, true to form, my annihilate-your-intellect show went on as expected.

"*Qu'est-ce que tu fais?*" inquired Michèle with a smile. (Huh? I shot a look at Alexandre. HELP!)

Alexandre said, "They are asking you what you do." *Excellent!* I had cleverly anticipated this question and memorized my response: "*Je suis une peintre*" (I am a painter). But with my terribly ineffective use of accents, I obliterated it into, "*Je suis peinture.*" (I am paint.) Smiles turned to quizzical expressions as they looked to Alexandre pleadingly. "What in God's name is she saying?"

Thus beginning a tag-team relay of French questions in slow motion to me, my desperate look to Alexandre to interpret, my response in Retard French, then Alexandre's reinterpretion into *actual* French. Oh yes, this was going to go along speedily; after two or three hours we'll have established that I'm from New York and my age, and clearly that I have the language skills of a doorknob.

Luckily, the opportunity to sit down to eat arrived and we all were seated before a beautiful table heaped with what I thought would be a plethora of simple subjects to discuss: bread, wine, etc. Looking down at my plate I quickly realized that, no, in fact, this dinner was just another opportunity for me to (1) speak mangled French and (2) in short order, exhibit my lack of understanding of French dinner etiquette. I mean, come on, where is the spoon, for starters? Okeydokey, there it is, apparently *above* the plate and horizontal. Who'd have guessed. All right then, let's get started. Oops, bringing my half-finished aperitif to the table was a no-no; I guess I was supposed to leave that behind on the coffee table. For the love of God, someone pour the wine, I'm dying over here. Okay, let's see, and exactly what do we have here? Saucisson and radishes, followed by andouillette and salad with strips of gigot. That's cow, pig, and sheep—terrific, bring on the whole farm! I'm a vegetarian so this will all be unbelievably pleasant, and I'm sure my gag reflex will just add to everyone's enjoyment of the meal. Wonder if there's any chance I could take a pass on the meat and nibble on radishes all evening. *Pas possible*. I immediately shoot a look at Alexandre that screams, *Don't you dare tell them I'm a vegetarian or I will knock you off your chair and withhold sex for a month.*

He smiles in understanding. Thank God, because I completely *know* I couldn't withhold sex from him for so much as a day. Munching away on the white fat of a sausage, I felt oddly disappointed there was no horse on the menu: it was one of those precious few words I knew. How scary is that?

I made silent prayers begging God that Alexandre's family preferred meals eaten in silence, but my hopes were dashed when conversation resumed. And not only resumed, but accelerated. I tried desperately to process this barrage of words, trying to grab hold of a word here and there, and piece together the general idea. A blackboard with it all written down, or a plane flying by with a streaming sign—nothing could've assisted my brain cells when there was absolutely no chain of comprehension.

I gorged myself on andouillette (which *completely* resembles the leftovers of a rabbi's handiwork *après* a circumcision) in an attempt to appear too busy enjoying the bovine entrails to chat, but it still was becoming almost unbearable to *not* follow the conversation.

I decided they were either discussing spaghetti Westerns of the 1950s or Jacques Chirac's tax policy. It occurred to me I could just wing it and jump in with vague positive comments like "*C'est vrai*" (That's true) or "*Ah, bon?*" (Oh, really?), but that could possibly lead to a question or comment directed at me. Crap. Serious crap.

Then I realized that I did, in fact, have options! I could (a) go to the toilet and hide there, hoping my absence wouldn't be noticed until well into the espresso service, (b) feign cardiac arrest and exit by way of an ambulance, (c) fake-choke on a hunk of meat and fall into unconsciousness, which might have the added effect of everyone forgetting my "I am paint" announcement, or (d) just smile and nod through—Christ—the next two hours. I chose *d,* the smile-and-nod option. My inoperative mental translation button, which had been straining to work for the last hour, switched officially to OFF and a peaceful calm set in. It all just became buzzes and whistles and I fell into a reverie.

In the still of my quiet mind (with the distant sound track of a French sitcom in the background) I found I now had the time to mentally compile my grocery list. Just as I was about to tackle Fermat's enigma, I suddenly became aware all eyes were on me and my . . . knife. Alexandre whispered, "You've just used your cheese knife to try to cut the sheep." Oh God, call the gendarmes! Have them drag me away by my chemically enhanced American blonde hair! What kind of imbecile am I? From their expressions, I took this knife confusion to be a major faux pas, possibly punishable by guillotine. Fine, add another hash mark to the long list of foolish errors I've made this evening. But please leave some space available, since here comes dessert, and I'm bound to come up with some more clever and impressive moves.

I thought I had wised up to the process of waiting a few beats and allowing everyone else to help themselves, and then mimic whatever culturally ingrained ritual was *de rigueur* for each course. But now I thought, *This is just fruit; a simple apple. I think I can be trusted to eat an apple without setting off the trip wires of impropriety.* But again the conversation faded as my cutting the apple into segments with—God forbid—the skin still on was silently put into the category of Uncivilized American Apple Consumption.

My three French dinner partners were all following the French set-in-stone rule of peeling their apples of their "unsavory" skins into perfect spirals. *Aha!* Okay. Whatever. I surrender. I've been raised by wolves in the deep woods of Wisconsin, do you understand? I grew up eating most of my meals with a plastic "spork," if truth be told. I bet no one at this table even knows what a spork is.

Coffee was served back on the couch. I helped Michèle prepare the tray to bring over to "the men." Then she took me aside to show me something.

"Viens avec moi, Klein. J'ai quelque chose à te montrer."

I knew enough to follow her gesturing hand. Michèle, in all her graciousness, opened a little box to reveal its precious contents to me. The small wooden box was overflowing with little ceramic figurines and charms. She carefully handed me a few of the tiny porcelain animals, a sheep and a cow, as well as a small cross and a minature loaf of bread. The little charms were indeed pretty but I was *so* not getting this. If I marry your son is this my dowry or are you offering me these to never see him again? Somebody throw me a clue over here.

Alexandre saw my pantomime of understanding and chimed in from the couch, "They're charms from the annual Galette du Roi. Each January we celebrate the new year all month by eating a round pastry filled with *frangipane* (marzipan) and there's always a little charm hidden somewhere inside. Whoever finds the charm in their slice is crowned king and wears a gold foil crown that comes with each cake."

Wow. I *so* wouldn't have guessed all those shenanigans. Never. What a charming idea. Once I got it, I spent the better part of a half hour examining and complimenting Michèle's collection (probably with far more enthusiasm then is necessary. But hey, Michèle and I were bonding, and if it had to be over miniature cake charms, so be it.)

Next, she offered me a tour of the apartment and I followed along happily. Anything with visuals, I'm *all* for. She showed me the little room that used to be Alexandre's and that she'd now made into an office. Funny to imagine the huge, sexy man in the other room, all curled up in his bed here, waiting for a good-night kiss from *maman*.

Michèle continued to show me family mementos: photos of Alexandre as a child, pictures of her with Claude when they first met. She was obviously a wonderful mother and I was quite touched that she was being so kind and warm to me.

Back we went to the living room, where I struggled with a few more words to say to Claude about the interesting paintings they had, and I thought I made a smattering of sense. Or maybe they'd all just given up on me and were being polite. Alexandre stood up as the clock chimed midnight and we began the long drawn-out process of saying goodbye, French style. Which entails a lot of standing around smiling, intermingled with earnestly looking at one another, visibly expressing great appreciation of the efforts made. It's complicated and that you can't seem too in a hurry to leave is the essence of this twelve-inch dance-mix exit. My *"merci beaucoup"* and *"au revoir"* went off without a hitch, by the way.

In the end, I survived. No one was injured or killed (except of course for the large farmyard of animals served), and while I didn't exactly wow them with my witty repartee, everyone seemed happy in the end. When Alexandre's parents gave me a warm embrace and kiss and invited me to join them in August at the family's country house, I knew on some level I had been accepted. Even if "I am paint."

A FEW SLIGHTLY ANNOYING DETAILS I DIDN'T ANTICIPATE

The mail delivery. I will receive absolutely nothing for ten days then, like clockwork, my mailbox will suddenly be chock-full of junk mail, flyers, letters, and bills. It is so obvious to me that my postman (postperson, if you want to be politically correct, but no one is in France so, postman), is spending a good deal of quality time at home and then, overcome with guilt for his inefficiency, drags himself out three times a month to distribute mail to us helpless souls.

This total absence of a sense of urgency is one thing you can absolutely bank on in France. It's killing my lifelong commitment of sending birthday presents to my family on time. I'll send off a care package *prioritaire,* opting for the most expensive, fastest service and the damn thing will, without fail, arrive weeks late *or not at all.*

I'm convinced that after I've paid and departed *la poste,* the conversation goes something like this:

Counter clerk: "Ha-ha, another sucker who fell for the priority service! Anybody here know someone going to the US anytime soon.? Anyone? *Non?*

Voice from the backroom of coworker (busily shredding freshly stamped mail): "Oh, I have a cousin who's thinking about going to Florida in the spring."

Counter clerk: "Yeah? Hey then, take this box and *if* you see him ask him if he'd consider taking this Stateside when he goes. Of course, *only* if it's not too much trouble."

Shredder garçon: "I'll try to remember. Leave it by the incinerator, *d'accord?*"

Counter clerk: "As you like. Don't knock yourself out or anything."

Recently I also sent a letter "priority" delivery to a company a mere five blocks away and it casually arrived twelve days later. But there *is* an upside, rent checks due the first of each month can and will be forgiven as late as the twentieth of the month. So you can buy yourself some time and blame it on *la poste.* Hmm. I'm convinced the French invented the expression "the check is in the mail." *C'est très possible.*

SUBLIME PLEASURE DU JOUR—OUTDOOR TERRACES

It's just like I imagined. Strike that. It's *better.* Romantic evenings on a classic Parisian terrace, under the stars, a glass of Sancerre in hand, a beautiful man at my side . . . sublime indeed. Thanks to the phenomonally generous and cultivated Alexandre, I have been able to experience this long-awaited dream at some of the most beautiful terraces in all of France. I offer the following list of venues for an enchanting evening or a long decadent lunch in the sun. (Need I even repeat Café de Flore and Les Deux Magots?)

La Fontaine de Mars: Lively old-fashioned bistro fare on checkered tablecloths bathed in sunlight on a tiny square facing a quaint fountain. Excellent cassoulet and tarts, not to mention, count on charming street musicians to meander around the tables playing Edith Piaf.

Le Restaurant du Palais Royal: In the gorgeous enclosed gardens of Louis XIV's childhood home. A great escape from street cafés and excellent cuisine. Romantic? *Oui.*

Laurent: A flower-filled garden and two-star cuisine in a historic pavilion in the gardens of the Champs-Élysées. Gloriously elegant. A personal favorite *when someone else pays.*

Jardin Plein Ciel: A superb roof garden at the top of the Hôtel Raphael. Chic to die and an astonishing view of the Arc de Triomphe. Fabulous buffet at lunch plus hot men in suits.

River Café: Outdoor dining on the deck of a *péniche* (barge) in the Seine. An experience unmatched. Great wine list and desserts. Not as fussy as Laurent; could wear jeans.

Flora Danica: A bucolic country garden terrace in the quiet private courtyard of the Maison du Danemark, just off the Champs-Élysées. Minimalist elegance and superb service. If you ever find yourself craving reindeer this is your place, believe it or not.

Café Marly: Under the arcades of the Louvre facing Pei's pyramid. Absolutely breathtaking view and romantic to the extreme. A good place for "popping the question." Or at least it's occured to me (hint, hint).

Café Costes: Enclosed garden terrace with Napoleon III decor in the trendy Hôtel Costes. A forever star-studded crowd. Food's mediocre and expensive but the scene is the draw.

FRIEND COUNT

Stella and I are inseparable. Both of our boyfriends are convinced we're falling in love with each other. They just don't get that a great female friend is more important than a boyfriend, because as we all know boyfriends come and go (literally, in some cases) but girlfriends are the emotional glue that keeps us from total breakdown. Stella and I have kind of set up a pattern of meeting every afternoon, after she gets out of classes and I've hit some wall painting.

Lately we've been meeting up at Café de la Marie in front of Saint-Sulpice for our *de rigueur* daily debriefing sessions. We constantly consider trading in our boyfriends for whatever monumental error they make next, but we also know we're unbelievably sexually satisfied so the next one has a goddamn hard act to follow.

We spend hours trying to analyze just how much compromising we, as expats, are required to do. It's bloody exhausting to live in a culture that never lets you put your guard down. Don't even *think* of wearing mismatched pajamas, your glasses, and dirty hair in front of your boyfriend. Because for some ludicrous reason this just "isn't done" in Paris. There is always some girl around the corner ready to be perfect 24/7.

We laugh like hell at the idea that after spending a "relaxing weekend" with our boyfriends we'd kill for another couple days to just exhale that belly, wear ugly but comfortable underwear, chuck the heels for sneakers, scrape off the Chanel lipstick and just chill.

Stella and I so look forward to going home to the States for just this reason. We readily admit we also kind of love it—I mean, the challenge, the pressure of living here. You sure as hell don't move to Paris to let yourself go physically or frankly, in any way. *Non, pas du tout!*

Sexy Shoulder Hair, Tantric Sex Guide, and the White Painting

February

MONSIEUR RIGHT REPORT

Alexandre and I are clipping along on auto pilot, I think. I spend virtually every evening with him and while it's totally fucking fun, I'm bonkers in love and he's just, well . . . fine. I *so* don't get it. He will *not* fall madly, crazily in love with me. And like hell *I'm* going to say it first. *No way*. It's like I've lost my touch, that magic fairy dust I used to sprinkle on whatever man I chose, and *voilà!*, we'd be an insta-couple, *crazy* about each other. Who knew there was an expiration date on that power to enchant? That's so not fair that when you hit your midthirties and you *finally* know who you are and what you want, *that* is the age when men start looking at you like, *Well, whatever. You're okay, I guess*. That's a crap deal.

Alexandre is holding back, making me feel like I'm just some pit stop on the road to something better. In truth, I think he might even be cheating on me. Oh, I know I'm infamous for my paranoia and mistrust, but let me lay out the reasons and tell me I'm not justified.

In the last month I've discovered, *chez* Alexandre: (1) My toothbrush was wet four days *after* I used it last and the day after he said he'd gone to a party with *friends*. Do a road test; toothbrushes normally dry in twenty-four hours unless, perhaps, you're in the rainforest. (2) A huge red wine stain on the carpet on my side of the bed. He said he brought a glass to bed one night and knocked it over turning off the light. We've never in all our alcohol-intake marathons brought wine to bed, so that's a toughie to swallow. (3) Alexandre handed me a polka-dot disposable lighter, saying, "You left this here." Ah, that would be unusual because it's not even mine. What can I do? I ask (more like *grill* him) about this stuff, but as much as I doubt his answers, I can't really leave over a lighter or toothbrush, can I? So I let it lie. *Lie* being the operative word. I hate this feeling. It's like waiting for a train to hit you. You know it's coming, you just don't know when. The jury is officially out. Big time!

Not to mention, the whole Jekyll and Hyde Le Bon Alexandre–Le Creep Alexandre extravaganza continues. Take last weekend; we had a fabulous time. He picked me up at seven o'clock and we zipped over to La Grande Épicerie de Paris at Bon Marché (a wicked-chic grocery shopping joint on the first floor of the fabulous department store). We filled our basket with half a dozen marvelous cheeses, three bottles of excellent wine, a beautiful rosy salmon from the *poissonnerie,* a couple of great baguettes, and some fresh haricots verts and piled everything between our legs on the motorcycle as we sailed home past the sparkling lights of the place de la Concorde. (Have I mentioned the unbelieveble, incomprehensible pleasure of holding on to his waist as the landmarks of Paris whiz by? I want to scream, "Vive la France!" at the top of my lungs. There is simply no greater happiness for me on earth.)

Back *chez* Alexandre, I'm in charge of music and setting the table as he assumes the regal role of *le grand chef.* I light candles as our favorite eighties CD from Tears for Fears blares in the background. Alexandre never fails to amuse me while he's deboning, chopping, or sautéing—usually a few absurd dance moves or a brief lip-sync bit with whisk in hand. He is a genuis chef and can make fucking corn from a can tantalize my palette so I'm always blown away. *Could I be any luckier?* I think, sipping Champagne. *He's hot to die. He loves cooking, kids, fashion, modern art, architecture. He is full-on, hands-down, "the One."*

After dinner we sit around on Alexandre's couch talking about ideas for creating a collection of furniture. Me, drawing and him, pulling books from his library for inspiration. My bare legs are slung across his lap. Both of us slightly drunk, surrounded by stacks of books on Dupré-Lafon, Prouvé, Giacometti, Arbus, and Royère. We pull pages from old Christies catalogues and from *Elle Décor.* I'm the designated artist and he leans over my shoulder suggesting ideas for furniture.

"Here, Klein, try drawing the couch lower and smaller like the scale of this one from the forties," he says as we both go to kneel over the coffee table. My sense of perspective never fails to go out the window when I'm drunk and if *ever* I'd like to impress Alexandre, it would be with my drawings, strangely enough.

"Yeowts! Sorry, this is looking more like a life raft then a sofa, baby. I'm a little too hooched for drawing. That second bottle definitely blew out my sketching skills." We kick back onto his groovy saddle brown and chrome Marc Newson chairs and light cigarettes.

"What do you think if I made a collection of armoires and *bibliothèques* (book shelves) in wrought iron, very simple lines, but elegantly made? With this whole obsession in interiors of *cabinets de curiosités,* that's all anyone asks for at the gallery these days," he says, full of enthusiasm.

"Cool, I love the idea. But you should build a *group* of like, five or six pieces, a little cohesive story. For example, an armoire, a floor lamp . . . maybe forties apothecary or pharmaceutical in feeling . . . an ottoman or two, and a killer chair and side table. Don't you always tell me side tables blow out of the gallery?" I say, gesturing wildly, excited to be talking *passionately* with him, even if it has to be about lamps.

"Klein, you're great. I have never been with a woman who gave a *damn* or knew anything about furniture," Alexandre tells me as his eyes sparkle in the candlelight.

"That's because you always date models, you poop, and they *are* like furniture. Duh?" I say reaching over to tickle him, which I know he loves-hates. Mister Huge Sexy Guy is reduced to a screaming, writhing little boy. "Stop it! Stop, Klein!"

I'm relentless, enjoying that for one whole minute I finally have a smidge of power over him. I climb on his lap and tickle him with abandon as he flails his arms trying to grab my hands. His kick-boxing skills kick in and I'm instantly pinned to the ground, arms over my head, held down as he straddles me.

"Baby, I give up," I say, laughing and loving that he's back on top being Mr. Über masculine.

Clearly some internal mechanism alerts him: "defenseless woman, passably fuckable, lying beneath you" and a wave of desire sweeps across his face. He leans down over me, pulls up my shirt and puts his warm mouth around my nipple. He flicks his wet tongue in quick strokes . . . I am . . . just slowly . . . melting. This nipple move, as most women would agree, is an instant all-access pass to your entire body. Take me *or just kill me* because this desire is going to kill me if you don't fuck me right this second.

Alexandre tears my pants off and then his own as I look on in unspeakable apprecation. Wow, cowboy, you were *seriously* put on this planet to please women. The whole thing you do with antiques? A total waste of time; *this* is your calling. With one hand holding my wrists together above my head he slides inside me slowly and gently, taunting me as I raise my mouth to meet his parted lips. He holds his mouth just above mine, exhaling soft, warm breaths and then teasingly pulls back as I try to kiss him. As his hips find their rhythm and press with increasing force, I grab his ass with both hands and pull him deeper . . . He comes with a shudder and a silent low carnal moan. No one as far as I'm concerned *ever* made a more beautiful sound. He collapses on top of me for a moment, and I smile with a secret pleasure in feeling his heart still race against my chest and the intoxicating fragrance of his sweat-dampened neck. It does not get any better than this. I know this much for sure.

We sleep all night like exhausted love cats, and the next morning Alexandre awakens me with a soft kiss on my brow. I smile before I even open my eyes. He whispers, "Baby, keep sleeping. I'm going to get some stuff and make you breakfast. *Je vais retourner tout de suite.*" And leaves blowing me a kiss. I roll over onto his pillow, dreamy with happiness and inhale his smell embedded in the warm linens. I could subsist on his smell alone. God, how ga-ga am I?

Alexandre quickly returns and, after a quick peek at me through the bedroom door, scurries off to make *petit déjeuner pour deux*. I giggle when I hear him try to be quiet as he slides plates slowly from the cupboard and gently plucks silverware from the drawer. How adorable? Love him.

He reappears with a large teakwood tray overflowing with goodies, a basket of still-warm brioche, a tub of his mother's genius cassis confiture, fresh-squeezed orange juice, and a fragrant mango cut into a fan motif and sprinkled with juicy framboise.

"Klein, you up? I thought you'd like to have breakfast in bed," Alexandre says as places the tray on my lap and sets about taking off his clothes to climb back into bed. Mmmm. Hot naked boyfriend and French breakfast. *Perfect.* We devour every last crumb and, hands still sticky with mango juice, indulge in yet another mind-blowing sexual romp.

All good, right? *Not so fast.* Because Alexandre puts the word *fun* in dys-*fun*ctional. Guess what he threw into my lap that very same night? This is priceless, quintessential Le Creep Alexandre. Around nine o'clock we took his scooter over to the famous Le Dôme restaurant by Montparnasse after having a glass of wine (okay, a bottle) at my apartment. He seemed withdrawn and distracted and, frankly, was hardly any fun. What the hell, he'd been a loving smooch machine when we'd woken up that morning. So I asked (bad idea, I know) and this is what he told me.

"Klein, I think I've got a serious problem," Alexandre announced as his eyes filled up with tears. Jesus, this is where he tells me he's gay. I always *thought* this was going to happen, but *how* can he be gay? *No* gay man fucks like that. Then again, I really don't know whereof I speak. Maybe they can. Yikers!

"What, angel? You can tell me anything. Oh, darling, don't cry, it's okay. What's wrong?" I plead, bracing myself for the worst.

"Don't hate me . . . but I want to be honest . . . (Long pause) . . . I was on my scooter after having lunch with Pierre in the Marais and I saw . . . this re-ally pretty young model. And I . . . I knew what I was doing was wrong, but I couldn't stop myself and I stopped and went to talk to her . . . (another long pause) . . . And asked her for her phone number. I threw it away five minutes after, but . . . I don't know, she was just so beautiful. I'm afraid I just can't stop being attracted to other women. Really, it's terrifying me." (Yeah? Well? I'm not diggin' it much either. I almost wish you'd said you were gay. And did you *have* to say "*so* beautiful"? Couldn't you just have said "attractive"? Grrrr.)

"Oh. Wow. I'm speechless, and that doesn't happen much. This is . . . well, not great news, but I guess I'm glad you told me and that you *don't* want to be like that anymore . . . (long pause) . . . Uh, it's okay. Listen, as long as you know it's a problem, I think you can get a handle on it. Your friend Pierre is married, right? And he's only twenty-eight years old, right? He must struggle with that same problem sometimes. Perhaps he can offer you advice on how to let go of the compulsion that you have to shag every beautiful girl you see."

How am I *not* flipping into a rage and storming out of here? I swear to God, if he weren't crying, I'd kill him. Hello? Hey, idiot, didn't we just spend the great-est night together? God damn it, talk about out of sight, out of mind. Christ!

Amazingly enough, we managed to salvage dinner and Alexandre complimented me by saying I was the *kindest* woman to stay by him as he struggled through his fixation on models. I don't know about being the *kindest;* maybe the most *stupid*.

Some strange unknown force commits me to staying with Alexandre. I'm clearly caught up in a powerless state of complete and total obsession. There are just a scant few (I think you'll be with me on this) times in your life when you are so drunk with love and desire for someone that you find what would normally be repulsive, sexy and appealing. With Alexandre, I'm that lost; he has a few dark long hairs on his shoulders that would, in any other circumstances make me puke, but with him I don't just tolerate them—I *love* them. (And I thought I was getting wiser with age. Hmmm, I'm not so sure.)

A FEW SLIGHTLY ANNOYING DETAILS I DIDN'T ANTICIPATE

Parisian dinner parties boggle my mind. One of the most pronounced differences between Parisians and New Yorkers is that we Manhattanites never cook. *Never*. Not breakfast, dinner, brunch, nothin'. We will gladly fork (gotta love that pun) half of our income over for dinners out for the convenience and perhaps, if truth be told, to keep our glamorous kitchens pristine and photo ready.

Personally, I have long found dishwashers to be wonderful additional sources of storage for things like tax receipts and old Madonna CDs. I am also a believer that ovens have an excellent dual use as a home to unsightly books with embarrassing titles like *10 Days to Thinner Thighs* and *Your Guide to Tantric Sex* (a gift, I swear).

Parisians, on the other hand, cook with abandon. It's built into their DNA to know at least twelve varieties of oysters and just how long to cook a soufflé, so they give dinner parties constantly. They will gladly run a rigorous grocery-acquiring gamut and cook for eight friends at the drop of a beret. Since I've moved here I've been to a handful of dinner parties and I've noticed the following: They always involve (1) a *ridiculous* amount of wine consumption (as though prohibition were going to be reinstated in the morning), (2) total disregard of time, often breaking up in the wee hours, even on a "school night," (3) absolutely zero attention to aesthetics. Numbers one and two on the list I'm completely cool with but three totally kills me. Maybe my mother shouldn't have given me that subscription to *Architectural Digest* for my tenth birthday because I turned into a ruthless Aesthetic Policeman forever on "critique alert." (Which is not to say I won't occasionally still eat pasta directly from the pan, sitting on the floor reading crappy magazines.)

I will definitely assume responsibility for putting too much emphasis on the word *party* when invited to one of these so-called dinner parties. Arrived at one of my first dinners in a sexy black Dior slip dress and Michel Perry heels (aka fuck-me pumps) only to discover everyone else was wearing beat-up jeans and pullovers. A few women raised an eyebrow, asking condescendingly (oh, the French do that so well) if I was going to the opera or ballet later. Note to self: Parisians may look terribly chic out on the streets but once at home, the comfort clothes come out big time. Americans do the reverse; we schlep around all day in Dairy Queen–stained sweatshirts and pull it together when guests arrive, dragging out a party dress from the back of the closet. Cultural difference no. 10,500. Or is it no. 10,501? I've lost track.

I felt like such a Franco-failure. Sadly, I was never given the secret manual *Blending Seamlessly into Hipster Parisian Life.* So now it's obviously just a hands-on, trial by fire, crash-course deal. I had clearly become the experimental guinea pig providing amusement to the citizenry of France. I guess I wasn't surprised I'd set Paris on fire with a stream of faux pas. But I didn't think it would be twenty-four hours a day, for God's sakes.

Back to that dinner. I'd brought a great bottle of Veuve Clicquot for the host (as I had learned from a guide book not to offer the host an ordinary bottle of wine; it's considered as inelegant as bringing Velveeta cheese to a New York City dinner). In keeping with the hyper-casual tone of the evening, the host (who shall remain nameless) quickly shelved it for a "special occasion" and handed me a plastic cup of Muscadet wine (which is the French equivalent of the almost undrinkable box-o-wine that we have back in the United States).

Bummer, as I'd envisioned a constantly replenished flute of Champagne as my escort through a somewhat nerve-wracking evening. I tried (pathetically) to downgrade my outfit by kicking off my Michel Perrys and going barefoot. I sauntered into the dining room where we were all being encouraged to sit down. I stopped in my tracks to behold a motley menagerie of folding chairs, mismatched stools, and an odd beat-up ottoman set around the Ping-Pong–cum–dining table. I had envisioned elegant chandeliers, calligraphied place cards, and finger bowls. All that went went flying out the window as I took my seat. Which was, *I kid you not,* the step-up pee ladder of the host's three-year-old. How he managed without it, those six endless hours, I don't really want to know. Wonder if that explains the puddle by my discarded heels in the hall. *Great.*

We all looked positively ludicrous perched at different heights. Poor Gaston was on the low ottoman and must have got neck cramps trying to see above the mismatched cutlery. I felt I was trapped inside a French version of the *Charlie Brown Thanksgiving* cartoon I grew up watching. In real life it loses some serious charm. When the paper towel roll was tossed to the table to use as napkins and a bag of white bread had been distributed, I came to the distinct conclusion to lower my expectations of a "French dinner party" next time around.

SUBLIME PLEASURE DU JOUR

One evening at about six o'clock, Monsieur Despont called me and simply said, "Come to the gallery, okay?" *Yes, master.* I sped over to the rue des Beaux-Arts. I assumed he wanted to chat, go for an aperitif, maybe fill me in on some exciting ideas for selling my work. But when I got to the gallery he barely acknowledged my presence. He nodded hello and continued talking to the *beyond* bourgeois woman already engaged in conversation with him. I stood around, looking at the other work in the gallery: gorgeous bronze sculptures of museum quality, a marble foot carved by Camille Claudel. Thirty minutes later Despont was still ignoring me and wouldn't even make eye contact. He just kept chatting away, showing pieces in the gallery to the rather unkempt-looking woman. *Fine, I don't know what I've done wrong, but I'll hang around until she leaves. Maybe I sent one too many potential boyfriends to the gallery to see my work. Geez, I don't know.*

Then Madame Bourgeois went and stood in front of my white painting. She said to Despont, "*Qui est l'artiste?*" (Who is this artist?)

Like an overexcited idiot I raced over and proudly declared, "*Moi.*" She asked if it was painted on wood or canvas (because of the texture it really resembled wood and though it was entirely a mistake I'd made, it ended up being the coolest thing about it). She calmly said she liked it very much and once more I, the insecure fool, said, "Really? Tell Despont, would you, please!" (Because I thought he'd be impressed and that was a top priority to me.)

She went back to him, said a few words, bid us both goodbye and left. At this point I was a little miffed Despont had made me wait around for an hour, but I hoped the lady had told him she liked my painting, even if she did look like a dreary secretary.

Then Despont said to me, "Do you know who what was? That's the richest woman in France!" (No shit, really, wearing that cheesy headband and bad suit?) Apparently Monsieur Despont had made the quick call to me because she'd expressed interest in the white painting and he wanted her to meet me, and yet I understood none of this and foolishly—Christ, did I really?—I asked *her* to tell Despont she liked the painting as though what *he* thought was more important than talking to her. Actually, it was probably better I didn't know who she was or I'd certainly have made an even bigger fool of myself blithering away in nonsensical, awful French.

So I sold my first (and thus far, only) painting to the wealthiest woman in France, completely against my own pathetic self-marketing skills. Despont and I went to la Palette (the artists' bar up the street whose walls are decorated with palettes of famous painters), to toast, and to agree that in the future he'll do all the selling and I'll just shut up.

FRIEND COUNT

Plenty of friends all of a sudden. My social cup runneth over! From an art dealer, midfifties, to an American girl, thirties, to a gay Dutch aristocrat, forties. God, if I just had an income or a command of the language, you could almost call this a real life.

The Return of the Big-Shot Ex, My Tree Nest, and a Family of *Canards*

March

MONSIEUR RIGHT REPORT

It seemed like a great idea at the time. My ex from New York City, the Big-Shot French Industralist, called to say he was in Paris and did I want to spend the day together. Hell, yes. After a year in Paris I was dying to see a familiar face, someone I just plain *adored* and who "knew" me. Plus, I thought, it would be marvelous to show him how I'd made my new life, new world, and that I was no longer the young girl who always felt she was tagging along as he steamrolled through life, everyone groveling at his feet. I felt proud of my little apartment, my new paintings, shedding my confident New York City skin for being a vulnerable, anonymous expat. So I didn't miss a beat when he called at eleven one morning. I answered without a thought, "You're *here*? I'd *love* to see you. This is so fabulous, meet me at Café de Flore at noon!"

I knew as soon as I hung up the phone, this day had the potential to be a real mind-fuck. But enough time had passed that I knew this man and I had such an extraordinary rapport and powerful bond, I could never pass up an opportunity to indulge in it. Having said that, I guess it's no surprise that this is the *only* man in the world that I will do the shot-from-a-cannon race to get ready to see.

Christ, I have one hour to get ready, minus the ten-minute walk to Flore; just fifty short minutes to become *the most beautiful* version of myself. C'mon, you get this, a date with "ex"? You want to look drop-dead fabulous. You want to be at your peak of beauty, your all-time wittiest, your most self-assured, utterly glowing in a state of total life fulfillment and inner peace. Even more so if it's entirely not the case.

I look in the mirror: a few gray hairs shimmering in the overhead light, a tiny spot, sure to double in size over the next twenty minutes; an imprint from my pillow still emblazoned on my cheek, and my face swollen up from last night's Chinese food binge. *Merde,* this will *never* work, *even* if I had a team of stylists, a hair and makeup crew. Oh hell, I love this guy but I need like a good *week's* notice to prepare physically and mentally to see him again. Dammit, I said yes and now I'm screwed. Okay then, let's get this shit under way.

I find I'm actually sprinting around my apartment in an semipsychotic excited frenzy (Puccini hiding under the bed, all the hair on his back sticking up like a stegosaurus). Everything's a blur, as I'm trying to concoct some glorious outfit that reeks of elegance while trying *not* to look like I've given it too much thought. Standing before my closet, I'm grabbing possibilities with both hands: the brown Dries Van Noten jacket or the black Ghost coat over a pair of low-waisted Gucci pants? Fuck, this is all old, really out-of-date stuff he's already seen a hundred times. In fact he bought it *all* for me, for crying out loud. I should wear somethinge NEW, the "new" me . . . All right, that's tough as my only new acquisitions are flannel pajamas from Monoprix (the upscale grocery store) and a belt with a gigantic buckle (the size of a Roman sundial, really; it was a bad purchase). Oh bloody hell, times a wastin'.

I throw on my new favorite CD to, in theory, relax (Coldplay, number five on the disc) and thoughtlessly start slapping on makeup with a trowel. With my mind racing searching for a slew of clever, intelligent stories to tell him, I discover, that just on complete autopilot, I've applied the equivalent of my sexy evening makeup and it's 11:20 a.m. What the *hell* am I doing? Not a woman in Paris would be caught dead even wearing eye liner, and I've just put on enough makeup to easily be mistaken for a transvestite returning home after a long night.

This is nuts. Why am I wigging out? I used to let him see me in my queer glasses, eye cream, and dirty hair—and he loved it. Or at least he said he did. I am nervous as hell; this is weird. I thought I'd taken on a rather self-satisfied sense of cool regarding splitting from him. And now I'm racing out the door, flushed and wildly anxious, dressed something like a Barnum and Bailey (sorry, make that Cirque du Soleil; this is France, I forgot) circus act. This oufit completely confirms that I'm the *only* person who moves to Paris and LOSES her sense of style. Like an imbecile, I've thrown on a short gray skirt, knee-high suede boots, a Helmut Lang sleeveless tank, a long red Fortuny scarf *and* a navy casquette (little French hat). *The scarf and the hat are ridiculous together, Klein, one or both of them has* got *to go.* I ditch the hat, jam it in my mailbox as I'm already in the lobby of my building and have zero time to race back up the stairs again.

In a half-run, half-jog to Flore I'm trying desperately to simmer down: *Okay, Klein, just because your ex is always the most exquisitely gorgeous man in any country doesn't mean you have to feel any pressure. He used to love you madly; he's always wonderfully adoring. Relax. (Shut up! I can't.)*

As I push through the doors to Café de Flore, I realize I feel nothing but the rapid, painful beating of my heart. And then I see . . . HIM. Sitting off to the side, calmly sipping an espresso, looking absolutely . . . perfect. With his ruthlessly sensual face in repose, his simplest gesture a study in elegance, his salt-and-pepper hair thick and in sensual tides of waves . . . and that nose, the definition of a classic French nose, his marvelous impeccable suit, the languid way he crosses his legs. I'm floored to think if I didn't know him I'd still fall in love with him at first sight. A sexy, sly smile washes across his face as his laughing eyes watch me walk thru the café. Dear God. Why did I ever leave this man?

I sit down, knocking over a chair as I try to negotiate my gigantic purse onto the floor. I'm forever clumsy and it's classically "me," when he says with a smile, "That's my Klein." My mind floods with all the times I've heard him yell out to me "Klein!" requesting I come see some marvelous object he's just come across while we're shopping, or "K!" calling to me to come watch some show on astronomy with him. Just smiling, we reach out for each other's hands and suddenly I just want to be back, with him, in that love. I've spent one year in Paris being either mistreated or simply not adored enough by virtually every man. And it just seems to be futile (no, it doesn't "seem" futile, it IS futile) to ever find a man like him again.

I try to dredge up the number one reason I left and put this file in the forefront of my mind. *Don't forget, Klein, he didn't want children and refused to consider it. That's why you are now dating men who are commitment-phobes and buying your clothes at grocery stores. You wanted desperately to have children and you had to leave before you lost the opportunity.* Christ, these children of mine better be pretty damn happy to be alive because letting go of this man ain't easy (I'm kidding).

It was obvious, we're both just elated to feel that intimacy and extraordinary bond just being in each other's presence. He immediately leans over and kisses me, gently brushing back a hair that the wind has blown across my cheek. Oh god, I'm dying . . . The smell of his cologne, the warmth of his face, it all comes back like it's yesterday. "Klein, you look radiant, more beautiful still than the day I met you."

"You are *far* too kind, please. I know I'm an absolute wreck today, but I wouldn't dream of missing a chance to see you, *mon chien*." (Yes, I call him "my dog." Don't ask. It's a long story and not what you think. *Okay, it is what you think,* but it's still a long story.)

"The usual, Klein?" he asks with a knowing smile, his piercing eyes penetrating to my core.

"*Bien sûr, mon ange.*" (I'm foolishly eager to speak French to him now, as sadly the whole time we were together I was too self-conscious and terrified to even try.)

"*J'adore ta souris, mon chien,*" I tell him, thinking I'm the wunderkind of speaking French, believing I have just told him how I adore his smile.

He roars in laughter and I look at him like, *What? Why is that funny?*

"My dear K, I think you'd better keep up with the French studies. You just told me you love my *mouse. Souris* is 'mouse' and *sourire* is 'smile,' darling."

"No! Really? Oh Christ, I'm trying, but I'm forever screwing it up. It's so humiliating. Thierry, give me an A for effort?" I say, flushed red with embarrassment and trying to charm my way back to a smattering of self-respect.

We order our traditional Kir to drink (white wine with a splash of crème de cassis) and he begins the conversation with his usual question.

"So what's his name?" Every phone call from him is the same; he wants to know immediately who I'm dating and if it's serious. I understand that he just hates the idea of it and has to broach the subject as quickly as possible. As is always the case, I respond honestly and tell him about the Alexandre situation and how he treats me more like a fuck-buddy than someone he passionately adores. I lay out my doubts about the wet toothbrush and the wine stain story as well, because I bet one Frenchman can smell the trail of a cheater in another Frenchman.

"This Alexandre doesn't sound like he's good enough for you. He seems to not make you feel you can trust him, as well as being very immature. You know I just want you to be happy. Remember, Frenchmen at thirty years old are like American men at twenty. Trust me, I speak from firsthand experience, darling," he says with a seductive, knowing smile.

"I know, I know. I didn't really believe you until *now*. I speak from firsthand experience too now, unfortunately," I say, making him chuckle.

I play along and bounce the question back to him. "So then, monsieur, who is *she*?" entirely expecting his usual response of a sincere, "No one, honestly I'm just working my ass off."

This time he *just* smiles. NO. NO. NO. Excuse me, this is where you jump in and tell me no one can ever replace me. I'm waiting. Somehow I hadn't ever anticipated this. For a whole year he didn't have anyone and now he has a new girlfriend. I feel like someone has punched a hole in my chest and cold air is whipping through it. This is totally unfair as he was supposed to become celibate for life and create a shrine to me that he worshipped at twice daily (that's minimum, three times would be better). I push on with questions as he gets a bit evasive and keeps smiling. (All right, I'm starting to hate that "cat that swallowed the canary" smile, you jerk.)

"Really, a new girlfriend? Do tell, is she anyone I know?" (Meaning is she famous? For fuck's sake, don't let her be some famous actress or model, and I'll have to see photos in magazines of the two of you *gallavanting* in Mustique.)

A couple more Kirs and I get it out of him: he's involved with a *married* woman with three small children. Her name is Ruth. It takes all the discipline I have to *not* cattily say, "Yeah, and like that's a sexy name?!" Apparently she's my age, and also tall and blonde. This is not good information. I don't want to know this; she gets three children *and* you? Amazingly, I also hold back, "She must be a fairly crappy person to cheat on her husband, with three little kids. I mean, really!" But you can damn well bet I made it clear with my appalled expression.

He turns the conversation back to me and now I'm supposed to rattle on about how great my life is. Hmmm. That will be hard to do as I'm still trying to process the married woman story and my recent accomplishment of finally learning how to work my French oven seems rather unimpressive.

"Well, as I told you, I made my first bronze and that was just such an amazing experience and I . . ." (So, you're fucking somebody else? You actually must be in love or you wouldn't even tell me. Someone else gets all the sweet love letters, incredible days and nights of your hilarious brilliance? Can I please just stop talking and curl up under the table in a fetal position?) ". . . am thrilled to say I finished reading the seven-book series by Proust. Wow, that was pure heaven. What an insightful, extraordinary man . . . blah, blah, blah."

"Klein, I'm so proud of you. Of course I know how hard it is to move to another country, an entirely different culture. You're flourishing, doing wonderful, brave, courageous things." (Yeah, well then, why do I feel like running back to you, leaving this *all* behind, even Puccini *and* that so-called boyfriend of mine? And your true and generous constant encouragement and enthusiasm? No one I know in France is as kind and inspiring as you are being right now. I miss that. I miss you. Waa-aa-a!)

"Thanks, it's sometimes hard but it's been intoxicating every day." (More like I'm getting intoxicated every day to get through these unbearable moments of self-doubt.)

I notice he's *not* smoking as I pound through cigarette after cigarette. He tells me he's quit finally, after smoking twenty-five years. Lovely, he's the one who smoked when I met him, and I got hooked after holding his cigarette one time too many. Perfect, leave me with a smoking habit, no kids and replace me. This is terrific. I can hardly speak, as all the little voices inside me are arguing with each other, and then he pulls out a wad of new euros to pay our bill and hands the waiter a five-hundred-euro note.

Hello! I live in Europe and haven't even *seen* a five-hundred-euro note before. Yes, I guess I'd kind of forgot: not only are you perfect, creative, and brilliant but you're rich to die. Lovely contrast to my current existence, as I just spent the past weekend on the phone yelling with Nicolas who demanded I pay him back the ninety euros for a coat he bought me six months ago. Now that I have a new boyfriend he wants me to reimburse him. Blechh! I am not sure this new life I've so brazenly chased is really so much better, or any better really.

We get up to leave and he says, as he's helping me on with my coat, "Madame Tease-n-Taunt, (again, private nickname, fairly obvious in its conception; no apologies offered or needed, I presume) I need some new shirts. Do you want to go across the street to Armani?"

"*Bonne idée!*" I say, slightly tipsy. Really, fine by me. Shopping with him was always such a blast. He'd pull some stunt or other and either have everyone in the store dying with laughter or drag me into his dressing room for a ridiculously obvious quick shag. (And, no, we can never step foot in the Fendi boutique on Fifth Avenue again. Don't ask.)

We run across the street hand in hand, dodging oncoming traffic, and stumble into the Armani boutique in giggles. I can't afford anything so I'm not even perusing the racks, just looking on as he, as is his routine, charms the pretentious staff to the point they virtually are on their hands and knees spit-shining his thousand-dollar John Lobb shoes. Two salespeople are beckoning at his slightest whim as another has gone to fetch us espressos. Funny, the one time I was here before no one so much as said hello.

He piles stacks of shirts in his size on the counter: ten identical white dress shirts, six in the same style, in French blue; four new variated stripes; and three ties. Mr. Big-Shot Industrial Pants never fails to offer something for me, forcing me try on a short-waisted tuxedo jacket with satin lapels.

"Klein, that's beautiful on you. Do you like it, darling?"

"Uh, yes, it's really gorgeous, but . . ."

With its narrow sleeves and tapered waist, it fit perfectly and of course looks a zillion times better than what I'd been wearing. (Damn, this is so chic, it would look killer with a pair of jeans.) Just as he says, "We'll take this jacket, and do you have it in white too?" to the saleswoman, I'm struck by that old crazy feeling I'd long forgotten. Because I'm clearly the less successful of the two of us, and fifteen years younger, I think that, yes, I look like a young tart with a rich man. I remember watching other people look at me that way when I first started dating him. At first it made me uncomfortable and mad because our love wasn't ever about money (I SWEAR), and now I could see it *again,* the way other people perceived us, me, in this relationship. I'm old enough now to not really care what other people think, but I don't love that perception and I was glad it wasn't my *life* anymore. Plus, he insisted on buying me the two new jackets so I didn't exactly have a leg to stand on to pretend I *wasn't* being given gifts by my Mr. Perfect Ex-Boyfriend.

Sauntering out to the street, armfuls of bags in tow, he offers, "Why don't we put this stuff in the car and drive over to rue de Seine and check out some galleries?" The car? Right, you're one of those men with the "black town car and driver" whole deal. I had left that life back in New York City and now it seemed a million years ago. I always felt a bit too fortunate, a bit guilty asking the driver (generally a father of four living in the cheaper suburbs, struggling to pay for his kids' tennis shoes) to go as fast as he could up to Barneys so I could pick up a dress and shoes and then wait while I got a manicure. It just felt like the epitome of vulgar and I hadn't even thought about whether I missed it. (*Well, maybe once.*)

The driver takes the obscenely unnecessary purchases and holds the door open for us to climb into the backseat of the obscenely shiny black Mercedes, just like the good old days. The difference being, after he leaves, my life goes into retrograde motion and Cinderella has to go back to being a little maid. And his just carries on, opulent luxury at every turn. Good for you, you lucky bastard. Honestly, he worked hard as hell to get his success and you know what? It suddenly occurs to me it's much more thrilling to earn my *own* money, buy my own jackets, and make my own version of success. I remember watching his credit card almost catch fire as we'd rip through store after store in Madison Avenue; I enjoyed it but never felt proud of myself for accepting such expensive gifts. And now I feel positively creepy and vow to return the next day to Armani to return the jackets and credit his account. Man, I *am* different now. What is this about? Integrity? Principles? How startling.

Driving down boulevard Saint-Germain, he turns to me, while looking deeply serious. "I have to say, Klein, I miss you. Just the other day I was remembering how we used to have our our little private-theme dinners. Remember 'the white evening,' or *'la fête du rouge'*?" Oh, God, do I ever! Because we were always so happy to just be *alone* in each other's company, no one to distract or enter our private world, we'd make these special nights that were pure magic. At least once every couple of weeks, we'd pick a theme. It could be a color or an opera, anything really, and the whole evening would be dedicated to that idea. The clothing, the elaborate meal, the music, the interior, all would be hired, purchased, and employed to set the scene.

It went like this: one of us would call the other and say something like, "So what do you say we do a full-on Japanese night?"

And then because there was never any doubt—it wasn't really even a question so much as a call to action—we'd take the afternoon off, get the car and driver, and head up to Takashimaya on Fifth Avenue and buy absolutely everything that was Japanese. A couple of embroidered silk kimonos for each of us, a pair of Japanese slippers, rich satin obis, oriental jewelry, black laquer trays, tea sets, and tiny bonsai trees and bouquets of Chinese blossoms from the florist Christian Tortu on the mezzanine level. On the way back downtown, he'd call over to the chef at the famous Nobu around the corner and have an opulent feast for two (don't even try to get them to deliver, it was by "private arrangement") delivered as we lit green tea candles and set the room with tatami mats and kabuki masks. We would get ready separately and agree to meet at eight o'clock in the grand salon where he would await me, standing in some getup, both of us bursting into laughter upon seeing each other.

Inevitably, he'd have chosen some rare CD of seventeenth-century Japanese wind instruments or *Madame Butterfly* and decorated the room with Japanese fans and hand-painted umbrellas while I'd been struggling to fix my hair into a tight chignon with a beaded hair stick. I think you get the idea now, why this man and I are so extraordinarily bound to one another. It was all a dream. No, *better* than any dream I'd ever imagined and here we were together again, a year later, two people who should by the laws of nature be together completely and forever.

It all felt a million miles away *and* yesterday and I wanted to rip his clothes off and take him right there in the car *and* I wanted to beat the living daylights out of him for never wanting children.

"*Arrêtez ici, monsieur!*" he commanded the driver to stop and let us out as we passed my hangout, the artsy Café La Palette.

"Oh, look, Klein, this is where I used to hang out when I was a student in Paris thirty years ago. I brought you here once," he said to me, full of nostalgia for his college days.

"I know, baby, I come here all the time," I replied, feeling pretty damn cool. We went into the dark and smoke-filled café, him leading the way like he owned the place.

"*Bonjour, Klein. Ça va, ma belle?*" said the proprietor Jean-François as he leaned over the bar to give me a two-cheek kiss.

"*Klein! Klein, viens!*" A few of my scruffy artist friends were having a *pastis* and waved us over. Nice timing, guys. I couldn't have arranged it better if I'd tried. My ex was taken aback, looked at me and raised his eyebrows with a smile.

"It looks like you've settled in rather well. This is new. Suddenly I'm a no-body and you're the star. Well, well, well," he said with generous pride.

I introduced them to my Big-Shot Ex and you could see in their eyes, they couldn't believe I had once had a big-deal lifestyle (trust me it's blatantly obvious when you see him; he's on a different stratosphere, the discreet red ribbon in his lapel denoting his having recieved the prestigous *Légion d'honneur* is a clue) and that, to them, I was entirely *not* that kind of person. Hmmm. Cool. I was neither remotely embarrassed to show my ex my new unglamorous, unfabulous friends, nor uncomfortable to show my friends my ex and all that he represented. Two worlds collided and it was just amusing. We had a quick glass of Ricard with them and headed back out onto rue de Seine.

With the afternoon sun starting to wane and our spirits heightened with our usual joking rapport, we bantered and wallowed in a familiar state of bliss. Then, in the middle of the narrow street, he took my hand in his and wrapped his arm around my back, asking, "Shall we?"

"*Pourquoi pas,*" I answered in complete acknowledgment of the unspoken question, and we set about a small elegant waltz, always just a turn or two until we cracked up in laughter as people began to notice and look on in charmed curiosity. Yep, we do this spontaneous "waltz business," as he calls it, whenever, *wherever* the mood strikes us. While in hip waders fly-fishing or in the lobby of Claridges Hotel in London or in the middle of a crowded airport. It's to-die charming because he is such a clever, sophisticated man and *still* just a little boy from Lyons, France. (But then again, all men are really just little mama's boys in grown-up bodies, aren't they?)

Waltz concluded, we strolled, window shopping, and popped into a few furniture and rare book shops, many of which I'd visited in the last few months. But as expected (but *not* anticipated), arriving with my ex was an entirely different affair. Because he is plastered across French and international magazines constantly, celebrated for his creative genius, everyone in Paris knows *of* him. So there's a lot of ass-kissing and congratulations to him on that recent spread in *Le Figaro* or *AD* magazine. I'm smiled at and generally assumed to be the lucky young girlfriend to this genius. It was always kind of like dating a superhero, come to think of it.

Hey, hold your horses, cowboys! It's not the Big-Shot Industralist *and guest* on the invitee list anymore. I'm showing *my* paintings in an art gallery just around the corner, thank you. Grrrr. Living in the shadow and wake of all his admirers really could be pain in the ass, I remember now.

But he's being sweet and cute as hell, rolling his eyes at me, at the over-the-top attention. So I let this momentary lapse in our blissful happiness reunion evaporate. Flooded with all the adoration, he grabs my hand and makes a beeline for the exit, eager to escape the attention of strangers. I love that he doesn't need the praise or take it seriously anyway. Again, he's perfect.

"Will you help me choose a gift for Gaspard and Isabel's anniversary? They are celebrating their tenth year. I was thinking I could get them something at that shop," he says, pointing to a fossil and gem store just off rue Mazarin.

"Okay, I've always wanted to go into that store. So how are Gaspard and Isabel? I think of them often," I say, referring to his best friend and his wife, who I used to be close to.

"They're well. They just had a baby girl; they named her Victoire," he replies in quiet tones, knowing this will *kill* me. I'm surpressing a scream of old anger and envy as I grasp the news that his best friend (the same age as my ex) just fathered a baby. I'm dying to yell, "For fuck's sake, if he can have a baby at fifty, why the hell couldn't you? Why did I have to leave you? *One* baby, that's all I asked!" I let it blow over as we've had this conversation umpteen times and never got through it, so what's the point of arguing now. Hell, we've split up. It doesn't mean I'll ever let it go inside, but we've beaten that dead horse to death. Hey, suffering in silence? *Not* exploding given a perfect opportunity? The old me would've been all over that. (Mental note: Brace yourself, Klein, but you might just be maturing here.)

In the tiny fossil shop we're ranting and raving at all the gorgeous stones.

Eyeing gigantic agates, huge golden topaz, and jasper spheres sparkling with flecks of gold, dragging each other to come see this or look at that. My ex spots something in a glass case in the window and asks if it can be brought to him. The little old propreiter unlocks the case and presents it to us.

"*Vous avez un goût parfait. C'est la meilleure pièce de la boutique, monsieur.*" (The older gentleman tells my Big-Shot Ex that he has perfect taste. How many godamn times have I heard people say that to him? And once again, it's because he's chosen the most expensive thing in the shop. I'm starting to wish I'd gone shopping with a *normal* guy, because everything is always such a production with the Big-Shot. Tra-la-la.)

Like the supercool creative man that he is, he chooses an enormous amethyst as large as a basketball, all purple shards of reflecting light and crystal. I gotta give it to him, it's a killer gift. Everyone else will probably offer the couple gifts like a bowl from Tiffany, or an Hermès blanket. No, Mr. Perfect always comes up with something truly unique and memorable. I look at him as he chats away with the old man who's wrapping the amethyst for delivery, and I'm overwhelmed by a tempest of emotions. Pff-f-ff, he is *so* amazing, so clever, so generous, so refined, so sexy, and *so not mine* anymore. Hmmm. And yet . . .

I realize maybe I'm just happy I have been a *part* of his life, able to be inspired and forever connected to this fascinating creature. It's true, I miss being in awe of the man I'm with, amazed at his constant thirst for knowledge, excellence, creativity. But I *think* I can accept that happens unbelievably rarely in life and I am forever changed for knowing him. And that might be enough.

The present will be delivered the next day, so with that done we walk back toward the car waiting for us on boulevard Saint-Germain. It's six o'clock and the church bells begin to ring their longest song of the day. The hollow chime echoes throughout the neighbrhood as the sky travels quickly as if chasing after a raincloud. Smoke dances out of the chimneys and buildings become faceless silhouettes against the darkening sky. Stepping together across the cobblestone street of rue Bonaparte, I am once again swept up into the dream of old Paris, the magic of living in a place so rich in history, so compelling in its elegant, aging architecture.

"Klein, I bet I know what you're thinking," he whispers as we pass the little crêperie on the corner.

"Oh, you think so. Give it a try," I say with a smile at once caressing and challenging.

"You've got that quiet angelic look in your eyes. I remember it swept over you the first time we came to Paris together. Remember, by Saint-Sulpice with the snow falling? It's why you moved here; this is your dream, where *you* feel at home."

I look at him and feel such overwhelming acceptance and love. "It's amazing, you have always understood me, without my even speaking. I *do* love you, *mon chien.*"

"*Je t'aime toujours.* Come, let's go to my apartment, to rest and have some tea," he says, knowing he need not even wait for an answer.

We climb in his chauffeured car and whisk off to his glorious apartment on rue des Cases. It's a grand and regal *hôtel particulier* with a large arc-shaped portico. We push open the enormous green door, arms full of bags from Armani, and walk over the perfectly manicured courtyard to his door. I hit my head on the elevator door, as I always did, and if I'm not bleeding (no, luckily this time I was moving slower than my usual speed of sound; I guess I am getting older) it makes me laugh. Oh, the good old days, where after a long day of shopping I'd always give myself a voluntary lobotomy.

Once inside his apartment, all warm and smelling of those expensive Guerlain candles (I so covetted), I'm completely caught back in time to the first time he brought me here. I was just stupefied; everything amazed me. To keep an apartment, this beautiful, in Paris, empty but a few days a year . . . unreal. And then I remembered, even when he and I had been together four years, and I'd spent innumerable holidays with his children, his family, completely enmeshed in his life, he still never allowed me to stay in his Paris apartment without him. That drove me crazy; it made no sense. If I wanted to go to Paris by myself he'd adamantly refuse to let me use his pied-à-terre; I'd have to stay in a hotel. That's right, you were a bit of a kook. What the hell was that about, monsieur? This was turning out to be a great lesson. All that I missed wasn't even what I wanted anymore (with the exception of his spirit which is, frankly, irreplaceable). All of these thoughts are put aside as he suddenly sweeps me up into his arms and kisses me with abandon.

"*J'ai envie de toi,*" he murmurs in my ear. I love that; it's the sexiest, most polite way of saying essentially "I want to fuck you." To be honest, we'd made an unspoken tacit agreement to be lovers at every opportunity until one of us married. It's just understood. No man can match his talents in business or the bedroom. He has a singular talent for making me feel like the most beautiful, desirable woman in the world, and until the day some lovely man slides a ring on my finger I'm *so* not missing an opportunity to be bathed in passionate adoration by this man. Not to mention he does some skillful maneuver with that large Gallic nose that is not to be believed.

We fall onto the feather bed with its canopy rising up to the roof as the rain begins its melodious song dancing down the slate tiles. He bathes me with such divinely passionate kisses, so skillfully that I have not even noticed I am being tenderly stripped of my clothes. His hands, so strong and masculine, glide over my flesh with infinite grace. I slowly peel away the layers of his clothing, unleashing the hypnotic fragrance of his warm naked flesh. Eager mouths find familiar curves and hollows, rediscovering each other in heady delight. I lie beneath him almost breathless, engulfed with overwhelming desire . . . waiting. He immediately yields to me, pulls my hips up to his and slides inside me with tantalizing gentleness, quiet whispers of sensual elegance in tandem with graduating thrusts of ravenous desire. Cloaked in the scent of our bodies' alchemy, consciousness recedes into oblivion . . . And yet once again, he brings me to a mind-numbing ecstasy where I forget where I am, who I am, everything . . . and we fall asleep entwined in an exhausted embrace.

After a delicous nap, I wrap myself in a cashmere blanket, leave him dozing on the bed, and light a fire in the fireplace. With twigs crackling and a marvelously cozy scent filling the room, I tiptoe to the kitchen to make a pot of our favorite Lapsang souchong tea by Mariage Frères. I can still hear his deep sonorious breaths as I drop a few brown sugar cubes into my warm tea. I love that man. How is it that even the sound of him sleeping is elegant? Like a slumbering king after a long night at a decadent ball.

Tea in hand, I curl up on the couch and leave the window slightly open to hear the pattering of the rain and the doves cooing in the courtyard. I forgot how it felt to be so well, so content and peaceful. I light a cigarette and a Diptyque candle and settle into looking through a few of his beautiful seventeenth-century books. Jet lag or the rigors of sensual delight have clearly exhausted him, as he continues to drift in and out of sleep. Fine, sleep, *mon chien,* I need this time alone, to silently take assesment of this intensely emotional day. I need even to escape your presence, the sight and sound of you. Putting the books back in their glass vitrine, I take the candle and head down the tiled corridor, to the bathroom looking over the courtyard . . . my old sanctuary.

Drawing a warm bath and smiling to myself at how his apartment, his quintessentially French apartment *used to* astonish me and fill me with such envy. I glance around the bathroom with its wooden beamed ceiling and antique gray marble bathtub, noticing all the products and objects that I used to pine for. Oh, how I longed to possess a life that was inhabited by these details, the tall glass jars of fresh lavender to sprinkle in the bath, all the fabulous French soaps of exotic scents like Vetyver and water lily, the collection of Côté Bastide oils and creams he always had, and I always wanted.

Funny. Now its just reminds me of *my* own bathroom. Yeah, I even have little pillows of lavender to line my linen closet, just like his. I made mine with lavender I gathered when in the Basque countryside with Nico. That's even more charming than his, now that I think of it.

Stepping out of the tub, I wrap myself up in one of his Christian Dior white robes, trot back to the bedroom and put on Mozart's *Requiem* (like we always did). Hopping up on the small canopied bed next to him, I thought, *You know what? I have all of this* now, *right here in Paris in my own apartment, just a few blocks away. The singing doves, the big bath, the French soaps and oils, the canopied bed, the same tea, the sumptuous robe, the same music. Everything.*

That was great. A deliciously happy moment, to realize I didn't need anyone to offer it to me when *they* wanted to, and *refuse* it when they didn't. Ha! That was a moment of realizing, I guess, just maybe I'm *not* doing *everything* wrong. Give me a little more time and, who knows, maybe everything else I want will eventually come too.

Just then his girlfriend called and he groggily woke up and took the call and, shock of shocks, I was decidedly all right with hearing him speaking tenderly to another woman. What a surprise. I know that he and I have a unique bond that will *never* disappear, and I know he'll always love me as I love him. That's marvelous—and that's *enough.*

The next day I returned the jackets to Armani and never even told him. He'd always so enjoyed being the Big Shot who could offer me gorgeous treats, but frankly I didn't want to be that girl anymore. More to the point, I wasn't a "girl" anymore; without any warning I had miraculously become an independent woman. I guess the wrinkles by my eyes could've been a hint. But wrinkles and all, it felt good. Damn good.

A FEW SLIGHTLY ANNOYING DETAILS I DIDN'T ANTICIPATE

Listen, this isn't fair. Who can I speak to in the head office? My face has been an endless festival of breakouts since I moved to Paris. At this age, I *so* shouldn't be Clearasil Poster Girl. I think the constant ringing of my biological clock is enough torture, thank you. What the hell is in the water? I literally have tried everything; every damn skin repair regimen by Vichy, Biotherm, Carita (each product is about the price of my weekly food budget, so it's a *really* fun way to spend money).

Nothing's working. I even washed my face with bottled Evian water for a week. Trying to go out at night with confidence and find my dream man is next to impossible when it looks like a hot-oil popcorn popper exploded on my face. Really bad timing. God, what did I ever do to deserve this? Was it the time when I was ten years old and the next-door neighbor gave me the angel food cake to take home to my mother, and I sat by the willow tree and ate the entire cake and never even mentioned it to my mom? Fine. *Fine!* I'll come clean. I'm calling her now. I'll dash off a twenty-five year belated thank-you card to Mrs. Nordling, okay? Just call off the blemish brigade, will you?

SUBLIME PLEASURE DU JOUR

Sometimes on a Sunday, when seemingly the entire world has forgotten I exist (that happens a lot since I moved to France, come to think of it) I go out walking by the Seine. Sundays are the best, any time of the year, as the traffic along the river is quieter and it's infinitely more peaceful.

I cross over Pont-Royal bridge, down the stone steps to the cobblestone walkway right along the river. Hitting the last step, I'm met with the faintest smell of the seaside mixed with the fresh scent of budding green leaves and immediately feel a wave of tranquillity wash over me.

Walking along looking up at the beautiful Museé d'Orsay with its two enormous clocks, and the sun reflecting off the glass roof of the Grand Palais, I defy you to not smile in quiet happiness. I walk along on the smooth edge of the path, just feet from the lapping waves of the Seine, ducking under the dripping branches of the weeping willow trees (*saule pleureur* in French, gorgeous) or sometimes I walk toward Notre Dame to see if "my spot" is available. I know it's not just my spot because I've come to understand (much to my surprise) I have to share Paris with other people.

If you pass under the Pont-Royal bridge, noticing the richly patinaed stains and cracking stone on the right pier, you'll come upon a huge tree thrusting out into the river. Its roots are like thick fingers, sprawling in every direction and anchoring this majestic tree firmly in its elegant locale. If you follow around the roots to the side facing the river, you will see "it." An absolute nest of roots to sit in, they embrace you like a gentle, loving mother. I sit in this wood nest, often unseen by passersby on the stone path, and just breathe. To look up at the wonderful apartments lining the quai Voltaire on the other side of the river, watch the occasional barge pass by, listen to the birds in the leafy canopy. The tree listens to all your unspoken troubles and absorbs all your fears and worries. When it's time to get up and leave the nest, you feel entirely calm and serene. I promise.

FRIEND COUNT

Maybe you'll think I'm strange, but when I first moved to Paris I made a lot of important friends rather quickly. Is it a problem that they were all ducks? I didn't really plan on it, it's not like I'm a duck-o-phile or something. When I'd go for my morning run in the Tuileries, I always noticed the sweet ducks scooting across the water in the fountains, flapping around the gardens, and then I got to know them, to recognize them. *Hey, yeah, there's the albino teenager duck, and there's the mallard I once saved by pulling off a plastic bag that had been caught around its neck.*

I really grew fond of one little family of ducks in the fountain by the lion sculpture. It was impossible not to fall in love with them, a proud mama duck and her six little baby ducklings. The babies were tiny little fluffs of soft feathers when I first noticed them. Perhaps she had actually hatched these little angels on the floating piece of wood by the fountain edge, for they were always there, in the same spot.

As weeks went by I watched this attentive mother duck exhaust herself to feed each gawky hungry beak. It was beautiful, this maternal selflessness; her only purpose was to protect and nurture her helpless little babies. In time, they grew large enough to plop down into the water and flit about in frantic spurts of energy. Chasing each other, investigating the territory, and taking turns racing under the cascade of water that fell like diamonds in the sun.

One day it was quite dark and pouring with rain (this is really when I love to run the most, as the gardens are entirely deserted and the whole Tuileries is like my private world. With the rain pelting my skin and me fighting against all the internal voices that yell, *It's raining, let's stop running and go home to bed again,* I feel totally alive). I didn't think I'd see any living creature that morning when I looked over to see the mama duck standing firmly and defiantly on the wood platform in the fountain. She unfurled her wings to their full span, creating a warm, protective umbrella for all her shivering little babies. The rain was coming down in sheets and there she proudly stood; it was magnificent. I nearly wept.

Quickly they became teenager ducks and became more independent and brave. You could see the mama duck had assumed a different role, more of an encouraging overseer. I couldn't believe I was falling in love with ducks; wait a minute, didn't I come here for the men? Yeah, well, for the most part they were revealing themselves to be a hell of a lot less charming. Screw 'em. One morning, as I fought through a hangover to make even one lap in the gardens, I noticed, oh, God no, one of the little ducks was dead. The mother duck had obviously found one of her babies dead in the water and dragged it back, all soaking wet, onto the wood platform. She nudged the little pile of lifeless feathers with her beak. No response. I absolutely crumbled. Without even noticing, I was just sobbing; I couldn't bare it, the heartbroken mother duck was desperately trying to revive her child. I cried all the way home. Even today, I'm still so moved by the beautiful image of what it is to be a mother, instinctively and naturally, so giving and loving. Is there anything so wondrous and beautiful as motherhood?

Flavigny, Madame Gueneau's *Fromage Blanc*, and Fanny Ardant

April

MONSIEUR RIGHT REPORT

When a beautiful Frenchman invites you to his family country house in a little hilltop French village, you don't really have to go through the pros and cons of such an idea before you respond. It's one of life's easier questions. And thank God, since, I had just received one of life's little curve balls smack in my forehead. (And I'm not talking about Alexandre's dinner with another chick, I got over that. Or more to the truth, the night with my Big-Shot Ex made us even-steven.)

I had spent the previous month working day and night, designing a collection of jewelry I hoped to produce in France. Like damn near everything in my life (with the obvious exception of learning French), I had just decided, "This is what I'm doing next!" I'd designed jewelry and sold a few pieces when I lived in New York City, so I was fairly sure it would be one of those entrepreneurial endeavors that (1) I was obligated to try as I couldn't work legally in France and (2) I could possibly pull off and earn at least "lunch money," as my cash reserves were dwindling scarily.

The collection was enormous—one hundred pieces inspired by Art Nouveau furniture and 1930s art. Delicate dragonfly brooches inlayed with ruby eyes, thin chains of innerlinked twenty-four-carat gold lotus leaves that were sprinkled with tiny seed pearls, and bracelets in bold geometric forms inspired by the famous inlayed spoon by Josef Hoffman. I was crazy about every piece and got into sketching with a passion, delaying the reality of just how exactly I was going to get all these delicate things made until the last minute. That minute had arrived.

Alexandre had a good friend, Caroline, who was an expert in the luxury jewelry business. She agreed to meet with me and offer advice. Portfolio of drawings under my arm, I marched over the Pont-Royal to meet her at her office in Place Vendôme. Caroline met me at the door of her office and had me wait while she finished a meeting. Fine. I had gotten slightly better at waiting since I moved to France. The office was fabulous; everywhere you looked were velvet trays laden with antique and contemporary jewelry. Two big black safes held trays of loose diamonds wrapped in fine white parchment. The phone rang off the hook. Messengers came and went. This girl clearly knew what she was doing.

Caroline was finally free; she waved me into her office to present my work and my hopes for my new venture. I unpacked my drawings and began to explain each one. Wait, is that my voice cracking and, for God's sake, is that my hand shaking? What, am I, twelve years old? I guess it had been a long time since I had presented drawings to anyone, yet didn't I used to do this for groups of twenty to thirty high-powered people and feel totally at ease? Christ, I'm nervous. Fortunately, Caroline loved a lot of the pieces and said, "This is really a great collection, but I have to be totally honest . . ." (I didn't like the "but" lead-in. That's never followed by good news like, "but you're just far too clever and talented . . ."). Caroline continued, ". . . but, if you want to do this collection, Klein, you could very easily manufacture it, for, I'm guessing here . . . about a hundred thousand euros and then not be able to sell it to a single store." She expanded, saying that French department stores and boutiques will rarely carry any unknown designer, especially American, and that most likely the companies who would actually make the jewelry would take my drawings and sell them to other designers and manufacturers to take advantage of the small-time inexperienced girl that I am. *Super* news. Hmmm. Okay, I guess I can understand that. My entrepreneurial luck has run out and I'm completely at the mercy of the French system, no arguing with that. (Not that I could have, *in French anyway*.)

I gave Caroline the bottle of wine I'd brought to thank her for her time, jammed that folder of intricate, beautiful sketches back under my arm, and flew down the stairs onto the street. I mean really, what did I think; they were going to applaud, hoist me onto their shoulders, and carry me around Place Vendôme chanting, "Vive Klein!"? Okeydokey, that little plan will have to sit on ice until some unknown future date where I've either got a hundred thousand euros, *or* some genius connections, *or* perhaps just command of the language.

So when Alexandre invited me to the countryside, I was entirely ready to put Paris in a rearview mirror for a while.

We all have images in our mind of a quaint little French country village, from books or movies, so I felt a vague sense of what to expect. But when Alexandre told me, "Did you see the film *Chocolat* with Juliette Binoche and Johnny Depp?" (Yes.) "It was shot in Flavigny-sur-Ozerain, where we are going." No way! That storybook, movie-perfect little village, *really?* My consolation prize for the failed jewelry endeavor was going to be a little piece of Gallic gorgeouness. The entire movie played through my mind and I couldn't quite believe that in three hours I'd actually be there, in an idyllic, perfect twelfth-century village perched on a hilltop in the Burgundy countryside.

I dragged my box of country clothes out from under the bed. All the stuff I used to wear when I'd go to my other French boyfriend's country house, you know, the Ex–Big-Shot Industrialist. He had a great (*such* an understatement) house on a little island called Belle Île off the coast of Brittany. "Hi, you guys!" I exclaimed to my old wool fisherman sweaters and pea coats. "We're going to the country again." I arranged for my friend Stella to come by and feed Puccini while I was gone and threw a bunch of books and my camera in my Tumi luggage (after the Basque countryside weekend with Nico I've learned to leave the Vuitton *chez moi*). At about eight o'clock on Friday night Alexandre came to get me in his cheapo Twingo car and as I threw my stuff in the back I realized I couldn't have been happier. Adventure. Cute boy. Crap car. Let's go!

It's a wonderful drive out of Paris. Slowly the city fades away, the highway gets more and more deserted and you see the occasional old château appear in the distance. A big red moon began its climb just in front of us as we made our way from the modern world to antiquated little towns that had just two street lights, one *boulangerie,* a single *boucherie* (butcher shop), and little else. In the heart of France, the people still go to bed early. By ten o'clock, we were the only ones on the little back roads and tree-lined *allées.*

After three hours, we were driving in virtual darkness except for the red moon now joined by thousands of glistening stars, when Alexandre said, "It's just there on that hill." I looked up to see the city walls of Flavigny magnificently illuminated from below and the bell tower of the tiny church silhouetted against the moon. Brilliant. I never looked at the skyline of New York City and felt such awe. *And I loved New York City.*

I'd trade any Central Park penthouse for this view, hands down. To me, this is *living*. We drove past a little farm with a stone cottage beginning to collapse into a stream, one little light inside and smoke dancing out of the chimney. We passed little enclosures of gardens, small sheep huddled together, and two old horses that woke up to watch us climb up the twisting dirt road on the side of the hill. We drove through the twelfth-century gates of the city, past a little convent with all the lights out.

We were being gently tossed from side to side inside the car as we trundled up the little cobblestone path to his *maison de campagne*. It's completely silent except for the sound of the wind twisting a weather vane on its iron perch. A few bats swooped down and glided past the car as our nocturnal welcoming committee. The cool air was crisp and smelled of dry leaves. We parked the car by the side of his stone house in the heart of the village. Wild cats scatter at the unexpected disruption and a couple of enormous crows stare down at us inquisitively. I was completely enchanted and excited beyond words. Alexandre and I grab our bags and with one turn of the large, rusty key—like a prop from a movie set!—the heavy old door glides open to invite us in to another time, another century. *Voilà!*

Their house is from the fifteenth century; Alexandre's parents have spent decades restoring it to its original floor plan and preserving its bones. It smells marvelous, like an old, wet castle. It's not an opulent house, just a beautiful, classically French country home. The kitchen is the first room through the door, with a huge fireplace for cooking bread and a large weathered stone hearth. There is a long wood country table with two long oak benches on either side. On the table sits a big bowl in provincial yellow pottery with old potatoes growing limbs and spines. The kitchen cupboards are open and stocked with tins of sardines, pickled vegetables, with dried handfuls of thyme, fennel tied with a thread, and a mortar with black peppercorns half ground into a fine dust. Each year Alexandre's mother makes her famous homemade confiture with the gooseberries, raspberries, and currants she grows in her garden, and the shelves are bursting with "*groseilles 2004*" and "*framboises 2005.*"

On the hearth a large dark clay pitcher is overflowing with various sizes of whisks, wooden spoons, and carving knives; everything is old, used, adored. Every single item, from the cutting board to the stained old teapot, has a long and beautiful history. Ah, the meals that have been made here! This kitchen fills me with wonderful visions of steaming hot onion soup served in chipped old crockery, with its bubbling cheese blisters and warm onion vapors rising up to your anxious mouth. France just knows what's important. Food, wine, and sex. *And any combination thereof.*

I look over at Alexandre and he's so pleased to see that I'm just beside myself with happiness. He lights a fire in the large stone fireplace and puts on a CD by Erik Satie. As the firewood cracks and sparks, releasing its moisture, the house is filled with the warm, comforting smell of oak. Mmm, now that smells like the country.

Alexandre says, "Come with me," and leads me by candlelight down a dark staircase into the cobwebbed, dusty wine *cave*. There are old crates of Burgundy wine half empty here and there, bottles piled on top of cardboard boxes, everything covered in dust and labels turning into unreadable seals of unknown promise. We choose a bottle of Haut-Medoc and duck under an enormous spiderweb as tiny gray mice scurry from corner to corner. I scream as I notice a huge white spider, his body as big as a man's watch face, suspended above me. Alexandre taps it with his finger and we realize he is frozen and just harmlessly beautiful in his icy tomb. We open the wine and let it breathe while we unpack a large cardboard box the neighbor has left for us on the front step.

Madame Gueneau, the eighty-year-old woman who lives next door, has wrapped many of the jewels of her garden in old newspaper and packed this box of goodies as her traditional welcome gift. Madame Gueneau has lived all her life in this tiny village, tending to her gardens of fruits and vegetables and each day making her own bread and cheese. For thirty years Alexandre's family has been connected to this fragile, sweet soul whose husband still works each day from seven in the morning till seven at night at his small farm at the base of the village. He has about twenty cows for milking and sells the milk, cheese, and *fromage blanc* to neighboring villages. The old Gueneaus' lives are the same today as they were forty years ago; they have never left the area, never been to Paris, never seen a television. The box of fresh provisions she has left us is fragrant and smells like the pure earth; there are huge flowering cabbages, gnarly pale carrots, bundles of white asparagus, a large heavy round of dense country bread, creamy Époisse cheese bundled in fresh green chestnut leaves, and one Cavaillion melon that promises to drip with sweet juice. It's all unwrapped and sitting haphazardly on the old oak table and I think, *My God, is it not a still life by Cézanne?*

She has also included a small tub of her freshly made *fromage blanc*. Alexandre is crazy for it and insists I try it, here, this minute. As he pulls off the plastic wrap and unveils a beige lump of curd floating in a pool of murky white juice, I'm not sure I'm going to be as crazy for it as he wants me to be. He grabs two small bowls and scoops the white curd into piles of quivering gelatinous mass. Is this cheese? Is it sweet? How the hell do you eat this? Apparently it's eaten like yogurt, with heaping spoonfuls of coarse brown sugar sprinkled on top. It's really not at all like yogurt and tastes so fresh-from-the-cow, so animal-sour, it's clearly an acquired taste which my super-American taste buds don't appreciate. When Alexandre turns his back, I pour even more brown sugar in mine to make it slightly more palatable.

We saw through the giant round of bread, slicing thick slabs, which Alexandre examines with the eye of a surgeon, for uniformity. He cuts a small clove of garlic and rubs it vigorously across the bread. The bread is gently toasted, drizzled with olive oil, and served on an old cutting board. He tells me this intensely pungent smell and the serious kick of powerful garlic is the breakfast—yes, breakfast—of choice for local farmers, generally accompanied at six o'clock with a big glass of homemade red wine, to kick-start their energy for a hard day's work. With breath that would wilt flowers, we devour the crunchy bread and take deep sips of the warm red wine. The local Époisse is untied from its shroud of leaves and sliced through the soft chalky skin to its creamy core. We slather this smooth beige cheese onto bread crusts and now *I've* found the perfect country meal. It tastes like wood and grass and nuts and the sun. As I'm smiling in heavenly appreciation, Alexandre jokingly says, "You Americans love things creamy and crunchy together." He often points this out, since I pour granola into yogurt or peanut butter on green apples. Before Alexandre, I never thought about how our surroundings form our tastes for food.

At times, I'm slightly embarrassed by my underdeveloped sophistication regarding cuisine. On evenings we spend apart, I'm utterly content to have a bowl of cereal for dinner, and if I happen to ask Alexandre what he's making for his own dinner-for-one, he'll usually say something like "baked sole with baby red potatoes" or "grilled salmon on a bed of arugula." I'm always amazed and utterly impressed with the effort French people will exert, for clearly every single meal is to be celebrated and savored.

Once the fire has turned to burning red embers and we've polished off the wine, we climb the creaking wood stairs to the second floor. Alexandre chooses among the three bedrooms, his favorite, what was once his grandmother's room. It's a small room with sloping wood floors and one large window that faces north out over the valley below. The wallpaper and drapes are in a matching, faded red toile de Jouy peeling away from the wall by the ceiling and lightly stained by tobacco and the smoke of many fires in the fireplace. The bed is soft and quickly absorbs us into its nest; the cool crisp sheets are softened from years of wear, and a little lace embroidery trickles around its edges. With the sound of the wind whistling through the trees and an owl in the distance we curl up against each other. We laugh hard as we try to kiss, but the potent aroma of garlic has won the war against toothpaste and overpowers us. We sleep like logs with the exception of Alexandre's trice nightly glass-shattering festivals of snoring, during which I have to literally push him onto his side and whisper, "Please roll over, Monsieur Ronfleur (snorer)." He never remembers this by morning and denies it vehemently.

At ten o'clock he still refuses to get up, so I get up alone, wrap a large old blanket around me, and quietly shut the door behind me as I climb the small curving staircase to the roof terrace. The little village is already in full swing, which amounts to a few older women standing in the street gossiping, the Gueneau's cat stretched out on the warm stones in the garden, the swallows gliding back and forth from the church bell tower to the roof peaks of the convent. The view is amazing. All blue sky, hills and valleys as far as the eye can see, dots of sheep and cows along the river below and the calm cooing of doves. The village itself is composed of perhaps thirty stone homes and buildings. A monastery was built on this hill in ninth century and this small village grew up around it. The monastery still exists, still is inhabited by about sixty young monks who remain very much to themselves.

I make a *chocolat chaud* as Alexandre has taught me, using boiled fresh milk from the Gueneaus and melting down half a bar of dark chocolate. Slowly adding the warm chocolate to the simmering milk and stirring constantly is the secret. The bells of the church strike eleven, and repeat it after a short pause, in case you lost count the first time. The bells of the convent and the monastery follow suit, in unison. It sounds like it's a coronation for all the ringing and celebratory music. The peace permeates my skin and I realize I am smiling with pure contentment.

Alexandre wakes up and, bleary-eyed, comes up onto the terrace. He's eager for a fresh coffee and more of that *fromage blanc* business. I'm generous and offer him my share (hardly a selfless act). I toast some of that hearty bread and pile on spoonfuls of his mother's cassis confiture. (This is my new obsession; I beg shamelessly for him to sneak a big jar of his mother's cassis jam for me to take home.)

We both take icy cold showers, as the hot water is volatile and unreliable, and throw on light sweaters and light silk scarves. (Remember, this is France; scarves are *de rigueur* and frankly everyone looks great in them.) Alexandre and I lock the big wood front door with the rusty old key, although it's laughably pointless. Even the monastery and the *boulangerie* leave their gates unlocked.

We head out to take a little tour of the village and greet the locals. Walking along little stone paths and cobblestone streets we encounter sweet little old dried-up people whom Alexandre greets with great affection and warmth. I like him better here, in the country; he's incredibly calmer and more expressive. Le Creep Alexandre seems like he could never have existed. The little old couple we meet by the church are amazed that I'm American. The United States is so far away and so exotic to them. They look at me intensely as though I'm an oddity, amazed that I found my way to this medieval village. I can't understand the *slightest* thing they are saying, as their French is entirely unique with its local regional inflections and sharp accents. I begin to understand only when they start to gesture to Alexandre and make references as to how they knew him when he was just a little tiny boy, riding his bicycle dangerously fast around the church. (Now he's a huge boy driving dangerously around Paris.)

We walk on, the sun warming our wind-kissed cheeks. All of the small stone homes are quaint beyond words: ivy crawling up the exterior walls, flowerpots blooming on the windowsills, carved stone signs in lieu of street signs. I see the little shop in front of the church that was Juliette Binoche's chocolate shop in the movie. Amazingly enough, it stands empty, even after its movie debut. It seems incredible to me no one has ever thought to actually buy it and open a little chocolate and bonbon shop there, then I realize that's my American capitalize-on-an-opportunity mentality. It doesn't exist here; this is a town of farmers, their wives, and a handful of monks and nuns. Suddenly I notice the distinct smell of anise is everywhere, and I realize this little medieval town not only looks perfect but *smells* perfect too. Alexandre tells me the only business in the village is the famous anis bonbon factory on the west wall of the village. We stroll over to take a look; it's a three-story nineteenth-century stone and plaster building, with large gray shutters and a few women moving about inside. They wear knee-length white aprons, like characters out of a Merchant-Ivory film. Fantastic. So this is where all those oval tins of anis de Flavigny are made. For years, charmed by their utterly French packaging with fleur-de-lis, old drawings of Marie Antoinette, and little villages on the front, I'd bought dozens of little tins as gifts on visits to Paris. They even sell them at the Charles de Gaulle airport for about two euros a tin. And now, here I was, surrounded by the sweet smell of licorice and watching the little round white bonbons pop out of the turn-of-the-century shiny bronze machine. This is great, so great.

We walk along the city wall, past the monastery where a young priest is mowing the lawn, head to toe in a brown monk's robe and large cross around his neck. He looks up and smiles gently. I try to fathom his life, the solitude, immense silence and piety. It's in total contrast with my own and I can only imagine how pure his thoughts and life must be. The six daily masses, beginning at five-thirty, the hours spent in quiet reflection, the absence of distraction, of any vestige of modern life. I have enormous respect for that kind of commitment. It's beyond my comprehension and, I admit, the twisted part of me wants to know just where they pack up their libido. That's got to be the trickiest detail about being a monk.

We walk on to the old gated cemetery that's just on the edge of the village, virtually falling over into the valley below. Alexandre unlatches the tall iron gate and we walk among lichen-encrusted tombstones to the farthest stone in the cemetery. Here lies his grandmother. Alexandre kneels and puts a few wildflowers we've picked along our walk on the granite stone. It's touching to see this lady-killer, the stud of Paris, so moved by memories of his gentle old grandmother. I give him time alone to say a few words in privacy.

A horse whinneys as we walk back onto the main road and we are met by a dirty gray horse on the other side. We pluck crab apples off a nearby tree and open our palms to the horse's eager nibbles. Alexandre tells me this is a son to a bigger horse that once threw him off in the valley when he was ten years old. He walked, tears streaming down his cheeks, holding his broken arm cradled in the other, back to his house and his mother's arms. She had to take him over an hour away to find a doctor who could set it in a cast. An endearing story and I find, in this moment, I'm more in love with Alexandre then ever before.

We rule out an impromptu bareback ride in the interests of safety. (Thank God, because I have no idea how to ride a horse and it would be humiliating like hell, because I always pretend that "I ride, sure I do.") Alexandre takes my hand and says, "Come, you've got to see this," as we stumble together down the steep hillside, catching branches to steady us as small pebbles make their best efforts to catapult us into the brambles. About three hundred feet down into the edge of the valley stands a rectangular white stone building, open to the front and back so trails of water can flow throughout. "This is the old *lavarie*," Alexandre explains. "Come on."

Apparently it's the old laundry outbuilding, sheltering a low pool, perhaps three feet deep, long and rectangular, where all the villagers would come and kneel on the stone ledges and wash their laundry in the fresh stream running down from the forest edge. I bend down to touch the water; it's freezing and the whole structure feels like an ancient public Roman bath in its elegant simple design.

As expected, Alexandre starts a seriously vicious splashing competition which I definitely lose. I'm sopping wet, in smelly wool and with dripping hair. These few minutes of water warfare in the sun, without a soul around, laughing like kids, are among my fondest ever. I do not want for anything. Life seems so pure, simple, and carefree. Love, the sun, and laughing. Nothing else matters.

As we begin our ascent back to the village, a farmer's guard dog decides we need to get moving a little faster and chases us all the way up the hillside as I howl with fear and laughter. Breathless, back in front of the monastery, the clock strikes two and the fragrance of licorice mixes with the wet wool. We head back home for lunch. I look over at Alexandre, jeans wet from the *lavarie,* sweat on his upper lip from the dog chase and in this moment I know, for all the frustration and struggles in moving to France, it's all entirely worth it. *Love* this man. *Love* this country.

A FEW SLIGHTLY ANNOYING DETAILS I DIDN'T ANTICIPATE

One of the lovely perks of my new telephone is the approximately eighty calls I get each damn day for the Banque Populaire. Obviously my number was once for some—you guessed it—Popular Bank. Aptly named, I must say.

I am not embarrassed to tell you as I have now grown tired of the daily conversation with Puccini on the pros and cons of French cat food versus American cat food (frankly, you can only debate that subject two, three days, tops). Thus, I am *desperate* for the phone to ring. When it does, I'll pretty much drop everything, leap up, demolishing any obstacle—cat included—to pick up the phone. How excruciating it is each time to be dealt the crushing blow: *"C'est Banque Populaire?"* Part of me wants to scream "No!" and slam the receiver into a kajillion pieces, and the other part wants to keep them on the phone for a little social visit.

The French are a curious bunch. Even after I've pitch my well-rehearsed rendition of "No, this is in fact an apartment, not a bank" they, without fail, ask if I have the bank's new phone number. As though I might have chosen to work on a volunteer basis for France Télécom's rerouting system. While I'm always polite and explain that unfortunately I don't have the much desired new phone number, it is getting to the point where I am strongly considering suggesting that they can go ahead and send their cash deposits to my address. Oh, that good old American entrepreneurial spirit can't be suppressed by a small thing like French legalities.

There is one French-made appliance that I covet and that has so far eluded me: the ever-so-chic top-of-the-line Magimix coffee machine. While its name is very circa-1950s Betty Crocker, it's an amazingly elegant contraption that makes brilliant coffee. I have a huge love-hate relationship with the Magimix. I would *love* to have one and I would *hate* to pay for it. They are like five hundred euros and you could buy a scooter for that price but, frankly, really good coffee is top priority in France.

Having arrived in Paris with my Bodum press-pot coffeemaker, I thought

I'd cleverly side-stepped the whole voltage-difference dilemma. For a while, I was fine drinking coffee that tasted like hot water with a brown Crayola melted in it. But after offering cups of "my special American brew" to French friends and watching them recoil in horror at the smell alone, I've abandoned the press pot altogether. I'm offering lots of tea these days *chez moi* and while many girls marry for money, I intend to marry someone with a Magimix. *And you think I'm kidding.*

SUBLIME PLEASURE DU JOUR

Without question one of the greatest pleasures of living in Paris is the fashion. Growing up in Madison, Wisconsin, I always yearned for the day when I could live somewhere with more sartorial options than the local *Farm and Fleet* collection. Let's just say that fashion takes a big backseat to comfort in the Midwest.

Since I moved to Paris, I love to go back home for the holidays for a dose of culture shock in reverse. Each time I arrive at Mitchell Field Airport I'm (1) delighted to see my father and (2) convinced I've stumbled upon the Overeaters Anonymous tour group in baggage claim. Everyone in Wisconsin has apparently happily agreed to eat with abandon and embrace any clothing with elastic waistbands. I'm at once jealous and amazed.

The fashion (again, in the general sense of the word) rolls right along with expanding girth. The sweatshirt has become a kind of uniform that somehow is considered acceptable for every occasion. Throw open the closet of a Wisconsinite and you might hear the following as you look upon the sea of fleece: "Well now, here are my daytime sweatshirts in pink and yellow with flowers. Those are for afternoons at the mall or lunch at the Olive Garden, and these red ones are for state football games. Oh, and this one with the glittery snowflakes is for Christmas and . . ." You get the idea.

Growing up I always knew I didn't fit in. Why didn't other kids call in sick when they couldn't find just the right taupe sweater to go with their corduroys? I actually used to make charts in my closet of possible options and ensembles. Choosing what to wear for the class picture threw me into an absolute tizzy. None of my friends understood my obsession but now, living in France, I can gloriously unleash my lust for fashion. When I throw myself up against the store window at Emanuel Ungaro in ecstasy, it's completely understood (they did actually request that I refrain from that behavior in the future, but I'm sure I was not the first).

It is such a pleasure to see streams of elegantly clad people striding down the street. On chic avenues like rue du Faubourg Saint-Honoré and avenue Montaigne, it's like a never-ending runway show. I adore that there is an across-the-board, ageless appreciation of dressing well. Men, women, and children, all have an innate sense of style and poise.

I live just down the block from a preschool and each day at three o'clock the young bourgeois mothers wait outside for their children. It's an amazing spectacle. The women are all, without fail, perfectly coifed, quietly elegant in chic cashmere twinsets, Hermès silk scarves, and camel-hair coats, a Birkin bag in the crook of their arm as they lean against their Façonnable umbrellas. Not to mention that they will casually stand *in the rain* in lamb suede heels (I am a witness), as though they're disposable. Amazing.

Their children run out into their arms, squealing with joy (hey, I would be too if I had their clothing budget), decked out in four-hundred-dollar Bonpoint hand-knitted sweaters, corduroy jodhpurs, Baby Dior boots, and leather knapsacks. It's so out of Central Casting perfect, that the first time I happened upon this scene, I thought somebody must have been doing a photo shoot or shooting a commercial. Nope, it's just a different mentality that's built into the society.

Equally divine is to see women age with grace and style. European women just don't flock to plastic surgeons in a frantic race, trying to nip, tuck, and Botox every wrinkle the way American women do. I see so many women of "a certain age" who are exquisitely dressed in age-appropriate Givenchy, with perfectly applied makeup, proudly presenting their rich crow's feet and smile lines. It's so pleasing to see these women, so dignified and regal, accepting their wrinkles as a visual testament to the lives they've led. (I try like hell not to think about their husbands and the strong possibility of a twenty-year-old mistress.)

There are always exceptions, like Catherine Deneuve, who, sadly, has done so much "work" her eyes are now almost on the back of her head. But more typical is the gorgeous actress Fanny Ardant, who I recently had the pain and pleasure of sitting next to at l'Esplanade restaurant by l'École Militaire. In her fifties, she is *so* ravishing, so sexy, that both my date *and* I were in love with her.

Women like Fanny (as though I'm on a first-name basis with her; who am I kidding?) are gorgeous role models and honestly make getting older seem quite appealing (feel free to call me back in twenty years to see if I'm still so jubilant).

But I have to get back to the clothes, that drug that is couture. The extraordinary quality, the fine craftsmanship, and the unbelievable creativity that come together at Lacroix, Galliano, Lagerfeld, Chanel, and Givenchy. My mouth is agape, every time I stand in front of the windows, in a rapturous desire that I imagine is something like the way a ten-year-old boy, in front of a stack of porn magazines might feel: *physical need tinged with the brutal reality that it's completely* not *going to happen, but it's still fun to look.* The French even have a phrase for this delicious experience: *lécher les vitrines.* It means "to lick the windows." Sexy, *non?*

One day I popped into the Galliano boutique and I decided to "play it up." Being ignored by the dismissive staff resulted in my assuming a new identity. I was going to be jetting off to Venice for an extravagant ball and I'd be needing a few gowns—*such* an outright lie, but it was fun to suddenly see the saleswomen shut off their cell-phone calls and exert a semi-believable amount of interest. (I don't want to say the saleswomen in Parisian boutiques are aloof, bitchy snobs, but I think it's safe to bet they weren't voted Mademoiselle Congeniality in high school. I can also say that if you're concerned about the expression "In a country where you don't speak the language, you appear as though your IQ is halved," don't worry because you still come out far above the sales creatures. All right, I will say it—they have the intelligence of Camembert.) And yet there is an upside. If the staff comes to the conclusion you're possibly in the position to purchase something, they frequently will offer you an espresso or a glass of Champagne.

During my performance at the Galliano boutique I accepted the free Champagne as though it were my due and slid into a couple of magnificent beaded gowns. What a dream to see myself in a sixty-thousand-euro duchess satin ball gown with a train. And when you know this *so* isn't going to happen ever again, you savor every second. When the pressure to choose one and "call in the tailor" was getting a bit heavy, I proclaimed none of them suited my needs and tried to make a convincing exit empty-handed. Warning: the complementary alcohol has obvious drawbacks. Not so long after my arrival in Paris, I indulged in a few too many *gratuit* glasses at Jean Paul Gaultier and got a little caught up in the moment. By the time I got home and sobered up, the fur-lined suede shorts did seem a bit hard to rationalize. Oddly enough they don't offer you much Champagne when you return things. Take note: life in a foreign country is often a fun excuse for creating a more glamorous version of yourself; no one will leap up and point out that you were once a waitress at Chi-Chi's Mexican Restaurant and had to wear a name tag that said "I'M SEÑORITA LAUREN, ASK ME ABOUT OUR CHIMICHANGAS!"

FRIEND COUNT

Stella and I have now altered our routine to include the they-could-only-be-Americans activity of jogging together. I'll run over to her apartment by Théâtre de l'Odéon, pick her up and we'll head off for a couple of laps around Jardins du Luxembourg. Running *and* debating whether our boyfriends are good enough for us is doubly exhausting, so we generally poop out after two rounds, head back to her apartment, and refuel on Lu Biscuits (at the fabulously cheap one euro per package of eighty, it's very easy to rationalize eating all of them in one sitting), accompanied by cup after cup of *chocolat chaud.* Calories burned running equalized *tout de suite.*

If we're too bloody tired for running, we park our slothlike derrières in a beautiful velvet seat at Ladurée on rue Bonaparte. This is the girliest, most fabulous tea and pastry shop in Paris, anywhere, positively. Ladurée is so classically old France with its red damask and velvet interior, it's as though it's been there since the "Let them eat cake!" revolution.

The experience is entirely elegant—tea for two with the whole Limoges tea set and its vast array of accoutrements. *J'adore!* A charming three-tiered pastry stand piled with delicate napoleons, cream-filled religieuses, and divine cucumber-salmon tea sandwiches is brought to your table, and that's just the beginning. The macaroons, in fourteen scrumptious varieties, are positively orgasmic.

It's virtually *all* women in the afternoon and feels like an elegant women's club. Stella and I try to make the trip at least once a month to pamper ourselves, dress up and pretend we're in the *beau monde* of nineteenth-century Paris. Then it's back to our apartments, jeans and sweaters and Coca Light.

I'm so loving having a girlfriend again. It's imperative to have someone to call when you're in an absolute panic because you've found some girl's phone number at your boyfriend's apartment. You'll be on the verge of flipping into a violent rage and you need a friend to say, "Be cool, casually mention it and see what he says, then call me back and we'll devise a plan to attack or disarm." Stella's treasured advice has kept me from making the zillion hypersensitive accusatory attacks I made with Nico. Thank God, since the woman in question's phone number turned out to be Alexandre's travel agent. *Phew!*

Eau de Poire, a Whirling Dervish, and Christian Louboutin

May

MONSIEUR RIGHT REPORT

I'm just whipped about Alexandre. It's gotten quite out of hand because he's not exactly poster boy for Perfect Boyfriend, as we know. We spend most evenings laughing and fucking like minks after drinking the equivalent of the entire state of Nebraska's annual alcohol consumption. Fantastic dinners at the pricey le Voltaire and the inexpensive le Petit Fernand and great times zipping all over Paris on his motorcycle. Then, just when I'm lovin' him to no end, without fail, he'll revert to Le Creep Alexandre.

Par exemple, I offer you the latest saga: I thought we'd be having one of our little romantic dinners at home, and he calls as he's leaving his gallery and says, "Klein, we're expected for dinner tonight at Patrick Lafon's house. He's having a small dinner party for some of us *antiquaires.*" Okay, maybe I'm crazy, but isn't he supposed to ask me if I want to go before confirming? It's not like we are an old married couple. And doesn't he know by now I hate having my life planned for me? (By the way, "the creep" part is still to come; this is all just the pre-creep portion) I snorted and huffed a while, then finally gave in as I've been dying to see this famous *antiquaire*'s apartment and chatting with other people in Paris *can* be quite fascinating.

Alexandre walked over to my house and hung out looking at my books and playing with Puccini while I got ready. "So who else will be there tonight?" I yell from the bedroom.

"Ah, I think, Claude, this successful editor, his wife, Sylvie, a curator . . . another couple, both in antiques, and Marcel Causans who has a gallery on quai Voltaire and his boyfriend, some decorator."

"Well, should I wear a dress or what?" I say standing in my underwear realizing the guy who lives across the street has a killer view of my bare ass at this very second, unlucky soul.

"I don't know . . . a skirt, pants, whatever," he says, apathetically lighting up yet another Gauloise.

"Oh, you're a big help," I mumble under my breath. I grab my pinstriped Dolce & Gabbana suit and a simple white cotton shirt to wear underneath. Once dressed, I step into the hall. "Alexandre, hair up or down?"

"Up! You know how I like it, side part, low ponytail." (Yeah, you make it really clear you find me, what is the phrase? . . . "*très désagréable*" any other way, you poop.) Catering to Alexandre's desire, I throw my hair in the low ponytail, whip on a dash of mascara, and smear a dab of water lily oil behind each ear and I'm acceptable.

"Okay, I'm done. Ready, Freddy?" I announce as I stand in the hall, clearly hoping for some sort of comment like, "Wow! You look fabulous," which never has fallen out of the mouth of my Mr. Stingy on the Compliments boyfriend.

"Yes, Fred." He laughs. (Sometimes I teach French guys American slang and they extrapolate into complete foolishness. Not that "ready, Freddy" is elegant prose to begin with.)

We walk out together onto charming rue de Beaune. It's quiet and the street is virtually empty save an old couple out strolling. Spring is in full force; the breeze is warm and smells of the afternoon sun. All the flower boxes in the neighborhood are blooming with cherry red geraniums and pale pink petunias. This neighborhood never fails to astonish me; it's picture perfect. So is Alexandre, actually. My crabbiness dissolves. *Mmmm.*

"Hey, we should bring some Champagne," he says, so we head over to the liquor shop, Nicholas, on rue du Bac just before they close. The young clerk knows us on sight as the couple who is either addicted to or bathing in Ruinart Champagne on a nightly basis.

"*Une bouteille ou deux ce soir, monsieur?*" he inquires.

"*Seulement une, merci beaucoup.*" We pay and walk hand in hand over one block to rue de Lille to Patrick Lafon's apartment just up the street. I look over at Alexandre. Damn, baby, you are so beautiful. He is dressed with such style, in a beige Paul Smith three-quarter coat, a vertical stripe dress shirt, gray narrow trousers that graze over his perfect ass and strong muscular thighs. And his shoes. This man has the coolest, sexiest shoes. Dior gray suede ankle boots with leather laces. Killer. I'm still such a terrible sucker for men who dress well, *obviously*.

"Gimme a kiss, kiddo." I demand, overwhelmed by his beauty. He stops, bends over and plants those soft, full lips on mine as the warm smell of his skin engulfs me. As always, my insatiable desire for him is in overdrive. I swear this man puts the O! in the word *libido*.

We stop in front of 97, rue de Lille, push the private door code and enter a gorgeous marble lobby, where a small garden in a courtyard peeks around the enormous curved staircase.

"Race ya!" I say, bounding up the stairs.

"Klein, it's on the sixth floor!" he yells after me, pushing for the elevator.

"Fine. I'll still win!" I yell back over the balustrade. Hey, wait. That actually means seven floors as the French never count the first floor. Fuck, sometimes this American competitive streak gets me into trouble. Winded, I still arrive first. "Ha! I win!" I say as he steps out of the elevator.

"Yes, but now you have a sweaty upper lip," he replies without charm.

Oh, here comes Le Creep Alexandre. I can just feel it. Patrick welcomes us into his grand apartment and offers to give us a quick tour. As expected, it's lavishly decorated with innumerable eighteenth-century marble busts, huge period gilt mirrors, beautiful moldings, and exquisite patterned parquet floors that creak with each step. How chic. Room after room of vast windows that overlook the Musée d'Orsay and out over the rooftops of Saint-Germain. Elegant to die. The best Charlotte Perriand tables mixed with rare André Arbus chairs and amazing museum-quality art. It's like a showroom at Sotheby's, for God's sake.

"Killer!" I whisper to Alexandre as we follow Patrick back into the grand salon. Apparently we are the last to arrive and introductions are made (I believe "*enchanté*" was spoken ten, twelve times in a row; hey France, work on getting another acceptable greeting, just a thought) to the six other guests including Patrick's wife, Cécile. Surprisingly, she's an unfriendly hausfrau, which I didn't expect as her husband is an elegant, friendly soul. (That's one thing about French couples, sometimes you just cannot see how they suit one another. Maybe it's that old yin-yang thing.)

Alexandre and I gladly partake in the Champagne and sit down together on a large beige velvet couch. It seems like we're falling into the cushion for hours, it's so plush. Jesus, this thing must be stuffed with only the precious feathers of the underbellies of baby ducks; talk about sumptuous, man, my ass is sunk about twenty inches deep into this thing. (I feel like Lily Tomlin doing that routine where she sits in an oversized chair with a lollypop.) The editor Claude is hot, sort of a French Ralph Fiennes. And the wife is pretty if you like women whose hair looks like they've just put their finger in a light socket. (Somehow the frizzy-hair thing is big in France. I don't get it.) As expected, she's a bitch to me. Clearly she thought she'd be the "pretty woman" here tonight.

The gay couple's a blast, witty, effervescent, and darling together. The *antiquaire* couple, both in their midforties, seem to have a cumulative IQ of nine and all the social skills of a matchbook. God, don't let me be seated next to one of them at dinner. I've discovered just where you're seated at a dinner *entirely* dictates how the evening will go. Nothing worse then being seated next to a dullard as the rest of the guests banter enthusiastically and keel over laughing.

"*Plus de Champagne?*" Patrick asks.

"*Oui, merci,*" I say, desperately trying to follow the group's bullet-fast banter in French. What the hell are they talking about? It could be furniture or possibly politics. This is France so it very likely is sexual, or possibly politically sexual furniture. Beats me. Crap, clearly no one got the memo, "Klein's French sucks, so everyone speak in English tonight," because this is starting to look like another night of smilin' and noddin' over here.

Patrick kindly notices I'm lost in trying to follow the conversation. "I'm sorry, Klein, we're just talking about our friend Fabrizio's new book. Apparently it's just been nominated for the prix de Goncourt," he informs me.

A strange wave of pleased recognition runs through me. Hey, I know that name . . . Fabrizio, that's Mr. Handsome Smug-Pants from Sebastian's birthday party. I giggle to myself. *Well, well, well, good for him. France's biggest prize for writing? Surely, he'll be even more insufferably smug now. Wonder if he's still with that sourpuss chick?* Hmmm. Alexandre leans over. "Grab your glass. We are going into the dining room."

"*D'accord,*" I answer, lost in thought for a second. And we all noisily retire to the adjoining dining room. Dinner is served in their elegant red *salle à manger*. A set of three gorgeous red coral candlesticks sits in the center of the table, the flickering candlelight illuminating the raw silk wallcoverings and the small Legér painting over the fireplace. By luck, I get to sit next to Alexandre and the Hot Editor guy. We're off to a good start.

La cuisine est formidable: les huîtres farcies (oysters stuffed with Gruyère cheese) to start, followed by *filets de Saint-Pierre à la Deauvillaise* (filets of haddock in an onion cream sauce), ending in a bountiful tray of a cheeses— Cantal, Brie, Mont d'Or, and various Chevrotins—with rich petit cups of *mousse au chocolat à l'orange* for dessert. Divine. Obscenely hedonistic and beats the hell out of franks and beans back in Wisconsin, for damn sure.

Alexandre's drunk. Not even caring that I don't have a clue what's being discussed. I know it's my own damn fault. At least the Hot Editor broke into English and chatted me up for five minutes before his wife glared him into submission. For all her crabbiness, Patrick's wife, Cécile, seems to be an ab-solutely brilliant cook; therein may lie her appeal. Hmm, my theory has al-ways been, "The way to a man's heart is through *his pants*." Maybe that's where I'm going wrong. (Mental note: *Look into cooking classes at the Cordon Bleu*.). Cécile clears the dishes silently and returns to the table, presenting a large glass decanter with a hand-written label Scotch taped to it. How cool. Obviously bought at some countryside backwoods distiller. Suddenly, all at once, the group says loudly, and in unison, "*Eau de poire!*"

Well hot damn, gang, what's the hoo-ha? Alexandre finally remembers I'm alive and still in the room. "It's pear liquor, dangerously strong stuff really." And with that he goes back to to drunkenly telling some story to the two ab-solutely entranced gay men. The Hot Editor leans over to me and says, "You've got to try it, Klein. It has the unique effect of catapulting you into a virtual hallucinatory state."

"Like absinthe?!" I ask excitedly, referring to the now illegal wormwood alcohol that great poets like Verlaine and Rimbaud used to drink and write marvelously decadent poems about.

"Hmm, no. But here, I'll pour you some," he says, taking the large bottle of clear liquid and pouring it into a tiny glass with a gold-painted rim. I smell it. It damn near melts my contact lenses and certainly curls my nose hairs.

"Yeowch!" and I drink it all in one brave and foolish shot. By the time I get to the bottom of the glass, I've lost all feeling in my face. Once the flames in my stomach extinguish, I think, *Well, that really wasn't so bad.* The taste is akin to formaldehyde (I'm guessing, no firsthand experience as of yet). I suddenly realize Alexandre has said all of three words to me since we arrived, one of which was "shush" when I tapped his arm once asking for a brief translation. Hey, rude boy, we came together, remember? I swear to God this man only comes alive around gay men and female models. Why do I put up with him? I glance down and notice the tremendous bulge between his legs, and his thighs straining against his pants. Right! *Now* I remember. For the first time in my life I'm a slave to my desire (how ridiculous) and Le Creep Alexandre has emerged again.

My already seriously drunk boyfriend is now simultaneously eating the remains off people's plates and guzzling *eau de poire* like water. Chic. Dude, slow it down a notch, you always get stupid drunk and we end up having to taxi back to your apartment.

Everyone's partaking in the vicious *eau de poire* and stumbling toward the salon. I stand up and realize, *Wow, this is good stuff, this . . . what's it called again? It seems to have the effect of halving your intelligence with each sip. Who are these people? God, I'm so drunk it's like they're speaking a foreign language. No, they* are *speaking a foreign language . . . wish I knew which one. Hey, this is cool, I live in Paris. How neat.* "Neat" . . . *that's a very seventies word. This is a great apartment. Is that drunk sexy guy over there my boyfriend? Hmm. Why is he over there?*

Someone puts on a CD by Blondie. Loud. *Very* loud. I can't even make out the words (and I *know* the words). We're all suddenly dancing like complete fools and as the French are hands down the worst dancers on the planet, we look like a rejected group auditioning for *Dance Fever.* Although I gotta say the gay guys are moving with the rhythm and lookin' kinda cool. Alexandre's dragged the evil *eau de poire* into the salon and is still guzzling with gusto. Oh, this is going to get *très* messy later, no question about it.

Patrick's jumping up and down on all the furniture with abandon. Yes, I'd say he's definitely smashed if he's stomping around on his $150,000 Jean Prouvé coffee table. I'm dancing like a maniac, shakin' it like there's no tomorrow when . . . *Ecch! . . . errf, I donf feelf sof gut . . . ouf! mef sinks Imf goo-oona beef si-ckk.*

It seems my whirling dervish dance moves have taken their toll. I make a mad dash to the bathroom down the hall to—how shall I put this?—relieve the discontented *eau de poire* into the *eau de toilette*. Lovely. I've had more elegant moments. I throw cold water on my face and rinse my mouth and try like hell to get a grip. Am I dying? I feel like death is moments away. Oh my God, *again?* Yaaacck! Another Technicolor yawn and I'm shakey with the chills. I stagger back to the party that's still in full throttle, if not hyperspeed. God, could you all stop moving around? And turn that music off or I'm going to upchuck all over this 200,000-euro Aubusson rug and it ain't gonna be pretty. I whimper over to Alexandre, who is now hip-thrusting into Sylvie with the Afro.

"Alexandre, I feel sick, can we go? I'm going to throw up." He keeps dancing, nods and turns back to Sylvie. "Alexandre, *really* . . . I'm going outside to get some fresh air. I'll wait for you, but I have to go, okay?" Again a nod and, *"D'accord!"* he yells above the music.

I leave in a hurry as I'm feeling yet another cresting wave of nausea. I can't wait for the elevator. I can just imagine: me, vomit, a contained space—bad idea. So I approach the stairs, glancing over the bannister. Oh my God . . . circles! I don't even believe, seven flights of circles, oh yeah, that's helpful.

Finally I make it onto the street just in time to "repaint" a Fiat in oysters and sole meunière. This is humilating. Stylish exit? *Not.* Okay, Alexandre, anytime now. I've just finished barfing up that amazing meal (which in fact is good because that was about ten thousand calories I didn't need). I wait leaning against a car, weak and shivering. Fuck, it's been fifteen minutes. I call his cell phone. It's off of course. Twenty-five minutes. What an asshole, he's obviously just ignored me and is having such a good time hip-thrusting Sylvie, he doesn't even give a shit I'm sick to die down here. Le Creep Alexandre, indeed.

With a vengeance, albeit a shaky vengeance, I hike back up the seven flights of stairs, again. FUN! FUN! FUN times seven. Pushing open the door to the apartment, I go back into the salon to see the following unimaginable sight *(and clearly, I have a fucking creative imagination)*: Alexandre is now standing on that Prouvé coffee table, wearing nothing but his tiny, *very* revealing underwear, stripping off all his clothes to the cheers of the group of drunken revelers. Now there's an elegant man for you. Do I have more exciting nights like this to look forward to in the future? Hey, thanks a million for rushing to my aid when I'm ill. And the disrobing bit, *really* refined.

Alexandre—get this—*still* wouldn't leave. Unreal. I yelled a weak *"merci"* to Patrick and Cécile, took my fourth trip on those fucking stairs, and walked home. At four in the morning, Alexandre drunkenly rang my door. Like hell I was going to let him come up. He yelled, "Klein! . . . What's your problem? . . . Fine. I don't want to be your boyfriend. You're a bitch!"

Lovely. What a romantic. In closing, I have to offer a new theory: Frenchmen are a gift. But they are one of those gifts that look so good on the outside, perfectly wrapped, marvellously inviting and *can* be quite disappointing once unveiled. I may be the first person to equate Frenchmen with a well-wrapped box of socks. I realize that in doing so I'm eliminating my chances of winning both the Pulitzer Prize and the Légion d'honneur. Fine. Someone had to say it.

A FEW SLIGHTLY ANNOYING DETAILS I DIDN'T ANTICIPATE

I don't know what the story is with the guy who lives on the floor above me. He looks normal enough, even dresses quite elegantly. But for the love of God, he spends ALL DAY, day after day, walking in heavy-footed circles. Literally at 7:00 a.m. on the dot I can hear him slide out of bed, slip on what I can only guess are gestapo-era steel boots, and commence his "Stalin march" daily rotations. The same pace, the same boots, eight hours a day. I'm going to kill him!

I try to figure out if he's an absent-minded telemarketer with extra energy, or perhaps he's training for some walkathon, or it's some new Zen religion where he must emulate a celestial orbital path. I can't decide if I should donate a rug to him to cushion this maddening rhythmic beat or just discreetly oil the stairs so he takes a nasty fall thereby giving me some fucking peace while he recuperates in a leg cast. It's an ongoing debate. I'll keep you posted.

SUBLIME PLEASURE DU JOUR

There is a gorgeous caramel-colored eighteenth-century building directly across from my apartment that has always been a source of charm to me. Looking across rue de Beaune into this building, I see into the apartment of a classic young bourgeois family. They are a handsome family of four: a young teenage girl, a boy of about nine, and their elegant forty-something parents.

It's a large and beautiful apartment with a mural painted on the ceiling of the *salon* and chandeliers throughout. If I had a family, this is precisely the apartment I'd want, so it's like watching a movie of the life I *should* be having, which is both charming and painful. For example, each Sunday is family day and they all stay home, throw open the lead glass windows and spend the whole day together. The young girl will set up her music stand and play the violin as her younger brother accompanies her on the flute. It's such an enchanting visual. The parents sit on the old Parisian club chairs and listen to their talented and pretty children practice Mozart and Bach. And as the neighborhood is so quiet and deserted on Sundays, the music from this charming duet fills the quarter. Occasionally I'll see a lost tourist stumbling around on their way to Musée d'Orsay and I get to watch them fall upon this experience serendipitously. They'll stop and look up, listen while a smile passes across their face and think as I do, *This really is the most extraordinary city in the world.*

THE FRIEND LOWDOWN

Stella wins the Bestest Girlfriend award for listening to my ongoing ranting and ravings about Alexandre. When your best girlfriend says, "He *so* doesn't deserve you," it's as good as your mother's hug when you'd skin your knee as a kid. Stella's boyfriend seriously doesn't deserve her—jobless, cheap and with crusty hair-goo in his ears, I can't believe she puts up with him telling her she should lose weight. She's five foot seven and a size 6. He's good looking and that seems to be his only positive attribute. Still, she loves him so I'm going to support her in all this until she decides *she's* ready to move on. I bet that's kind of what her attitude is about me and Alexandre, come to think of it. We have totally opposite taste in men, frankly, and neither of us can quite figure out why the other is so madly in love. Especially when we agree on everything else from movie reviews to the best French birth control pill: Diane (it makes your boobs big and clears up your skin. How cool is that? Let's put another hash mark in the "yes" column for France).

We bought Lotto tickets today after a day of shopping in Saint-Germain and discovering everything we want is completely out of our price range. If I win (oh God, could I even claim the reward as an illegal expat?) I'm heading straight over to Kenzo for that sheared beaver coat with embroidered cuffs and the gigantic fur purse with jewelled closure. Then a pit stop at Christian Louboutin for the precious red-soled slingbacks. Ohmigod, I *can't* forget that new lingerie shop on rue Bonaparte, Carine Gilson. Their stuff makes La Perla look like the concierge's housedresses. I literally almost wept caressing a piece of pearl gray pure silk. What? Were the silkworms fed Champagne? The nightgowns are all handsewn with the most beautiful delicate lace ever held by human hands. I was actually afraid to even touch the exquisite little bra and underwear sets, so perfect, so heavenly. Is there a woman lucky enough, somewhere in this city that she just *stocks* her boudoir with these museum pieces? Sex in these exquisite creations would be out of the question . . . even sweating would be tragic . . . just *standing* in them might be risky. I'd be like, "Okay, you've seen it, now it's coming off and going back in its velvet bag. No, no, don't touch *for God's sakes*. This was five hundred euros! Unfortunately I have about as much of a chance of winning the lottery as waking up fluent!

Frankly, *both* would be great.

Zeffirelli, Shoulder Slams, and a Facial at Carita

June

MONSIEUR RIGHT REPORT

Just when I was starting to accept that life with Alexandre was going to be an ongoing emotional roller coaster, he actually took my advice! He went on Prozac. In a month's time, everything miraculously changed. He stopped his anxiety attacks, his confusion faded, and he was finally happy and alive! Alexandre began to work hard at his job, became a lot more thoughtful and was almost, God forbid, like a *normal boyfriend*. He started leaving me little notes in the morning when he'd leave for work before I got up, and did very un-Alexandre things like suggesting we take a bubble bath by candle-light. I was stunned. Delightedly stunned, but the weird thing is, I wasn't convinced this was going to be in *my* best interest as I'd come to believe he only liked having me around because he didn't have his full strength to chase models. Something inside me feared now that he was happy, he'd take his happy perfect ass and leave me in the dust. Still, I wanted him to be well, even if I got the shit end of that stick.

We hadn't seen each other for a couple of days (I was trying the "absence makes the heart grow fonder" theory as my most recent strategy to kick him into high gear) when Alexandre called me one sunny Sunday afternoon.

"Klein, it's me. Are you busy? I need to see you."

"Hi, angel, no, I'm just reading the newspaper with Puccini. What's up?"

"Do you want to meet at Hôtel Montalembert for tea in an hour?" he asked impatiently. Referring to the über-chic modern hotel a street away from my apartment.

"Okay, pumpkin, *à tout à l'heure*," I answered. Even though we always speak in English, I like to drop in a few—okay, *the only*—little bits of French I know, as a gesture. I feel it's nice to occasionally express that I haven't entirely forgotten I live in a foreign country. Thoughtful, *non*?

I hung up the phone wondering what was on his mind. With him you never know, so no sense spending too much time trying to figure it out. I changed clothes from my in-house uniform of paint-spattered jeans and a sweater to a more Alexandre-friendly (read: sexy or tighter, or sexy *and* tighter) ensemble of a hypershort suede skirt and tight cashmere V-neck with high brown boots. A quick spritz of the water lily perfume he loves (which, come to think of it, is the only thing he's ever complimented me on), and I stroll over to the hotel down the street.

Hmm, that's wacky, it's not even four o'clock and his motorcycle is already parked. He's astonishingly on time; this ought to be good. Alexandre is sitting in the back by the fireplace, looking his usual breathtakingly sexy in jeans and a pale blue Dior shirt with cufflinks. (*Love* that look. *Me-ow!*) Looking up, he flashes *that smile*. Jesus. His smile is so gorgeous, so brilliant, it makes Tom Cruise's look like a painfuly repulsive grin. No lie, I've seen Alexandre pass nuns in full habit at Sacre Coeur, and they damn near got whiplash doing double takes.

"Hi, baby, I've missed you," Alexandre says. (A rare moment of expressing any attachment whatsoever to me.) We share a brief kiss and sit down to order two glasses of Champagne, despite the fact it's four in the afternoon and thirteen dollars a glass.

"So, how was your weekend, kiddo? What did you do?" I ask, assuming he probably hung out with his friends Pierre and Cédric.

"Well, this is what I need to talk to you about. You're not going to like this, but . . . I saw my ex-girlfriend. You know, the one I was with when I met you."

"Ah . . . um. Okay," I reply. (Is it too late to change my drink order to a double whiskey?)

"Don't get mad, but . . . we slept together, and I realized, I felt *nothing*, that I could think of nothing but you and I realized . . . that I . . . love you," he said with an eager smile, as though I'd be just as thrilled by the first part of that story as the last. So he went back to his perfect-boobs model and now he "loves" me? This was a little much to stomach all at once. I sat with a vague smile in stone cold silence.

"No, it's really exciting, don't you see, Klein? I've never told ANYONE that I loved them and I'm so happy, so proud that it's *you*." By some seriously twisted network in my unconscious, I filtered out and tossed away the fuck-fest with the ex bit and just homed in on the delicious, long-awaited profession of love. He *loved* me. Ha. Finally. This is it, this is *everything*. Now I can breathe again. He loves me back. Like the romantic love-struck idiot that I am, I swallowed up this news and fell into a passive state of contented bliss. *He loves me,* was all I could think as I looked at him sitting there glowing, looking at me through new eyes.

We drank a couple more glasses of Champagne and reveled in this thrilling moment. (Each of us for very different reasons, as it turned out.) It was as though a floodgate had opened. He was so animated as he leaned in and offered endless invitations to all kinds of upcoming trips and parties, vowing to introduce me to a sea of people he'd previously held at bay. I was "in." Miraculously, the love of his life. The center of his world. "Cool beans," as we say in Wisconsin.

Alexandre paid the bill and we went back to my apartment. I grabbed an overnight bag, jamming in more of that water lily perfume, a bottle of Vichy body oil, and a fresh pair of underwear *pour demain* as he bounced around, and then we jubilantly sped back to his apartment to make love for like, ten hours, thank you. P.S.: If I thought he rocked in bed before, well . . . Oo-osh! Apparently being *the love* of a man's life is a massive aphrodisiac. He created a new benchmark the likes of which I'd never imagined. The French *ooh-la-la—la la* was born for a reason. And yes, the last two *la-la's* make *all* the difference.

For days Alexandre was the sweetest love bug to inhabit the planet. It was "*I love you*" and "*je t'aime*" at every turn. Because he'd never used the "love" word before, he'd tell me constantly, so delighted he actually felt it after so many years and *so* many women. My delight at hearing it only made us both all the more ga-ga. You know, the whole "I love you" . . . "No, I love you *more*" . . . "No, I love *you* more" shenanigans. The six months of waiting made it all that more delicious. Finally, all the pieces fit together. I was ecstatic, and Paris was a dream realized. I patted myself on the back for my courage in thinking it was all possible and that my energy and perseverance had been rewarded. A real, honest-to-goodness delicious Frenchman loved me back and I was *thrilled*.

A week later, Alexandre and I took a trip to Brussels to go to another antique fair (I should tell you that these aren't low-brow, audition-for-*Antiques Roadshow* affairs. They're *really* chic. You could find yourself knocking over a vase and being told, "Madame, that was a wedding gift from Napoléon to Josephine." Oops, *sorry*.)

We drove on Alexandre's motorcycle in the rain to Gare du Nord, to catch the train, getting absolutely soaked to the bone but, as always, laughing hysterically. We were running late because of the torrential rain-paralyzing traffic, dramatically leaping aboard just as the train to Brussels was pulling out of the station. And while I may have got over the sex-in-train-bathrooms fixation, I quickly replaced it with a more generous gift of giving him pleasure as I pretended I'd lost something in his lap. (C'mon. There's nothing men love more, and to play my part in the movie we'd created was always a pleasure . . . Well, *almost always*.)

The next day we got up early, wolfed down a couple of croissants and coffees and taxied to the exhibition hall. It was a dark and still chilly morning when we arrived at seven. Alexandre's few disciplines in life are waking early and making sure he is one of the first to view whatever antiques are exhibited. He has the knack of always being able to talk his way past the other *antiquaires* queing at the front gate. Or, I don't know maybe they just let him in first because he's so damn *gorgeous*.

We excitedly raced in together, both of us scanning the halls for the elusive and important piece that just leaps out from the vast sea of mediocrity. In the last week of our love-induced hysteria, we concocted a fantasy of the two of us moving back to New York City and opening a gallery of furniture and art together. We were going to name it Alexandre Klein—our first "baby," so to speak. *Or so I hoped*.

The joint business venture made complete sense, as we share the same taste and always are drawn to exactly the same object at every fair, exhibit, or show. So later that morning when we came across a 1930s oil painting of a truly beautiful and elegant Asian man, we instantly agreed: it was fabulous, modern and we had to buy it no matter the cost. It would be the first acquisition for our new store, our new life. The dealer was a tough old specimen from Amsterdam and wouldn't budge on the price. A steep four thousand Euros. A glance between us confirmed that this was to be the first challenge to be surmounted by us as a couple. We had to buy the portrait as a sign of our commitment, so we each paid half. Alexandre put the painting under one arm and me in the other, and we promenaded around the fair in elated triumph and in love.

Everything seemed surreal. How could life *ever* be any better then *this*? My dream man smothered me in kisses. (Whereas the pre-Prozac Alexandre could go a whole night without so much as holding my hand.) I could hardly believe how much everything had changed in just a month. I had everything I ever wanted: a sexy, intelligent man, a cool creative idea for a new business, a man who adored children. I was drunk with happiness.

After the walking on air through the rest of the fair, we decided to go celebrate our purchase at a chic little café on the Grand Place. Alexandre, the Asian guy, and I grabbed a taxi and arrived at place Sablon just as an incredible double rainbow arced over the twelfth-century church. I'm fairly sure Franco Zeffirelli was in charge of the sets that afternoon as everything was bathed in a golden light, sparkling in a light mist. We looked at each other in awe, thinking, *Man, what an amazing day*. We ordered Champagne with our Asian man leaning against our table, and the future before us. Sitting by the window to glimpse the fading trace of the twin rainbows, Alexandre asked, in the most charming voice, "What do you call (in English) the wife of my brother?"

"Sister-in-law," I answered without looking up, perusing the menu.

"Klein, would you like to be the sister-in-law of my brother?" (A bit roundabout I agree, but darling.)

I just sat there a second computing if *he* understood what *he'd* just said when he repeated it in more crystal-clear terms: "Would you be my wife?"

I'd never wanted anything more in my life. I felt like I'd won the Lotto, jackpot, Pulitzer, Oscar, and Nobel prizes all in that moment. Delirium.

"You're serious? Really? Oh my God, YES!" I said not even knowing if Alexandre still really knew what he was asking. But he did. And he ordered a bottle of Champagne, telling the waiter, "I just asked her to be my wife!" An older couple at a nearby table overheard and offered their sincerest congratulations. The whole restaurant got caught up in the beautiful moment as word and congratulations spread like wildfire.

Alexandre called his father to tell him. I called my father and mother. I felt like I was on Ecstasy. I couldn't stop smiling, couldn't eat—which if you know me had never happened before or since. We took the train back to Paris that evening, laughing all over again as we arrived to another rain storm, this time with the Asian-man painting in tow. We wrapped him in our coats on the motorcycle (*and* with our luggage, it was like a Chinese acrobat show, swear to God) and we froze to death in the cold rain, wearing only T-shirts. Oh, who cares?! Give me pnuemonia, whatever, my life is *perfect*.

There is a photo of me taken that night, seated below the painting we had just unwrapped and hung on Alexandre's living room wall. I love it, as I am the vision of happiness incarnate (albeit a bit bloated from a lot of Champagne imbibing). My smile is the purest I have ever seen captured on film, my laughing eyes looking into the lens at the man I had loved from the first moment I saw him. That night I fell asleep smiling in his arms with his even warm breaths against my neck.

Now this, *this* is why I moved to Paris.

A FEW SLIGHTLY ANNOYING DETAILS I DIDN'T ANTICIPATE

I think it's safe to say French girls don't like American girls. They may not even like each *other*. Because it can't be screamingly obvious (or *can* it?) that I'm American and I'm getting glares and the evil eye constantly from these chicks. Not to mention they have an amazing way of slamming into you as you walk past on the street. It's not even like the streets are crowded, and time and again I will be ploughed into with a razor -sharp skeletal shoulder by some beautiful *parisienne* creature.

I wonder if it's something they are trained and coached at in grade school: "Listen my little mademoiselles, whenever you should see an attractive girl coming in your direction in the future, remember always to slam into her shoulder with great force. And never—I repeat, never—apologize. To do so would negate the intended hostility."

Now when I see a *parisienne* of a certain type coming, I slam her back with equal force. Gone are my old American apologize-for-what-is-not-your-fault *pardonnez-moi*'s. Forget it, I'm starting to look at these encounters as (1) a good workout and (2) a confirmation that I've put myself together rather well that day.

SUBLIME PLEASURE DU JOUR

I don't know who he is, but an old man passes under my window each and every night whistling such a beautiful little song. Lying in bed, every night at

1:00 a.m. on the dot, I hear the faintest gentle whistle floating through the air and into my room. Then after he passes, it fades slowly away. It is so unbelievably charming, this joyful little tune. At first I was tempted to look out and see him but I stopped myself and decided I adore the idea of not knowing what he looks like. How enchanting, to be entertained by this elderly man who goes out for a private stroll, enjoying his solitude, filling the neighborhood with a bedtime lullaby.

THE FRIEND LOWDOWN

Well, everyone's pretty bloody excited for me after watching my agony of trying to get Alexandre to let go and fall in love with me. It's such a shock for me and all my friends that I've finally landed my love. Stella's a doll. We've already marched through every damn bridal salon in town together.

"Would you like to be a bride festooned with ribbons and enough bows to wrap all the Christmas presents of France?" (At Lacroix.) Or perhaps the first in your family to don a virginal sadomasochistic buckle sheath dress?" (At Gaultier.) What an absolute gas this all is with a girlfriend! If I hadn't met Stella, I'd be lost. Maid of honor, definitely.

Stella and I had to do something to celebrate, so we decided to scrimp on our daily five-euro tiny cups of espresso for a week and splurge on facials the following Tuesday, at the famous Carita Salon on rue du Faubourg Saint-Honoré. She came over in the afternoon and we sat around dishing and made our way through of a plate of pistachio and framboise macaroons from Ladurée tea shop.

"Man, these are luscious, what do you think, two, three hundred calories each?" Stella asks, licking the cream off her fingers.

"I choose not to even think about it, otherwise it kills all the pleasure. All I know is, life's short and you gotta live hard. Abstaining from moments of delicious decadence is way overrated," I offer as justification.

"I'm starting to think that's your motto in life!" she replies with a tinkling little laugh.

"Oh, you kid, but *I'm* the one making the big leap to get married, so my days of 'indulgent activities,' shall we say, are coming to a welcome close."

"We'll see, girl. Have you and Alexandre decided where you're going to get married? I have always dreamt of a wedding in France."

"Oh, I didn't tell you yet? You're going to love this: at his country home in Bourgogne. In Flavigny, the little twelfth-century village from the movie *Chocolat*. You saw the movie, right? In the very same church. God, it's going to be a total dream with all the little old villagers and the ancient bells chiming. His mother's already busy arranging everything. She's lovely. I lucked out there, I have to say, I *really* like her."

"I've got to hand it to you. You know, I've always thought your commitment to him was extraordinary. Even crazy. But it's amazing now how he's changed. I could not be happier for you. What does your father think?"

"Thanks, sweetie. But, yeah, I have to say, it's a little dicey with my father. On one hand, he's happy because I'm out-of-my-mind elated, but he also remembers every time I've called him upset about something Alexandre's said or done. He says he's reserving judgment until he meets Alexandre."

"So, when is your father coming to Paris for the all-important meeting?"

"I think in the next two months. Yikes! Alexandre better be charming to die, and if he drinks on Prozac . . . oh Jesus, it's hilarious. He's like a gigantic, disoriented child. The other night I had to carry him by the scruff of his neck up the stairs. Not pretty. Hey, it's almost five o'clock, we have to go. The appointments are at five-fifteen, right?"

"Yeah, when was the last time you had a facial, a real one?" she asks as we grab our purses and traipse down the narrow stairs of my building to the street.

"Don't ask . . . *years*. How scary is that?" I answer as we begin the ten-block hike over to the Right Bank and up rue de Rivoli. "And you?" I add.

"Would you believe never? That's why I'm so excited."

By rue Saint-Roch Stella and I happen upon a seriously beautiful male model leaving an office building with his portfolio tucked under his arm. He's staggeringly pretty, with baby-smooth skin the color of mocha and probably all of twenty years old in his chiseled perfection. We stop conversation (totally) as he passes, devoting all our energy to this feast for the eyes.

"Holy shit! That guy was unreal. Isn't it funny when you see someone so beautiful your brain just goes into an electrical storm like, *I need that, get me that*. What are you going to do about *that* when you're married, Klein?"

"Trust me, when you get to be my age and you've sampled at least a nibble of everything on the buffet, shall we say, you've had your fill. Now it's just fun, just pleasant to glimpse gorgeous men. I really don't even feel tempted anymore. Frankly, they start to fall into variations on a theme. You know, like okay, *he's* the "twenty-year-old sexy stud, a brain like putty, a body like a rock, and zero idea of who he is" type. And then there are the older ones, for example, a Frenchman, late forties, recently divorced, has a few kids, confident, self-assured but sick of being a father-husband and wants to be a playboy again. He's craving stupid undemanding conversation and breasts that defy gravity. You gotta run in the complete opposite direction of them. And there's guys like your boyfriend, who you know I like, (lie!) but he's a mama's boy, young, hardly knows how to live alone, wants you to cook each night, be an insta-wife and mom. Those kinds of men need an enormous amount of attention but the upside is they generally have respect for women. The ones you've gotta stay clear of are the sexy woman haters. You know, the dudes with Porsches or *worse,* the Ferrari-owning men; they're all about trophies. Generous with lavishing attention on women *but* also obsessed with the physicality of women. You can't trust them as far as you can throw 'em. God, I could go on and on."

"Klein, you kill me. I guess I see your point. Tell me honestly, do you think my Antoine is *good* for me?" she says as we turn onto rue du Faubourg Saint-Honoré. "Hmmm. Yes and no. He's committed to you, this I'm sure of and that's hard to find, as we both know. And in many ways he's a 'combination platter,' full of good intentions, handsome, active, and sweet, but I really think it's totally shitty that he tells you how to dress, that he doesn't like you to go out with your friends. He should give you more freedom and make you feel like you're beautiful. He's fucking lucky to have you and he should worship you and—super important—make you laugh."

"Yipes, you know, you're right. He's not very funny, but he thinks he is, which is so-o-o annoying. If he tells that story of how he used to seduce rich women in LA that hired him to teach them French . . . oh, I'll kill him. *Not* funny, not cool. Hey, at least he'll never give me laugh lines," Stella says with a giggle.

"And *voilà,* we're here. How cool," I announce as we walk the long elegant corridor to enter the Carita Salon. "I kinda feel like we're off to see the Wizard."

"You're nuts," Stella answers as we proceed through the glass doors held open by the uniformed doorman. We give our names to the woman at the *accueil* (reception desk) and are told to go upstairs to await our aesthetician.

"This is chic. It's like a cross between a palace and a sanitarium, a little 'sterile white' for my taste but if they throw in a free dash of electroshock therapy I won't argue."

"Klein, do you *ever* shut off? Keep your voice down," Stella says for the umpteenth time since I've met her, always thinking we have to speak in little whispers so no one knows we're American. I could care less and refuse to become a quiet little mouse just because I live in a different time zone. We ascend the winding staircase to the boudoir–changing room to exchange our carefully chosen we-live-in-Saint-Germain ensembles for luxurious white robes and matching slippers. A little woman in a boxy white linen uniform (*très* Cardin), with a complexion like a bowl of cream offers warm tea with lemon. We sit on luxurious couches, waiting a few moments until we are escorted to our private *chambres*.

"Bye, Stella. When you see me again, I will be unrecognizingly radiant, a mere teenage version of the haggered, leather-faced creature you see standing before you."

"Oh, Klein, please," she whispers as she is whisked off by a small Filipino attendant.

My aesthetician invites me into the dimly lit room where the sound of tides from the white-noise machine creates a quiet hush. She is a formidably built woman of "a certain age," with expressive eyes and a warm, comforting smile. With her golden hair held back in a serious chignon at the nape of her neck and her starched white smock coat, she has the look down right to her soft-soled white shoes. She speaks in calming tones and suggests I slip out of the robe so she can cover me with warm towels. I get naked and catch a glimpse of her eyeing the tattoo on my shoulder. I instantly think, *Listen, sister, don't ask. I got it when I was twenty-two years old. Can we just carry on here?*

"*J'ai un tattoo aussi, une petite poire sur ma hanche.*"

No way, you've got a little pear tattoo on your hip, grandma?! You *are* a hip grandma! Wild. That's the thing about tattoos, you are forever amazed by who has them. I have a hunch Prince Charles has "Camilla Forever" tattooed somewhere . . . my money's on his inner thigh. C'mon it's totally possible. Remember that whole audio tape of their phone chat where he told her he yearned to be her *tampon*? See, a royal tattoo isn't so hard to believe now is it?

I quickly relinquish my general state of heightened nervosity and let myself be lulled into a peaceful state of calm. Frankly, being bundled in cozy towels with a kind, maternal figure caressing my forehead, I feel like I've gone three decades back to being a little infant pampered in my crib. I never want this to end, this is sublime. I'm pretty sure this isn't sexual (well, *pretty* sure?), but the smell of her hands, the respectful gentleness as she strokes my neck? I swear I could almost kiss her. Damn, I could get addicted to this. How expensive could that be? Note to self: *Make enough money one day to pay this woman to come live with me.* I wallow in pampered peace through the hour-long ritual of a milk massage, a *noisette* (hazelnut) scrub, and a *thé vert* (green tea) moisturizing mask after the warm beeswax peel. Apparently the whole bloody garden was dragged across my face. Fine by me, I never felt so, well, *lovely.* We emerge from our dens of serenity, glowing with the skin of babies' bottoms and feeling like princesses. I meet up with Stella already getting changed in the boudoir–dressing room.

"Wow, how are *you*? I'm in la-la land. That was amazing, better than sex with . . . well, most every man I've ever met," I say by way of greeting.

"It was great. I feel so *clean,* like I should just drink water and eat fruit for the rest of my life," she replies with a radiant smile.

"What? Did they give you a high colonic or something?"

"Gross! Shut up. Come on, don't you feel so fresh? We have to do this again, next time my treat," she says as she zips up her boots. Stella and I put our slippers and robes in the lockers and glide down the circular staircase. Arriving at the cashier, I catch the first glimpse of my facial after-glow in the mirror behind the counter.

"Stella! What the hell?! I look like a third-degree burn victim! My face is neon red!" I say in a total panic.

"Yes, I noticed that, but you seemed so happy, I didn't want to ruin it for you."

"But your face doesn't look like raw beef, why does mine?!" I race back up the stairs and hightail it to the aesthetician, who is tidying up her little *chambre.*

"*Pardonnez-moi, madame. Regardez mon visage. C'est comme une tomate. Qu'est-ce que c'est le problème?*" She comes a bit closer to examine my face, which is now turning a molted shade of violet-orange. She smirks, steps back a step and offers, "*Et voilà. Apparemment votre peau est très sensible, évidemment. Peut-être vous êtes allergique à quelque chose. La noisette ou le lait, je ne sais pas. Pas grave après un jour ou deux.*" And with that she scoots off behind some door labeled PRIVÉ. Charming. I'm allergic to nuts, or milk, or pampering? Oh for God's sake, now I have to prance down the hoity-toity rue du Faubourg Saint-Honoré like a giant tomato head?! In Wisconsin I wouldn't even leave the house. This is so "me"—my tremendous luck. I trudge down the stairs and meet up with Stella who is buying some product or another. She's clearly in deep.

"Sure, give them *more* money. *What* are you doing? Look at my face! Can we just go?"

"Oh, Klein, it'll calm down. It's already just . . . really rosy?" Stella tells me with a half smile.

We leave the famous Carita Salon, apparently less well known for its "mincemeat facial" than for its soothing environment. Walking through the Tuileries just as the red afterglow of sunset spreads across the sky, Stella looks at me and begins to laugh. "Look at it this way, you are the color of the radiant sun setting in Paris," she says animatedly, flourishing her arms in the air.

We stroll back to the 7th arrondissement roaring with laughter, knowing that in life there are good days and bad, but it's still always better to have a bad day . . . in Paris.

A Skaggy Whore, Proust, Palais Royal, and Sexy Boys

July

MONSIEUR RIGHT REPORT

Like the third act of a tragic love story, everything began to spin out of control. My control, that is. Alexandre went off Prozac too soon, claiming the sexual side effects were frustrating. And panic set in. He went through a phase that I can only imagine a lot of men experience: "Am I supposed to be with just this one woman forever?" It was horrible to watch. And more horrible to be that one woman! He stopped telling everyone we'd run into that we were getting married. He postponed the date from four months away to ten. After four weeks we were starting to argue and after dinner one evening, *chez* Alexandre, he found himself compelled to tell me "something important." (I hope you're sitting down.)

Having just polished off a bottle of Brouilly and a great dinner of fettuccini with gorgonzola sauce (calorie count: don't even fucking calculate it), we took up our usual positions in the living room. Me on the black 1950s couch and him on the Marc Newson leather chair. I felt the alcohol just enough to think I could deal with whatever he was going to throw at me. Frankly, being sedated by an elephant tranquilizer dart would've been more helpful than three glasses of wine.

"So, kiddo, what's the big, important thing you want to tell me?" I said casually as I lit my traditional after-dinner cigarette. Alexandre just sat there on his leather throne, staring at me with a sad, pained expression. He tucked his legs up under his body like a little boy, and wrapped his arms around his knees. *Okay, he's going into a fetal position, this isn't going to be good.* The smile fell off my face, and I suddenly felt like I knew what was coming—but I didn't. Oh, not by a long shot.

"You know I love you, right?" Alexandre said, grimacing.

"Yeah . . . ?" I mumble, terrified. (Now what? Why do I feel this is going to kill me? I have only had, like, one month's happiness with you. What the hell are you doing now?)

"Baby, listen, I'm not saying that I don't want to marry you. I just think it's important that I tell you I'm having a bit of a hard time with an aspect of this whole . . . *'une femme'* thing."

I nod, feeling all the blood drain from my face. Okay, asshole, let her rip.

"I have to tell you, you are not exactly . . . physically . . . my, how do you say? . . . my *fantasme.*"

"You mean 'fantasy'? I am not your physical fantasy?" I say, not even believing I'm having this conversation.

"Yeah, that's the word. It's maybe . . . strange to you but I've always been attracted to women who were . . . sort of perfect . . . physically. Dark hair, olive skin, dark eyes, and . . . bigger breasts, to be honest. You're beautiful, really, but not what . . . I prefer. Do you understand me? I just am struggling with that . . . because . . . I'm in love with you, but I'm not . . . attracted to you."

"What . . . what are you saying? You're NOT attracted to me? Then why do you fuck me all the time? Trust me, it's almost impossible for a guy to fuck someone he's not attracted to. What the hell? For my age (God, am I really old enough to start putting that in conversation as a defense?), I rock! I run every day, I'm five foot ten weigh 126 pounds with a 34C cup and that's not okay? (My voice is starting to get louder as I sift through the reality of this insanity and, frankly, cruelty.) You are so fucking full of shit, if you think the exterior of someone is that important. Fuck!! You've told me so many times how you were bored to tears with your last girlfriend. For all her fucking physical perfection you said it got so unbearably dull and now . . . now you tell me my skin is the wrong COLOR? You're fucking crazy! That is so shallow and . . . so bullshit. You have a REAL problem, kiddo. A REAL PROBLEM!"

I was shaking with rage. At my bad judgment, at my stretch marks, at my pathetic, shaky voice yelling at him, trying to defend my body. What in the hell has happened that I've spent my whole life growing to accept myself, my flaws and choosing to focus on becoming an intelligent, self-sufficient woman, who's a great sister and friend, and here I am, being made to feel bad because my eyes are green and not brown. This is beyond my comprehension. God, even in the fifth grade, no boy was so cruel and judgmental. And back then I looked exactly like a boy with short hair, a sway back, and legs like sticks. And now, at this age, someone's trying to diminish me. NO FUCKING WAY!

I get up and, without another word, haul ass into the bathroom, throw everything that belongs to me in my purse and plant myself in front of a stunned Alexandre, still sitting in the chair. He speaks first.

"Klein, I never said I didn't love you. I just thought that it was occasionally a problem and would get worse with time, and that we should start talking about it, because I still . . . fantasize about that 'ideal woman' and—"

"You know what? Fuck it. Forget it. You are far too immature and have no right to make me feel bad about myself. You're not perfect, not MY fantasy (okay, I'm so lying here and that's what's really killing me, you ARE my fantasy, and that's as screwed up as my not being yours; oh, the irony) and I love you for WHO you are, not just how you look (this is true, I'm half redeeming my integrity). I deserve better and while I may not be your fucking fantasy, I am somebody's. And I'm going to find him. I'm going home. Don't call or come after me." With that I storm out the door, getting increasingly pissed as he doesn't yell "stop" or come after me.

I walk home the twenty blocks from the 17th arrondissement to the 7th. The streets are empty except for a few cars and late-night revelers and I slowly begin to calm down. In the 17th, I'd been in my initial phase of screaming out loud, "What a motherfucker!" In the 1st arrondissement, I was in tears, and by the 7th, silent fury. The whole gamut of mourning in a single three-mile walk: denial, sadness, acceptance, and anger. As I'm walking over the beautiful Pont-Royal, dazzling in the mist, I think, *we used to call this "our" bridge. Fuck that. I claim this bridge in the name of ME, for all that is decent and good, goddammit!* Queer of me, but I felt better.

The next evening I refused to see Alexandre. I stayed at home trying to plot a strategy to repair my heart and tried to figure out a way to continue to walk the planet, when he called. I told Alexandre he was "free" for the evening, he said, "Free forever?"

"God, I don't know. Whatever. I have to think," I replied limply.

I hashed this out with my friends (long distance at one euro a minute sobbing the entire time—getting depressed as an expat ain't cheap). Everyone I knew concurred that Alexandre was one seriously immature boy. And if I cherished a scrap of doubt, by two o'clock the next day, the diagnosis was confirmed in stratospheric proportions.

The following morning was a Sunday. I woke up awash in panic. I didn't know why, but I had to talk to Alexandre. I didn't want him back, I didn't want anything specific. I just had to hear his voice. His phone was shut off. Weird for noon. No one sleeps that late. Especially Alexandre. I decided to go to his house. I had never ever done that unannounced before. I was drawn to find him, to see him. I just threw on a cheesy pair of corduroys (don't get me wrong, they were Helmut Lang; crazed or not, this is still Paris) and a denim jacket and jammed some money in my pocket.

I fled across the Tuileries to catch a cab on rue de Rivoli. After a heart-racing taxi ride, where I just sat in the backseat in dazed silence, I arrived at the front of his building. Alexandre's motorcycle was still there, so he was inside. I called to announce myself—phone still off. I buzzed the door buzzer—no answer. I yelled below his window—zip. Okay, maybe he walked to the *boulangerie,* or he's running, I'll wait.

I sat on his motorcycle and waited. After forty-five minutes, the door to his building opened. I looked up to see a slightly dishevelled dark-haired woman walk out and pass by me with an evil, knowing smile. We both turned to look over our shoulders at each other as she passed. Then she laughed and crossed the street. *That's it, that's why I'm here. No, this is crazy. She wasn't even remotely pretty, and bowlegged to boot. Yeah, but in a rather exaggerated way that suggests men slide between those thighs with great frequency.* (Allow me to be catty; this woman just fucked my fiancé and I knew it.) She laughed! That bitch looked at me and laughed. I broke into a sweat, a stupor of nausea. I was going to wait out this ugly scene at all costs. About twenty minutes later, Alexandre came out, looked at me stunned, and burst into a big, nervous smile.

"Klein, what are you doing here? What a great surprise."

"Oh come on, Alexandre. You didn't hear me buzzing your door? Yelling your name? Don't fuck with me. I saw her leave," I reported, thinking, *If I'm right, he's trapped, there is no way out of this.*

Making a face like, *Oh you silly girl,* full-on with a tilt of the head and that heart-melting smile, he said, putting his arms around me, "Klein, I love you. I was in the shower. Why would I not answer if I heard you? I was playing music. Come on! There was no woman, don't be paranoid, you never trust me. Let's go for brunch, I'll take you to that place you like on rue Cherche-Midi. Come on, here's your helmet," he said, getting on his motorcycle.

I didn't buy it, but I couldn't be sure and I knew the only way to be sure was to spend the day with him, to watch him. I was just going to buy time to get into that apartment and find the clues that probably were scattered all over his ever-so-groovy apartment. At dusk we went back to his apartment. I have to say he did a pretty good job of obscuring evidence. But I was on a mission. Let's see: two coffee cups in drying rack, fresh sheets on bed, two towels in the bathroom drying, and—the pièce de résistance—a woman's name and phone number tucked in his bag (can you blame me for looking?), written with the same red pen sitting on the coffee table. My heart sank. I stayed at Alexandre's that evening simply because I was too paralyzed to move.

The next morning he gave me a ride on his motorcycle back to my house and I tried to play it cool, holding back the flood of tears until I was safely back at home. He didn't deserve to see me crumble in front of him again. As I walked up the stairs to my apartment, I realized I could hardly lift my legs, barely focus on putting the key in the lock. The minute I got inside, I did the worst thing I could've done. But it was the only iron-clad way to confirm what I knew to be true, short of a confession from Alexandre himself: I called this skaggy whore, Carine. Incredibly, "Cah-reene" confirmed it all, evidently enjoying it more then a little. "*Oui, j'ai passé hier soir avec Alexandre. C'était un plaisir.*" And with that, she hung up on me. Fine, bitch, it's not like I was going to invite you over for tea.

I felt betrayed and beaten, lied to and unattractive. I could hardly breathe. I didn't deserve this; I gave that creep more love then I ever gave anyone— real, total, unconditional love. I couldn't stop thinking of all the times I helped him out of his dark thoughts, all the times I played cheerleader to his every idea. What a waste.

Now that I had the confirmation and the evidence, "dying" was on the agenda, but first it was time to fuck with him. Pity he's a kick-boxer, I have a right hook that is so wanting to make impact. Or at least I think I do, never had an opportunity to test it. Maybe I've just bragged about it so long, I've even come to believe it. I digress. sorry. It's an attempt to avoid the painful reality. I threw on my coat, left my purse on the floor, and ran back to his gallery to confront him. Damn near shattered the glass door as I blasted into the gallery and yelled, "Alexandre! I've got to talk to you. NOW!" Waving in his face Cah-reene the skaggy whore's phone number, written in his handwriting, I demanded, "So, Alexandre, wanna tell me who the hell Carine is?"

He tried to say she was "just a friend" (does anyone actually ever buy that story?), that she gave him her number at the party he'd gone to the night before. I knew that was coming, and I was ready.

"Nice try, smart guy: red pen from your house and written on your notepaper!"

He pathetically attempted a counterattack. "You went in my bag?! I can't believe you dug through my bag!"

"Oh, please, Alexandre, give me a break. Give it up. You're so fucking busted," I said in a rage so fierce, my temples were throbbing.

Finally Alexandre admitted it. And I unleashed hell. I screamed like a banshee in front of his little world of fellow *antiquaires,* "You are such an ass-hole! Take your fucking models and go fuck yourself. You'll be bored to tears and you'll have lost me, you shallow piece of shit. Fuck off!" After my Tourette's-like curse-fest, I flew out the door and ran back to my apartment where I called his parents and then mine, told them what had happened, and sobbed that obviously the wedding was off. Hanging up the phone, I wished I were dead.

Devastated, I couldn't imagine my exile from happiness would ever lift. It was practically impossible to peel myself off the floor. So much time and energy wasted on such a worthless man.

I tried to call Stella but her phone was off as she was in class. Floris, my savior, rushed over and comforted me. After a few hours of shrieking in anger, mixed with intermittant crying, I finally took a muscle relaxant Floris gave me, called Klonopin. Stopped sobbing, pulled myself into my bed, and slept like a log. The next day I woke up—no, woke is too strong a word; crawled into consciousness is more like it—feeling like I'd been dragged from the depths of the sea. Apparently the name Klonopin is an abbreviation for KLobbered ON the head with a rOlling PIN. My conversation was limited to such intelligent witticisms as "Blerrggh," "Slarrghha," and "Kahgnd." I sounded like a drunken Viking. For once, I was glad to be alone.

But there was still no escape from the pain. All my usual distractions— alcohol, cigarettes, books, food—nothing could ease my misery. Frankly, I could barely lift my arms. No wedding, no boyfriend, and every beautiful memory destroyed. All my faith in life, in love, in men has just been washed away in a huge, destructive flood, leaving nothing behind but rotten tree stumps, cigarette butts, garbage, and dark clouds. I don't care if I get fat, die of starvation, get hit by a truck . . . nothing.

To my astonishment, life just continues to chug along, bringing with it wave after wave of sadness. I go stand on "our" bridge, the Pont-Royal (I know, bad idea), which has never failed to fill me with serenity. This time, I feel nothing. This is the first time Paris has failed to lift my mood. What a shitty experience. No, really. I wouldn't wish it on my worst enemy and, frankly, for all the character-building maxims like "What doesn't kill you makes you stronger," I could have easily taken a pass on this experience.

A FEW SLIGHTLY ANNOYING DETAILS I DIDN'T ANTICIPATE

Could it be more obvious? Having to carry on after being handed the Cheating–Marriage Over card really sucked the big one. I had to crawl back into the reality (at least the one I live in) that at age thirty-five I wasn't exactly a *poulet d'été* (spring chicken) and couldn't lick my wounds too long. The proverbial biological clock is like a fucking gun to my head. And thanks, *Time* magazine, for that timely article about early infertility I read over breakfast at the Flore. That's a real help.

SUBLIME PLEASURE DU JOUR

Have you ever read the book *How Proust Can Change Your Life*? I had seen it umpteen times in the bookstore and dismissed it as a hokey idea. (Yep, that's probably the first time Proust and hokey have ever been mentioned in the same sentence.) But what I once thought was a crock of shit appears to be surprisingly possible. Without a television, *beaucoup d'amis,* or a sex life, I've spent a helluva lot of quality time with myself delving into every French author I can get my hands on. And I can confirm that Proust is a Genius, with a capital *G*. (As if you need me to tell you that.) All those references to *Remem-*

brance of Things Past suddenly make sense. I had always been intimidated and daunted to delve into even one of the seven books before. To read it now, while living in Paris, is perfection.

His perceptions on emotions, the innermost depths of human thought, are just astonishing in their precision. Each sentence is so eloquent you want to read it two or three times, savoring every word. I'm one of those people that abhors bending a corner to mark a page. I shriek if so much as a crumb falls into one of my precious books, but with Proust I'm compelled to get out the old highlighter and mark up the whole damn book to fix each beautiful phrase in my memory. Looking back now it would've been wiser to highlight what didn't enchant me—the whole book is now neon yellow and ravaged from thumbings and rereadings.

THE FRIEND LOWDOWN

My buddies have rallied around me and, like the true friends they are, cursed Alexandre and condemned him to hell. Stella's been a good egg, immediately bringing over Rice Krispie treats, As you can imagine, it's almost impossible to find the ingredients for them in Paris. *Quelle amie!* And Stella and I have taken up playing tennis. Which, mind you, I was once very good at. And now? It seems I lost that skill about the same time I started wearing a bra. (Come to think of it, at about that same time I also lost the ability to look great in boys' jeans, to wake up "cute," and to have flawless skin. Puberty. What a raw deal.)

We play on the sun-splashed courts in the Luxembourg Gardens. It's so gorgeous that it doesn't matter that we spend all our time yelling to each other, "Oh, sorry!" It's so not about exercising. (What am I saying? Of course not, this is France where you only break a sweat uncorking a stubborn bottle of wine.) But like everything in France, playing tennis involves a little bureaucratic, time-consuming nonsense. *Mais, bien sûr.* Don't think you just stroll up to an empty court and start playing. Oh no, you've got to go to a little ramshackle booth by the courts, pay five euros, prove you live in the area (Stella does), and then put your name on the bottom of a long list for that day and then find a place to wait in the vicinity until they call out your name. This extravaganza takes the whole afternoon. Fine by us, because we get to sit, gab, read French *Vogue,* look at men, get tea at the snack bar and, well, pretty much hang out all day in our tiny tennis skirts. Two tall, blonde girls in tennis skirts, in Paris. This is rare in Paris and, frankly, with my beaten-ego-care-of-Alexandre, I soak up the attention like a desperate sponge. Embarrassing to admit but true.

And Floris, my angel, has taken me out to get "air" and on one occasion to just sit at Bar du Marché getting stupid drunk. With a bottle of rosé on ice, we sat and watched all the really cute boys saunter by, taking turns grabbing each other's knees in a frenzy. "Ohmigod, look at HIM!" Floris bellowing, "Now that one. Oh, dear me, I believe he's carrying a hammer in his pants." And we howl with laughter. But you can't blame us, the sexy young garçons at Bar du Marché are just scrumptious to ogle. In their groovy jeans slung low on their skinny hips, tight white T-shirts and lithe bodies, mmmm. It's extremely easy to forget that lump of shit Alexandre with hair on his squishy shoulders. (Then later I sober up and cry for hours missing him all over again.) Sobriety is evil these days. To be avoided. Recently I stumbled upon the marvelous poem "Be Drunk" by Charles Baudelaire that hit a note:

Be drunk, always. Nothing else matters; this is our sole concern. To ease the pain as time's dread burden weighs down upon your shoulders and crushes you to earth, you must be drunk with respite.

Drunk with what? With wine, with poetry, or with virtue, as you please. . . . But be drunk.

Mr. Catch-o-Paris, Cinderella, and *Escargots*

August

MONSIEUR RIGHT REPORT

After the ever-so-fabulous morning of catching my fiancé sleeping with another woman, I realized I could either go blind with rage, hole up in my apartment devouring pastries day in and day out, or choose to go on. In truth, I did all three, in exactly that order. Amazingly, it is possible to tire of buttercream and pure dark chocolate. Who knew? Stella commanded me to pull myself together and leave the safe confines of my apartment. What? Do you mean there's a problem with spending all your days and nights trying to teach your cat French? At least it was a project, okay? Not to mention I still hadn't quite finished that voodoo doll I was so busy with.

"Klein," she said, "getting fat and agoraphobic isn't the best revenge; happiness is." "Oh, I was under the impression looking good was. But all right, I'll put on a good front and get back in the saddle."

Stella lured me out with an invitation to accompany her to a birthday party of, supposedly, the greatest catch in Paris. Meaning: an elegant, prominent, single, successful businessman who happened to be both wealthy and, for the moment, unattached. This would be like competing for the Ironman Triathlon with a hangover. I was feeling neither desirable nor social, so pulling myself together was going to be a tremendous effort.

"Stella, I know it sounds like a fun party but what I don't need is to meet some fabulous man when I have all the confidence of a bird that's just flown into a plateglass window."

"You're coming. And by the way, his name is Charles. Charles Barthes. I'll pick you up at eight o'clock." Click. Hmm. Maybe it would be fun to wear something other than pyjamas. And I have actually finished organizing my teas by country and region, so I guess I'm free tonight. All right, then. Onward!

I am going to give you the "highlights, evening wrap up" about this whole Mr. Catch-o-Paris night. Frankly, I only have retained a few, fleeting images of recollection. It went something like this: Stella picks me up in a taxi, I attempt to finish my eyeliner in transit, taxi hits a pothole, and I end up blacking out a tooth with eye pencil, consider leaving tooth black just to see reaction from the Parisian Elite crowd, Stella and I laugh until we almost pee our pants at the idea of it, abandon idea as way too dangerously wacky for this group, clean tooth, powder nose, and arrived at fabulous party *chez* Charles's opulent apartment which overlooked les Invalides' glittering gold dome. We were greeted warmly by a room full of wealthy Frenchmen in their midforties, scowled at by their French wives and girlfriends in their midthirties, and spotted and made a direct beeline for Mr. Catch-o-Paris. Nice surprise in that he resembled the sexy actor Jean Reno, got wind of his easily "the worst on the planet, damn near set my eyebrows aflame" breath (bad surprise). He launched into a soliloquy of his pretentious stories—"I do so enjoy to charter a Gulfstream to take my friends on holiday with me. Frankly, if you can't go by private jet there is really no point in going"—which made me further recoil, back pedal, and seek gasps of fresh air on one of his five beautiful terraces. I sent Stella back over to him for breath confirmation, reached full agreement on said issue of fatal halitosis, scanned room for possible Plan B. Man, out of luck. For distraction consumed mass quantities of sushi from silver trays, tried to appear fabulous and happy, failed on both fronts, drank flute after flute of Champagne, accidently responded honestly in a conversation when a flirtatious troll asked, "Where's the most exotic place you've ever had sex?" Answered, "The church of Saint-Sulpice." Cringed, wished I could've hit the erase button, graciously gave Mr. Catch another go, discovered his breath from hell was made now exponentially worse when combined with his cigar. Made mental note: *Bad breath is the assassin of desire regardless of all other attributes, including appearance.* Vowed to carry Altoids at all times. Drank more in attempt to revive faux "fun mood," moderately successful, left by midnight à la Cinderella (if she were drunk). I managed to not yell at Stella when she told me in taxi on way home she gave Mr. Murder by

Breath/Catch-o-I-Think-Not, my phone number. Unlike Cinderella, but rather astonishingly, given my condition, made it home with both shoes but, alas, no prince. Fell into bed, still unable to shake the feeling that over-whelmed me: missing Alexandre.

A FEW SLIGHTLY ANNOYING DETAILS I DIDN'T ANTICIPATE

While, yes, it was unbelievably great and convenient to live one short block away from Alexandre's antique gallery when we first met, now that we've split (breakup no. 10,792 I think, for us) it's not so funny-fun anymore. To be forced to see your fucking ex-boyfriend by chance five or six times a day is torture. If I go to the corner grocery store, go for cigarettes, go for lunch, go to the Sennelier art supply store, chances are pretty rich we'll smack right into each other. Usually Alexandre's surrounded by a batillion of fellow *antiquaire* friends, all laughing and relaxed, and I'll be making a mad dash to the phar-macy to buy Maalox in some bedraggled state.

So now I have to try to look perfect every single goddamn time I step out-side my door between eleven in the morning and seven at night. Just in case. And seeing his motorcycle still parked in front of his gallery at seven-thirty makes me want to throw up, because it reminds me of his (our) habit of invit-ing girls (me, at the time) over after closing for a glass of Champagne, roman-tically nestled on some eighteenth-century daybed with five sparkling chandeliers overhead. My mind turns inside out thinking, *Who the hell is he with? That bitch. That bastard. You can both go to hell.* (Clearly not quite over the breakup just yet I suppose.) Note to self: *Don't date men who live, work, or habitually hang out within a block's radius! The money saved on taxi fare is so not worth the trouble.*

SUBLIME PLEASURES DU JOUR—TROIS!

• The cleanliness of the French métro. With the elegant Art Nouveau signs (at least the old ones) at the entrances, and its quiet efficiency, I'm *très* impressed. The Paris subway is so vastly superior to the New York City subway, which is always filled with such a glum and de-pressed group it's like climbing aboard the Suicide Express. The métro is sparkly clean, with fun jump seats that can be pulled down, and, thank God, no one cutting their toenails or stretched out dead drunk on the floor. The only slightly disturbing thing may be a group of musicians with an accordion, bellowing out an old French tune. That can get a wee bit old if you're battling a hangover. (*"Monsieurs, there's five euros in it for you if go you to the next car, ça va?"*)

• *Escargots.* I never quite understood their appeal until I came to France (the same goes for the bidet!). I am now addicted to those tiny little devils drenched in parsley and butter, served on a bed of coarse sea salt from Île de Ré, and washed down with a cold, dry white wine. (*"Les escargots à la Bourgogne pour moi, s'il vous plaît."*) People say oysters are erotic—oh, not to me. I feel like I'm choking down the phlegm of the sea. No amount of lemon juice or chili sauce can convince me otherwise. Plus it's a hell of a lot more fun to say *"escargots"* than "oysters," which sounds like a belch in comparison.

Le Procope in the 6th and Brasserie Lipp on boulevard Saint-Germain do *escargots* to perfection. Little tip: They taste best when you're dressed to kill. And feel free to borrow a pretentious lap dog as it's a *de rigueur* accessory *chez* Lipp.

• I simply adore the honorific title "Monsieurdame." It is used to address a man and woman who are quite obviously a couple, perhaps as they enter a restaurant or walk down the street together hand in hand. *Par exemple, "Bonsoir Monsieurdame, vous êtes vraiment élegants ce soir, vôtre table est prête."* Somehow, it sounds so regal; as though you're being announced to "The Ball" at Versailles, amidst a blast of trumpets. Of course, it's just *Monsieur* and *Madame* combined, but it connotes a special union, addressed with respect. I am a sucker for that stuff, you know.

THE FRIEND LOWDOWN

Stella's taken a job part-time at the Bibliothèque Nationale to bolster her resume. Since we are stuck together like glue, I come to her for her lunch hour. I'll grab a couple of *baguettes de thon* from the *boulangerie* and scurry over to the gardens in Palais Royal to meet up with her. Sitting by the gorgeous circular fountain, the sun at our backs, in traffic-free peace, we settle in for a high-speed chat. There's a lot to cover in just under an hour so the conversation is a tag team of updates.

"So, Klein, what's the latest? Or should I say, who's the latest?"

"Very funny. I'm just completely over this dating business. So over it. Did I tell you the text message that guy Stephan sent me last night an hour before I met him? He actually wrote, "Wear the highest heels and the shortest skirt tonight." Come on, how offensive is that? It's like saying, "Listen, you are an object to parade around, is that clear?" Oh, VERY. I was going to text back, "Go straight to hell, do not pass Go or collect two hundred dollars." I wanted to entirely cancel on him, but then I thought, *No, "one better" is to go, wear the heels, the skimpy skirt, look fabulous, and don't so much as even give him a kiss. Just look fabulous, torment him and say, "Thanks for dinner, you can drop me at home now."*

"Klein, did you actually do that?"

"Yeah, I just left him—in dire need of a very cold shower. Fuck Stephan, he's got a warped image of women."

"You poor thing. You have the worst luck with men. Hey, cool bag. Is it new?" Stella asks about my black leather purse with white top-stitching leaning on the foot of my chair.

"Yeah, would you believe I found this at Agnès b. 40% off? Sold! It's really great. Check this out, it has a pocket for your cell phone, a place for your credit cards. Groovy, no?" We shift our metal chairs to face the sun directly and the chair legs scratch on the gravel as we turn. We gobble up our remaining sandwiches, alternating with sips of Coca Light and brushing baguette crumbs off our laps.

"Hey, what ever happened to that guy you met at Café Marly a week ago . . . Olivier?" she asks.

"You know, I liked that guy. He had a shot. He was really elegant and distinguished, and shy, which is a rare combination. We met for brunch at Flore last Sunday and when he sat down I damn near fainted and fell over because in broad daylight, he had all these repulsive veins all over his forehead." Stella breaks into laughter.

"No, really, Oh my God, Stella, it was like his skin was paper thin and completely transparent. I could almost do a visual white blood cell count!"

"Klein, you are the absolute meanest."

"And I'm not even telling you about Mr. Vellum Head's lo-o-ong nose hair."

"Stop! I beg you, I'm eating."

"Oh, I know I'm terrible, doing exactly what I hate in men, judging guys on their looks. But you know, he was probably looking at me thinking, 'Wow, I didn't realize she was so haggard. She definitely looked better in dark lighting.' Listen, I'm not looking for the handsomest man on the planet, but I don't think I can stomach being with a guy where after dinner I'd have to say, "Honey, you have mustard on your nose hairs.""

We laugh together and Stella takes out her compact to reapply her perfect cinnamon mauve lipstick. I reach for my Dunhill Super Lights. "Let's switch chairs so I'm downwind or the smoke will blow in your eyes," I suggest.

"No, it's okay. Sometimes cigarette smoke smells strangely good." I light up as she tilts her head back for maximum sun exposure.

"And what about that Italian writer guy? Fabrizio? You once spent an entire weekend talking about him. How he was so 'maddeningly interesting' to talk to and all that, I swear you seemed quite smitten."

"Did I? *Au contraire,* Stella. I'll admit Fabrizio's smart as hell and gloriously handsome but he made me absolutely crazy. I walked away from him feeling this dizzying mental storm. That can't be a good thing," I say, making a smoke ring in the air.

"No, I suppose not. Klein, do you ever think we should just move back to the States and find good American men?"

"I never thought I'd say this, but, yeah, maybe. Whenever I talk to my friends at home, like, Charlotte or Yasmin—I told you about them, right? Both fashion designers? They're both married to lovely men. Smart, wonderful, kind men who worship them and when I tell them my horror stories, they just say, 'God, what are you doing? Come back!' "

"Oh, I know. My friends back home are all with their 'soul mates,' buying houses, having chidren, and here we are with men who tell us precisely what they don't like about our bodies, telling us how to dress to please them. God, did I tell you Antoine asked me, if he'd pay for it, if I'd have breast implants. Isn't that revolting?" Stella says, taking off her sunglasses.

"No way! Stella, that's it! I can't believe you don't just tell him to go to hell. That's repulsive!"

"Not only that, but he wants me to be a D-cup. I just got up and left him in the middle of dinner at Le Petit Zinc, I swear to God he wants me to look like a complete bimbo—arghh!"

"Plus, with his crappy paycheck he probably could only afford one boob!" I say, trying to make her laugh.

"So true. Life in Paris is pretty frustrating sometimes."

"Yes, but it's so unbelievably beautiful!" I reply, gesturing to the fountain and the rainbow that had formed in its mist, with the opulent arcades of Palais Royal as a backdrop.

"I know. I can never imagine actually leaving . . . Can you?"

"Never. I'm completely wed to Paris, regardless of the constant frustration with the men. Hey, what if we stop thinking about men all the time? Let's just focus on our work, making our own lives, doing all the things we like to do," I say with real conviction, grinding my cigarette out in the gravel.

"Yes, dammit! We're great . . . To us!" Stella replies, lifting her Coca Light can in a mock toast.

"Yes, to us! Two blonde American girls trying to make a go of it! We shall persevere, or die trying!" I declare, feigning Napoleonic seriousness.

"Crap, it's two o'clock. I gotta get back to work," Stella says, gathering her purse.

We stand up and smile at each other, a quick double-cheek air kiss, acknowledging we have another bitch-session under our belts and are stronger for it. Thank God for that girl.

And I'm also delighted to report, I've done the impossible—I've made friends with a French girl. Her name is Albertine. We were introduced by Floris at one of our *apéritif rendez-vous* at L'Hôtel on rue des Beaux-Arts. With her long mane of dark cascading hair, perfect full ruby lips, and flawless skin, Albertine is so fucking beautiful. I find myself thinking, *God, what must it be like to be her, to look in the mirror each morning and say, "Ah yes, ravishing as always!"*

And I admire her enormously, not only for being open-minded enough to tolerate my terrible French-studded-with-English chatter, but for being wise beyond her years. Her attitude toward her husband and men in general is so self-assured and simple: "Just love them and they will love you back. Nothing else matters." I would need a genetic transplant to ever adopt that attitude. Though, God knows I'm trying.

Monsieur Murder by Breath,
Bon Courage, and Andy Wahloo

September

MONSIEUR RIGHT REPORT

Why am I doing this? I've gone through the whole hoopla of getting dressed up and have come to Café de Flore to wait for a man I don't even like. I'm probably doing it because I spent the whole weekend alone, painting in a silence so complete I could hear myself blink. So I've agreed to dinner with Charles (Monsieur Catch a Whiff of That Vile Breath), who turns out also to be a crashing bore. Even the fun of dragging out my chic clothes to give them a night out doesn't seem worth it now that I'm here, waiting for that breath to clear my sinuses—if not the entire room.

Christ. Whatever. I can suffer through an expensive dinner. Definitely clever of me to arrive a half hour early, so I can indulge in a pre-aperitif aperitif. Charles will be infinitely more tolerable viewed through a drunken haze. I'm evil. Or honest. Or maybe both. God, if only he'd do something about that vicious breath. Charles is really handsome, elegant looking, single . . . even rich. But ble-e-e-ch. I guess he'd be a catch if you had no olfactory or auditory sense receptors. Hey, what if maybe that foul respiration was a one-time thing? Perhaps tonight he'll be palatable. No, because that absurd pretentiousness would still be hardwired like . . . OH MY GOD! Check out that guy!

Sitting four tables away is a truly handsome creature. Now him, I would kill to meet him. Why can't I be with a guy like that? He is staggeringly attractive, with thick brown hair and luscious dark eyes that stand out against heavy, tired eyelids. Cool eyes, they give him sort of a lazy-sexy-puppy-dog look. Oh, come on, you know what I mean. He's sitting in profile to me, surrounded by files and documents, talking on a cell phone while his (clearly British) pinstripe suit (possibly Paul Smith), falls slightly open revealing a lipstick-red silk lining. He's just my cup of Earl Grey. All right, I'm staring. No time to be a shy girl once you hit thirty-five years old. Dude! I'm over here! Dammit, he doesn't even notice me. I'll stand up, take off this black-and-white houndstooth coat with a flourish and make such a scene, I'll look like I'm leading a drum and bugle corps.

Foo-oo-sh! Yep, that did the trick. *Bonsoir,* gorgeous. Thank God, he caught my eye. I give him one of those looks that screams, *I'm alone, you're alone, I want you, but I'm trying to play it cool.* I'm madly loving him, that nose, dear me, so regal. Classically French. Fantastic, he's finally off the phone. The waiter brings him a large glass of white wine and places it on the table among his huge stack of papers. A Workaholic-Alcoholic? Hmmm. Could be my first. Why not? Why are you working on a Sunday night at eight o'clock, gorgeous? Oh, I've got a few questions for you all right, like do you possibly harbor a lifelong unfulfilled dream of marrying an insecure American girl and having loads of kids? God, maybe he's an overworked businessman who never took the time to realize how devastatingly beautiful he is.

He looks over again. But, man, he's discreet, not even a smile. Maybe I don't look that great tonight but I'm (head check) the best thing here, so look alive, kiddo. Let's see here (time check) I've got a good fifteen minutes until über-punctual, über-repulsive Charles arrives. Times-a-wastin'. What to do? I'm ordering another drink. To solve this I need to be under the influence of Bacchus. I have to meet him; I haven't been so intrigued by a man in months. Waiter with the expected smug attitude arrives after I hail him down with a wave of my empty glass. *"Oui, madame?"*

"La même chose, s'il vous plaît." Ha! The American accent works again. Mr. Regal Nose has turned around to glance at me after hearing my shitty French. For a nanosecond only, but it counts. It's a distinct acknowledgment of interest and—OH SHIT!—Charles has arrived.

"Bonsoir, Klein. Tu es très belle ce soir, chérie."

"Bonsoir, Charles. Merci beaucoup. Ça va?" (Would you be okay with just waiting outside for say, five or six years?) I stand up to greet him with the usual cheek-kiss and . . . Dammit, unbelievable! He didn't fix the horrific hal-

itosis. His breath still smells like elephant feet. Jesus! Well, at least now I'm with an elegant-looking man, and hopefully that cancels out any impression I might have given Mr. Regal Nose that I'm on the hunt like a sex-starved carnivore of men. Even if it is entirely true, one hates to be blatant.

Then the fire-breathing dragon roars, "So, Klein, shall we have a drink and then go over to Lipp for dinner?" (Sure, how about you go snag a table and I'll catch up with you? And on the way, why don't you go have your mouth jet-blasted with industrial-strength mouthwash.)

"*Parfait!*" I answer, lying through my teeth. For once I could care less about food. I cannot let Mr. Perfect Nose escape. I must not let this become another one of those occasions where you pseudo-connect with a beautiful man and never see him again. I've got a mental back catalogue of about a hundred of those, already, thanks. Ah-ha! I've got it. I know just what to do. It's preposterous but could possibly work.

"*Excusez-moi,* Charles. I'm just going to dash to the ladies room for a second." Charles, ever the formal gentleman, stands when I get up and watches me as I scoot off to the bathroom. If I can pull this off, I'll move from the Junior Leagues of dating to a certified professional title. Wait, that's a scary idea . . .

"*Bonsoir, madame. Pardonnez-moi, avez-vous un stylo pour une seconde?*" I score a pen from the female bathroom atendant, grab a napkin, and with not a moment to spare, set about writing a note to Mr. Regal Nose. Okay, this is GENIUS! An official thank you to the two glasses of wine that have inspired this clever—or is this a totally absurd—move? Just how will I even get this note to him? I could so easily get busted by Charles. Fuck it, you only live once. And in the words of Proust, "Boldness rewards those who know how to seize their opportunities." Right on, Marcel. Here goes. I write, "Sorry not to be brave enough to speak with you, but I see you are quite busy. I am an artist and would be honored if you'd allow me the opportunity to paint your portrait in the future. (Well obviously in the future. Duh! God, what am I doing? This is insane. True, but finish it, Klein.) "Call me if you would. Klein, 0671882643." Okay, I'm nuts. I don't know if this is an all-new low or a stroke of genuis. I give the pen back to the attendant, fix my lipstick, powder my glistening cheeks, smile, and say to myself, *Klein, you are positively bonkers, but this IS hilarious!* I scamper down the stairs, honestly not even feeling the ground beneath my feet, back to Charles. He stands up at my arrival. Oh, sit down, you big oaf!

We make small talk for about ten minutes while he finishes his wine and I knock around ideas of just how, exactly, I'm going to get this message over to my Alcoholic-Workaholic Dream Man. I'm smoking a cigarette and plotting my next move when Charles fires at me an exhalation of stench. "Shall we go, Klein?"

"Yes, let's." I reply, instantly thinking, *Yes, let's see if I can pull this off.* Charles helps me on with my houndstooth coat and as he retrieves his coat from the checkroom, I nervously kneel down alongside Mr. Regal Nose. Yeowts. My heart's pounding furiously and suddenly this seems like mission impossible, but here goes.

"I have a note for you," I say quickly, trying not to blush crimson red. He "gets it," opens his hand, puts the note in his jeans pocket without even reading it and smiles broadly, saying, *"Merci."* FABULOUS! That so worked. I stand up (spring, really), say, *"Merci, bonsoir!"* to the waiter, and Charles arrives just in time to take my arm and escort me out the double doors onto boulevard Saint-Germain. Yeah, baby! That's spur of the moment creativity, all right. Love that shit!

"Klein, did you know that man?" Charles breaks into my mental celebrations to inquire. (Rats. He saw. Apparently, more quick thinking is required.)

"Oh, yes, he's an old friend. I'm starving, let's go," I say, taking his hand and racing across the boulevard to Brasserie Lipp. (By the way, this all completely clairifies that the "he/she is an old friend," story is the biggest crock of shit in the history of the world.)

I got through "the last supper" with Charles only because I was enjoying an ongoing mental debate that was infinitely more interesting then Charles's drone. I kept saying to myself, *I did it! Mr. Regal Nose is going to call; he's got to . . . What if he doesn't call? Oh, that would set me back light-years in the confidence dept. He'll call. Fantastic, my adrenaline's racing so fast, my metabolism's sure to make this crème brûlée evaporate. Tra-la-la, then I'll be skinny for my date with Mr. Regal Nose!*

The next morning when soberness set in, I felt more than a little foolish. I realized that I must have unquestionably come off as a two-timing vixen and had put my head on the guillotine to be terribly disappointed. Yikes! Maybe after I left he took out my note, read it to the waiter and they fell into gales of laughter as he then went on to set it afire in the ashtray. Horrors.

But, get this, he called that night and we set up a date to meet the following evening at les Deux Magots at seven o'clock. After I got off the phone I did a victory dance around the apartment as Puccini looked on with an expression of, *Oh no, she's hornswoggled another guy. This never ends well.*

Wait. I wonder if Mr. Regal Nose gets that the whole portrait thing is a ruse, right? Of course, please, who really offers to do portraits of strangers?

The next night, around six-thirty, I put on my low-waisted black Gucci pants (circa 2004), high black boots, and a simple charcoal cardigan, unbuttoned just enough to hint at my black lace La Perla bra (gift from the Big-Shot Industrialist) underneath. With my heart racing, the ten-minute walk is a blur. I arrive, take a deep breath, and put on my habitual false sense of calm and confidence. All righty, here goes nothin'.

He was already sitting having a coffee, and stood up as I came to the table. Hmmm. He definitely seemed taller three days ago. I was a healthy four inches taller in my snakeskin boots, but who cares? I can't be such a bitch as to see that as a problem, can I? (Okay, I could but I'm learning to be more accommodating as my body careens toward infertilty.)

We transition quickly through the *bonsoir*s and chitchat and are just making our way to the "so you live in the 7th arrondisment" when he says, still smiling confidently, "I'm married, I should be home by eleven o'clock. So do you want to go to your house or a hotel to fuck? I'll do whatever you command."

What?! My eyes fell out of their sockets as I leaned over to pick my jaw up off the floor. You'll do anything I command?!

For a moment I considered telling him to take off all his clothes, put his underwear on his head, and crawl around quacking like a duck, then I thought better of it. This isn't what I want. Oh, not at all. Bravo, Klein, your over-the-top note resulted in an over-the-top proposal. Nice work. All righty then. I simply replied, "You know, I just don't think that's what I'm looking for in life. Sorry to have troubled you." And I put down a five for my coffee and trudged home in a sea of karmic payback. But maybe that's kind of what I deserve for being a full-blown sneaky, aggressive chick. Okay. Noted. What goes around comes around, yeah, yeah, yeah. Fine. But you have to admit it could've worked—if, say, he wasn't married and a cad? I vowed not to track, chase, or attack men anymore . . . for a while at least . . . unless I feel really sure it'll work . . . and I'm certain he's single. I swear . . . sort of.

A FEW SLIGHTLY ANNOYING DETAILS I DIDN'T ANTICIPATE

That my lightning-quick, tried and tested "make the first move" approach with men is going over like a lead brick in France. In New York City it was a win-win–no-fail strategy. After years of honing the clever tactics to speak to a man and building enough confidence to apply "the go after what you want" approach, I'm back to square one. That whole strategy is too American and backfiring all over the place. Crap-*merde*. I don't think I even have it in me anymore to try to wait passively, play coy and bat my eyelashes. How in the world am I going to figure out how to attract a decent man? And by the way, why am I dying to marry one of these guys when he'll probably just cheat on me?! Oh, this is fun. I'm just loving that the "Frenchmen cheat" cliché is confirmed left and right. Grr-rr.

SUBLIME PLEASURE DU JOUR

I can't get over what a dream it is to start each day with a run in the Tuilerie gardens. As I walk over the Pont-Royal with the sparkling Seine flowing below, I hear the caw of seagulls that have snuck a ride inland on one of the long barges and sweep through the sky in balletic turns. I always pass the same young red-haired girl, who has set up a little display of her colorful hand-painted scenes of Paris and sits on a small stool, palette in hand, quietly at work on yet another. She always looks at me in a curious way, as many French do, as though exercise was the most absurd notion imaginable.

Once on gravel, I break into a run and begin the game of dodging between the odd tourist and the little old ladies feeding the ducks in the fountains. Making my way to the rue de Rivoli side, I sprint past an old crippled drunk man, with his chin on his chest, who yells, "*Bon courage,*" to me with a sudden burst of energy. It never fails to charm me. I've also come to know the thin Asian man who practices his daily tai chi under the shadows of the trees. His graceful, controlled gestures are so exquisitely calming and so in contrast to my morning regime. And still, when he hears the thunder of my sneakers on the dirt, he pauses to smile and gives me a low-waisted wave. I'm honored.

I continue past the Belle Époque merry-go-round where children are always clamoring to ride the pristine white horse with golden bridle, past the six miniature ponies that are always standing, tethered together waiting to make their laps around the gardens with children in tow. Continuing, I loop the lower fountain where the ducks flit around searching for a discarded end of a baguette or simply paddle about in the sun. Just beyond the tall wrought-iron gate is the glittering place de la Concorde and behind it, the Tour Eiffel looms behind like a chess piece you could almost grab in your hand. Dashing under the canopy of leaves in the long *allée* of trees, I venture by the two small restaurants, where servers clad in white aprons tied at the waist are lazily getting the patio tables set for the lunch crowd and taking their morning coffees together, chatting and smoking the first Gauloise of the day. The magnificent smell of warm, freshly baked croissants floats through the air; I take deep lungfuls. Mmmm, that is a reason to be here, huffing away, to be able to devour a warm croissant slathered in confiture upon my return. The handsome young waiter, Marcel, will offer me a Perrier if it's hot and I look like I'm going to collapse. I am amazed that so many people take the time to be warm and friendly; the old saying that the French are rude is just simply not true. Back out into the middle of the gardens now, the view of the Louvre dead ahead, Sacré Coeur peeking over the tops of the Haussman-era imperial buildings, the endless sky above . . . It all conspires to urge me to make as many laps as my legs will bear. A perfect beginning to any day in Paris, rain or shine, hot or cold. Sublime, indeed.

THE FRIEND LOWDOWN

Still hangin' with my buddies. Can't even imagine how I'd find time for adding any friends to the list. And the ones I have, especially Stella and Floris, are all I need. When I meet a potential new friend, I have a test. I ask myself, *Will I come home after seeing them and regret not spending the evening reading?* If the answer is *maybe,* forget it. Life's too short to spend time with people you don't just adore.

Floris has so definitely made the cut; we try to meet up at least once a week for an aperitif. Well, since we've never just had just a single drink, make that several aperitifs. Last Friday after making an appearance at La Palette, we needed an excuse to scooch around town in Floris's fab Jaguar, so we decided to hit the Marais and check out this late-night hot spot, Andy Wahloo. I may be a proud monthly-pass *métrocard* carrier these days, but I still have to admit that zipping through Paris at night in a Jaguar rocks. With Donna Summer blaring on the CD player, beautiful monuments at every turn, and Floris taking the corners at the speed of sound, I'm in heaven.

A half block before we even arrive at Andy Wahloo, we can spot it by the hip-to-die crowd milling around outside smoking. And unlike some trendy temples in Paris, the exterior is not subtle in the slightest; the entire facade is one large glass window stocked floor to ceiling with hundreds of Pop Art products like wacky Brillo pads, Andy Warhol–esque Campbell's soup cans, and little boxes of weird hair dyes, but all in Moroccan. You do not get groovier than this.

"Floris, is this not so cool?!" I say, so uncooly, as we pass through the crowd and up the steps. Always publicly more discreet than I, Floris simply nods and holds the door open for me. Once inside we plop down on a crazy orange banquette along the wall and check out the scene. There's a long bar along the back wall, gigantic gold hookahs sit on small tables where people are smoking fragrant apple tobacco, and a dozen people are writhing on the tiny dance floor. Beautiful thirty-somethings clad in everything from Helmut Lang leather motorcycle pants to Chloé slipdresses lounge about drinking "knock you flat on your back" moijitos and mint tea. A gorgeous Moroccan boy with mocha muscles and long hair tied with a ribbon works the bar and yells, "*Bonsoir,*" in our direction, over the pounding bass beat of the "Maroc-techno" dance music.

"Klein, I lo-o-ve this place. Fabulous. They're playing Rachid Taha, let's dance!" Floris pulls me out onto the dance floor without waiting for an answer. We're dancing wildly as always, creating a scene as we gyrate and undulate like Moroccan gypsies in a trance. We may look ridiculous, but it's all hilarious to us and we're having a ball. Floris spins me around and dips me, leaning over to kiss my neck.

"What are you doing, you madman?" I say as he pulls me into him and throws his head back laughing. I'm just about to tell him, "Let's order some drinks," when I look over his shoulder and see someone I think I know. Yes, it's him: Mr. Smug-Pants. Fabrizio. That handsome writer from the dinner at La Grande Cascade. He looks different, and better. Apparently he ditched the bad suit and found some pretty cool jeans. That works. He's dancing? Who knew he danced? God, he was so much work. Smart though, maybe too smart. Saw right through me and unnerved the living hell out of me.

"Floris, order us some margaritas, okay? I'll be right back." And I walk straight up to Fabrizio and say, "Hey you, aren't you that Mozart nut?" (After all the wine at dinner, I'm drunk. This is me thinking I'm being clever.) He looks back, smiling broadly.

"Hey you, aren't you that American artist who wears alfalfa sprouts?" My mouth drops open, but I burst out laughing.

"Ohh, how could you bring that up again? Soo-oo embarrassing!"

"I enjoyed it. It was . . .'a look,' I'll say that," he says, putting his hands in his jeans pockets and leaning against the bar.

"And since when do you know anything about 'a look'?" I say mockingly, checking him out from head to toe. (Hey, where did he get those cool shoes? They are Prada, I know it. Alexandre had the same pair.)

"Ah, I think you know, I would never profess to know anything about Fashion" (he says with a capital *F*). I point challengingly at his shoes, raising my eyebrows. "Oh. These? What? They are comfortable, that's all. When I was on my book tour, I did a little shopping in Italy," he says, looking a tinge proud. "I'm not giving you full credit here, but maybe, just maybe, your fashion critique made me rethink my wardrobe."

"Say it's not so! Those 'pleather' loafers were so working for you. Hey, congrats on the whole prix de Goncourt nomination. That's way cool."

"Way cool? I didn't win," he replies, letting the "way cool" slide but clearly not impressed with my drunken slang.

"I thought winning was only important to Americans, Fabrizio."

"True. It's an honor just to be nominated," he says sarcastically.

I suddenly realize I'm leaving Floris too long. "In fact, I really should get back to my friend. Hey, where's Céline? Are you here with your girlfriend?"

"Gone," Fabrizio says curtly.

"Gone?"

"Gone, on business in Geneva. And where's Alexandre? Are you with your boyfriend?"

"Gone," I answer.

"Gone?" he asks, with an arched eyebrow.

And once again, we resume that tennis game–like banter we had from moment one.

"Gone, as in gone. He was the kind of man who liked Kylie Minogue too much. You know what I mean?"

"Yes, I'm sure I understand. Sorry. You okay? (I nod.) Well, you look great, Klein."

"Thanks. Don't look now, Fabrizio, but you're making polite conversation." We laugh and I shake my head, feeling an amused confusion. Hmm. Maybe he's not so smug-uptight. Funny, he bought new clothes. That's pretty cool—for Céline. I scoot back to Floris.

"Who's that guy, Klein? From here it looked distinctly like you were unabashedly flirting."

"Pff-f, just some guy. A writer. He's not bad though, is he?" I say as we both admire him at the bar, talking animatedly to a male friend.

"Klein, he looks like Alexandre, only younger. You see that, right? You have such a 'profile' when it comes to men," he says, slightly jealous.

"Not true! What about my ex, Thierry? He's like the dead opposite of these guys: gray hair, Savile Row suits, distinguished, a million years older," I say, starting to laugh at the truth of what Floris's saying.

Then I hear a voice behind me at the same time a warm hand falls on my bare shoulder. "I still think you should stop smoking." Without turning I know it's Fabrizio.

"Well, you still insist on telling me what to do and, frankly, who asked you?" I say over my shoulder, feigning indignance. Floris and I look at each other and smile.

"Dance?" asks the Italian voice.

"*Pourquoi pas,*" I answer, standing up. We push onto the tiny dance floor and start moving, neither of us really looking at each other, just skanking to the intense beat. I push away a bit from the crowd and glance back at him. He's all taken up by the rhythm and dancing in a surprisingly free, astonishingly sexy way.

"You're not bad, kiddo. Be careful, I have a hard and fast theory about men and dancing," I say as I move past and behind him, still dancing. (15-Love)

"Really? What's that?" Turning around to face me. (Returned serve)

"Ever since I moved to France, I've discovered men who dance well are terrible in bed," I say, being far too drunkenly overt. (30-Love)

Laughing, he comes back with, "Well, I'm not French, remember." He smiles as he dances and moves slightly away. (Ace! 30-15)

"You got me there. I will have to have a chat with Céline. You did suggest we speak together, didn't you?" (Lob!)

"Go ahead," he adds, all cocky and self-assured. "But you're going to have to improve your French. She doesn't speak English." (Returned)

"No? How appalling. Haven't you ever told her you're terribly unimpressed with women who don't speak several languages?" (40-15)

"Ah, you got me there, Klein." We laugh together and finish out the song smiling at each other to the last remaining beats. When the song ends, both of us stand around awkwardly, waiting for the other to speak first. He finally breaks the tension. "*Merci pour la danse.* Unfortunately, I really have to be going now. The friend I came with has an early meeting. It was very nice to see you again, Klein. You know you really are . . ." he says, trailing off, in search of the word.

"What?" I ask, curious as hell. (Foot fault)

"Different," Fabrizio replies just as his friend arrives, clearly trying to accelerate their departure by nodding and heading to the exit to wait for him. (40-30)

"Is that a good thing, Fabrizio?" He doesn't answer, taps me gently on the chin with his finger.

"*Ciao, bella.*" He smiles mischievously and the door closes behind him. (Deuce)

Different? What the hell? This guy and his judgmental comments make me bonkers. Jesus, why am I even nice to him? But, actually, he was surprisingly fun tonight. Still, always the challenging comments. Not to mention that he's Italian, taken, and too much trouble. Okay then, back to Floris and another margarita.

We dance another couple of hours until we're absolutely exhausted. Collapse on a couch, drink huge glasses of cold mint tea, and decide it's time to pay the bill and head back to Saint-Germain. Driving over Pont-Neuf, happily tired and delightfully drained, I say, "Floris, great night, *non*? Thanks so much, you're my favorite dance partner ever."

"Really? The way you were dancing with that Fabrizio, I was convinced you'd cast me off," he says, playing the slightly jealous role.

"*Floris, arrête! Tu exagères. Je n'aime pas Fabrizio! Pas du tout. Il est vraimant trop compliqué!*"

"Me thinks thou dost protest too much, and look who's working on her French suddenly!" He sweetly gives me a kiss as he drops me at home. But suddenly I'm not so sure that it's Floris I want kissing me.

Fake Diamonds, My Sexual Peak, and Sleeping with Floris

October

MONSIEUR RIGHT REPORT

I was tiring of the Crusade for Monsieur Right, so I stayed in an entire week and threw myself into a marathon of reading. Reading *The Story of O* may have been a wise choice; in a quick 203 pages, it definitely kick-started my dormant hormones, and resurrected the crusade. Yep, dreamy romanticism had been replaced with raw, voracious desire.

So when my new French friend (brag, brag: c'mon, it took me forever to make one) Albertine invited me to go with her to a *vernissage* by Drouot, I jumped at the chance. All the galleries in the antique furniture and art district near the famous Drouot Auction House open their doors two nights a year in a civilized version of an open-house street party. I had already been to Carré Rive Gauche openings in my own neighborhood, and I had an idea this would be similar. I could bank that it would attract a sophisticated, diverse crowd (a sea of possible Monsieur Rights) and, equally important, offer free-flowing Champagne and even the odd oyster on the half shell.

As luck would have it, I was enjoying one of those very rare "I feel and look good" evenings (and, yes, they get rarer every year, damn it). That very afternoon, in an act of dangerous spontaneity, I had chopped off my waist-length hair in an act of rebellion against my ex, Le Creep Alexandre. A sort of "I don't need you, or my hair, which you loved" stunt. As often is the case with this kind of thing, the new "do" had come off looking not quite as chic as I had envisioned it in my mind's eye. It was a bit Betty Boop crossed with Gloria Vanderbilt (and sadly not even Gloria Vanderbilt in her heyday, but her now, aged eighty). But in spite of the flip hairdo from God knows what era, I felt confident and decidedly pretty as I set out to meet up with Albertine. As I've said, Albertine is one of those exquisite young Frenchwomen in whom all of nature has come together in celebration of beauty. She is completely ravishing with no makeup and quietly elegant in every respect. A sort of French Audrey Hepburn with the voice of an angel. Of course, at age twenty-five, she had already found and married a truly lovely man, rounding out a perfect life. Yes, I know it's probably terribly unwise to go out with a girlfriend who's better looking than you are, but I told myself we were opposites, so get over it. Albertine is a dark-haired, dewy olive-skinned nymph-gift from God and I'm, well, you know what I am already: a tall blonde American from hell—something for everyone. Plus, I needed a wingman.

We walked together from my apartment to the 9th arrondisment, enjoying the sultry violet sky and the pleasant stillness of the air. Paris at night is always an orgy for the eyes, every monument and building brilliantly illuminated, and everyone embracing the arrival of night. It's one of those cities, like Rome or Amsterdam, where a scrim of sensuality cloaks the air once the sun has fallen. It's palpable and intoxicating. Albertine and I talked about the United States. She's never been and I find it's always quite entertaining to hear foreigners' perceptions of America.

"These 'malls,' are they places where you drive through and shop from your car? In photos, they're huge with so many cars everywhere," Albertine asks so charmingly I could kiss her.

"Trust me, you have missed nothing. I spent all my weekends at malls when I was a teenager and all I learned was how to steal obscene amounts of makeup and curling irons."

"Curling irons? Are they to 'make fitness'?"

"You're adorable. No, not a bad guess actually, but curling irons are for your hair."

"Ah, I see. Tell me what are *baskets* called in the US?" she asks with charming sincerity.

"Baskets?" I look at her questioningly as we pass the Molière sculpture.

"*Baskets.* You know, shoes for fitness. They're called *baskets* in French."

"Sneakers?! Oh, right, because *panier* is the French word for what we call a basket. The American version, you know, a straw carryall or container?" I say, thinking this is getting crazy confusing and a fairly ridiculous conversation.

"*L'anglais est très compliqué, non?*" she says.

"*Non, je pense que le français est plus difficile, mon ange,*" I say, laughing. She giggles in her charming quiet French way that is the complete opposite of my glass-shattering uproar, and before we know it we have arrived at the soirée.

Flocks of well-dressed Parisians mingle among the rows of galleries, spilling out onto the streets in jovial groups. An animated trio of musicians marches around playing old French tunes. Vespas and scooters are parked in rows along the street, while a golden light falls upon the scene making everything look like a sequence in a film from the seventies. Albertine and I meander among the antique galleries, dozens of them. Me, with one eye on the Ruhlman banquettes and the other eye out for a stray, single Frenchman. Quite frankly, these antique gallery openings are a little like being on a museum field trip in grade school. You see numerous beautiful old objects, learn a great deal, eat a little, and walk a lot. The difference is now you're a lot taller, smoke cigarettes instead of chew gum, and you're not satisfied attracting just any boy without braces on his teeth.

We chose the most beautiful gallery to ensconce ourselves in, La Galerie Philippe Derain. An easy decision, as they have the most magnificent tapestries, and the best Champagne, not to mention that and the ratio of men to women was easily ten to one. (Factoring in the clear preponderance of gay men did handicap the ratio a bit, to be honest.) The crowd is a writhing mass of chic hipsters with a smattering of moneyed geezers. We each see a few people we know, which soothes my insistent little internal voice, which always says, *I don't belong here, let's go home and eat cookies.* I am having a great little chat with Céleste, an expert gem dealer, until she spies my ring of brown diamonds and finds it necessary to comment.

"Well, those are interesting. You know they almost look real. They're synthetically enhanced you do realize?"

"Oh, are you sure? I bought them for myself from an art dealer in New York City about ten years ago," I reply, hoping she's not entirely sure.

"Without question. Sorry to be the bearer of bad news," she answers, with a flip of a wrist that of course is dripping with sparkling jewels. Poop. That's a nasty blow, as I'd saved and saved and bought the ring for myself to celebrate life after a breast biopsy came back negative when I was twenty-five. Pure crap-a-rama. If I ever go back to New York City I'm gonna kill the guy that sold them to me.

I was just verging on a descent into "officially glum" when I caught sight of the handsome Fabrizio breezing into the gallery. Make that Mr. Ex-Smug-Pants, now almost palatably friendly if memory serves correct. He was alone and seemed somewhat rushed, but he approached me immediately. "*Bonsoir, Klein, how have you been?*" He looks fabulous . . . and fabulously distracted.

"Hello, Fabrizio. What a lovely surprise. Last time I saw you, you were dancing like there's no tomorrow, and then you disappeared like Cinderella," I say, immediately regretting it. (*Quelle idiote* I am. Klein, if you're going to refer to childhood stories, at least pick something French-intellectual like La Fontaine. Where is my brain? And lately I can't stop referencing Cinderella. What's that about?) (Bad serve!)

"I see you're still American to the core," he replies, looking over his shoulder. (Love-15)

"And I see you're still failing charm school." (15-All)

"And you're still smoking," he says, taking the cigarette from betwen my fingers and putting it out in an ashtray on the ledge. (15-30)

"And you're still pedantic and rude," I reply, lighting up another, even though I don't even want one. (30-All)

"And you're still not speaking French," he says, going in for the kill. (30-40)

"I'll have you know I've taken a tutor." (40-All)

"It shows," he counters, sarcastic. (Ace!)

"*Touché.* You win that round. Tell me, are you ever cordial, Fabrizio?" I ask. (But what I'm really thinking is, *Damn, I never noticed before what a pretty mouth you have . . . lips so full and well defined . . . I want to just run my finger over them.*)

"With people I don't know, I am. Klein, I went to your gallery on the rue des Beaux-Arts and saw your paintings," he says, smiling in that way of his that is a blend of condescending, sexy, and impossible to decipher.

"And? Do I need to be sitting down to hear your review?"

"Actually, I thought they were surprisingly intriguing. Not bad work, Klein."

"You're kidding?" I am positively stunned.

"I don't kid. *'Risus abundat in ore stultorum,'*" he replies, stepping out of the way of someone passing.

"Okay. Obviously it's Latin, but remember I only really speak pig latin fluently," I say, laughing.

"Laughing comes from the mouth of fools," he states, looking quite serious.

"Gosh. Sorry, I just thought my pig-latin thing was silly."

"No, the quote. That's what it means."

"That's a little harsh, don't you think? Don't forget, I have seen you actually laugh. I have witnesses. And as far as Latin, Mr. Academia, I frankly prefer, *'Carpe diem quam michemum creula potrero.'*" I am so grateful to have an occasion, this occasion, to use the single Latin phrase I know, the long version of the old "Carpe diem" motto from my New York City life.

"Not bad, Klein, and spoken like a true decadent. I have to go. Céline will be livid if she sees me talking to you. I just saw you through the window and wanted to say hello." Fabrizio sweeps in for a quick cheek kiss and rushs outside, melting into the crowd without another word.

I stand there a minute scanning the crowd for Albertine and thinking, *Well, that was weird.* Très *condescending Latin quote, but he liked my paintings. Ha!* But he can be *so dreadfully serious, and talk about pussy-whipped. "Céline will be livid." Please! A spineless Italian who quotes Latin, I don't need.* He looked amazing, though. No, he's all wrong; we'd end up strangling each other after twenty minutes together. And who could ever unravel that tangled skein of a personality? *Pas moi.* What am I saying? He doesn't even like me; he's in love with Princess de Rivatives anyway. But he has a point, I do have to speak French more. What's his problem? Why does he always have to nail my most sensitive issues? My nervous chatter, my love of designer fashion, being hyper-American, not fluent . . . The audacity!

I walked back over to Albertine and we concurred we'd given the night our best. I put my lovely Parisian friend in a taxi to go home to her adoring gorgeous husband, and I dragged myself through the streets of Paris, to go home to eat cookies. Lots of cookies.

A FEW SLIGHTLY ANNOYING DETAILS I DIDN'T ANTICIPATE

The realization that the whole "find Monsieur Right get-married and have babies" thing is going to take a bit longer than anticipated. While there is definitely something to be said for taking one's time, sowing one's oats (and I be-lieve I've sowed enough oats to supply bread to all the third-world countries), and allowing for self-discovery before making the all-important leap, it does kind of seem rather cruel that once one has done all that, the buffet of good men has all been eaten up, and you find yourself competing for the remaining losers with women a decade younger who are all light and carefree and not in a mad panic to have kids. Yeah, I'd say that's a crap deal I didn't expect.

SUBLIME PLEASURE DU JOUR

I would be remiss (not to mention beheaded) if I didn't go on record with the most vital piece of information you'll get from this book (go ahead, laugh out loud); Frenchmen really, truly are the best lovers. Hello? Why do you think I'm still here? I'm at my sexual peak. I'm not going to beat around the bush. Let's just say I've done a fair amount of traveling and certainly dipped my toe into the pool of International Men on more then one occasion. (While ad-mittedly taking a huge pass on my long-held sexual fantasy of fucking a Ma-sai warrior. C'mon, that one's far sexier in theory than in practice. Once on safari in Africa, presented with the opportunity, I was like, "Sex? No, no, no. Hate it, not really interested, thanks. Love your necklace though, and great loincloth. It could use a cleaning, but nice, really." As a rule now, I try to keep my sexual fantasies free from involving spear-wielding men who favor clitorectomies.

But frankly, Frenchmen have (and I'll even throw in Italian men because there are similiarities) some marvelous innate sense of how to please women. From the passionate, breathy whispers in a language foreign to your own ("I have absolutely no idea what you're saying, young man, but by all means, carry on") to the right-on-the-money targeting skill of hitting the G-spot dead on. It's not the way it is with some men (I'm not naming specific nationalities as I'd like to continue my global studies in this arena), where it's like that children's game we all used to play in the swimming pool—Marco? Polo? Marco?!—where someone's trying to find the target with their eyes closed. C'mon, admit it, we've all spent more nights than we'd have liked with a boyfriend drop-zoning in the wrong hemisphere, and you find yourself just wanting to scream, "Go left, down 30 degrees, and conquer! For God's sakes!"

Frenchmen have the passionate talking thing (usually full of metaphors involving references to (fruit, flowers, alabaster, the sea), the magnetic-field internal compass to Pleasure Central AND (as if the first two wouldn't get you though a night) the consummate skill of endurance and enthusaism. I may never research a cure for cancer (I'm guessing here, but "stop smoking" might help), but I've done my share of hands-on technical research in this field, and I confirm that Frenchmen are worth the trouble. Definitely.

THE FRIEND LOWDOWN

Floris is funny these days. For some reason he's decided he loves me. Which is great; I love him too. But no, he says, he loo-o-ves me. Okay. He's decided he literally loves me, and we should sleep together. Hmmm. I've given it some thought. I think I'm to blame for this whole situation. When relaxed I'm terribly tactile and affectionate, so I pretty much hang on him wherever we go, and we've gotten so flagrantly flirtatious it's getting out of hand. Everyone's questioning, "Is Floris really gay?" "I think they ARE sleeping together," etc. Being rather dramatic, for fun, we've played it up and now he's telling me every day, "We should sleep together! Tonight?" Frankly, after Alexandre telling me I wasn't physically exactly what he desired, the idea of letting a gay man see me naked seems downright . . . masochistic.

Saint-Germain's Liz and Dick, a Proposal from the Big-Shot Ex, and Colette

November

MONSIEUR RIGHT REPORT

L et me just preface the following report with an apropos quote from the philosopher Leibniz: "The way is long from logic to the heart."

Alexandre. In a word. I beg you to hold off on the lecture. I missed him, okay. So he jerked me around for months, asked me to marry him, fucked another woman, and then lied through his teeth. What? Is that so crappy? Right, it is shit, and he was a chickenshit poop-head. But my chickenshit poop-head, okay? True, not mine all the time. But, like a bad song on auto rewind, I found myself back in throes of the Alexandre experience, which was honestly just getting embarrassing. My insatiable desire for him was like a stone tied around my neck. As I believe I've mentioned, Alexandre is a very bad dancer, if you get my drift. Come to think of it, for the first time in my life I was beginning to understand why men often stay in relationships with dumb women who are great in bed, because I was constantly returning to this relationship and he wasn't exactly setting me on fire with his intellectual capacity. My body had made some secret pact, unbeknownst to me, to endure any emotional turmoil to return to that bed of his. I was starting to understand how people get addicted to things they know are bad for them, because, like a heroin addict, I kept going back for my fix only to find myself craving it in consistently increasing doses. Who the hell had I become? I was losing time and had nothing but rug burns on my knees to show for it. Was I regressing or just enjoying the freedom to fuck the way men do for the sake of selfish pleasure? Hmmm. I know, you've got to be shaking your head in disappointment at my predictability. You're not alone.

You know when French friends say to you, "You two are like an episode of *Dallas*," your love life has become a bad joke (gotta love that *très*-current reference care of Cédric; it still makes me laugh). Alexandre and I played the roles of a couple, going to parties together, dinners, but it was really like beating a dead horse. Probably my appeal (to him) was just that I was a bottomless pit of compliments and adoration and a cheap substitute for his therapy.

But I'd always keep an eye out for an escape hatch, a possible knight in shining armor to rescue me from my ever so apathetic boyfriend. Apparently my knight was having a hell of a time getting into his armor because he wasn't showing up. So we officially became the Saint-Germain version of Richard Burton and Liz Taylor. Complete with excessive drinking, dramatic exits, and serious weight fluctuations (for once, I can proudly say that was his problem).

Frankly, all his problems were starting to seem minor in comparison with the gang of idiots I'd been meeting. And I could not fathom going out and trying to drum up someone new. Nope, that idea seemed as enjoyable as swallowing a wasp.

He welcomed me back with a celebratory reunion that was decadently memorable, only to be followed in a week's time by his standard routine: "I don't know who I am, I don't know what I want, I need time to think." It had gotten to be such a frequent statement, I was tempted to engrave it on a sign that he could just carry around and hold up when the moment struck him. So we've split again. For the last time, I swear. I knew going back was a dumb idea.

Then one Sunday afternoon I was having my usual *petit déjeuner chez moi*, reading the newspaper and trying to pretend that being alone for the gazillionth Sunday was fine, just fine, when suddenly my Big-Shot Ex, Thierry, called from New York City.

"*Bonjour K. C'est ton chien.*"

"Oh, Thierry. God, it is so good to hear from you," I say, instantly soothed by his familiar voice.

"How are you dahr-ling? I have no news from you for ages."

"I know. I'm sorry. I've been through the ringer lately. There's been a revolving door in my love life lately, with a constant stream of idiots passing through. And I thought I should just pull away and leave you with your girlfriend . . . Ruth?" I reply, saying her name as though it tastes like a rotten egg.

"Mmm, this is amusing timing then."

"Why? What do you mean, Thierry?"

"Because just when you let me go . . . I . . . I want you back," he says, in a voice that is so vulnerable and so *not* him. "Klein, I miss you."

Stunned, I answer, "I miss you too, terribly."

"Are you in love, K?"

"No, I'm alone. Aren't you with Ruth anymore, *mon ange*?"

"No, she was a pale substitute for you."

Touched, a small giggle escapes me. "That's so sweet. My little heart needed to hear that."

(Long pause on his end.) "K, I want be with you, I want you to come back. Will you? We could live together, maybe even get married, if that's still important to you." (I just sat silently, with my eyes popping out of my head and thinking, *Am I dreaming?*)

He continued, "What we have, our connection is so rare. And now you've been to Paris, followed that adventure. Can't you come back now? Be with me. I can offer you everything you've ever wanted. I can take care of you. I promise even to let Puccini use my bespoke trousers as a scratching post, as he used to like to." We both collapse laughing, remembering how Puccini always clawed his pant legs into shreds. Jealous cat, he always chose the most expensive to destroy.

"Thierry, you know what I'm going to ask, don't you?" I say, certain he knows already.

"Yes, and no. No, I am sorry, I still don't want to have any more children. Is it possible for you to give up that dream? Sometimes in life you don't always get everything you want."

"Oh, really. Coming from you," I gently chide him, "that's rich. You have everything you want, don't you?"

"Everything but you, Klein."

"*Mon ange,* let me think. I know my life . . . my life in Paris hasn't turned out as I had hoped on every level, but I'm not sure I can give all this up," I say as I look around my apartment and think, *All what? A tiny apartment, an uncertain career, a crap love life?*

"Even for me? A life with me? Remember how happy we were? And you'd never have to worry about anything again." (My mind floods with what that all means. And that he knows I am living on the end of my meager savings.

That I never go away on glamourous vacations anymore, can't buy any designer clothes, and can barely even afford to take a taxi. Maybe it would be nice to be loved and treated like a queen again. To feel totally accepted and adored. And I have never loved any man like I love Thierry.)

"*Thierry, je t'adore.* Thank you for being so romantic and for this . . . Obviously I need to really give this some thought. I do love you. I always have. I need some time, okay?"

"I've already waited two years, I can wait a bit longer. The offer stands. A week? A month? Come back when you're ready. But, really, know that I am serious. I want you back in my life. *Je t'aime, my K.*"

"*Je t'aime, mon chien.* I will call you soon."

"Goodbye, dahr-ling."

"Goodbye, *mon chien.*"

Click.

Wow! That knight I was waiting for to come and save me? I think that his name is Thierry. I got off the phone and scooped Puccini into my arms and sat down on my chaise in shock. I needed to think. Seriously.

For as many people who have sided with me—"If Thierry really loved you, he'd give you a baby because he know's how much you desire to be a mother"—there are an equal number who know us, the magic of our chemistry and say, "Klein, don't walk away from a love like that, a lifestyle like that for the idea of children. There are no guarantees in life and you'll regret it."

And I have regretted it at times. All the times that these Parisian men and I locked horns over ridiculous cultural differences. All the times I'd be with some man at a dinner and be thinking, *Damn, no one is as interesting, as funny, as elegant, as adoring or as thoughtful as Thierry.* And when I hear my New York City friends going on and on about buying a country house, jetting off to St. Barts, etc. I do miss it sometimes. The ease of life, the safety of being part of a couple, God, just the idea of having a man I can trust again. Or even enjoying the calm of knowing I can go to a dinner party and be able to speak intelligently, for Christ sakes, which is never a certainty in Paris with my nonfluency.

Maybe this whole Paris dream thing is a dream, an unattainable dream. When is it time to throw in my chips and call it a day? I have tried so hard, for so long. Gilles, Nico, the married Count Jean-François, Alexandre, Monsieur

Murder by Breath Charles, and a smattering of faceless others. Is it time to go back? To say I gave it my best shot here? Is Thierry "the one" and this is my second chance?

A FEW SLIGHTLY ANNOYING DETAILS I DIDN'T ANTICIPATE

I miss my family a lot. It's so damn pricey going home to the States that I only get to make it two times a year if I'm lucky. And I'm always so bloody jet-lagged the whole time that I end up having all the personality of an amoeba in a coma. So not only am I aching to make a family of my own, I'm aching-missing my real family in Wisconsin. Mother of God, what stress and pressure!

SUBLIME PLEASURES DU JOUR—DEUX

• Check this out. Monsieur Despont (the owner of the gallery where I exhibit) gave me a call today. I sold another painting! Hurrah! The small pale gray abstract one. It didn't sell for a bunch of money, but it will pay the rent—for the next month at least. Since last time it was positively thrilling to discover who the purchaser was, I asked, "*Monsieur Despont, est-ce que c'est possible de me dire . . . qui a acheté le tableau?*"

"*Un homme italien. Je crois qu'il s'appelait . . . Fabrizio, ou quelque chose comme ça.*"

Is that not amazing? Mr. Smug Smarty-Pants bought one of my paintings! He just gets curiouser and curiouser, that boy. Ha! Now Céline, Princess de Rivatives, must positively hate me. I gotta admit I miss that verbal tennis stuff with him . . . sometimes. A little.

• The boutique Colette is my obsession. This multilevel emporium of cool is just a short walk away on rue du Faubourg Saint-Honoré. Some cutting-edge fabulous music's always blaring at dance-club decibels (which surprisingly never sounds half as cool in my apartment once I've sprung for the CD and brought it home, come to think of it) and the employees are the smuggest, hippest group I've ever seen.

You know this place, right? They sell the most prized aesthetic objects of the design and fashion world, all placed *par hasard* (randomly). So you'll see some tricked-out pair of neon orange Nike sneakers next to a forty-thousand-dollar watch, next to an Italian sugar bowl, next to a Swedish-designed ashtray. I've got a theory (bear with me on this) that while Catholicism fades from importance, a new modern religion has been born complete with its pious followers (moneyed tourists in the know and hipster French), and its holy site is Colette. Popping into Colette is akin to a pilgramage to worship at the modern basilica of cool.

Just when did the world change into a place where we all must have designer toilet-bowl brushes, five-hundred-dollar toasters, and diamond-encrusted cell phones? I find it all terribly entertaining, the extreme seriousness of the cultlike clientele as they hover over a two-thousand-euro tea set made from recycled bottle caps, frantically vying to be the distinguished owner of one of the "limited edition of a precious five." Go hard, lady, I've got a hunch that will be so over in about a week, you won't be able to give it away. *Amusant, non?*

Colette also has a "water bar" in the *sous-sol en bas* (basement) in which to take communion. (Literally, well almost. I'm tired of the religion metaphor, aren't you? Let's abandon it, shall we?) They stock over a hundred different brands of water, all of which are packaged like entries in a design competition. (Two favorites are a Tasmanian brand made with 4,875 drops of rainwater and bottled water from Wales, said to ease a broken heart. I'll take a dozen of those, thanks.)

You can plop down at the communal table to rub shoulders with fellow groovy Parisians, eating yummy plates of couscous and hummus, or indulging in Pierre Hermé's famous pastries washed down with four-euro bottles of imported Icelandic water. These days I can't afford a bloody thing at Colette, so if I leave with anything at all it's a bottle of Nicofluid water. (And no, my ex, Nico, hasn't bottled his love juice. Though he could probably could and make a pretty penny.) It's refreshing as all get-out, and flavored with menthol and licorice and a lot less trouble than Nico!

THE FRIEND LOWDOWN

Stella and I have chosen a new venue for our support group meetings, the café Au Petit Suisse. Kitty-corner (who the hell made up that phrase?) from the le Théâtre de l'Odéon. It's tiny, with just four tables on its triangular corner and the best damn *omelette aux fines herbes* you can get for five euros. It comes with a little salad, the traditional basket of bread and, being the cheap-demons we are, we round it out with a plain old *carafe d'eau*. This economizing meal gives us the right to justify our outing *après les omelettes*. Destination: shoes.

Paris is a haven for all women's obsessions: hot men, great chocolates, scrumptuous pastries, sexy lingerie, cool clothes but, as any shoe-o-phile knows, this city is a hotbed of fabulous shoes. I'm forever seeing female tourists from the four corners of the world making their pilgramage around Parisian shoe stores. All women will agree, it is absolutely worth the trouble of dragging around enormous bags of shoe boxes all day, when you know the blissful rush that awaits you when you unpack them. But it's quite torturous in my current situation; I can't plop down a *carte de crédit* and acquire yet another pair of simply divine, utterly unneeded heels. So, once again, I'm Stella's consultant and scout while she contemplates the pros and cons of a beige mule. From my extensive and thorough research I offer the following *gratuit:*

A Girl's Guide to les Chaussures de Paris

For those with trendy taste and small wallets, aka cheap-to-die verging on disposable footwear. Shop at Jonak, André (both on rue de Rennes), Mosquito, Eden Shoes (both on rue du Four), Thierry 21 (rue du Bac), and Zara (rue de Rennes).

Midrange shoes, meaning will survive more than one season and won't deconstruct in the rain. Shop at Kevin Dorfer (rue du Bac), Heyraud (rue du Four), Marisa, Jet Set, and Parallèle (all on rue de Sèvres).

Spendy-Glamourpuss, meaning try to get these as gifts, or plan to take a mortgage on your apartment. Shop at Bruno Frisoni (rue de Grenelle), Christian Louboutin (rue de Grenelle), Sergio Rossi, Prada, Miu Miu (all rue de Grenelle as well), Rodolphe Menudier, Alain Tondowski, Pierre Hardy (sold at Maria Luisa boutique on rue Cambon, which also carries Manolo Blahnik), and a personal fave, Michel Perry (rue des Petits-Pères).

Cabaret, le Bigfoot, and Drunk Man Below

December

MONSIEUR RIGHT REPORT

She said 7:30, right? It's now 7:50. What? Was everyone put on earth to test my patience? This is my traditional "waiting for Stella" part of the day. Always the same drill, just playing it out all over Paris at different locations. Tonight I'm standing in front of Christie's auction house on Avenue Montaigne.

Love this girl but she is always late. Funny, though, I realize I'd wait for her longer then I'd wait for most men. It's okay, it's beautiful out. Yellow and orange leaves blow gently down the wide avenue, a dry cool wind caresses my face. The golden glow of the streetlights makes it feel as though I've stepped into an old Brassai photograph. I love Paris in the fall. Love it all the time, really.

Tonight we're off to yet another "happening." This time taking a welcome pass on antiques and checking out the high-end art galleries. Even if I wasn't an artist, it's still a reason to dress up and gallivant from chichi gallery to shasha gallery, partaking in free Champagne and high-brow culture in equal doses. There's the added bonus of a high concentration of chic men packed into a two-block radius. With the proposal from Thierry in my lap, I still need to make a final effort. See if there is a needle (a decent man) in this haystack, (Paris). And yes, I am aware that Paris has probably not been metaphorically referred to as a haystack before. There she is, finally.

"Hi, girl!" I say with an intonation that she instantly understands.

"Klein, I'm so sorry! I broke a heel getting into the taxi. Had to go all the way home and grab these ugly pumps instead. They're queer as hell, aren't they?" she asks. (I gotta give it to Stella that this is a new one in her never-ending series of excuses. This girl must keep a database of explanations for being late and cross-check every time!)

"Well, they do kind of look like Pan Am stewardess shoes, but you can pull them off. C'mon, let's go." We link arms and head over to the atrium just down the street where the crowd awaits.

"So how are you? Did you have a good day?" she inquires.

"Oh, I'm okay, spent the day painting. Still struggling with the big gray painting—"

"The spider?" she interrupts to ask.

"No, Stella, it's a biomorphic form, not a spider!" I say, jokingly chiding her.

"Right, right," she says, fishing for a breath mint in her purse.

"And then I went running, followed by crying in the bathtub. The usual," I conclude.

"Klein, tell me you are NOT missing Alexandre! C'mon, he's such a shit. You know that. I don't believe you."

"I know, I'm trying. Hey, I'm here, aren't I?"

We approach the inner sanctum of the art galleries; there are people packed shoulder to couture shoulder, wall to wall. Looking through the floor-to-ceiling windows is like looking into an aquarium; all the colorful scarves, brightly colored dress shirts, sparkling jewelry, the flurry of gestures.

"God, what a scene. Are you ready to dive in?"

"*Absolumment.* Is my lipstick on my teeth?" replies Stella.

"Nope, is my mascara under my eyes?"

"No, you go first," she commands. We push through the revolving doors and are immediately greeted by two burly Asian men guarding the door in formal red jackets and discreet earphones.

"*Bonsoir, mesdames.*"

"*Bonsoir.* Let's go this way, against the stream," I suggest, pushing through the sea of camel hair and fur. We check out the exhibit of Otto Dix and Munch paintings and press on to the next gallery.

"That was depressing stuff, eh?" Stella comments.

"Seriously. Gorgeous, yes, but not exactly joyful. The curator must be sui-cidal," I say. Stella laughs and we move on to a photography exhibit of a fa-mous lensman, who shoots exclusively beautiful nude women. This small gallery is jammed with models and sexy young men clad in the grooviest combinations of black leather, denim, silk camisoles, and chunky jewelry.

"Oh Christ, supermodels," I whisper. "Stella, brace yourself."

The photographer, a sixty-year-old gray-haired man with *beaucoup d'attitude,* stands in his black sunglasses and wool cape (yes, cape) surrounded by a throng of admirers and hangers-on. It's like a world to which we are uninvited and where we will go unnoticed. So we quickly scan the huge black-and-white photos of amazing physical perfection, look at each other, look back at the crowd . . .

"We're outta here," I say, about to drown in insecurity. We dash out into the courtyard. "Okay, that was just a little too young and groovy for me. Was every chick in there nineteen years old and six feet tall or am I wrong?" I ask.

"Ple-e-ease. I can't bear that every man thinks he should be with a model. Let's go to the bar and get a drink. They're free, aren't they?"

I nod and we join a swarm of people hovering over the bar that's been set up for the evening in the courtyard between galleries.

"Hey, I know that guy!" Stella suddenly exclaims. "See the guy over there by the geezer in the hat hitting on the model? He's a hottie, isn't he?"

I try to follow her gaze while maintaining my spot in the drink line. Stella and I never agree on men so I'm not too optimistic about this "babe."

"Whoa, Nelly, you know that guy?! He is handsome to die. Ah, *deux coupes de Champagne, s'il vous plaît.*"

I take the drinks, hand one over to Stella, and we extricate ourselves from the tide of the drink line and proceed to assume our positions (standing in a semi-arc, almost side by side, to check him out.)

"How do you know him? Tell me everything," I ask before sipping.

"His name is Pierre and he's a really successful antique dealer. Shy, thirties. I met him at one of Catherine's parties last year," she reports. I look back at the subject at hand. Dark brown shiny hair, a chiseled, expressive face adorned with a slight stubble of a beard on his creamy ivory skin. In truth, he's a little short for me, five foot nine to my five foot ten. But that's outweighed by the fact he's dressed terribly elegantly in a gray single-breasted wool suit (I'm detecting Lanvin) with skinny pants. I love narrow pants on men. If the body is right (and it has to be for a man to wear them) . . . Ooph! They do it for me everytime.

"Not another antique dealer, Stella! God, he'd be my third. I gotta date

someone unconnected with the world of chandeliers and sconces. It'll just remind me of Alexandre. But he is hot. He looks like a mini version of Pierce
Brosnan, no?"

"Klein, come on, I'll introduce you." And Stella takes my arm before I can
even answer. We move so fast across the room I feel like it's a blur.

"*Bonsoir,* Pierre, do you remember me? I'm Stella, we met at Catherine's."

"Of course, how are you?" he says with a divine accent, as they do the *de
rigueur* double-cheek-air-kiss bit. Right side first, then left.

"Very well, and may I present my friend Klein. My dearest friend." Cool, I
get the kiss move too and a brief waft of his fragrance. Vetiver by Guerlain, I
think. Dee-lish.

"*Enchanté.* Stella tells me you deal in antiques. What period do you spe-
cialize in?" I ask, drinking my Champagne a little too fast and, of course,
chickening out of speaking in French.

"Louis XVI. In fact I'm just publishing a book about it." A pause as Pierre
looks me up and down and then smiles to Stella. "I'll have to invite the two of
you to the book party next month."

"Lovely, I look forward to it immensely," I say, all stupid-nervous, which
as a rule results in my assuming some absurd British accent and speaking like
a stilted sixty year old.

He and Stella catch up as I vow silently to shut up and quietly drink Pierre
in . . . Oh yes, you'll do, shorty. I love that he's a bit shy and reserved. Not one
of those hipsters from hell, like at the photography exhibit, posing and on the
prowl for overgrown teenage models. And he has great shoes; I'm such a
sucker for great men's shoes, it's so rare really.

"So what are you two ladies doing after this?" Pierre asks, looking at each
of us in turn. Stella and I look at each other like, "Fuck, we have no idea.
Should we have a plan?"

"Ah, I think we're going to have dinner at Market around the corner," I
lie, hoping Stella will back me up. Ha! As if we'd ever go to have dinner there,
just the two of us. It'd be like three hundred euros, approximately thirty times
the cost of our usual dinners of *croque monsieurs*.

"Yes, Market, lo-ove their salmon. And you, Pierre, where are you off to?"
Go, Stella! You're coming along nicely in the spontaneous-lie department,
good student.

"Frankly, it would be my pleasure to invite the two of you for dinner, if you'd allow me to accompany you."

Score! Stella and I glance at each other with the understanding that if we were alone we'd be high-fiving. We take Pierre up on the dinner invitation and also his offer to go to the bar and retrieve us all a last round of Champagne.

"Damn, that went like clockwork. How great. You know, he's exactly the kind of man I should be choosing: timid, elegant, serious, and a gentleman," I add, as if I've never laid eyes on a man with these qualities before.

"Exactly, Klein, let go of that loser Alexandre. He made you crazy with all his "I want you, I don't want you" nonsense. And Thierry, he refuses to have kids. That's just selfish. Whereas Pierre, he's—"

"Stella, he's coming. Shhh." Pierre arrives balancing three flutes together by their stems in one hand.

"Well there you are, and one for you," he announces, handing me a glass. Clink! We toast, and for once I remember the set-in-stone rule of looking into the eyes of the person you are toasting. Not so tough, as Pierre has beautiful laughing blue eyes I could fall into.

By ten o'clock the three of us have polished off a third round of Champagne. We decide to walk over to La Maison Blanche for dinner, just a few blocks down on Avenue Montaigne. Sitting atop a grand building, La Maison Blanche is famous for its two-story-high windows that command a stunning view of the Seine, the shimmering dome of Les Invalides, and the sparkling lights of La Tour Eiffel. A *très moderne* (the extra *e* on that word is imperative in France to indicate the extra elegance, I'm guessing) interior that is all-white floor to ceiling. It's like eating in a cloud with one of the most amazing views in all of Paris, and has a two-star menu to boot.

The three of us climb into the tiny elevator and zip up to the top floor where the doors open onto a dazzling white cloud of luxury. Four pale gray banquettes face the view like private alcoves. They are the choice seats. Pierre asks for the maître d'hôtel right away and secures one of the coveted alcoves for dinner. I keep an eye out to make sure he doesn't resort to the cheesiness of palming the maître d' a fifty or something. Nope. Phew. That would've killed my image of him right out of the gate.

Meanwhile Stella and I are completely assuming our new roles as *très* feminine dainty girls and speaking in that aforementioned refined diction that really only emerges when we are around men we don't know. We find ourselves saying things like "this is positively splendid" and "why ever not?" as though we had been educated at Oxford. Queer, I know.

Pierre sits down next to me and his knee brushes mine a little. Hello, Sexual Rush Department? This is Klein's libido; message recieved. This is definitely one of those moments where I thank the almighty God for making me a girl, because if I were a man I'd have levitated the table with my rush of desire. How men deal with that whole insta-uncontrollable hard-on thing, in public, I'll never know. Let's hear it for being a girl!

Pierre chose a bottle of Ladoucet Pouilly-Fumé from the *carte de vin* and politely asks Stella and me if we approve. It's a lovely gesture, as most men choose themselves, and it's a surprise when it arrives to the table. We settle into a genius meal of foie gras in a *noisette* cream, coq au vin, a baby artichoke engulfed in steamed *petits pois* with a just a whisper of cilantro, and I clean my plate of every last tasty morsel in record time. (Dammit, I have to remember to turn off my automatic eat-like-a-truck-driver switch. Haa-o-oonk! Wait! What the hell was that?)

Pierre is laughing at a joke of Stella's and, for God's sakes, it sounds like someone is stepping on a goose. Ha-oo-onk! That's one wacky laugh, mister. His laugh à la poultry is quickly forgiven as he's been charming and endearingly inquisitive all evening. Not to mention that his upper lip has the most beautiful curve to it, with a pale outline that accentuates . . . lips, shoes, noses, narrow pants? . . . I'm attracted to the stangest things.

"Klein?" (Right. Back to reality already in progress.)

"Yes?"

"Pierre was just asking if you want to go next door to Hôtel Plaza Athénée for an after-dinner drink," Stella says, urging me with her eyes to "say yes!"

"Love to."

I've never been there. Read about it in *Paris Match* and *Hello* magazines a zillion times in the waiting room of my bikini wax salon. Always the glitterati, fashionista types having their after Fashion Week parties. Should be cool. Not sure I'm dressed fab enough. Wish I could cut about seven inches off the hem of my skirt right about now. How dumb would it be to take off my shirt and toss it in the garbage, just wearing my black bra under my jacket? Cool like Gucci? Or queer and pathetic? Who knew this night would require either cleavage or leg exposure? I'm sporting neither. I so cannot compete with young models wearing this . . . blouse. Like that even sounds sexy: "blouse." No, "blah-z" is more like it.

Stella and I go through the age-old dance of pulling out our wallets when the bill arrives. "Ladies, thank you, but no. I wouldn't dream of letting you pay." Pierre says, placing his credit card on the small silver tray for the waiter. That phrase is like Mozart to my ears now that my bank account has lost about three zeros and a comma. We thank Pierre profusely and sincerely and get up to leave. Wow! Hey, standing up is overrated. Guess the alcohol has kicked in. These are my shoes, right? And my feet? 'Cuz we're not walkin' so elegantly over here.

Stella and I take the offer of Pierre's arm, one of us on each side, as much to steady ourselves as to put him in the middle of a blonde American sandwich. That's right, he's the delicious dark filling. All right, I'm drunk. In the elevator I whisper to Stella, "God, I wish my skort was shirter." We explode in laughter at my intoxication-inverted phrase. (You know you're smashed when what would normally horrify you suddenly seems like the funniest thing you've ever uttered. Funny how alcohol always has that effect.)

Once outside, back on the avenue, the cool crisp air is a godsend. We go left, to make the all-of-twenty-foot walk past the long line of limousines and chauffered cars to the elegant entrance of Hôtel Plaza Athénée.

The interior is exactly what you'd imagine. Ubiquitous gilt and warm peach lighting, huge crystal chandeliers, a plethora of overstuffed Louis-something chairs, and floral arrangements the size of helicopters dripping with lilies and orchids. (I'm leading our group. Why am I leading? I have absolutely no idea where I am headed in this vast interior. The music's coming from the right; my best bet is to turn ninety degrees and proceed.)

I assume a stupid, phony air of "sure, been here a million times" and lift back a large velvet curtain assuming (hoping against hope, actually) that it leads to the bar. Nope. The coat check. (None of us even have coats. That didn't work. Drop back, Klein. Discreetly let Pierre barrel ahead before you make a total ass of yourself.)

We pass small groups of handsome men with white hair and white teeth, deep tans and deep pockets. And we're here. Cool as hell. Versailles meets a futuristic *Blade Runner*-esque nightclub. And on our left, my friends, you will see the clichéd bevy of young models surrounded by playboy types, who are easily their fathers' ages. Oh, and the same goes for the group on our right, *mesdames, monsieurs.* Right. Wall-to-wall models! Didn't I just escape a pack of you earlier this evening? To be fair, this is a nightclub and nightclubs are their natural habitat. Sorry, what was I thinking?

The three of us saunter up to the long glass bar, which is illuminated neon pink, and in about twenty seconds I'm fine, relaxed. Oh, who gives a fuck about teenage models? Screw 'em. Plus, Pierre's being a total gentleman and not even glancing at them despite the fact we're surrounded by them. We order Champagne (hey, there's a new idea), this time with raspberries, and I pull out one of my many antique cigarette cases in a feeble effort to make my disgusting habit seem somehow retro-chic. The sterling silver 1940s case with the little built-in clock gets 'em every time.

"This is a beautiful object, Klein," Pierre offers, "as are you."

He takes my cigarette case, turns it over to admire it, then places it back in my hand, brushing my open palm with his warm fingers. Mmmm. I know it sounds cheeesy, but Gallic charm has to be witnessed to be understood. (Much like the appeal of a Bateau-Mouche boat trip down the Seine. Looks foolish, but is divine in reality.)

"I'd love to see your work. I'm crazy about large abstract paintings, love them in rooms full of, say, 1930s furniture. You know . . . Ruhlman, Prouvé." (Oh, do I ever. I love that shit. Lo-o-ve talking about paintings, interiors, stuff like Jean-Michel's use of shagreen, Franz Klines' obsession for indigo blue. Bring it on!) Pierre and I are way engrossed in furn-o-speak, Stella's content with her boyfriend on her cell phone and enjoying the silent attentions of about twenty guys who are staring at her. Another flash of Pierre's credit card and it's suddenly 1:30 a.m. None of us can stop smiling and laughing, and we're all in silent agreement this is "one of those nights."

"Let's go to Cab!" Pierre announces.

"Yes!" Stella chimes in. I'm thinking, *To cab? To take a taxi? I have had a great time tonight. Yeah, I could skooch on home now.* But suddenly I realize they are far too giddy at the idea "to cab," so maybe we're not talkin' taxi time.

" 'To cab' is what exactly, Stella?" I whisper, turning my head out of out of earshot of Pierre.

"You know! The club Cabaret, silly. By Palais Royal, killer dance music?"

(Right. Heard of it. Have never been there. Maybe I spent too many nights with Alexandre, a DVD, a bottle of Champagne and somehow fell out of the cool loop.) Just then. Pierre takes my hand in his and pulls me in gently for an awfully surprising slow, soft kiss. Perfect timing. Okay! All night this man hasn't made one error, one false, slightly less then perfect move, gesture, or phrase (goose-giggle aside). Dammit, it is about time I met someone like you. Even as we leave, passing through the crowd of nubile beauties, he doesn't twitch, doesn't divert his attention from me for a second. Bravo! Pierre, you are a rare Frenchman.

We grab a cab and fly over to Cab, the three of us bouncing around in the back of the Renault. Stella yells, "Great song, turn it up!" to the young Rastafarian driver. It's Eminem belting out, "You better lose yourself in the music, the moment, you own it, you better never let it go." Right on! What are you, a modern-day Arthur Rimbaud? Just as I'm committing the song lyrics to memory, we arrive.

A Champagne-induced confident stride past the four huge gorillas-in-suits doormen and down through the mazelike labyrinth to find a private banquette to hold court.

(All righty, an even younger crowd here, if that's possible; I could be babysitting this group of kids, for crying out loud. But Pierre's still completely attentive, so I don't feel like quite the gravity-ravaged grandma I normally would.)

The bass beat of the music throbs in our chests, the club is all a blur of rotating, flashing lights, perfumed sweat, intermingling flesh, wet lips and gyrating hips. The sexual energy is so thick you could cut it with an Opinel knife. I'll take two slices, please. We all throw ourselves into a deep white leather alcoved banquette, order another bottle of Champagne (hey, you gotta keep your blood alcohol level equal to your age), and force our way onto the dance floor. Claiming our rightful territory—age before beauty, gang—skooch over, club kids. I'm hiking up my skirt virtually to my hipbones, trying to create an insta-minskirt like an idiot, as I grab Pierre's perfect waist from behind. (Let's see if this guy has any rhythm. Whoa, kiddo!) For all his shy, discreet, fine manners, this boy's an absolute freak on the dance floor. It's like he's morphed into a Chippendale's stripper. Talk about alter ego. Somehow cute. Like getting two men in one. And given my new theory of wacky bad dancer=good lover, I'm lovin' Pierre's crazy dance moves.

By 5:00 a.m. we have all completely exhausted ourselves, drained our reserves, killed the Champagne, and possibly lost five pounds in sweat. One quick check of my dance-till-you-drop-full-stop reflection in the ladies room and I realize, *Oh boy, is it time to go home.* We drag ourselves outside into the refreshing predawn air to discover it's misting out and a magical fog has swept over Paris. It feels like we're stepping out of one dream and into another. Pierre takes charge, beckons a taxi with a single gesture, and the three of us collapse in the back in spent bliss. The foggy, glistening streets of Paris are practically deserted at this hour. Pierre drops Stella at her apartment first, then whisks me to my front door. Pierre and I exchange a quick salty kiss. I happily relinquish my phone number and climb the stairs to my apartment, exhausted but a smiling girl: Pierre has potential, big time.

Pierre called the next day and invited me to an exhibit at the Palais de Tokyo the following Saturday afternoon. It felt great waiting for him in front of the Hôtel de Crillon and watching him approach, women's heads turning like tops as he elegantly glided by.

Short? Yes, but sexy, this new almost-boyfriend of mine. A big *bonjour* kiss in the warm sunlight of a gorgeous day, and we took our jubilant selves off to the museum. The exhibit was crap. We critiqued and ridiculed every piece, laughing in complete agreement. (It's easy to bond over the ludicrousness of a pile of Barbies labeled as important post-*moderne*—yep, there's the extra *e* again—art.) We held hands, snuck kisses, went for a great lunch at Bar du Théâtre, and just generally fawned all over each other for hours.

This was the beginning of many fabulous days and nights together: drinks at the Hemingway Bar at the Ritz, brunch at Flore, dinner at 1728, a clutch of cocktail parties, and several openings together. We never had a single cultural snafu or miscommunication, amazingly enough. Everything about dating Pierre was smooth and light, so different than dating Alexandre. And we were establishing ourselves around town as a happy new couple thrilled to have found each other.

Pierre was such a gentle and kind man, a brilliant kisser, and impressed me (not easy) with his expansive and enthusiastic knowledge of French history. I was, I suppose, quite happy. Not really in a I-want-to-tear-my-clothes-off-and-take-you kind of way, but something more, evenly balanced pleasure in continuity and, I thought, something more grown-up. Something that never existed with Alexandre.

After a few weeks of kisses goodbye at my front door, the time had clearly come to do the sleepover. The adult version. Not the one we used to do at age ten, where we'd put the hand of the first person who fell asleep in warm water so they'd wet the bed. Though, come to think of it, the adult version also often results in wet linens. (I think the similarities end there.)

The fateful evening started with dinner at a perfect old-fashioned bistro, La Fontaine de Mars, just steps from La Tour Eiffel and beautifully situated on a small old square with a monumental fountain. Red checkered tablecloths and the traditional French fare scrawled in chalk on a blackboard propped on a rickety wooden chair. *Très charmant.* Serving old-world cuisine like *cassoulet, steak au poivre, tête de veau,* and *blanquette de lapin.* (The last is a roasted tiny bunny rabbit. How ghastly is that? Pass!)

At dinner, I was a little anxious, as I'd come to realize I didn't have the craziest passion for him (have I mentioned that?), so I prolonged dinner by eating an exorbitant amount of food. After an eggplant and goat cheese terrine, Breton sole meunière, and an insanely decadent prune and apple tart, I couldn't have eaten another bite, and I knew a sexual romp of uncertain appeal awaited me *chez* Pierre. For some reason, I just didn't have a raging desire to sleep with Pierre. And that ambivalent voice needed to be swayed, or drowned. I needed something.

"Why don't we order some Calvados?" I ask, a little insistently, deciding that being a bit tipsy could help.

"Klein, I've never seen a woman eat or drink like you. Where do you put it?" Pierre asks with a smile.

"Hollow leg," I reply automatically, having used that joke ad nausem times before.

Pierre and I kick back two enormous snifters full of the warm apple liqueur and grab a cab back to his apartment. In the taxi I'm feeling maybe this is all going to be fine, great even, as he kisses like nobody's business and smells like heaven. We arrive *tout de suite* at his building. Note: climbing four flights of stairs really makes it crystal clear how truly drunk you are. The Calvados would've been a good idea, if speaking was no longer required. *Now I tink I feel properwy rweady. Eesa nof like hees nof attraktif. Whas my prwoblam? Woopfs, meight've drwank troo mouch.* I say to myself, holding on to the bannister like a rope tow.

Once in his apartment Pierre turned on the TV (not exactly foreplay, in my book), and we settled in to watch a crazy old Bette Davis movie. Lying together on the chicest Louis XVI *canapé* (that's a couch in French, not a plate of hors d'oeuvres), we laughed at the ridiculous dubbing where Bette's mouth kept moving long after the speaking stopped. Our legs tangled up on the couch, we somehow began kissing with unexpected (to me) ferociousness. The passion jumpstarter? In a word: Calvados. Never did see the end of that movie. I vaguely remember the sensation of dragging him off to the bedroom—nothing like becoming the aggressor to shake off uncertainty—followed by the flash of a clock radio glowing in the dark, and the realization I was wearing just heels and a thong. Another blip of thinking, *Why is it during sex with short men I always feel like a giant love panther eating my kill?* Then . . . nothing.

The morning came pronto and when I woke up, I couldn't for the life of me pinpoint the apartment. *Okay nothing's familiar here, not one damn thing . . . and this dark-haired body? . . . Let's see . . . oh yeah . . . Pierre.* I think I'll quietly slip out and put on my ridiculous evening ensemble and stagger home. I never quite know how to deal with these awkward morning-after scenarios.

Sitting up, trying not to wake Pierre, I thought, *Jesus, did we or did we not? I think we slept together . . .* Oh, it's coming back . . . We did . . . I think . . . Yes, we must've, *there's a condom wrapper. Hmm. Clearly nothing to write home about (not that one would anyway and obviously not to family!), but that's probably entirely my own fault. Pierre is lovely, so smart and sweet. Why'd I drink so much? He deserves better . . . a semiconscious girl at the very least. I vow to be sober-girl at the next sleepover.*

I managed to find all my clothes and even the two earrings I'd apparently flung, midfuck, to opposite corners of the room and got as far as the front door when . . . Christ . . . how does this goddamn door work? Turn that, pull here . . . and . . . no luck. Okay, calm down, you can get out. Try this knob . . . No! Pause. Crap-*merde!* Only available option! "Pierre!"

He got out of bed all childlike and sleepy-eyed. Fatigue was immediately replaced with a crestfallen expression when he realized I'd tried to make a silent getaway.

"Why don't you stay for breakfast? I could make you an omelette, tea, or I could run to the *boulangerie* and get *vienoisseries* (pastries)?" he offered, standing there buck-naked.

But I'd made it this far and knew, just knew, my makeup was a mess and that I had turned into Bette Davis as Baby Jane herself, so staying for breakfast was a distinct nonoption. And, frankly, I just wanted to get home and drink about a liter of Evian and take a couple handfuls of aspirin.

I declined, I hoped, graciously. "You know what? I have a million things to do, and I should just get of your way. Go back to sleep, angel. So sorry to have awakened you." Stepping away so he could finagle the door and—dear God— I found I was standing behind Bigfoot (of course a shorter French version).

Jesus. Pierre was either wearing a mink bathrobe or he was the hairiest boy I'd ever seen. In the early-morning daylight, his pale white skin against this mat of dark thick hair was positively scary.

I tried to swallow my gasp, kiss his cheek goodbye, and make it down the stairs before the gasp returned with such force I almost inhaled the bike parked in the courtyard. Yeeowts! I had spent the previous night with Le Bigfoot. Who would've guessed? There were no clues; it wasn't like he had big hairy knuckles (vomit) or chest hair creeping out of his turtlenck (gag).

Despite having discovered Pierre was really Sasquatch in a suit, I liked him. I thought this was a perfect opportunity for me to improve myself by curbing my instinct to be a shallow bitch and chuck him just because he had a permanent fur sweater. In fact, I thought myself, rather the generous soul. *I'll compromise, accept him as he is. Make peace with the whole hairy deal.* Très *big of me,* non? And I figured, in time, I could possibly discreetly slip a cer- tificate for a free waxing in his coat pocket.

Pierre and I agreed to meet up a day later—Friday night—and with Stella in tow, go off to the nightclub La Suite for the usual Champagne–dance ses- sion soirée. La Suite is a fairly cool club; it looked like a 1970s interpretation of a twenty-second-century space station, in a good way. Sort of chic *Star Trek* with an enormous aquarium thrown in and a constantly changing trippy light- ing system. The evening was as sublime as it was expensive. Very.

Stella and I dance fast and furious, Pierre holds the table and chats with César, another young *antiquaire* (who happens to be crazy-sexy, seriously more famous in Paris for his beauty than his eye for furniture) and has joined our table with his beautiful girlfriend, Katya. Stella and I take a breather to re-join the group and replenish our diminishing body fluids. Icy cold explosions of tiny bubbles going down your throat when you're so hot your clothes are glued to your flesh, well, it's intoxicating, a completely perfect elixir. I sit down between Pierre and César and take my darling Pierre's hand in mine.

"Angel, you're not dancing tonight. Are you okay?" I ask.

"Yes, I'm just tired. It's okay, you're having fun. It's great to see you and Stella out there." Good answer, boy. You rock. I look over at the delicious César and he catchs my eye and winks. Oh God, don't. I'm just not strong enough to refuse you. His girlfriend trots off to chat with a friend and César turns toward me as though he's about to say something. I lower my ear to his mouth and César just leans in and exhales slowly against my neck. ME-E-O-W! Not fair. That was too sexy for words. And despite the fact I'm still drip-ping with sweat, I am instantly covered in head-to-toe goosebumps. I glance over at Pierre, who seems oblivious, watching the crowd on the dance floor undulate and swell in its debaucherous revelry.

"I love your shoes, Klein," César says, seductively running his eyes down my legs and resting them on my black four-inch Roger Vivier heels with criss-cross lacing up the back.

"Ah, thanks. They're killing me but I'm a slave to—" Grrhhh . . . grhhh. César has taken an ice cube from the ice bucket and quietly slid it up my bare leg to my inner thigh and, after a pause, lets it drop against my already wet un-derwear. Oo-ooph! Wow! Oh dear God! The internal mechanism that sig-nals, "Leap up, for God's sakes, it's ICE!" is not operating in lieu of, "Let your whole body melt into those fabulous shoes." Silence. For once in my life I'm speechless.

Pierre. Oh Christ, did he see? I look over at him slowly, full of apprehen-sion, and he . . . glares back at me. Well then, I guess that's a yes. I choose to laugh it off, making light of it as my best defense.

"Oh, César, you're so bad. Run along now and leave me with my love," I say with what I hope is a tone of casual dismissal. (Totally ineffective and unconvincing, I might add.) I reach for Pierre's hand as I say, "Gosh, darling, he's a bit crazy. Do you know him well? That was really bizarre. Sorry, I can't imagine what he was thinking." (I'm definitely talking too fast. WAY too fast.)

"I'm going home, Klein. As I said, I'm tired," Pierre says as he stands up, serious and cold, not even looking at me.

"All right, honey, I'll come too. Bye, Stella, we're off. Pierre's pooped and I'm a bit miffed at César."

"What? Why?" She glances at Pierre's expression and sharp cookie that she is, immediately intuits plausable scenarios. "Oh, okay, call me tomorrow." Double-cheek air kiss and we leave La Suite without saying goodbye to the frightfully dangerous, sexy César and his girlfriend, who are now on the dance floor writhing away.

Out on the street, Pierre says nothing, hails a taxi and with the door open behind him announces; "It's over. You need more attention than I can give you." He gets into the cab, slams the door and speeds off, leaving me standing sweat drenched in my fabulous shoes. I am utterly astonished.

Damn, boy, you took the ice cube thing ridiculously hard. I didn't even do anything. Okay, maybe I shuddered in ecstasy at another man's sensual gesture. But that's forgivable, right? Okay, maybe not.

I walked home the ten blocks, punching his number on my cell phone to try to talk to him and get everything straightened out. As my name popped up on his caller ID, he clearly relished not answering my calls. He even ignored my text messages, would not return my calls and—just simply disappeared.

I'd been dumped. This was new, and despite having said I love new things, this wasn't cool. This wasn't on my list of "things to do in Paris"! Definitely not. Get on first-name basis with the famous Colin P. Field of The Hemingway Bar at The Ritz? Yes. Dumped? Nope.

Three weeks later I finally reached Pierre. (From a pay phone, so he couldn't detect it was me. (Creative but pathetic, I know.) Rather than attempt a conversation, I just plunged into a series of bullet points that had been running through my head the last couple of weeks: "Hi, it's Klein. Sorry to bother you, I just thought it was really rude of you to dump me so abruptly. I didn't really do anything. I mean, you're acting like I did something criminal. César was just joking around. I miss you." (Easy, girl, desperation is just pouring through the phone. Find some dignity, fast!) "Can't you give me another chance, Pierre?" (All righty, dignity officially buried under groveling. You know you're going to regret this, Klein.)

"Listen, Klein, I'm sure we'll see each other 'out,' cross paths, and we can be friends but no. Hey, someday you will thank me. Okay? Well, take care." Click. Jesus, he actually threw the "take care" at me. Yuck I got dumped and then gave him yet another shot at rejecting me. Oh what a clever girl I am. Pff-ff-f.

Pierre, wherever you are, let's get something straight right now: if anybody's going to do the dumping, it's ME. And the "some day you'll thank me" line? . . . Nah, that day will NEVER come. I've had enough blows to my ego lately; I didn't need this one. And to think how forgiving I was to you with your unbelievably revolting Bigfoot fur festival!! Hrmph! Dumped. "Humbling" is an understatement. My flabber is gasted. Frankly, returning to the Big-Shot Ex is becoming really tempting.

Parisian men! I swear to God I'd become a lesbian now, but French-women seem to hate me with such intensity I think I'd be rather unsuccessful at it. Although it would be really great to be able to share the same wardrobe with a girl—and a French girl, at that. Think about it, if I found a great girlfriend, and we moved in together, I'd instantly have double the clothing, perfume, handbags. Hmmm. It's something to consider . . . Nah, there's no way I'm sharing my Jimmy Choo heels.

A FEW SLIGHTLY ANNOYING DETAILS I DIDN'T ANTICIPATE

I saw it coming. They guy downstairs from me has gone off the deep end. Far too many times I've left my apartment, just moments after he's passed through the building lobby and . . . Ooof! The cloudy haze of exhaled alcohol is so strong I literally wait until I'm outside to light a cigarette for fear of becoming a human torch blown into smithereens. But now he's drunk twenty-four hours a day, hanging out the window at nine in the morning, yelling to me, "Come up for a drink!" as he spots me coming back from a run. Oh sure, a shot of whisky would be genius after an hour running. Just what I was craving. Poor soul, he's about forty-five, not bad looking, just lost. God forbid, he'll see me at Café de Flore, raise both arms over his head and yell, "My American neighbor!" then pull up a chair, joining me and whomever I'm with. Once I was on a first date and he pulled this horrifying move, wrapping his arms around me saying, "Give me a kiss, c'mon. No? Okay, touch my arm. TOUCH IT! I've been working out. Touch my leg, it's rock-hard. TOUCH IT!" Horrifyingly embarrassing.

Last night at 4:00 a.m. I heard a car door slam, then yelling and a scuffle below my window. With the sound of hands making impact with flesh I went to my window to see Drunk Man below trying to run away from paying for his taxi ride home. Just pathetic, as he feebly clawed at the air as the driver smacked him in the head. I ran down in my robe, paid the driver who kept yelling, "*Putain!*" and dragged Drunk Man to his door thinking, Good Samaritan that I am, *I've done my work here, he's capable of getting in his own door and throwing up in his own apartment.* I passed him curled up on his floor mat as I left this morning. I'm hoping he doesn't ever remember my good deed and think to invite me over for a drink to repay me. Note to self: do not befriend alcoholic, lecherous male neighbors.

SUBLIME PLEASURES DU JOUR—A BIG FOUR THIS MONTH

• Adopting the French *laissez-faire* attitude to life. There is absolutely no sense of frantic energy the way there is in New York, where you feel guiltily decadent if you actually leave your office to get lunch. I love the slow pace of each day in Paris—lunch for two hours, no morning rush hour; it's a calm transition from one activity to the next. No multitasking here.

Admittedly, the old impatient me still rears her ugly head occasionally, in lines at Monoprix grocery store thinking, *All right, everybody, let's pick up the pace here, I'd like to get through the line before my milk turns to cheese. Can we just scooch along here . . .* "

• The French way of saying *oui*. It is done while inhaling, almost gasping in air, and charms my pants off (not literally; okay, maybe once).

• The black licorice, sold like penny candy at the small *épiceries*. Black licorice was also a favorite of the Marquis de Sade, who is starting to seem like a charming dream date compared to some of my recent boyfriends.

• The sexy silver helmets (think *Rocketeer*) and the black leather jackets and boots of the *pompiers* (firemen). Their uniforms are so drop-dead sexy that I've often considered setting my apartment ablaze just to see them in action (it's still a possibility).

THE FRIEND LOWDOWN

Floris saved my ass. No really. We were at Bar du Marché last Thursday around eight in the evening and I was just telling him my predicament that Thierry wants me back and that I was dumped by Pierre after Alexandre left me again, when he said, "Uh-oh."

"What?" I said. "Klein, you are going to have to be cool. Alexandre just arrived—with three women." No fucking way. I felt all the blood drain from my limbs and my mouth go dry. Floris cleverly sat me down at the first available table on the terrace close enough for me to check out the scenario, but seated so that if I fainted I'd just slide a little rather then fall facedown. Yep, motherfucker Alexandre had taken a table four feet away with three dark-haired, un*baisable,* aka unfuckable (if you're shit drunk, maybe) women. I sat in a trance and tried to cope. It wasn't pretty. To see Alexandre laughing and pouring wine for this committee of women, all clearly dying to get him naked . . . nauseating. Presenting the final show of Le Creep Alexandre, come one, come all! Performing in full form a new all-time low of creepy-crappiness. Who knew he had such an evil side? Guess the cheating could've been a hint. Floris held my hand and demanded, "Klein, listen, we have to put on a big show here, like we're having the time of our lives." Right.

So we gestured wildly, keeled over in exaggerated laughter, and tried our damnedest to make Alexandre feel stupid. And intermittently I'd sneak peeks and try to ascertain which of these ho-bags was Alexandre's target, the intended fuck. I ruled out the oldest: with her pale skin and bad fashion sense, no way he was going there. It was a toss-up between the skinny chick who looked like she ran headlong into a wall at a hundred miles an hour and the nondescript woman with the head wrap.

"Floris, can I march over there and say to him, 'Please. Three ugly chicks don't add up to one me, you idiot!' Or is that just bad form?"

"Klein, he wants to hurt you, that's why he's here with them. The coolest thing is to act like you could care less. C'mon, we can play his game and play it better!" Floris said, laying a tender kiss on my hand.

"Okay, you're in charge. My brain has gone to mush," I replied, reeling from this whole nightmare.

Floris ordered two bottles of Chinon and invited every damn cute boy he knew in the place to join us. Our table became a smorgasbord of the hotties of Paris. With this flock of male beauties in attendance, I endured and began to feel slightly better. I noticed Alexandre began to look progressively more and more sad and quiet—exactly the effect we'd hoped for. Perfectly predictable. He soon left with the three mediocre babes, and I flourished Floris with friendly kisses for helping me put on a show and gracefully survive the night. Of course I went home later, belabored calling Thierry and declaring, "Come get me! Take me away from this insanity!" I was still wildly unsure whether leaving Paris was the answer, so I didn't call and opted for vicious anxiety coupled with massive insomnia—and the finale: throwing up from stress. You can only feign nonchalance so long.

Dating Three Men Named Jean, *Ménage à Quatre*, and MITH

MONSIEUR RIGHT REPORT

France needs to come up with a few more names for men. No question. It's as though there are only ten options, so you find yourself meeting several Nicolases and a handful of Philippes and an obscene number of Jeans. The Jeans are where I got into trouble.

I had met, over the course of six months, three men, all named Jean. The first (strap on your thinking cap, this could get tricky) was a very handsome male model, last August at Castel. We'd had a quick chat at the bar where he'd offered, how shall I put this? Okay, he said outright, "Dump your boyfriend, come with me tonight. I know a great party where a bunch of models get together every Thursday and everyone gets naked and it's like a wild Roman party." Hmmm. Tempting for a nanosecond, until something kicked in to remind me that I'm (1) a bit too busy looking for "The One" to sidetrack myself with le group sex gig and (2) if you think I'm getting naked next to a nineteen-year-old female model from Denmark, you are so off-base. A masochist I am not. So I just smiled and slithered back to Alexandre. Of course I immediately told him about the proposition, thinking it'd make him jealous, possessive, maybe even proud? The sum total of his reaction: "Oh."

Chatty guy, *non*? Anyway, I'd taken Jean's phone number simply to fill my cell phone log up . . . I think that was the reason . . . I swear I never called him. I swear. Okay, I texted him, "thks 4 the offer" and that's how he got my number. Innocent, really.

The next Jean—Numéro Deux—I had just met a few days before, at the very-serious-intellectual-bookstore la Hune on boulevard Saint-Germain. Dark haired, in his forties, a distinguished businessman (the whole cuffs and under-stated cufflinks, pocket square, French sleek-suit business-guy look), a bit shy. Feel free to imagine a dapper Harrison Ford sort with a Gallic accent. This lovely creature helped me find the section of Baudelaire and, charmingly, even offered to buy the volume *Flowers of Evil* for me. (Sure, buddy, go ahead). We'd only had that one chance meeting followed by a coffee at Café de la Marie by Saint-Sulpice. Jean Numéro Deux quickly became the central figure of hope in my current love life. We exchanged phone numbers and I, of course, built a universe around the fantasy that he could become serious boyfriend material.

Jean Numéro Trois was an attractive, struggling artist I'd met a couple of weeks before at the Laundromat on rue du Bac. My washing machine at home had spun itself into a hypnotic frenzy and exploded. I hadn't quite managed to embark on the hellish mission of hiring a repairman. (The complexity of that task seemed as difficult as, say, trying to read Sanskrit—in the dark.) Jean de la Laundromat (he should be so lucky as to have a title, even if it is linked to lint traps) was friendly, if a bit strange. And of course, sexy, in a Mad Max kind of way. The only two people there, folding our sheets side by side, we got to talking. Turns out he was also an artist, so I of course asked the question, "So what kind of art do you do, Jean?"

He replied, "Social, conceptual art."

"Interesting, could you be more specific?" (You're going to love this . . .)

"This . . . this conversation, the act of doing laundry, the process of liv-ing . . . this is my art." Trust me, I was as confused as you are.

"Let me get it straight: every moment you're, for example, reading the pa-per or, I don't know, buying cheese, this is your art?"

"Yes," Jean said. I was dumbfounded. I'd been to my share of outrageous and bizarre art exhibits in New York City and met a lot of artists with cre-atively absurd concepts of "making art," but this took the *gâteau*. Talk about taking the pressure off—if just sitting staring into space is art, I'm a prophetic artist. I knew this Jean was harmless, if not totally bizarre, but we exchanged cell phone numbers anyway. I thought if some afternoon I was bored out of my mind, a conversation with him would be hilarious.

So there I was with all three Jeans entered into my cell phone directory and no idea I'd manage to get them all wildly confused. I'd frankly completely forgotten about Jean Numéro Trois after I told absolutely everyone I ran into that week about his theory of art, just to see my friends try to get a handle on the concept. It never failed to elicit, "You're fucking kidding me!" I loved that.

It all really started with Jean Numéro Deux, the new prospect, calling to invite me for dinner that coming Friday evening. Since I'd already spent some serious time imagining what our children would look like (I was banking on my height, his bone structure), I was looking forward to it with anticipation bordering on impatience. This Jean Numéro Deux was a refreshing contrast to recent boyfriends in that he was older, had a serious job at an embassy, and spent his nonworking hours "reading voraciously," as he put it. Despite my love for dancing until I can't stand up, I preferred the idea of a man who didn't find himself sitting next to Kate Moss at nightclubs.

The trigger that set the three Jeans into a collision course was when Jean Numéro Deux called me the Thursday before our dinner to postpone. He told me he had an "unforeseen situation" at the embassy and needed to take an official out for dinner. (C'mon, it's pretty hard to argue with that excuse.) *Très* disappointing. *Très*. The glitch lay in the new cell phone number Jean Numéro Deux gave me to reach him. As I entered his new number, I completely forgot about the other two Jeans. And didn't even think to write his last name on my log. Just "Jean." Hence, the presence of three Jeans in my phone memory. Since that Friday evening was open now, I called Floris.

"Darling, it's Klein. Drinks *ce soir*?"

"Absolutely. Pershing Hall? I'm loving that place lately. You know Andrée Putman did the interiors?"

"Hmm, love it too, but I've been there too much lately. What about Hôtel Costes? Always a chic crowd, and if it's lame we could go to The Hemingway Bar at The Ritz."

"Oh, hell, let's just go to Café de Flore."

"Perfect," I say, somehow knowing we'd end up there anyway. We arrived at eight o'clock and got so caught up people-watching and snivelling about our crappy ex-boyfriends, we blew off dinner and just drank more wine. And more wine. I'd just been telling him the story of Jean Numéro Un, the sexy, beautiful model with blonde shoulder-length hair from Castel. Floris scolded me for being too puritanical and said enthusiastically (and drunkenly), "Let's call him, ask him to join us and, who knows? Maybe the night will take an interesting turn."

Being a slave to every whim of Floris's, I pushed "call Jean" on my phone, and asked him if he would be interested in coming to Flore to meet us. Maybe I should've thought it strange that he was free, as he was in the top ten sexy-men-o-Paris, and that he leapt at the idea, but instead I just snapped the phone shut triumphantly and announced to Floris, "Done! He'll be here in half an hour."

Floris and I share all the details of our love affairs (fair warning, future boyfriends), so we spent the next thirty minutes sending ourselves into a frenzy about whether one or both of us would sleep with the drop-dead sexy boy who was due to arrive any minute. We refused all other invitations, lying in wait for what we were sure was going to be *un petit scandale.*

Toasting our bravado and thirst for life, I hear my name and look up to see Jean. A Jean, but not *the* Jean. Standing before me is Jean Numéro Trois, kooky-wack job of an artist (who's latest masterpiece, *Opening the Door to Flore,* was obviously overlooked by everyone present).

What the . . . ? Wait a minute. Nothing quite computed until I said, "*Bonsoir, Jean,*" and then it hit me. I'd invited and built up and awaited with bated breath . . . the wrong Jean. After telling Floris how Jean had delicious blonde hair and was a model, he looked at me like, "What? This guy's cute, but a bit of a scruffy ragamuffin!"

The three of us made polite chitchat, and I tried to make the best of it by bringing up the subject of art, but when Jean Numéro Trois went to the men's room I couldn't explain fast enough. "Floris, I'm such an idiot, I've absentmindedly—all right—drunkenly, invited the wrong Jean. Do you believe this?"

"Klein, you are stark raving mad!" says Floris, as he raises his glass to toast my apparent insanity. We laughed until we teared up and I vowed to erase Jean Numéro Trois's phone number that instant.

The next Jean snafu was far less innocent, unfortunately. The next week I received a phone call from "Jean" who said we hadn't spoken for a while and that we should catch up. I didn't know his voice very well after just one meeting, so I assumed this was Jean Numéro Deux, the Embassy Guy. (In fact, it was Jean Numéro Un, the sexy blonde model.) I was happy to hear from him, and while he did seem more chatty then I remembered, I racked that up to the fact we were going into week two of knowing each other. He asked if I wanted to meet for dinner on Thursday evening. So, on Thursday, this Jean Numéro Un (sexy blonde) calls and we make a date to meet at a place on Île de la Cité at eight-thirty. Keep in mind, I'm convinced I'm on my way to meet the businessman.

I spent a solid hour choosing just the right outfit: the gray Dolce & Gabbana suit and black Kenzo choker. A half serious–half sexy get-up designed to do the trick for Embassy Jean. I allow a half hour to make the long but beautiful walk to Île de la Cité and entertain myself the whole way thinking up names for our children. I'm kidding. *Oh, you so know I'm not.*

Arriving at the Le Vieux Bistro at precisely eight-thirty, I go inside to wait for Embassy Jean. Ten minutes, twenty, thirty. I walk through the café and don't find him anywhere. So I call, of course. His phone's off. Lovely. What the hell is going on? I just cannot be be stood up. No! I feel like just leaping into the Seine. Okay, thirty-five minutes, thirty-five FUCKING minutes! I decide to leave a message because this is just unacceptable. "Hi, it's Klein. Ah, I'm at the café and YOU are not. It's not terribly polite to not at least call and let me know you weren't coming. Well, take care." Click.

I had to add that little "take care." It's so insincere and cutting, frankly. God, maybe he did come, saw me at a distance, decided I was a troll, and shut his phone off and left. Yep. That's probably it. What a nightmare. Now what? Just then I look up to see the gorgeous blonde model (Jean Numéro Un) strolling my way. Hmm, haven't seen him in a long time. Man, is he beautiful or what?!

"Hey, *bonsoir*, Klein," says the hot blonde model who doesn't seem the least bit surprised to see me.

"*Bonsoir, Jean, ça va?*" (Yes, being distracted-dumped-girl, I have absolutely zero awareness of the ironic double-Jean situation I have stepped into.)

Suavely cavalier man that he is, he doesn't say a word about being late, he just leans in for the ubiquitous kiss on both cheeks. He smells amazing. Mmm. And his soft, warm cheeks, really nice. I am not about to tell him I've just been stood up, so I ask how he is, and what he's been doing lately. Meanwhile, minutes are passing and Embassy Jean is still NOT calling or showing up, and the little girl in me wants to burst into tears.

After we stand around catching up for twenty minutes, Jean Numéro Un invites me to a dinner he is "making with friends," and I accept. At the minimum, to not have to go home shattered and at the maximum, to at least be pursued by one hot man, even if he isn't the Jean of my hopes. Jean tells me he lives just over the bridge.

"All right, lead the way," I say with a final look over my shoulder to see if Embassy Guy has made a late arrival. Nope. Oh, he's a dead man. Jean and I walk together through the little winding cobblestone streets, past the exquisite *hôtel particulier* where the artist Camille Claudel lived, and passing over the little bridge to the Île Saint-Louis.

"This is my building, come on," Jean says, pushing the door code of a handsome eighteenth-century building with double glass doors. We walk through a huge courtyard filled with tall oak trees that surely witnessed the Revolution and past lichen-encrusted sculptures that stand as silent guards in the pretty winter frosted garden. After yet another ornate door and three flights of a wide marble staircase, we arrive at the enormous panelled door to his apartment. Jean stands aside to allow me to enter first.

"Aren't you the gentleman. *Merci,*" I say as I step into an octoganal foyer with twenty-foot ceilings. Mother of God, this is insane. Opulent to die. It's just precisely like stepping into a castle in 1789.

"You want a tour?" he offers with pride, well knowing this is pretty much where every man, woman, and child becomes putty in his hands. When most hosts offer a tour, generally, it's tongue in cheek, followed by, "And this is the breakfast nook, here's the broom closet, and this is the dining-bedroom-office." But not here; this is a literal tour (it ought to have professional guides) involving "wings," servants' rooms, and an entire room for, get this, ironing sheets. Hello? MARRY ME!

Without question, Jean had one of the most amazingly beautiful apartments I have ever seen in Paris. It was huge and even had an enormous circular balcony that looked directly onto the buttresses of Notre Dame. Damn, boy, nice lifestyle. Four vast bedrooms, a two-story library, three large bathrooms each with marble bathtubs sitting on lion's claws clutching crystal globes, a light-filled office set in a turret overlooking the garden. I tried to keep from (1) fainting and (2) falling at his feet, groveling to be his wife, mistress, love slave—maid.

Did I mention, it was perfectly—no really, perfectly—decorated with gigantic modern paintings which I loved, geniusly chosen Italian contemporary furniture in sombre tones with an occasional splash of pumpkin as the accent color. And then there was Jean, who was also absolutely beautiful. Jean Numéro Un blew my mind with his exquisite taste: every chair, every object, was expertly chosen. We went into the kitchen (slightly larger then my apartment); the walls were covered with every size, every type, of copper pan and skillet. It was a gourmet chef's paradise: a wall of at least seventy different knives, two Gaggenau stoves, a huge steel refrigerator with double glass doors (admit it, you've always wanted one too). Two fellow model friends of his— Michel and Bruno (thank God no more Jeans. Christ.)—had arrived earlier and were busy in this culinary paradise whipping up something for dinner.

Michel and Bruno were about the same age as Jean, early thirties and apparently single to boot. Michel was taller, about six foot two with dark thick hair, brilliant green eyes, and an ass to kill for. (Enough said). Bruno was a dirty blonde with a swimmer's body, handsome with short, short hair and long hipster sideburns. Looking at the three of them all standing around talking, I thought, *For crying out loud, this is like a casting call for a men's fashion show. What a stroke of good fortune to find myself, by chance, in this scenario.* I was sure this was going to be a far more interesting night than I would have had with the goddamn businessman anyway. As six different pans simmered and sautéed, all my senses were tantalized. I was definitely up for the Cristal Champagne Michel was uncorking. Bring it on!

Champagne in hand, I went to the balcony to drink in the view and check my cell phone to see if Jean Numéro Deux had finally left some excuse or apologetic message. Nothing! Hate him. So I began leaving what turned out to be a series of progressively nastier messages for Jean Numéro Deux (was it the Cristal talking?). That should do it. There was not the slightest chance he'd miss that I was pissed as hell and not going to let him treat women like this. Lesson delivered, I went back to the three Graces in the kitchen.

All three gave me so much attention that, caught up in my emotional state of being dismissed by the businessman, I was practically giddy. I didn't even find it strange to be the only woman on board. When dinner was announced, the four of us sat down in that ballroom-sized dining room; the table was set with candelabras (Italian, Murano, 1960s, of course) and five wineglasses each, of varying delicacy. We sampled Châteauneuf du Pape, Pétrus Pomerol, Château d'Yquem, you name it. The great vineyards greatest hits, to be sure. The *veau* with white truffles was beautifully served and damn, if all of these men weren't handsome, clever, and complimentary. Somebody pinch me. No, on second thought, somebody ask me to move in.

"So, tell us, Klein, how is it that you're not married yet?" Jean asks me. (I could not be more sick of this question. I ought to have a dossier with photos and reports of each man I've dated, clarifying the reason each of them got his walking papers.)

"Well, I guess I'm waiting for the right man and I'm not really in a rush." (A cliché and an outright lie. What? Do you really want the truth? I'm in full-blown panic every waking minute to start a family. But let's not kid each other, if there's one thing I know, it's that saying that out loud would clear the room *tout de suite*. Still, I have a feeling this probably fools no one.)

"But you're so beautiful, you must be mobbed with men," offers Michel, obviously drunk. (No, in fact, I believe I was stood up tonight, so I'm afraid that would negate that theory, cowboy.) By the way, charm + Champagne + stood up = dangerous night.

After about two hours of banqueting like Romans, we were all drunk as skunks and laughing like we'd had laughing gas for dessert. And drunk. (I guess I mentioned that. It just really needs to be restated as a semi-disclaimer.) My "dangerous seduction incoming" antennae had long since fallen off and the four of us drunken, laughing heathens went into the grand salon to light candles and put on some Moroccan dance music. I need to get something straight here. In the beginning it was just sensual dancing with the three very sexy men. Innocent aerobic activity, *non*? But ever so expertly I was soon bathed in kisses and caresses. The night went on, the clothes came off, and I was definitely in the midst of the single most erotic evening of my life. I was laid on a long leather chaise and attended to like the queen of Egypt. Unfathomable pleasure. Never in my life did I think I would find myself in this position (actually all positions) with three luscious men and the breathtaking image of Notre Dame in the background.

I will admit, I generally enjoy being the center of attention, but this was even beyond my wildest fantasies. The highlights (and by the way, there were no lowlights): a sensual storm of six strong masculine hands caressing me absolutely everywhere, light kisses, and wet, probing tongues pulling me into virtual unconciousness, three mouths, three very hard, throbbing French sceptors of desire, beautifully executed, perfectly paced, and with an undulating rhythm. Moans of pleasure in waves of their different voices and exquisitely timed. Exhausted, I'd yell, while laughing, "Time out! I need to rest a second!" and a tray of refreshments (never has that word been more appropriate actually) would appear: Belgian chocolates, cold milk, handfuls of grapes; gold chocolate wrappers all over the floor, empty glasses shattered in the fireplace, peals of laughter, candles burning to the quick. Then we'd go back and resume our fabulous orgasmathon.

After hours and hours of this and the sight of the first rays of sun starting to make their way through the silk curtains, I thought perhaps it was time to call it a night. A fucking AMAZING night. But if I ever wanted to walk again without the aid of prosthetics, I knew I'd have to let the curtain fall on this performance.

"Gentlemen, I think it's time for me to take my leave," I announced with a smile and a dramatic flourish.

"Are you quite sure?" asked Bruno pleadingly, from the floor at the foot of my chaise.

"Yes, I should go," I said, feeling like a carnal Cleopatra in the center of these three examples of male perfection splayed across the floor. Finally coming out of the tunnel of delicious hedonism, I looked around the room—what a state it was in. Everywhere I looked, bonbon and condom wrappers, emptied Champagne bottles strewn about, abandoned and crushed sprigs of grapes, piles of jeans and dress shirts, some tossed-over chairs, the odd cufflink underfoot, and a single sock flung onto the fireplace.

"Thank you for this. It's been . . . a pleasure," I said formally, as all four of us burst into exhausted, contented laughter. They all pitched in to gather my things and with sincere tenderness helped me back into the same clothes they had so beautifully stripped me of six magnificent hours ago. I gave them each a kiss on the forehead and took my quite satiated self home.

I walked slowly, dazed and in a delicious trance. Shaking my head every few steps and often bursting into self-astonished nervous laughter. *Now that, Klein, that is LIVING,* I said to myself as I watched the sun majestically rise, turning the sky from violet to amber. I went through the entire next day with a huge Cheshire cat mischievous grin. What a secret I had. I told no one, not even Puccini. And certainly not Stella; she was a tad on the conservative side, and if I had told her my latest exploit, her head would have fallen off.

Fleeting images of tongue baths and spine-tingling pleasure ran through the cinema of my skull, making it impossible to rest and recover. I took a warm bath, sipped tea, and basked in the aftereffects of it all, totally relinquishing myself to the erotic automatic playback that ran through my thoughts. (The word *sublime* falls far short. Ridiculously short.)

Jean Numéro Un and his two friends called me that afternoon to invite me for a spontaneous weekend for four (*mais oui*) in Marrakesh. I was flattered, exhausted, and knew no matter how pleasurable it could be, I wasn't going to make a repeat performance of that oeuvre again. Once was perfect and enough to live off forever. Frankly, I'd completely forgotten about Jean Numéro Deux until he called that evening to say, "Hello, Klein. I'm sorry, I'm very confused. Why did you leave me so many rude messages last night?" I was pleased to finally have him on the phone to let him have it for standing me up, when he added, "I've been in London all this week and just returned this morning to your odd messages." (That explains why his phone was off.) And then it hit me: oh dear God, I did it again, I got my Jeans mixed up. The sexy blonde model was the one who called Monday and invited me to dinner, and—No! Oh, yes—who planned the whole *ménage à quatre* evening. It wasn't just a chance meeting on the Île de la Cité, it was already set up: a group-sex soirée. Eeeeck!

I cowered in my apartment with shame. How did I miss all the clues? I took a new vow of celibacy and stayed in all weekend, staying out of trouble, escaping into books. I delved into literature with a vengeance, seeking poetical support for those fleeting moments of, *Jesus, what have I done? Am I a bad girl now? Or just really, really modern and sexual, à la a new millennium version of Anaïs Nin? Talk about getting sidetracked from my husband-baby mission!*

I repeated to myself a favorite rationalization I like to employ in such moments, the wisdom of my buddy Oscar Wilde: "The only way to get rid of a temptation is to yield to it." (You can borrow; it's terribly useful some morning-afters.) And my research also yielded these poignant lines of poetry by Guillaume Apollinaire:

Remember me you men in years to come . . .
I saw Paris already drunk in the vine
Was gathering the sweetest grape that the world knows
The marvelous fruit singing from the trellises . . .
O Paris we are you, your lively drinks
Great Paris, last refuge of leaving reason
Ordering our moods as your destiny compels . . .

And then, ever so fortuitously, I came across a phrase by Victor Hugo that immediately made me reconsider my self-imposed guilt-fest. In fact, I did a complete about face and let myself slip into delight all over again when I read, and committed to memory instantly, the following:

A woman with one lover is an angel,
a woman with two lovers is a monster,
but a woman with three lovers is a woman.

So French, non?

A FEW SLIGHTLY ANNOYING DETAILS I DIDN'T ANTICIPATE

My washing machine spun itself into a maniac state and damn near exploded. Do you know how long it takes to dry a towel that is soaking wet and weighs fifty pounds? Fuck. I thought, *Oh great, another Euro-obstacle I so don't need to deal with*. But I took on the challenge of trying to get it fixed. Well, sort of. I found the warranty manual, and found the Paris-based repair company phone number; even actually called them (pre-written, dictionary-prepared translation speech in hand). And what do I get for my efforts? A recording. Perfect. I've left ten messages requesting they return my call. Zip.

I'm sure in the year 2020 someone will get back to me. So it's back to shades of my college days, *chez le* Laundromat. It is positively *très* unchic dragging bags of laundry through Saint-Germain! Bloody hell!

SUBLIME PLEASURE DU JOUR

Have you ever wondered about the whole noncircumcised European men issue? Too shy to ask? Here's the deal. When I was about fourteen years old my best friend Kathy and I saw a photo of one in a medical journal of her father's, and I believe our howls of horror were heard in the next zip code. One of us (probably me, because I was more frigid and uptight) named this scarily unfamiliar uncircumcised penis the Man in the Hood, "MITH," for short. (You get it, it's kind of like a hood, the whole foreskin deal.)

Kathy and I used to sit around gabbing at the frightening idea of ever— GROSS!!—ever actually seeing one in the flesh. Of course at that age we hadn't seen any wholesome all-American circumcised penises either, but that didn't stop our unshakable vow to stay away from the MITHs. In fact, the Big-Shot Industrialist Boyfriend was my first MITH, and I can hardly remember ever seeing it in its flaccid foreign state of complete hooded cover. Plus, I have got to say there is seriously something about the intact foreskin that just makes sex better (for me, of course; I mean, they always come, don't they?). I don't need to see any research. Ladies and gentlemen of the jury, I offer myself as evidence. I am a devout worshipper at the shrine of MITH. So much so, that I vow to never circumcise my own sons as a pseudo gift to the future women in their lives. Not that I expect a daughter-in-law to ever actually thank me for the gesture, but it will be understood. So if you have been timid and reticent about partaking of a Man in a Hood, run, don't walk, to the nearest Frenchman. You can thank me later.

THE FRIEND LOWDOWN

Feel kinda crappy. Couldn't share details of the *ménage à quatre* with Stella. I wanted to, sort of, but she already thinks I'm a bit of an untamed filly, so I held my tongue. (Something I obviously didn't do during the raging romp with three male models. Ha-ha.) I did tell Floris about the three-men-on-me soirée. Floris took it as casually as if I'd said, "I just bought a new cutting board." I love a man who's seen it all and just can't be shocked. It's like, "Yeah, yeah, yeah. Three dicks in your face. Been there, done that. So where should we go for dinner?" Hilarious. (By the way, Floris has ended his campaign to sleep with me, phew! All is well again.) Although I do kind of miss the ego boosting, "I'm so fabulous, even gay men want me!"

The Journey Through the Wilderness,
a Go at Celibacy, and Sabbia Rosa

February

MONSIEUR RIGHT REPORT

So was I going to go back to New York and my Big-Shot Ex, Thierry, or not? I had spent months thinking, *I really should. I still love him madly. And this Monsieur Right search is just becoming a bad joke. I'm running out of money and time and what do I have to show for it? Just a plethora of anecdotes that make people laugh in horror at all my bad fortune and allow them to say to themselves, "Phew! I'm glad I'm not her."*

Skimming through my private journal one chilly gray Monday afternoon, I read my notes of story after story of hopes raised on the belief I may have found a decent man then always followed by a horrible, crashing descent. I looked over at Puccini and said out loud, "*Ça suffit!*" (That's enough!) I raced to the Paris phone book, scouring for numbers for shipping companies, jotted down two, and set up an appointment to have them come give me an estimate for hauling everything back to New York, back to life with the man who really loved me and I knew always would: Thierry.

I called my old design headhunter back in New York and told her to put out the word I was headed home. I fired off letters to all my Manhattan friends. "I'm comin' back!" I announced. Friends and family were all wildly supportive, even thrilled with my decision. I was just going on autopilot. Project: New York Return. Within that same week, I took Stella to lunch at Lipp and explained that I hated the idea of leaving her but I'd had enough. I wasn't going to let Paris ruin my chances of . . . POW! Then it hit me. I can't go back! This is my dream; I'm not done. So what? I haven't had everything fall into place instantly. There is still a chance I will find the right man who will love and accept me and will want to have children. And that "children detail" is one thing I know I will never get with Thierry. Right then, in mid-departure defense speech, I abandonned the idea of leaving. Happily abandonned it. No way I'm leaving. I've made a life here. I called Thierry and said a teary final goodbye and set him free. And in doing so, I felt that I set myself free too. It occurred to me, *It's not about the end result of accomplishing my big goal, it's about the journey. This way of thinking maybe isn't very goal-oriented-American, interestingly enough, but it's how I feel now. Who I am now.*

For all that I have done and not done, I have learned the most valuable lesson is to follow your heart, your own path. And to trust in that. Uprooting yourself from one country to another to chase a lifelong dream gives you an eternal sense of pride no one can ever teach you, take from you, or give to you. It's your little private joy. In the poignant words of Marcel Proust:

> *We are not provided with wisdom, we must discover it for ourselves, after a journey through the wilderness, which no one can take for us, an effort which no one can spare us, for our wisdom is the point of view from which we come at last to regard the world.*

Read it again. Let it settle in, it's that good.

A FEW SLIGHTLY ANNOYING DETAILS I DIDN'T ANTICIPATE

I can do it. It's not complete torture, but it's hard. After the final (I swear) breakup with Alexandre and the male model flesh-fest I've put my sexual desire/libido in a box under my bed and sworn myself to celibacy. I'm dedicated to protecting this precious pleasure. I've lived freely in this respect since the moment my Christian Louboutins hit the tarmac in Paris and I regret nothing. But I just feel I want to save myself a bit, for truly deserving souls.

Fighting against my own raging hormones is an exhaustive new game of discipline. Just because I'm in my sexual prime as "they" say (I'll be frank and tell you "their" studies were right on the money), I'm not going to jump into bed with any more merely beautiful men just to test my maximum orgasms-per-evening record. I'm going to work like a dog all day, drawing until evening, and then whatever meager strength is left in my hand shall be put to good use in the private confines of my bed-for-one, shall we say. And no more need to drag the mattress to the floor to accommodate another human being. Puccini and I are fine on our own, thank you very much.

SUBLIME PLEASURE DU JOUR

The search for Monsieur Right is on the back burner. I'm firmly placing myself in no-man's-land, literally. No men for a while, I'm pooped. I need to unleash all this energy in a constructive, creative outlet. It's time to draw. No question about it. As I have enough canvases done to fill every square inch of my apartment walls, I think I'll head over to the famous Sennelier art supply store around the corner on quai Voltaire to check out the pastel papers. They always have some new fabulous thing just off the boat from India: crazy-cool silk paper with real silk cocoons woven in or huge ombréd sheets specked with gold foil. Love this place, and finally after almost two years of shopping here, I'm on a first-name basis with the staff. I so get a huge kick out of buying pigments at the same place Picasso, Cézanne, and Gauguin used to buy their art supplies.

It occurs to me as I'm marching over to the quai Voltaire, *Funny, these guys at Sennelier only know me as a scruffy makeupless girl who goes in and belabours for hours over which verdigris to buy. They don't have a clue I clean up okay and ever had a whole glam jet-setty life. They just think I'm some poor starving artist who has probably never even seen the inside of a proper restaurant. I love that.*

Pushing through the old wood door into the quaint little nineteenth-century shop, I spot my guy, the one who helps me reach the huge tubs of polymer medium on the top shelf and steers me clear of bad-quality gesso.

"*Salut,* Émile!" I say, as I take the stairs two-by-two up to the floor that stocks watercolor paper, easels, and fine inks.

"*Salut, Klein, ça va? De quoi as-tu besoin aujourd' hui?*" he yells up to me.

"*Juste du papier, je pense. J'ai une nouvelle idée!*" I call back over my shoulder as I turn into the narrow room lined with large oak cabinets laden with hundreds of narrow drawers full of sheets of paper. There's paper everywhere, floor to ceiling. Sheets of vellum hanging in a hundred different weights, rolled tubes of thick white Chinese paper for calligraphy, heaps of bamboo, mulberry, and rice sheets, fibrous pressed cotton flocked with bits of pulp and bark. Heaven. I rifle through a drawer of pale gold sheets, delicate as powder. Nope, I need this particular paper to be able to hold up to a wash of ink and erasing and not buckle or warp. Oh, check out these raw eggshell colored ones; they're the perfect weight and the edges are fabulous, all haphhazard and irregular. Great, they have the same paper in a multitude of greens and sepia browns. Perfection.

I pull the drawer out so I don't forget where in this chaos I found them and go to retrieve Émile. I have to, you can't just take what you want to the cashier. *Non,* as with so much in France, you've got to go about buying art supplies in the most time-consuming and formal way imaginable. I realize I've gotten used to this process and it has a certain charm. With Émile in tow, I hustle up the stairs and point out what I want. Émile oh-so-gingerly rolls up the five or six sheets of paper, while simultaneously jotting down the prices for each on a small pad to his left.

"Tu connais que le vert est plus cher?" he says, explaining the green paper is more expensive. *"Parce que c'est avec des algues."*

"Mortal!" I blurt out. How cool, it's made with seaweed. Ideal for my idea of linear motifs abstracted from nature. With my tube of treasures paid for I troop out to the street and head for home. The sky is as gray as a sea pearl and dark clouds are rolling in. Gorgeous. I even love dark days in Paris. They are romantic, somehow poetic. Come to think of it, I've never once looked out my window and thought, *Ah crap, what a crap day.* This city is just magic; that's all there is to it.

Once home I give Puccini a proper three-minute shoulder massage, open the windows to clear out my "cigarette-smoke aromatherapy," and start about pulling my supplies out to work. After flicking on the CD player to the sound-track from the film *Farinelli* (my poor neighbors, who are forced to hear this day after day), I unroll and lay the sheets out on a large old chalkboard I bought for a pittance at *les Puces* (flea market). I gently Scotch tape the edges down to keep the paper flat and set the board at an angle against a wall. I'm aware sitting Indian-style on the cold tiles, with a bottle of Orangina by my side and a pile of pencils all over the floor, isn't exactly picturesque and light-years from comfortable, but it's the only way I can work. Even if I had a killer huge studio I'd still be hunkered down in a corner. Hey, you ever see Francis Bacon's studio? A tiny dump and it was the setting for creative genuis. In fact, some of the crappiest work I've ever seen has come out of those spacious light-filled lofts in Soho. (Smells like defensiveness, *non?*)

Puccini resumes his regal position on the chair next to me as I straddle the sheet of pressed seaweed, softly putting pencil to paper, barely making an image, just warming up, seeing how it feels, and trying to find my gesture. Far too often I've begun by working on studies and prep drawings and discovered that the very first drawing is always so free, loose, and relaxed and that for the life of me when I've tried to create it on the proper surface, it loses all vitality. So I've learned to just leap into it. Hit or miss, at least it won't be overworked or rehearsed. My cell phone rings and I see on the caller ID that it's Alexandre. Lately he calls and says he wants to be friends. Good God. Even if I could find it in my heart to be his buddy, not today, I'm engrossed in this project and my love affair is with the work.

The wind outside picks up and blows petunia petals from my flower boxes into the window as the singing castrato hits a high C. Well, that's certainly inspiring, for God's sakes, and how lovely. I smile to myself and keep drawing. Sweeping pale green pastel in undulating waves, innerweaving streams of color until the image appears to be sea anemone tentacles. It's coming together; this is what I was shooting for, gentle and graceful strokes, part balletic arabasques and part sea coral anchored in the waves. Reaching for a soft gray to highlight the edges and a moss green to strengthen the shadows . . . an hour passes, then another. I'm on to another sheet of paper, this one a swampy green with flecks of amber . . . a variation on the theme . . . a sprawling outline of a sea skate in motion, still abstract enough to be undiscernable . . . Then a cigarette break so I can step back and look at them from a distance. Not bad, could be bigger still and have more volume, but that's the idea. Man, I love this. Strange that I'm so exhausted and frustrated in my love life and the work is coming out so delicately ethereal and quiet. Oh dear, does this mean what I think it does? No men = good work.

Say it's not so.

THE FRIEND LOWDOWN

At nine o'clock this morning Stella called from a taxi on her way back from Charles de Gaulle Airport. She just arrived from a trip back home to the

States. "Are you up?" she says with muffled traffic as a background. "Klein, guess what?"

That's always a bad question to put to me, because I have an insane, twisted imagination and generally my guesses often are so over-the-top they destroy the intended impact. So I refrained from conveying my first thoughts, which were *You ran into Sean Penn on the plane and fucked him in the toilet* and *You found a Bulgari watch in the taxi,* and simply respond with a polite, "What? Tell me!"

"I got engaged." (Note the lack of an exclamation mark.)

"Wow." (No exclamation mark right back.) "Really? Tell me everything," I say, a little in shock. (Wasn't it just about three weeks ago we'd had that long, drunken heart-to-heart at Flore about her boyfriend and all their problems, and how he definitely wasn't "the one"?) At least I'm not convinced he's good enough for Stella. Did I get her so drunk she blacked out and forgot all the things she said? Impossible. Stella gave me the whole story and it goes something like this: She took her boyfriend, Antoine, back to Boston to meet the family and celebrate her thirtieth birthday. The parents loved him and he swooped in, took advantage of the whole celebration and warm reception, and proposed.

"Are you happy?" I ask, begging for the truth.

"Oh yes, it's just overwhelming."

"Yes, it is that," I respond, thinking back to each of the ten times I've been proposed to. (Don't ask! Only six of them were real, potentially worthy prospects and the others a smattering of fools. One who didn't even know my last name, another on the first date. You may wonder why I keep a list at all.) "We must celebrate, girl. Meet me at La Croix Rouge at one o'clock, okay?"

"Perfect," she says. "It's a date."

I walk over to La Croix Rouge ten minutes before one o'clock. I have to, the café is so damn cute it's always packed by lunchtime and I vow to never be one of those idiots who actually stand in line and wait to pay to eat somewhere. La Croix Rouge is smack-dab between Stella's and my apartments, on the little corner of rue de Sevres and rue de Grenelle. Conveniently located, I might add, in the absolute heart of power shopping in Saint-Germain. A stone's throw from Prada, Yohji Yamamoto, and MAC.

It's a pretty sunny day and, despite it being winter, the terrace is filling up fast with fellow thirty-something fashion types. I lay claim to the corner table drenched in warm sun and as private as it gets at La Croix Rouge. The tables and chairs are all crammed together and, with everyone sitting virtually on top of each other, privacy is in short supply. But then again, you don't go to a café to be alone, but to be part of a scene and to be seen. It's part of their charm really.

Stella arrives a smidge late, as always, breathless, apologetic, and the vision of femininity. In heels. She wears heels every day. Amazing. Stella and I scooch on our wicker chairs, sidesaddle, next to each other to people (men) watch and "get a little color," as she says.

"So, did he propose with a ring?" I ask right off the bat. Girls and rings, what sex-based genetic disorder exists that makes rings so ridiculously important and interesting? I don't know, but we all have it.

"No. No ring yet. But it was really sweet. He got down on one knee and the whole thing," she says. I give her a look; she knows I'm not convinced this engagement thing is clever.

"Oh, come on," she protests before I can even say a word. "He is so good to me. He always cleans, brings me flowers," (yeah, like twice) ". . . and I love his family" (true, but you don't marry the family) ". . . and I'm thirty now. I love him and I've got to try." Ah, there's the heart of the matter! She's panicking at thirty! If she were an old spinster like me, she'd probably slit her wrists. I've got my work cut out for me here, but the time has come. There is no way she can marry this idiot. Better take it slow or she'll defend him.

"Okay, we're here to celebrate. No diets. My treat. Let's eat until we're sick!" I say with faux enthusiasm. We order huge bowls of moules marinières accompanied by a plate of saucisson and radishes, followed by an *île flottante* (meringue-like baked Alaska swimming in creamy custard). Gluttony—one of my top three favorite sins (I'm sure you can guess the other two). And, of course, wine is ubiquitous. An hour later, *la bouteille de Sancerre* is history and the terrace is starting to empty. We're in great moods, two American girls slightly drunk in the sun, sitting on a beautiful terrace in Paris. It's a perfect setting to drink our way to the truth. "*In vino veritas*" I've always said (I'm aware I didn't make it up). So, before the espressos hit the table, I got her to admit her boyfriend's really a stinker. When you ask someone, "Tell me one thing, just one, that you adore about him," and they can't come up with one, the gig is up. We lay it all out on the table and I'm not going to let her pretend "he's really sweet" when he insists she come home each night after class by eight o'clock to iron his shirts and make him dinner. *Quel idiot!*

In between fits of laughter and sober (okay, not sober, make that fleeting moments of seriousness) she has opened her eyes. Being that I'm five years older than Stella, I don't want to watch her make a mistake I feel I can so easily see coming. She seems quite relieved, in fact, and despite saying we were meeting to "celebrate" her engagement, we end up toasting to her refusal. I happily put down my credit card; this was money well spent. We agreed, great lunch, bad boyfriend. Case closed.

What now? The obvious: two smiling girls with round tummies like little ponies head over to rue des Saints-Pères to window shop. Without a glance or a word Stella and I concur "no" to Ferragamo (too old lady–Japanese tourist), "no" to Versace (trashy nouveau riche). J.P. Tods gets just a nod at a great handbag, and the hat shop Elvis Pompilio gets a conspiratory glance and, "Oh yes! Let's!"

We leap up the stairs and in a blur each are trying on the most beautiful and ridiculous hats of this genius milliner. I'm trying mighty hard to rationalize owning a two-foot-tall madhatter in straw while Stella's sold on the pale yellow Ascot chapeau with an enormous bow in the front. We look at each other, then really see each other, our hats grazing the chandelier. "Oh, who are we kidding? We have absolutely nowhere to wear these." That never held me back before but with age, one gains wisdom—and less room in one's boudoir for eccentricities. One glance across the street at the yummy window of Sabbia Rosa and we're off. This lingerie shop is world renowned for its heart-stopping sexy lingerie. I own nothing, not even a measly stocking, from this store for the simple reason that the turquoise and cream bustier in the window costs the equivalent of my monthly rent. *Et voilà!* But take note: this is absolutely the best time to shop for ridiculously expensive lingerie, as after lunch you feel like such a bloated cow you are completely not able to envision yourself in a lace string and transparent lace bra. *Non, merci.* I would look like a walrus with two rubber bands around it. We hold up nightgowns of hand-embroidered lace that are so exquisite they should be framed instead of worn. We peruse the sexy demi-cup "merry widows" and "ooh" and "ah." Our excursion is fun but painful, which is in fact a constant theme of life in France.

Once back on the street Stella says, "Just who has the money and the body to wear those clothes? God!"

I mouth her our worst nightmare: "M-I-S-T-R-E-S-S."

"Argh!" She collapses in feigned agony. We walk away, arm in arm, safely single and knowing we'll live to shop many more days. Girlfriends: there's no substitute.

Wake-Up Call, Reality Check Time

One thing about "chasing a dream" that you can't escape is the fact that you have to occasionally sit down with yourself and assess your situation. Life will be pleasantly going along and then you will be jolted by some bump in the road. Sometimes it's something minor. For example, for me it's often a bank statement (I always open with one eye closed and sitting down), and sometimes they're major. The big ones make you realize you'd better take a moment to think about what you're doing and more important, where you're going.

But that particular evening, the wake-up call was strangely different. I had just finished reading *The Prime of Life* by Simone de Beauvoir and wasn't ready to go to sleep, even though it was already one o'clock. Routinely, when I can't sleep, I leave Puccini dozing on the duvet, and go open the large French windows (*mais oui*) in my living room to look out onto the silent streets below. I was used to lighting up a cigarette as my night-gazing prop but it was no more Dunhill Super Lights for me. I had finally quit smoking. So there I was with just my hands on my chin, elbows on the ledge . . . just me.

There was not a single light on in any building up and down rue de Beaune. All my neighbors must have been asleep or away. I was entirely alone. Divine. I leaned out over my flower boxes and felt the evening air on my face. I felt as though I was the sole inhabitant of Paris, with just the nocturnal chorus of the wind in the trees as my companion. If you love Paris, it has a soul that speaks to you in these moments, allowing you to see things with clarity and perspective. In the midst of the darkness, looking out toward the Louvre, I felt a surprising absence of anxiety and concerns. My thoughts were less racing, less anxious. I became aware of a palpable quiet not only on the streets, but in me. As powerful as the ephiphany I felt the evening in New York when I decided to move here, yet unique in that, this time, it was not a driving force to act but a silent awareness of peace.

After living in Paris for almost two years, that tranquil evening I knew I was forever changed. I had never cried so much in my life as in those two years but, I'd evolved into someone I sure liked a helluva lot better than I used to back in New York City. There was a "pre-Paris me" and "me now." And I could not go back to being that other girl.

When I first moved to Paris, I made a commitment to not have a television, and while I am sure it would have probably helped my French, I just wanted to force myself to be intellectually active, to have to entertain my own mind. Let's face it, I love going out and painting the town red, but I wanted to have a balance to those decadent nights. So life in Paris was immediately different when I stayed in; my options were music and painting or music and a book. I have never read so much in my life. When you have few friends, no TV, and you've walked all day until your feet throb, you have all the time in the world to read. I hoped that one day I would be busy with a family, a husband and kids, and this was (a rare) chance to read everything I ever wanted. To make good on the "one day I will attempt to read Tolstoy." I have read great stuff, serious stuff—every day for over two years. I have devoured virtually all of Balzac's *La Comédie Humaine,* Hugo, Proust, Dumas, La Fontaine, de Beauvoir, Huysmans, Sartre, Sand, Flaubert, Rousseau, Colette, Anatole France, Baudelaire, Gracq, Nabokov, Goethe, Rilke, Rimbaud, Hegel, Saint-Simon, Voltaire, Molière, de Sevigne, Daudet, Racine and read all about Talleyrand, Fouché, Mazarin, Richelieu, Napoléon, Colbert, and on and on.

For all my efforts, I cannot say I have any grasp or appreciation for Sartre's existentalism, nor Hegel, for God sakes. Leisure reading? Not so much. And if you ask me to quote Daudet I'll have to pull a "Nico" (a grunt nonresponse). But hey, I'm trying and that's what matters, *non*?

Could I be happy—truly happy—living in Paris without the Frenchman I came for? I knew I could be. My life was rich in what mattered. Truthfully, each moment living in Paris is like a surreal, lucid dream (or nightmare at times). From the moment I wake up to the sound of doves cooing and church bells ringing at nine o'clock, Paris is already working its magic, calmly, welcoming me into my day. Such a beautiful contrast to waking in New York City to the grating alarm clock, car sirens, and downtown morning rush-hour traffic.

Around ten o'clock I put on my (blatantly obvious American) running garb and jog over the Pont-Royal, past the Louvre to the Tuileries. (I used to grab a bagel and crap coffee at Starbucks and dive into the hot subway, simmering in a potpourri of urine.) My morning run these days is past the gorgeous fountains and Maillol sculptures in the Tuileries, past Vincent, who sets up the chairs in the morning at the outdoor restaurant in the park. He always yells out in English, "You are the champion!" How charming, and such a striking difference to jogging in New York City, where I'd dodge bike messengers and taxis, inhale toxic exhaust, and hear, "Hey slim, I fuckin' guar-antee you a good work out!" from truck drivers on the West Side Highway. *Mon dieu,* how appalling.

After my run, back home for a long, warm bath with a cup of tea. Taking a quick shower and racing back into society isn't even an option since I only have a bathtub, like most Parisians. Everything is slowed down here. This relaxed, lackadaisical approach to life just takes everything down a notch on the stress meter. It's not so important what you do, especially what you do for a living. It's just important that you *be*. Be in the moment, be who you are, be consistent in your rituals and habits instead of always chasing the trendy and new. That influence has also affected my painting. In New York, I painted large violent oils, but in Paris I find I'm making small gentle drawings inspired by a calm sea. It's as though they were done by two very different people, and in a way they were. I'm still a million miles from getting into the Venice Biennale, but I am proud of where they are going and I'll have a one-man—make that one-woman—show in April at Monsieur Despont's gallery on the rue des Beaux-Arts.

That night my mind ran through what are surely the classic memories of every expat: my first dream in French, or when I told my first joke in French. These moments I will never forget, and I'm sure that joke was about as impressive to my French friends as tying a shoelace, but for me it was a huge triumph.

My new schedule of working twice a week with a tutor has given me a sense of a door opening. A barrier has come down between me and what had felt like a play I had a nonspeaking role in. I can't honestly say I'm fluent quite yet. So obvious after going to see a movie in French recently. "What did he say? *'Crémaillère?!'* What the hell is that? Could the dialogue fucking slow down, please. What is going on? Arghhh!" (By the way, it means "house warming party.") But it's coming and it's exciting as all hell.

I miss having a little more money, but the upside is that now everything "luxurious" seems more precious and special, because it is so rare. To dine in a chic and gorgeous restaurant like Guy Savoy is—as it should be—a treat! In New York I was getting so jaded with all the expensive dinners care of my Big-Shot Ex, Thierry.

After my entire adult life spent feeling I had to have "the latest" everything, whether it be a designer shoe or a killer jacket, I rarely buy clothes anymore. I window shop with abandon, and maybe once a season I'll indulge in the big *soldes* (sales) and grab a classic belt or a skirt. In my late twenties I could finally afford things like makeup from Chanel, manicures at Elizabeth Arden, leg waxing at J. Sister's, massages, and personal trainers. Now my beauty routine has all switched back to how it was when I was a teenager: Maybelline, Gillette disposable razors, doing my own pedicure, stretching, and running outside. And I like it this way. It amazes and delights me to have walked away from being a high-maintenance diva. That girl was a bit of a demanding bitch and spent money on ridiculous things like Puccini's hundred-fifty-dollar silver cat bowl. So dumb.

Falling into the diva-no-more category? My friend Fabian called recently to make me a preposterously funny offer: "The guy who lives below me just died and has no family. Anyone who wants to can take what they wish." Morbid? Yes. Free stuff? Yes! The apartment had mostly been pilfered through by the time I got there, and it wasn't as though this guy had Fabergé eggs and Giacomettis, but I found a slightly used vacuum and literally went into ecstasies to have a free vacuum. Yes, the Klein who would go ballistic, insisting on sitting in the first-class cabin only, on the Concorde, was jumping up and down over a dead man's Hoover! You know what? I am proud of that (or maybe I have just simply lost my mind). But honestly, life in Paris quickly and quietly alters you in profound and pleasant ways.

And when you're living your dream, you can never say, "God, I wish I were in . . ." Rome or Paris or whatever beautiful locale again. When you're actually there, you just lose that way of thinking entirely. For example, having a screaming argument with your boyfriend in the courtyard of the Louvre still ain't half bad.

For all the painful misadventures I've had trying to understand Frenchmen (which is often like throwing yourself against a brick wall) I still wouldn't trade it for the world. I am all too aware that I am the last of all my friends, even the lesbian, to have children. But I have chosen differently, a path I had to take. I live by the motto "It's better to regret what you've done than what you have not done," which honestly is so exhausting to adhere to. I know I have aged twice as fast with all the wine, cigarettes, and stress. And I'm okay with it all. I have the face I've earned; I wouldn't dream of having it any other way.

It's time to accept my mistakes, like marching around for a whole year ordering "a Diet Coke and a blow job," or my blazingly absurd declaration at a dinner party, "*j'adore ma chatte,*" thinking I'm proclaiming my love for Puccini when in fact I'm screaming, "I love my pussy." (The men laughed and the women scowled, in case you're curious.) And I'll accept the mistakes I've made with men too—lots of mistakes.

I've probably spent too many nights dancing and drinking into the wee hours, trying to literally shake free the turmoil of disappointment I felt in men. And I know I pushed too hard (*par exemple,* the note on a napkin), have been too eager to find a man to bring me what I wanted and to solve everything. I have finally realized I am what I wanted: childless or not, I am enough. Yeah, I am a one-woman show all right.

That calm and quiet night at my window, I looked at the woman I was and the woman I've become, and I realized that I'm far happier in my skin than I ever have been, that I have never felt so conscious, so intensely alive. No man did that for me. Paris did. I did.

Café de Flore, My Stepmonster, and Magic Pants

March

MONSIEUR RIGHT REPORT

Held until the precious end. (And trust me, it's worth waiting for.)

A FEW SLIGHTLY ANNOYING DETAILS I DIDN'T ANTICIPATE

What I miss about the States . . .

My initial thought was to leave this page entirely blank, because at first I couldn't really think of many things I miss, even a little. And plus, wouldn't an entirely blank page in a book look cool?

But it turns out there are a few things I miss or even occasionally pine for: a weekly paycheck, Reese's peanut butter cups (I went through horrible, agonizing withdrawal), New York delis with their amazing salad bar buffets of food fixin's by the pound, Snapple Diet Lemonade, skim milk (doesn't really exist in France; it was categorized as "healthy" and thus immediately abandoned), my family, clothes dryers, those crappy frozen onion rings, Jerry Seinfeld, polite waiters, Silly String (I don't even know why exactly), being able to casually eavesdrop without having to filter everything through the exhausting translation sieve, bookstores where books in English aren't double the cover price, squirrels (I can't for the life of me find a single squirrel in France) . . .

The list is starting to turn ridiculous. I guess I'd better stop before I start adding things like "cheap emery boards." Obviously, I miss a few big things, and a few small things. It's a fair deal. I am staying put in Paris because I'm damn sure that if I left, the chapter "What I Miss About Paris" would fill an entire book.

SUBLIME PLEASURES DU JOUR

I never cease to appreciate that the entire population makes a conscious effort to keep the city beautiful. Shop owners create charming and endlessly creative shop windows, even if they just sell eyeglasses or paper. Parks and gardens are kept photo perfect and spotless. The streets are cleaned each morning, garbage is picked up every day, everyone sweeps in front of their buildings and fills their window boxes with little flowers or ivy topiaries. It's like living in a beautiful movie set where no one ever yells "Cut!" Paris is just a paradise for visual pleasures.

I could go on and on about the packaging and presentation. Every damn thing is packaged so beautifully, whether it's a few pastries you've bought at the *pâtisserie*, charmingly boxed and tied with a ribbon, or when you buy a gift from a little boutique. Each and every store is prepared to wrap it exquisitely for you, with ribbons and a gold seal. Did I mention that all this care and attention to detail is free? I laughed out loud the other day as even my bottle of "Ajax" was labeled "Fête des Fleurs" (party of flowers), prettily packaged in a floral container and smelling like a florist shop. Nothing escapes the French passion for beauty in the details. Even the man who comes to take the garbage from the storage room of my building always sprays—get this—an air freshener that smells of lilies of the valley. These small things make each day richer, and you find yourself just walking around smiling.

How lovely it is as well, whenever you encounter anyone on a Sunday, whether it be buying the newspaper or picking up a baguette for breakfast, you are sent off with the lovely wish of "*Bon dimanche!*" (Have a good Sunday!) Somehow it just seems more sincere and rings truer than the cashiers in New York City who, like robotic automatons, bark "Have a nice day!" with all the enthusiasm of a napping cat.

But in the Hall of Fame of charming phrases in France I adore the most, the "*monsieurdame*" greeting still stands alone. Remember? It's the title addressed to a man and woman who are clearly a couple in love. Just say it outloud once "*Monsieurdame!*" I beg you not to revel in the grandeur of the sound of it. I have yearned to be on the recieving end of that delightful phrase for so long. And I'm still waiting.

THE FRIEND LOWDOWN

Personally, I think I have a helluva nice group of friends. I can't begin to imagine my life here without them. Thankfully, Stella has come to her senses and broken up (entirely) with Antoine. It's a huge relief for all of us in her life, as we'd sooner throw ourselves in front of a firing squad than watch her become an unhappy wife. Better to be alone than suffer for the sake of doing the expected. I'd like to think I helped keep her from making a fatal error, because she's helped me get through so many trials and confusing moments. Where I would be without Stella? How did I ever survive this adventure in the beginning? I remember when I first lived here and didn't know a soul to so much as go for a coffee with. The phone never rang except when it was my father. Who, I must say, has been my absolute best friend through this whole Parisian experience. He still calls faithfully every other day and will always be the most supportive man in my life. He's never once made me feel that I'm anything but "a great kid." I'm so not a kid anymore, but sometimes it's great to be able to sob to your dad when the world has let you down.

My dad always has a marvelous phrase at the ready to, in one broad stroke, bring everything into perspective. Among my favorite Dad expressions (when I'm trying to decide whether to chuck a guy or not): "Lauren, a good mate is one that makes the good times twice as good and the bad times half as bad." (Alexandre had that first part down but failed miserably—he actually made the bad times twice as bad.) And what about this one? "Good judgment is the result of making a bad judgment and learning from it." Oh, yes, I think I can apply that one all over the place, thanks.

My dad has come to visit me three times with his wife, Jean, who I used to call my "stepmonster" when they first married (hey, I was eleven years old). But now I adore them both and find when any tiny great thing happens I race to the phone to share it with them. Having your dad as your best friend is just cool as hell. I'm about to call them right now because . . .

ENFIN, THE MONSIEUR RIGHT FINAL UPDATE

I think I quietly gave up on men this winter without even realizing it. Each day I would wake up and think, *Well, today is for me. I'm not going to drive myself wild looking for a man; I've got better things to do. Soon, maybe, if I feel like it, I'll get back in the game.* I painted with a passion, read voraciously, and went on long walks along the Seine. I really only saw my dear Floris, Stella, Albertine, and a couple of buddies, Fabian and Helena. I'd meet them for a drink (a Perrier more often than not these days) or for dinner in the arrondissement and would scoot home immediately thereafter to work or to read. Life was full; I was content and productive. And then? And then he pulled up on his bike and "reopened my eyes," as he likes to say.

That Sunday evening around seven o'clock, after a long day of painting, I'd just had enough being the captive painter. I put down my brush as the light was changing and was drawn to go outside by the golden reflections shimmering against the stone buildings. The air was just starting to smell like spring, all fresh as a green tulip stem. Mmm. I needed to get clean, get out and feel a part of the human race again. Maybe go for a walk, pop into a café.

Stripping off my splattered jeans and scruffy sweater, I wanted to feel feminine-pretty again. Reaching into my armoire I grabbed my new Corinne Sarrut cream cardigan and a pair of beige Helmut Lang jeans. *J'adore* this embroidered sweater; it's quintessentially French. For three whole months I'd desperately pined for it, every day when I saw it in the window of that charming boutique on rue du Pré aux Clercs while I'd be lugging groceries back from Monoprix. Finally it went 50 percent off and I splurged. "Splurged?" Yup, a thirty-five euro sweater is now a splurge to me. And these jeans I bought years ago in New York City, but they still work. Helmut knows what he's doing. I don't know what's with these jeans, but I have never had a bad time in them. Had 'em on the day of the marriage proposal from Thierry, on a beautiful solo walk in Central Park as the Chinese blossoms floated through the air, cracking up over something with Kathy over Bloody Marys at Odéon, the first kiss from Alexandre by the Seine . . . Yep, these are magic pants.

I cinch 'em tight with a beige piece of silk cord, something I saw in a store window in the Marais and not at all as Jethro Clampett as you'd think. In fact, it's downright chic. I'm sure of it. Toss on the old favorite camel-hair coat from Agnès b., and since no outfit's complete without the *de rigueur écharpe*, I wrap the cocoa beaded antique silk scarf I found at the flea market for a steal around my neck the French way (twice).

"*À tout à l'heure, Puccini*," I call out (Puccini speaks French now, *naturellement*), and without planning it I suddenly know I'm headed out the door for Café de Flore. A pale orange sun hovers on the horizon, as if hesitating to sink out of sight and end this beautiful day. The air is clear and refreshingly cool, whipping the ends of my scarf behind me like triumphant wings. Strolling up rue des Saints-Pères, my thoughts flow easily. *This has been a good weekend. Got a lot done. I should have about fourteen new paintings ready for that exhibit in April. It'll be great, an exposition of just my work; there's going to be a poster even! I can't wait to seen an* affiche *posted around Paris announcing my very own show. I've been craving that since the day I arrived. Not bad. Not bad at all. No boyfriend, to be sure, but serious progress on the "work front," as my father would say.*

Turning on to boulevard Saint-Germain, the wind blows my hair around wildly and I find myself smiling. What a simple pleasure: the wind in your hair. I realize I seem to experience everything much more intensely these days, from noticing the way the sunlight filters through the trees in the Tuileries, scattering kaleidoscope patterns on the soil that dance with the wind, to appreciating the delightful differences in accents from one French generation to another. Life has more texture, and it's the little things that are touching and make my day.

Tonight the sidewalks are almost empty and traffic is sparse. On Sunday evenings most true Parisians have headed home to prepare dinner *en famille*. Even at Flore there are only a few seats filled on the terrace. Good, it's quiet . . . I couldn't bear the big scene Flore can be, the way it is on a warm Saturday afternoon. Then it's such an extravaganza, everyone checking everyone else out, showing off their latest purse, diamond bracelet, fabulous car. Ecch. When that's going on, I just pass by and go sit alone in the little park of L'église de Saint-Germain down the block. Last time I sat there, I met a neat older woman, eccentrically dressed and wearing an enormous red hat, feeding the pigeons. She had marvelous stories of how she had been the perfume-bottle designer for Balenciaga and Jean Patou in the fifties. By the time we had finished speaking she'd even offered me an invitation to visit her in Montmartre one day soon to see her Suzanne Valadon drawings. I smiled the whole next day, I was so completely charmed by the experience. One of those chance meetings that could only happen in Paris.

On the terrace that Sunday, I take a seat near a charming-looking older man and patiently wait the traditional ten minutes it takes to be noticed. My favorite waiter, Maurice, arrives at last.

"*Bonsoir, Klein. Tout va bien? Qu'est-ce que vous désirez ce soir? Comme d'habitude? Une Sancerre, non?*"

"*Bonsoir, je suis bien, merci. Non, Maurice, peut-être je prend du thé avec citron, s'il vous plaît,*" I reply.

Opening a sketch pad that I'd tucked into my coat, I quickly abandon the idea of sketching and fold it shut. Instead I drum up a conversation with the sweet old British man sitting next to me. He's thrilled to be back in Paris, at Flore for the first time in thirty years. We talk about his memories of Paris, about a long-ago love affair with a Frenchwoman named Céleste, and how he's just beside himself that he still can't get a proper scone in France. Alistair was a marvelous raconteur, witty and fantastically interesting, and was just launching into his opinion of the latest Atget exhibit at the Musée d'Orsay when (a drum roll, *s'il vous plaît*) the clouds parted, the sun burst through, and *he* rolled up on his bicycle in a blaze of exquisite perfection. I must offer my apologies to Alistair, as I instantly shut down all communication and just stared at this incredibly beautiful man getting off his bike and carefully locking it up. Clad in indigo blue jeans, beige suede loafers (didn't I once say I hated slip-on shoes; forget I said that!) and a crisp white shirt, sleeves rolled up to reveal toned, strong arms. Pah! The vision moved with unconscious grace, and as he hefted the chain around his bike wheel, he didn't even see me. But I was riveted. I just devoured the opportunity to observe him unaware of my penetrating gaze. My eyes followed him as he headed into la Hune next door, (a small but intellectual bookstore) and stayed fixed to the door, impatiently awaiting the moment he would return to his bike. I tried to gather my wits and attempted to rejoin the conversation with Alistair. Feeble, as I couldn't concentrate, feeling my heart accelerate with every minute I had to wait to see him emerge. Five, ten, fifteen impatient minutes went by, and just as I was considering getting up to go hover in front of la Hune, he came out and stood directly in front of me.

Ah, there he is. Mmmm. No more than a dozen feet away, still not noticing me. One hand in his jeans pocket, the other holding a large bag of new books.

He cast a glance once over the terrace, clearly debating whether to stop in at Flore or to simply get back on his bike and ride away. Out of my life.

Finally he saw me. I looked up and smiled as he simultaneously burst into a delighted smile.

"*Bonsoir,* Fabrizio." (Yes. That Fabrizio.)

"*Bonsoir,* Klein." Not another word passed between us for a full minute. It seemed as though he stood there for an hour; everything but Fabrizio receded into a nonexistent blur. At last he walked over and I stood up with the same anxiousness. We both reached out for each other's hands at the same moment, as we leaned in for a kiss. Not a double-cheek air kiss but—surprising to us both—a real tender kiss. Fabrizio pulled back for a moment, looked into my eyes, and said, "Klein, we're definitely making a spectacle of ourselves . . . and . . . I don't . . . (I held my breath) . . . care at all."

He leaned in for another delicious kiss, then I slipped my hand into his. He led me inside and we sat down in a banquette by the window, side by side, the way only lovers do in Paris.

"So, it's nice to see you," I say, grinning from ear to ear.

"Oh, more than 'nice.' *C'est parfait!*" he says, still holding my hand.

"That was quite a kiss, mister. You'd better hope Céline doesn't hear about it."

"Not to worry, she's gone."

"Gone?"

"Gone. As in 'it's over.' "

"I'm . . . sorry . . . You okay?" He nods. My grin is just a little wider. Actually, there's a strong chance my face will crack. "Well, gosh, you look great, Fabrizio."

"Thanks. Hey, is it just me or have we had a conversation like this before?" he says, referring to the "Alexandre gone? Gone" exchange at Andy Wahloo.

"*Oui, déjà vu, non?*"

"Oh, and how that French of yours has progressed. Impressive," he jokes.

"Don't kid me! No, that's right; you don't kid, do you?" I say, noticing for the first time a fleck of dark gold in his amber eyes.

"Quite honestly . . . I have to tell you, Klein . . . I've been thinking about you. Is that reckless of me to say?"

"No. I like the new 'reckless' you." I'm both shocked that I'm finally holding his hand and hearing his voice again. And that Princess de Rivatives is no
more.

"Wait. Are you with someone?"

"Do you mean that guy over there?" I say inclining my head toward Alistair. "Or someone-someone?" I say, thinking, *Here goes that verbal tennis shit
I love.*

"Someone-someone?"

"A boyfriend? No. Why? Do you know anyone who'd be interested in
dating an American artist who wears alfalfa sprouts on her eyebrows?"

"I can assure you, I do," Fabrizio says.

"Do you really think he's right for me? I'm a little complicated."

"I am sure he'd find it scintillating."

"Really? Scintillating?"

"I would even go so far as to say . . . you might be the woman of his dreams."

"Dreams?"

"Yes. I said 'might.' "

"I should very much like to meet this delusional man. Can you arrange it?"

"Are you sure you're ready?"

"More than ready."

"I'll call him." And with that he pulls out his cell phone and begins to
punch random numbers.

"Hey!" I say, grabbing the phone, snapping it shut, and tossing it back in
his bag. "You always skirt subjects. You're very good at it. It's easy to hint at
things, difficult to say them. Be brave."

"You're right. Sorry. Okay, here goes. Um, recently, well, I realized I don't
want the 'expected' type of woman in my life. And you, Klein, are the totally
'unexpected.' " (I'm dying to leap up and do a victory dance but miraculously
refrain.)

"Ahh, a wall comes down. This goes back to the 'you're different' comment, I presume?"

"Every time we saw each other, you have to admit, it was like being caught
in a tempest. I just wanted to stay and talk to you for hours."

"I love to talk to you too—it has been the most fun I've had . . . with my
clothes on."

"Klein, you're bad!"

"Not bad, just truthful."

"*Oui,* and that's rare. A lot of women put out an image they think men want, and you just offer it up like, 'Take it or leave it.' It's overwhelming and difficult, but entirely honest and—"

"Don't get carried away. I'm not always honest," I interrupt.

"And then, when I saw your paintings—"

"Thank you. I know it was you that bought the gray one. I was touched—surprised as hell—but really touched." I can't stop interrupting.

"I saw a side of you that you don't reveal enough, a quieter version of Klein you didn't show me."

"I know I come off as a bruiser sometimes."

"A 'bruiser'? *C'est quoi?*"

"It means a bit tough, defensive. You have to admit, Fabrizio, there are so many things about me you didn't like," I say, noticing that the hair at the back of his neck has curled ever so slightly with sweat from his bike ride in the sun.

"Perhaps I wanted you to believe that. I'm sorry if I was critical. I was hard on you because . . . I think I just wanted to make an impression on you. I was sure all the men you meet must fall all over themselves with adoration and blind acceptance."

"Acceptance? No, I haven't got much of that since I moved to Paris. It hasn't exactly been open arms all around, to be honest." He's looking at me questioningly, expecting me to go on.

"And you know, you were right on so many points. It was pretty hard to hear things like, you should speak French, stop smoking, stop your nervous fidgeting. But I loved that you did. I needed someone to say it."

Fabrizio smiles, leans over and kisses me softly on the check. The slightest waft of his cologne lingers in the air after he sits back against the chair. Mmm, Héritage by Guerlain. I know it well, but it never smelled like this, so intoxicating. God, I'm so drunk . . . no, impossible, I've only had tea . . . how funny.

"Shall we order something? What were you drinking when I swept you away?" he asks. Alistair grins at the two of us knowingly.

"I was having tea, but—"

"Maybe *nunc est bibendum.*"

"Another Latin quote, I presume?"

"Yes. 'Now is the time for drinking.' Champagne, perhaps?" he offers, handing me *la carte*.

"Veuve Clicquot?" I ask.

"My favorite."

"Mine too. And I'm famished, let's get some, hmm . . . *saumon fumé, frites, et crème brûlée!*" I suggest.

"Surprising combo. I suppose I shouldn't be surprised," he says, laughing, as he motions to Maurice to come take our order.

"And seriously, if you really want to, you can smoke," he offers, sliding the ashtray to my side of the table.

"I've quit," I reply, drawing a smile from his exquisite lips.

"Really? Fantastic! Another surprise from Klein." As he finishes speaking, he gently gathers my wind-blown hair and holds it loosely in one hand. God, how lovely.

"Fabrizio, I have to know something. You've always given me such a hard time for being American. Really, do you have a problem with it?" I ask as the Champagne flutes and ice bucket are brought to the table.

"Um, no, that's not exactly the reason. It's not a fun memory."

"No, it's okay. You don't have to . . . really . . . another time. I'm sorry I brought it up." I nervously run my finger around the rim of the Champagne glass.

"No, I want to explain myself. I want to be transparent with you (that's adorable; Europeans always say "transparent" when they mean "clear"). Well, okay, let me tell you. Three years ago I fell in love with a woman. I alluded to it, I think, when we first met. A New Yorker, like you. I was madly in love with her. After about a year together, here in Paris, I asked her to marry me. Then two weeks before the wedding she left me for a man she said offered her a more luxurious lifestyle. I was more than shocked. I was devastated."

"Oh God, that's terrible. I'm so sorry for you. Thank you for telling me. Now I get why I scared you so much. You probably thought I was her times two. If it's in any way comforting to you, I've already been there and back."

"Yes, I know."

"You know? About my life in New York City?"

"Don't forget, we do have a few mutual friends."

"You've done your homework, haven't you?"

"I do when it's important."

It suddenly occurs to me I've got another question. "Hmm, tell me, why did you split with Céline?"

"Because she's not the kind of woman—how should I say this?—who has a tattoo . . . or has nervous habits like rearranging her silverware. You know what I mean?" Fabrizio says, putting his hand on mine as I'm caught mid fork-transfer.

He continues. "Céline was lovely, but quite safe and conventional. Then when we met, you and I, it occured to me that I'd been kidding myself."

"Ah. Really? So you do 'kid'—"

"I'm sorry I misjudged you in the beginning, Klein. I was just fighting with something inside me."

"Ah, yes, the internal battle. I know it well. But think of it this way: whichever way you look at it, you've won!"

"So optimistic, so American—I love it!" he adds, grinning.

"And don't worry about judgments, Fabrizio. I thought you were an up-tight intellectual."

"I am," he says, eyes sparkling, raising his glass of Champagne.

"I know. And somehow, I love it. You make me laugh with your silly Latin quotes. To be totally honest, I've been calling you Mr. Smug Smarty-Pants behind your back," I say, giggling behind my glass.

"No, tell me you're not serious."

"Don't worry, my friends all saw through my scathing rants. Apparently I've only been fooling *myself* about you," I tell him, relieved to be able to finally acknowledge it: I adore this man.

Fabrizio bites his lower lip shyly and wraps both hands around my waist, pulling me closer to him.

Beaming, I look down, notice what I'm wearing and I think, *Magic pants, indeed.*

We are still at Flore two hours later, as the tables begin to fill up with couples having dinner. Everyone and everything suddenly looks beautiful to me.

"What an amazing night! I don't think I've ever enjoyed an evening in Paris more," he says, holding me.

"E-may either-nay."

"Pardon?"

"Pig latin."

"Quite sexy."

"It is not."

"No, it's sexy that you . . . don't hold back. You just say everything," he says with a sweeping gesture.

"Sexy? I promise you it can get quite tiresome."

"Exhaust me, Klein. I beg you," he says.

"You sure you're ready?"

"More than ready," he says, raising his glass. I'm so happy I could cry.

We are still at Flore at midnight, watching out the window as the clouds move quickly across the new moon. Fabrizio's hand in my hair, tucking loose strands behind my ear tenderly. We are silent for a long time then, placing his warm hand lightly on my forehead, he says in almost a whisper, "You're lovely, Klein. And you know I don't mean just physically, but *dans ton esprit.*"

"*Merci. Toi aussi.*"

"Um . . ."

"Um . . . what, Fabrizio?"

"I still haven't gone on that trip to Madagascar."

"No?"

"No. I've been waiting."

"Waiting?"

"Like you said, waiting to go with . . . Klein, would you consider coming with me or . . . do you want to save it for someone . . ."

"Someone-someone?"

"Right."

"That someone-someone . . . I think I've found him. Yes, I'd love to go with you."

"Really?" he asks, all excited.

"Really."

"So perhaps it's true then . . . *Omnia vincit amor.*"

"Translation, please, Mr. Smarty-Pants."

"Love conquers all."

"Yes, I agree, ove-lay onnquers-cay ll-ay."

We dissolve into kisses entwined with laughter for a few minutes. Then just sit looking at each other, his hand on mine . . . completely still . . . in blissful silence.

Fabrizio unfolds my napkin and places it gently in my lap. It feels strangely familiar. We smile when we remember at the same moment that he performed that same gesture the night we met. Maurice arrives, tray in hand, arranges the two plates of crème brûlée on the small table and announces, "*Votre dessert, monsieurdame.*"

Monsieurdame. Finally.

Acknowledgments

First off, I must thank the exiled Prince of Greece, who casually mentioned to me at a dinner party in Paris, "You know, you should write a book." (And thank God he didn't suggest something else, like, "You know, you should really throw yourself into sumo wrestling.")

A special heartfelt thank-you to my editor, Elizabeth Beier, at St. Martin's Press, who graciously guided me through this process with inspiring enthusiasm and brilliant suggestions. I am forever grateful to her for making this experience one of the most exhilarating and fulfilling of my life.

A special thank-you to Michael Connor at St. Martin's for his extraordinary professionalism, hilarious e-mails, and for never telling me to go to hell as I'd barrage him with question after question about publishing.

And a huge thank-you to my dearest friend, Kathy Greenberg, who's been there for me through twenty-seven years, one growth spurt, nine hair colors, a gazillion men, and dozens of claims from me: "He's the One!" For all her invaluable advice, unflagging support, eternal friendship, and for hashing out the plot (Wha . . . ? There was a plot? You're asking!) over nine time zones on our cell phones.

To Amy Schiffman at Gersh Agency and Lauren Lloyd for generously taking *Paris Hangover* "to Hollywood" and pulling together the film and television deals.

To my agent, Lori Perkins, who laughed out loud at the *merde de chat*, bravely took me on, and brought me to St. Martin's Press.

To my *équipe* in Paris—all my friends who endured my constant "I can't go out, I have to write," as well as all my endlessly exhausting dating stories. The most amazingly generous friends, and my partners in crime: Helena O'Neal, Sabina Fogle, Floris Houwink, Nicolas, Cyril, Olivier, and the most lovely couple I know: Fabian and Lorene Edelstam. And on the other side of the Atlantic: my faithful and fabulous *amies*: Charlotte Tarantola, Katie Chebatoris, and Beth Bowley. And to TWD for his love and inspiration.

Merci to Renaud Vuaillat, for his devotion and for the endless laughter. To Oscar Whiskas, for the title and for entirely not believing I could do this, which provided much determination to prove you wrong. To my typist, Jessica Grandhomme, who somehow managed to read my handwritten book (I know, would you believe?!) with all its scrawlings and bring it to the printed page. To Xavier LeGrand of Castel, for letting me unleash my unbridled energy on your dance floor night after night.

To the entire staff at Café de Flore, for all their kindness and for making me feel "at home" in Paris. (And for keeping my table, replenishing the *cacahouètes*, and always remembering my favorite wine.)

The greatest and most sincere thanks go to my parents. My father, Horst Lobe, who has been my best friend and the most attentive, loving soul I could ever have imagined. For all his patience, understanding, counsel, acceptance, and love. And for hopefully agreeing to read only the blacked-out version I give him. Remember, Dad, it's fiction!

To Tony O'Hare, for all the loving support and incredible commitment to my mother and my family.

And finally, to my extraordinary mother, Susan O'Hare. My hero. Who showered me with never-ending encouragement, unconditional love, and adoration. And who showed me how to be a strong, creative woman and to live intensely, decadently, and with style. A greater role model in my life, I could not have had.

PARIS
HANGOVER